Druidess Found

Druidess Trilogy Book One

Machelle Hanleigh

Druidess Found

An Inhabitants at the Center of the Universe Novel

Copyright © 2020 by Machelle Hanleigh

First Edition, June 2020
Cover Design: Covers by Christian
ISBN 978-1-7348458-2-2 (Paperback)

Dear Reader

Thank you for taking a peek inside.

The novel in your hands, is the rewritten/re-edit version based on changes in our editing/writing processes to incorporate what we learned from the SPF Booklab 9 episode, private messages, and reviews. I am pleased with the final product and hope you will be as well.

For news of upcoming releases, free offers or simply keep up with what is happening in my world, please visit my website, machellehanleigh.com and join my newsletter.

As with life, writing is a journey. We will continue to grow with each published novel, and I hope you will join us on this journey!

Contents

Chapter One

Moto skimmed his fingers across the surface of the water in the delicately balanced bowl on his thigh. The surface of the water held an image forever burned into the very core of his being. He didn't know how one such as she had so profoundly captured his attention. There was nothing extraordinary about the girl. She lived on a world full of Inhabitants who lived without basic knowledge of the Universe they resided. Neither did the Inhabitants display any inkling of an ability to touch the very life-giving energy of their own world, let alone the rest of the Universe. She was not an exception. He took a deep breath.

If it had not been for his cursed travels from his home world, he would never have glimpsed her, and she would not have become a distraction from his quest for answers. He kept returning to her world either through his looking bowl, or in person when he could manage the feat without his absence being discovered. Kahoali did not leave their home world. If his off-world excursions were detected, regardless of his honorable intentions, there would be consequences. Even for him, one of four Chosen of the Queen, and her favorite.

He couldn't help himself. The cursed girl kept drawing him to her and had from the first moment his eyes caught sight of her. Something about her entranced him. Despite how many times he promised himself that he wouldn't return to her, he did. He couldn't make sense of why he returned. He shook his head. He didn't like when something didn't make sense. He needed answers, not more questions. He gazed out over Crystal Lake.

She was nothing, less than ordinary. Certainly not someone who could help him with his dilemma. She meant nothing to him. His eyes strayed back to the image in the bowl.

"If only you could help me." Moto caressed the surface of the water which held her image.

Her image turned towards his whispered words as if she'd heard him. He knew, without a doubt, that she couldn't hear him. The movement and timing were coincidence, an illusion, nothing more. She didn't know he existed. He'd been careful not to reveal himself to her. There were times it took all of his warrior's iron clad will power to resist the urge to confront her, demand answers. How had she beguiled him? How could he break the spell?

He slid his fingers across the surface of the water with his fingertips as if he caressed her soft fair skin. He imagined her skin would be silky smooth to his touch. He had absolutely no intention of confirming his suspicions. He would be content observing her from afar. Until he found a way to break this power, she held over him.

Even if she'd been a part of his world, she would have been an unwelcome distraction. She wasn't part of his world which further complicated matters. Outsiders were not accepted in any of the Kahoali Villages, and especially his. Unless he found a way to ignore the obvious connection between them, she would remain an intrusion in his life.

He smiled to himself. So fragile, despite the rugged crumbling ruins surrounding her. Too fragile to survive in his world.

"Lovely."

Moto dumped the water from his bowl. He opened a tiny portal to send the bowl back to his hut. He glared up at Shimani. His unawareness of Shimani's approach, gave evidence to the detriment his little distraction had become to him, let alone his quest.

Shimani sat on the ground next to Moto. He had the audacity to smile.

"What do you want?"

"Thought you might like some company," Shimani said.

"In other words, the Queen sent you to check up on me."

Shimani shrugged. "That too."

Moto shook his head and looked back out over Crystal Lake. The Lake and surrounding meadow provided him peace, usually uninterrupted. He turned back to Shimani. "Tell the Queen I'm fine."

Shimani's good natured smile faded. His features took on a serious demeanor.

Moto shook his head. "Don't."

One of Shimani's eyebrows shot up. "Queen Shakti has good reason to be concerned about you."

"You agree with her?" Moto's tone bordered on hostile. Normally, he tried to be patient with Shimani as he was still young, for a Kahoali warrior. This time, he didn't bother. He didn't like being checked up on, and he didn't like being caught admiring his distraction. His obsession with the girl was a weakness he never intended to display for anyone's scrutiny. Not even his protege's.

Shimani shook his head. "I didn't say I agree."

"Then what are you saying?" Moto didn't keep the harsh bite out of his words.

"Who's the girl?"

"No one." Moto hoped his tone communicated to Shimani his displeasure in such an intrusive question. "Don't change the subject."

"I'm not telling the Queen you're fine when clearly you are not."

"Fine." Moto stood. He started pacing back and forth. "I'm fine," he muttered to himself.

Shimani remained seated on the meadow's mossy ground.

Moto silently credited Shimani for his occasional good sense.

Shimani stood.

Short lived good sense, Moto thought.

"You're not fine, Moto." Shimani tried to put a hand on Moto's shoulder.

Moto shrugged off Shimani's attempted gesture of comfort.

"Your night terrors are preventing you from resting. You're venturing farther and farther away from Center Village."

Moto stopped pacing and turned towards Shimani. He crossed his arms over his chest.

Shimani shook his head. "No, I haven't told the Queen you're traveling off world, and I won't. You're ignoring your responsibility to our Queen and people, while expecting me to cover for you. You've stopped taking me off world with you."

"Enough!" Moto all but shouted at Shimani. He took a calming breath to regain a modicum of his warrior composure.

Shimani faced him, mirroring Moto's stance, including his crossed arms.

Moto impatiently tied his long, dark braids at the nape of his neck. He took a few more deep breaths. Shimani didn't deserve all of his anger, some, but not all. The girl on the other hand. He pushed his wayward thoughts to the back of his mind. "My apologies."

Shimani acknowledged Moto's apology with a slight nod of his head.

"What?" Moto demanded. Shimani could be as irritating as the Queen accused him of being on several occasions. He had no one to blame but himself for Shimani's attitude problem. What had he been thinking, taking him under his tutelage?

"What's changed?" Shimani asked.

Moto shook his head. "I don't know." That wasn't exactly the truth, and yet it was. He walked to the water's edge and stared down into the Lake's depths. Shimani had been correct. The night terrors were keeping him awake at night. He turned to face Shimani. "I don't know." He shrugged. "The night terrors remain the same. The six Outer Villages are abandoned, and the six Inner Villages are under attack. I never see who attacks. I feel the heat of the fire burning me, but I don't see the fire, ever. I hear the screams of pain. I feel the death and destruction of our people, all our people, Shimani." Moto shook his head. The night terrors remained the same each and every time they came to him, but something had changed. There resided an urgency inside him that grew more urgent with each passing day. "I stand in the middle of the destruction and am helpless to stop it." He lifted troubled eyes to Shimani. "I'm not a helpless Villager, Shimani. I'm a warrior. A Chosen One! In the night terrors, I stand there and do nothing. Nothing! Why would I do nothing, Shimani?" Moto ran his hand through his dark braids, untying them in the process.

Shimani didn't reply. He stood where he was, his eyes trained on Moto.

Moto turned his troubled gaze to the forest surrounding Crystal Lake's meadow. "I sense we are running out of time. I am no closer to finding anyone who can help me understand the night terrors. I don't know if they are real. I don't know if they are a vision of what's to come or simply night terrors without any meaning at all." Moto focused his attention on Shimani. "If they are not visions of future events, then I can rest in peace and endure the night terrors. But if they are visions," he left his words unspoken. He knew Shimani was aware of the implication if his night terrors were about future events. "How am I supposed to convince the Queen and Council to take precautions if I can't confirm if they are more than night terrors?"

Shimani opened his mouth as if to reply but closed it without saying anything.

Moto shrugged and turned away. There was nothing for Shimani to say. This wasn't the first time they'd had this conversation. The Queen and Council had rejected his suggested measures to protect the Villages. The Kahoali had lived in peace too long to take such things seriously. In addition, fore-visions were not a normal ability any Kahoali had ever possessed. Intellectually, he might understand their reluctance to take his night terrors as reality, but emotionally, he did not. Which prompted his current need for solitude. The urgency inside him was the source of his now daily conversations with the Queen in the hopes he might persuade her to his way of thinking. They had not. He was too emotional for a Kahoali warrior, he'd been told. The conversation with the Queen that morning deteriorated from there.

Moto walked over to Shimani. He laid a reassuring hand on his shoulder. "Thank you for your concern." He turned and started towards the closest stationary portal from Crystal Lake.

"Where are you going?"

Moto didn't reply or stop walking away.

"Don't forget about the evening repast." Shimani called after him. "You are expected to attend this one."

Moto lifted his hand in acknowledgment of Shimani's words before stepping into the portal. He understood that Shimani was just trying to help keep him out of trouble with their Queen. She was a patient woman, but he'd worn her patience thin of late. Still, he didn't require reminding of his duties towards Queen Shakti and their people.

He stepped out of the stationary portal and quickly opened his own portal before anyone, who might come around the Queen's hut, noticed him. His destination lay beyond the confines of his world. He would need the Ancestral Gateway for where he intended to traverse.

He exited his portal and stepped up to the large stone arch. He laid a reverent hand on the Ancestral Gateway. This was the only evidence he'd ever found that his people had once been more than the mere Villagers they were now. He could only imagine the kind of knowledge it would take to build such a magnificent structure.

He brushed his hand along the smooth tan stone towards a specific rune. He closed his eyes and concentrated. A familiar heat from the rune penetrated the center of his palm. The heat had not ever been too hot to bear, but neither was the sensation comfortable. He kept his hand pressed firmly against the rune while the energy of Ki flowed through, into the rune and infused the stone arch. When Moto sensed the energy vibrating against the palm of his hand as the residual energy started to flow back into his hand, he stopped pulling the energy from Ki. He shifted his concentration on his end goal of opening the Gateway to his desired location.

He opened his eyes and focused on the empty space inside the stone archway. The shimmer within the inner confines of the arch indicated he had succeeded in opening the Gateway.

He removed his hand from the stone arch. The last remnants of a silver glow that traced the lines of the rune dissipated.

Moto's gaze shifted from the rune to the inner archway. He took a deep breath to calm his mind, then stepped through the shimmering doorway of the Ancestral Gateway.

Once on the other side he closed the doorway and moved to crouch behind a partial crumbling stone wall. His speed came from practice over more visits than he cared to remember. Curse her for drawing him to her as she did.

He made his way towards the edge and knelt on one knee. He then peeked around the side. A barely audible voice in the back of his mind reminded him that a warrior faced his foes, not hide behind crumbling walls for a glimpse. He silenced the annoying voice.

His eyes landed on his prey. She stood partially turned away from his position which allowed him to take his fill of the sight of her. She talked to an elderly man he'd seen in the ruins before with her. He didn't know how long it would take her to sense his presence. Maybe talking to the elderly man would help give him time to study her. Somehow, she always appeared to sense his presence which perplexed him. The Inhabitants, herself included, simply did not have the skills to display any kind of ability to sense anything. Yet, she always became aware of him within moments of his appearance.

Something in her called to something in him.

He studied her, from her dark auburn short hair to her deep-sea green eyes. He longed to run his fingers through her silky strands. To crush a lock between his fingers and take her scent deep into his lungs. Her eyes were the same rich hue as the oceans of Ki. The same eyes locked firmly with his.

He vehemently cursed as he ducked behind the wall. She distracted his good senses too much for his own well-being! With a strength of will greater than it should have taken, he resisted the urge to take one last look. He hurried to the Gateway and opened it with haste.

He sank to the forest floor once he'd made it safely back to Ki. He took a deep breath and laid his head back against the Ancestral Gateway. "Fool," he muttered to himself. If he had any sense, he would let go of his obsession with her. Now, in this moment, she had no name he knew her by. He should leave well enough alone. But he couldn't. Something about her pulled him to her. He remained powerless to counter, despite his attempts to resist.

Each time he traveled to her world weakened his resolve. She captured a piece of him every visit, even though they had never spoken to each other. Even more disturbing was the piece of her he carried away with him.

Moto closed his eyes and savored the feel of her essence. He knew he shouldn't, but again, he remained too weak to withstand the power she held over him. A no-name girl should not have such sway!

It didn't help that he sensed a deep longing inside of her for something so profound he couldn't make sense of her longing. He didn't think she was aware of this longing inside herself. Then there was the deep seeded sadness buried so thoroughly that he knew she was not aware of it. If he focused too long on that part of her, tears would sting his eyes. If he didn't know better, he would think the Kahoali bonding process had begun between the two of them.

He shook his head against his ridiculous thought.

Kahoali only bonded with other Kahoali, and she was not Kahoali.

Moto turned his gaze to the darkening sky and cursed. He pushed himself off the ground as he stood. Too much time had passed. The evening repast would have already begun. Just one more example of just how much a distraction that girl was in his life. He had to find a way to break this control she had over him. He vowed to focus solely on his duty to his Queen and people. To not be distracted from his responsibilities or his quest for answers. His quest, after all, was the reason he'd found her in the first place. Finding answers about his night terrors had to take precedent, even over his little distraction.

He refused to let anyone have that kind of control over him, and certainly not a see-green eyed slip of a girl!

Chapter Two

A shiver prickled the back of Kaily's neck. She didn't have to wonder about the source of the sensation. She already knew who held the blame for causing her such discomfort. Her dark warrior! He had the strangest hazel eyes she could imagine. Imagine, because no one had those kind of eyes in reality. A silver spider webbing covered his irises. Those eyes haunted her dreams. During the day, her waking dream, for she knew no other way to describe his brief appearances. They were mere glimpses, phantom like. A glance caught out of the corner of her eye. But at night, in her dreams, he remained present long enough for her to study every chiseled edge of his finely honed body. A warriors form she'd committed to memory.

And most likely a delusion.

The cold shiver traveled past her neck down her spine to settle at its base. Her eyes strayed to the crumbling partial wall of the castle ruins. She turned her head ever so slightly to get a better look. She'd learned from experience to move slowly to keep her illusive dark warrior from disappearing the moment her eyes landed on him. She couldn't decide if he were real or a sign she'd lost her mind. The dreams of him seemed too vivid to be just an illusion, but then again, they were just dreams. Still, she couldn't accept that her dark warrior did not exist. She grew desperate to learn the truth with each encounter, be them waking or sleeping. He drew her to him, and she desperately needed to know if he were real or a product of her overactive imagination.

The hair at the nape of her neck rose to stand on end. Her eyes locked with his. For one brief moment, the ground shifted beneath her feet. She'd felt that sensation before as well.

She blinked.

Kaily lifted her foot to take a step towards the now empty space her dark warrior had occupied just moments before she'd closed her eyes.

"Are you listening to me, lassie?"

"Dammit!" Kaily muttered under her breath. She turned back to the older gentlemen she'd forgotten was present. "Aye. I'm listening." She glanced one last time at the crumbling wall.

"Humph!"

Kaily returned her full attention back to Mr. Ferguson. Her illusive warrior had already vanished. That fact wouldn't stop her from investigating his last known location, as soon as she had the privacy she required. She linked her arm with Mr. Ferguson's, and started moving them towards the path which led to home. "I am listening. I promise." The sooner she helped Mr. Ferguson go away, the sooner she could search for signs her dark warrior existed, and perhaps a way to locate him.

Mr. Ferguson patted her hand. "You spend too much time in this desolated place, lassie. Don't think I don't know about the other night you spent out here until the wee morning hours."

Kaily cringed. She didn't reply. She remembered that night. She'd caught sight of her illusive warrior, much like this time. He'd evaporated then too. She hadn't intended to be out all night, but, dammit, she stayed to wait his possible return. Instead of spotting him again, she'd ended up falling asleep, despite the bitter cold night.

Mr. Ferguson stopped them at the head of the path towards home. "I know today is especially hard on you, Kaily. Please don't forget you still have family who care about you."

Kaily hastily brushed a stray tear from her suddenly moist eyes. "I know I do. You and Mrs. Ferguson are wonderful family, truly. I just need to be alone today. Please understand." She didn't need to be reminded of how sad this day was for her. It was the fifth-year anniversary of her foster parents' death. She'd spent every year since their passing in the ruins they'd first found her as a child, alone, freezing, hungry, confused. They'd taken her in as one of their own. She shook her head and tried to give Mr. Ferguson a reassuring smile.

"We do understand." Mr. Ferguson patted her hand again. "Don't stay out her all night, lassie. We'd don't want to lose you too."

"I won't. I promise." She gently squeezed his hand. "I'll be fine. Really."

Mr. Ferguson hesitated a moment, his eyes locked with Kaily's.

She thought he might say more on the matter. She silently waited and forced her eyes to remain locked with his.

He didn't say anything else. Instead, he patted her hand again and unlinked his arm from hers.

Kaily let out a quiet sigh of relief.

Mr. Ferguson nodded, and then set his feet to the path home.

She watched him go just long enough to be certain he wouldn't return. A sadness squeezed her heart painfully tight. She couldn't blame him for being so worried about her, especially this day. She'd not been herself since the loss. She knew the Fergusons missed her foster parents as much as she did. They deserved more effort on her part, but she couldn't bring herself to allow the closeness that once existed between them back in her life. The loss remained too vivid, even five years later.

She took a deep breath and exhaled a long sigh. Perhaps she could try, she thought. She shrugged and turned back towards the ruins. At that moment, an elusive mystery required her attention. A welcomed distraction from her sorrow.

She ran to the last spot she'd spotted her dark warrior as best as she could. The path was steep so she couldn't run full on. Which probably didn't matter. He was gone, and like other times, she knew he wouldn't return. If he were real.

In truth, she didn't know if she wanted him to be real or not. If he was, then she wasn't losing her mind. But then there would be many questions to be answered. First one being 'what the hell did he want from her?' If he wasn't, well than she might spend the rest of her life chasing a shadow.

She hurried around the partial standing wall. No surprise! The space remained as empty as she'd expected to find it. Even if she'd left Mr. Ferguson mid-sentence to pursue her warrior, she wouldn't have found him. She never found him, just empty space. She leaned against the stone and slid to the dirt ground. She buried her hands in the edge of her bulky sweater and crossed her jean clad legs. She looked around the crumbling ruins and sighed.

Mr. Ferguson was probably right. She shouldn't spend so much time in that dilapidated place. But she couldn't help it. The castle ruins held a special place in her heart. Not only had her beloved foster parents found her there, but it was the first place she remembered of her childhood. For a child of seven, she should have maintained more memories, but she hadn't. The lack of her memories bothered her foster parents when she was younger. But as the years passed, they built new memories together, and the missing ones didn't matter as much.

She wiped at a stray tear. Her gaze drifted to the one thing in all those ruins which remained intact. Not one sign of decay. Across from her stood a stone arched doorway. The decay of the stone walls and other doorways was not surprising considering the age her foster father attributed to the ruins. The stone arched doorway should have been falling apart as well. It wasn't. Not even her archaeological foster father could determine what kept the stone doorway so pristine these countless centuries later.

Etched runes lined the stone arched doorway. Their lines remained as sharp as they might have been when first carved into the stone. Her foster parents hadn't been able to determine the origins of the runes. They didn't match any known historical peoples. Close to some, but not exact. A mystery they weren't able to solve before their untimely deaths' in a freak accident.

She wiped away more tears with the sleeve of her sweater as she pushed off the ground and stood. Her eyes remained fixated on the carved runes lining the sides and arched part of the doorway. She slowly walked towards it. Her gaze narrowed to one specific rune.

She frowned. Her eyes widened in surprise. She would have sworn she'd seen the rune glimmer for a brief second.

She stepped closer and reached out her hand. She brushed her fingertips across the cold stone. The stone was colder than other times when she'd touched it. Almost frozen. The rune which she focused on, glimmered again. This time the silver-blue glow remained. She knew for certain that it did glow, and it had not been her imagination.

Her eyes narrowed to mere slits as she focused on the glowing rune. She traced its lines with her fingers. The rune felt considerably warmer than the rest of the stone doorway. She laid her hand on the rune, covering it with her palm. The warmth of the rune penetrated the center of her hand. She pulled her hand away, shaking it out as if she'd received a jolt. She hadn't.

The glow of the rune flared. Kaily took a deep breath and closed her eyes. She opened her eyes and took another deep breath. In all the time she'd been at the ruins, before and after her foster parents' death, she had not witnessed any of the symbols glowing.

She placed her hand over the rune once again. The same warmth permeated her hand. She forced herself to leave her hand covering the rune. She didn't know what the warmth or glow meant, but she was determined to find out. A strange sensation flowed into her feet from the ground, despite the tennis shoes she wore. The sensation moved up her legs, and moved within her, much like the blood in her veins. The warmth of the rune under her palm intensified as did the sensation flowing through her. She yanked her hand away, unable to keep it in place. The rune flared brighter. She reached a hesitant hand towards it.

Mr. Ferguson called her name. She heard panic in his voice. She hurriedly turned to make her way towards him. He was not easily roused by fear.

Her foot caught on a nearby rock. She stumbled backwards. She grabbed for the sides of the doorway. Her hands slipped on the smooth stone, and she fell through it instead. Pain shot through her tailbone as she landed with a hard thud. She uttered a few choice words at her own clumsiness.

Kaily placed her hands on the ground to push herself up before Mr. Ferguson found her in such a state.

She froze in place. The ground beneath her hands was cold, smooth stone, not the dusty rock strewn floor she expected. She lifted her head and gaze. The same stone arched doorway frame stood before her, at least it looked the same, runes included. All except the solid mahogany wooden door within its frame.

Her heart skipped a beat.

She looked around her surroundings. She swallowed hard. Her heart skipped more beats.

She gingerly pushed herself to a standing position. She turned in a full circle. She repeated her full circle a second and third time. Her breathing became shallow.

Kaily no longer stood in a crumbling castle. Walls, ceiling and floor confined her in a somewhat small room. She uttered some more choice words as if they were a mantra.

She took several deep breaths. Turned another couple circles, staring in disbelief.

She bent and placed her palms on her knees. She took several long, deep breaths. Too many apparently as dizziness overcame her. She stumbled backwards until her butt landed against a solid wooden desk in the room. The desk and matching chair were the only pieces of furniture she saw. She held on to the edge of the desk for support.

Her brows creased as her frown intensified. This had to be a dream. The solid wood beneath her hands told her otherwise.

She hit her head, she surmised. She lay unconscious on the dirt ground for Mr. Ferguson to find. "Great! Just great!" She muttered. It had to be a dream brought on by an obvious concussion. Her eyes roamed the confines of the room. She shook her head. She hoped it was a dream, regardless of the panic Mr. Ferguson would feel if she were unconscious. It had to be a dream. She shook her head again.

Everything was too real for a dream, even one from a head injury. She closed her eyes and focused on breathing, inhale, exhale, and repeat. She had to be dreaming. There was no other explanation. Yet, she didn't believe she was just dreaming.

She forced her eyes open and looked around the room again. A sense of familiarity overwhelmed her. Kaily shook her head. She'd never seen a room like this before in her life, but she couldn't shake the familiar feeling. She stood and took another long look around the room.

One of the four walls held books from floor to ceiling. Torches were dispersed in various positions on the other three walls, and tapestries hung from two of them. The torches did not give off any smoke in spite of their medieval appearance.

The light tan stone of the doorway contrasted badly against the darker stone and mahogany wood of the door, desk and chair. She walked to the wooden door and ran her fingers across its surface. She placed her palms on the wood and pushed. She took a deep breath.

As much as she wanted to be dreaming, no dream contained the depth of solidness as reality. Not even her dark warrior dreams seemed as real, and those were real enough that she hoped her dark warrior existed.

This, she shook her head and turned in circles, this was too real to be a dream. She focused on her breathing and rapidly beating heart, willing both to calm down. She couldn't afford to panic now. Not when she had no clue what had happened to her or where she might be.

She shifted her focus to the tapestries. One held images too gruesome to focus on. She moved her attention to the other tapestry. The background held the same tan hue as the stone arched door frame. The scene on the tapestry depicted two planets, one silver and the other gold. A thin bronze oval encircled each planet and intersected in two places as if illustrating their planetary orbits in relation to each other. The tapestry did not show any other planets or celestial bodies. Embroidered below the planets was a map of sorts. The map appeared to be out of focus.

She walked closer to the tapestry while staring at the map. As she drew near, the map shimmered and changed. She stopped, took a step back. The map shimmered and changed again. Frowning, she moved closer.

The map almost looked three-dimensional and flat at the same time. When she was close enough, Kaily brushed her fingers along the map on the tapestry. To her surprise, static electricity zapped her fingertips. She yanked her offended fingers back and put them in her mouth. The shock had been stronger than a minor jolt. She hesitated to touch the tapestry again. Instead, she focused her attention on the rest of the room.

A large blood red satin pillow lay on the floor beside the chair. The pillow was big enough to sit on cross-legged and not touch the stone floor. She let out a heavy sigh. She would have sworn that she had never been in that room prior to now, except for the sense of deja vu invading her mind.

She shook her head. Her heart continued to beat rapidly in time with her quick breaths. Panic slithered inside of her. The walls closed in on her. Bile rose to the back of her throat. She needed to escape the confines of that too tiny room. She struggled to stave off a full-blown panic attack. Losing what little wits she possessed would not help her now.

She stared at the only visible door in the room. A really bad feeling kept her from opening it. Perchance it was because of what had happened when she accidentally fell through it in her clumsiness or possibly something else. Either way, she had no intention of going through that damn doorway again.

She turned her attention back to the tapestry with the twin planets. The middle of the tapestry seemed to quiver. She walked towards it until she stood within inches of the fabric. She held her hand up and hesitated. She sensed the electrical current humming through the cloth. The shock the first time still stung her fingertips. She braced herself for the shock she knew she would receive. She pushed her hand against the middle of the tapestry, expecting to come up against a stone wall. To her surprise the cloth gave way, and she did not receive a second electrical shock. She could feel the current vibrating in the tapestry. She shrugged, unable to make sense of it all. She moved her hand to other places while pushing firmly against the cloth. She soon discovered a portion of the tapestry seemed to have nothing behind it. She pulled the fabric aside to expose an opening which revealed a stairwell behind the tapestry.

She glanced again at the wooden door. She resolutely shook her head. She would take her chances with the stairs. She slowly made her way up the spiraling stairway. Torches, similar to those in the library, lined the wall. Each sprang to life as she approached them as if on some kind of motion sensor while still appearing to be medieval primitive. Fear and panic rose with each step as she ascended those stairs.

Finally, she came to a door at the top. She placed her hand on the door handle and paused. Kaily glanced back down the stairway, wondering if she should try the door after all. A lump lodged in the back of her throat, and stones in the pit of her stomach. An intense fear threatened to choke her senses. The torches began to dim. If she remained, she would be surrounded by darkness before too long. While she hated small places, she hated dark small places even more. The stairwell was not all that wide a space either. She took what little courage she had in hand, and slowly opened the door.

Her fear of the dark got the better of her. She hurried into the room and slammed the door shut. A sudden clatter of noises startled her. She shrieked and spun around. Two women in the room, appeared as frightened as she was. A man stood off to the side. Kaily stood paralyzed in place. Her eyes locked with his.

He broke their eye contact and turned his attention to the two women in the room. Kaily's mind numbed as she tried to make sense of what she saw in front of her. The women and man appeared to be right out of the medieval history books right down to their clothing and mannerisms. Which kind of made sense considering from all appearance she somehow landed in a medieval castle. The man barked what sounded like orders at the women. Or maybe it was the way they responded which made her think so. The words sparked a familiarity in the back of her mind, just as the tiny room had. His words were not ones she understood. But then again, her thoughts barely were coherent even to herself.

The man continued to speak to the women.

She continued to be frozen in place with fright. She tried to focus on his words as a way to distract herself from the intense fear coursing through her veins. As she focused on his words, Kaily soon realized that she could make out some of what he said. She thought perhaps he spoke an old English or Gaelic. The more he spoke, the more she could comprehend. She fell against the door to keep from falling down. Her eyes remained fixed on him, although he paid little attention to her. A cold chill ran down her spine. She shook her head. No, not old English or Gaelic, but the language of her childhood. The one she had spoken when her foster parents first found her.

The language held similarities to old Gaelic which is how her linguist foster mother had learned how to first communicate with her. It had been so many years since she last spoke the language, she would have thought she'd have lost the knowledge to understand it. Somehow, she still possessed enough knowledge to start making out the words he spoke. The more she listened, the more she understood. She gave a small shake of her head in amazement.

She turned her focus to the two women as her heartbeats began to slow. Strange how a familiarity with her childhood language could create a measure of calm in the myriad of chaos. Maybe not quite chaos, but close enough.

From the look and sound of what was going on, the two women were servants. Probably chambermaids from the look of the room she'd stepped into. A bedchamber, a sizable bedchamber with highly decorated furnishings. She frowned at the women as they curtsied to her and bowed their heads to the male. They left the bedchamber through another door than the one she still leaned against. The door was larger than the others and perhaps the main door to the chamber.

Her attention turned back to the man in the room. He definitely seemed medieval, sword and all. When their eyes met, he bowed his head, but not before she saw a puzzled expression cross his features.

"Forgive me, Mistress, for not having your chambers prepared for your early return," he said.

Kaily thought he might have repeated himself before his words penetrated her fear clouded mind. She couldn't determine if her mouth hung open, although she wouldn't have been surprised. She couldn't find the words to respond. Although she did retain understanding of the words spoken, she didn't have the ability to engage her wits.

He opened his mouth as if he were going to add more, but then closed it. He slowly raised his head and again his eyes locked with hers. He most definitely wore a puzzled expression on his facial features. His brows furrowed.

She didn't blame him for the lack of words or his bewildered countenance. She didn't know what to say or how to act either.

He stepped closer to her, but not within reach.

She absolutely preferred he kept his distance, sword and all. She couldn't take him down if he were to turn on her with intent to harm, and not just because of the sword he wore.

"Did your visit go well with your sire?" His expression remained perplexed. "Mistress," he said as an afterthought.

Her frown deepened.

"I only ask as we were not expecting your return for another fortnight."

"Ummm." Kaily couldn't manage to say anything else. She also couldn't take her eyes off him or his sword. Why was he acting like this? Like he knew her?

He didn't press her further. Instead, he walked over to a decorative crafted wooden chest at the foot of a canopy bed and opened the lid. The bedchamber furniture appeared to be made of a dark mahogany wood, like the desk and chair in the other room. He pulled some cloth items out of the chest, and then went to the wardrobe. He opened it and took something else out which he draped over his arm with the other items. Next, he turned back to Kaily.

"The serving women will return with food and drink before long. You must be tired after your long journey. I will place a change of clothing," he indicated the items he held, "in the bathing chamber for you to change into after your bath."

Kaily didn't respond. She simply watched him as he entered another door in the room. She glanced around the room. She counted three smaller doors and one larger door. There also was an alcove, of sorts. She made note of the shutters. Her attention snapped back to the man as he reentered the room.

"It will take the serving women time to draw your bath which will give you time enough to enjoy your repast." He piled wood into the hearth and started a fire. He pushed up a lever near the top of the hearth. "Both chambers will be warm before too long."

"Thank you." Kaily managed to say between beats of her racing heart. Her childhood language felt foreign on her tongue.

The man stood and turned towards her. He stared at her for a moment longer before speaking. "Will you be here long?"

"Ummm." Kaily couldn't find the words. What she wanted to say was 'hell no' but it would mean she knew how she came to be there in the first place and how to get out of there. Neither of which she had the slightest hint of an idea.

Before either of them said another word, the serving women returned with a platter of what appeared to be cheese, bread and a steaming bowl of something. She couldn't see enough to say for certain what it might be, and the smell wasn't a familiar one. The tray also held a goblet and pitcher. The serving women placed the items on the table near the hearth. They poured some of the contents from the pitcher into the goblet. When they finished setting everything up, they curtsied before entering the bathing chamber.

The man didn't speak to her or them. Instead, he stepped up behind one of the chairs at the table and pulled it out for her.

Not that the gesture had been necessary. The chair didn't exactly fit under the table. He watched her and waited.

Kaily glanced over her shoulder at the door she'd come through and still leaned against. She gazed back at him. She caught a glimpse of a small, amused smile curve his lips before suddenly disappearing.

He tilted his head towards the table and chair. His hands still rested on the top of the chair back.

She sighed and pushed off the door. She couldn't think of any other option to consider. She didn't know where she was or how she'd come to be there, other than a really impossible thought she didn't want to bring herself to accept. The man, scary as he appeared, offered her a measure of kindness. Not that she understood why, but she knew nothing of her surroundings. Really too bad all this wasn't a dream. She'd have far more courage if it were. She sat in the chair with another sigh.

The man stepped around to face her. He studied her for a moment longer before picking up the goblet and handed it to her.

"Thank you," Kaily said.

He glanced towards the partially open door of the bathing chamber before he leaned in close to her ear.

Kaily jumped, startled by the movement. Her eyes riveted to the hilt of his broadsword. She gripped the arms of the chair hard and pushed herself against its back trying to gain distance. It didn't work. She was confined. Her breath caught in her throat. She would have dropped the goblet had it not been for his quick reflexes as evidence from it setting atop the table once again.

"There is no need to thank your servant Jaren or the serving women, Mistress." Again, he seemed to add the 'Mistress' part as an afterthought. "Understood?" Jaren straightened and looked at her.

Kaily nodded.

"Is there anything else you require, Mistress?" Jaren asked in a louder voice.

"Nay." She suspected he spoke loud enough for the serving women to overhear.

Jaren mouthed a different phrase than her one word response and waited.

Kaily repeated the words aloud that he'd mouthed, she hoped. She was not the best at lip reading.

He gave her a nod, and then took his place by the door as if on guard duty.

Kaily gazed at Jaren and frowned. His eyes no longer rested in her direction. In fact, he acted as if she no longer existed or at least that's how it felt to her. She turned her attention to the food the women had brought. Her stomach protested. Still, she should try something to keep up her strength. She sniffed the contents in the goblet. The smell didn't offend too much. She took a sip and placed the goblet back on the table. The room temperature liquid tasted okay, but her stomach rolled and gurgled all the same. She broke off a piece of the bread and nibbled on the corner. She stared at the flames in the hearth.

She needed options, but she didn't have any. She didn't even have a clue of what she was dealing with there. Or even how the hell she'd gotten herself to that place. Where ever 'that place' was. She shook her head. That damn doorway and rune had something to do with it, despite how implausible.

All she could do was observe her surroundings, for now. She hoped sooner or later answers would present themselves.

She glanced towards Jaren. Somehow, he seemed to know her. As much as she hated to admit it, this place held no small amount of deja vu for her. She would swear she'd not been there before, but it felt too familiar for that to be true. She turned her gaze back to the blazing fire. She focused on her breathing and held back the tears threatening to fall. Kaily refused to panic or at least she would do her damnedest to keep the attack at bay. 'I'm not going to panic!' She silently repeated to herself in hopes that at some point her body would listen to her brain for once in her life.

Chapter Three

"You're late."

"Don't you knock?" Moto demanded.

"I did knock. Several times." Shimani shut the door to Moto's hut. "What are you doing?"

Moto let out an exasperated breath. "I can't find her."

Shimani frowned. He moved to stand across the table from Moto. "Find who?"

"The girl!" Moto glared at Shimani. He pointed at the looking bowl between them. "Don't pretend you don't know who I'm talking about." He knew Shimani was more than aware of what girl he meant. His wayward protege had caught him wasting his time obsessing over her on more than one occasion. He had to evade Shimani's incessant questions about her. Moto never gave any satisfactory answers to him. Figures that Shimani would feign ignorance when Moto was ready to talk about her, sort of ready. He was ready in as much as necessary to get help finding the girl.

Moto woke up early that morning, and went about his duties as he'd promised himself, he would. His cursed mind kept drifting back to his little distraction. As much as he tried, he couldn't ignore the impact she had on him. Each time their eyes locked, something indescribable passed between them. It would be better for both of them, if he could find the strength to let her go. But as the day drew on, an intense feeling of unease grew stronger inside him. He became less competent in his duties. He thought if he could just take a moment to check on her, the growing panic would ease up. Possibly gain a sense of peace which would allow him to focus on his responsibilities. An indulgence he should have ignored, but he hadn't. And now, he couldn't locate her, anywhere.

"Well, at least you're obsessing over something other than your night terrors."

Moto glared at Shimani. "There's the door." He pointed. "If you don't have anything useful to add, feel free to use it."

"My apologies," Shimani said with a slight nod of his head.

Moto sensed Shimani attempting to suppress amusement, and he didn't care for it. He glared at him.

"I'll help you look after the meeting," Shimani said. "You know our presence will be missed."

Moto shook his head and cursed. Shimani was right, and it irritated him. This wasn't just any meeting. It was a Council meeting with the Shanees from the other twelve Kahoali Villages. The meetings were held twice in an annual cycle. The

Chosen always attended by the Queen's side or rather at her back as custom dictated. The Chosen were the only males permitted to attend those meetings. He should feel pride in his being a Chosen, but at that precise moment he did not feel pride. He was annoyed.

Moto cursed. What if something happened to the girl? Since the first time he laid eyes on her, he never failed to locate her whereabouts. He often found the girl at her residence or the ruins. They appeared to be the only two locations on her world she inhabited. He couldn't understand why now all of a sudden, he couldn't find her.

"Moto!"

"I know!"

Shimani laid a comforting hand on Moto's shoulder. "I'll help you find the girl. I give you, my word." He started moving towards the door. "I'm sure she is fine."

Moto ran his hand over his face. "Thank you." He forced the words. He didn't have the same certainty as Shimani. He had no choice but to attend the meeting. Shimani was correct. They would be missed. "Duty first." Moto muttered under his breath. He turned away from the wooden looking bowl he painstakingly made. He followed Shimani out of his hut. He didn't bother to send back the water from Crystal Lake within the bowl. It would keep and he would try again at his first opportunity. After the cursed meeting.

At the Queen's hut, they moved around the side to where they entered through a back door. It wouldn't do either one of them any good to draw too much attention to themselves. The meeting would already be underway.

Shimani stopped him before they entered. "Try to control yourself."

Moto glared at him. He pushed his way past Shimani and through the door without comment. Kahoali males were supposed to be stone statues without a modicum of emotion or at least, none they displayed in public. It grated on his nerves that the women had no such restriction placed on them. To be fair, males were far more emotional than the women, but it still irritated him.

He quietly walked across the back of the dais to stand in his customary place beside Baridi. Shimani came to stand between him and Kesho. Moto couldn't see the Queen's expression as she sat on her throne in front of the four Chosen. He sensed the moment she'd become aware of their presence. Curse the Kahoali empathic abilities. It didn't help that his empathic ability was stronger than most. Her annoyance permeated all his senses. Moto took a silent, deep breath and focused his attention forward to those gathered in the throne room.

Fortunately, this would be a short meeting. The annual meeting usually lasted three days. The first day, which this one was, meant the meeting would be mainly pleasantries and mapping out the next two days. The subsequent meetings were where the twelve Shanees and Queen would get down to business. He would endure, Moto told himself. Not that he actually had a choice. The benefits of being a Chosen. He really should be more grateful for being selected to serve his people in such a way. But he'd found conforming to societal norms difficult. As a Chosen the expectations weighed more heavily on him. He loved his people, he just wished they would be a little bit more understanding of his unusual ways. He braced himself to endure the short meeting.

The meeting dragged on far longer than it was supposed to! Moto shifted from foot to foot. Baridi directed a low growl his way. Moto ignored it. He focused all his attention on not losing his temper. He hadn't been surprised when Shanees Tanyu brought up her request to be his mate to Queen Shakti and the Council. She'd promised him she would the last time he rejected her offer. However, he'd been shocked when the Queen allowed her to present her request before them all. His choice of mate was a private matter and should have been kept private! The Queen should have rebuked Tanyu or at the very least told her the three of them would address the matter in private!

"As your majesty is aware, only two of the last four Chosen are eligible to choose a bonded mate. Which is why I have brought my request before this Council and yourself." Shanees Tanyu inclined her head towards the Queen.

Moto's eyes narrowed to mere slits. He gritted his teeth.

"Moto!" Shimani said in a harsh whisper.

Moto spared Shimani a glance.

Shimani gave him a small shake of his head.

Moto took a deep breath and focused his attention on Tanyu. Curse her! He couldn't abide by her inappropriate behavior. Why was the Queen allowing her latest antics?

"With so few Kahoali developing abilities, our people are on a decline. We have no other Kahoali males who are capable of being a Chosen, thus our pairings need to be chosen with purpose. How else are we to save our waning abilities?" Shanees Tanyu asked.

Moto's nostrils flared with every word she uttered. He tuned out the rest of her words to try and keep his temper in check. She was spiteful. He'd made it clear the last time she approached him that he would never choose her as his bonded mate. Never! The Queen should have put Tanyu in her place. The fact she hadn't infuriated him. He took a deep breath as quietly as possible. He was vaguely aware that both Shimani and Baridi side stepped closer to him. He didn't spare either one of them a glance. His heated focus remained fixated on Tanyu. Surely the Queen wouldn't force him to bond with her!

Queen Shakti stood up from her throne. She held her hand up for silence.

Finally! Moto thought. He waited for the Queen to put Tanyu in her place.

"Thank you, Shanees Tanyu for your passionate argument and the honor you do Moto in requesting him as your bonded mate in such a public forum." Queen Shakti said.

Moto's mouth would have dropped open if he hadn't been clenching his jaw.

Shanees Tanyu opened her mouth as if to add more to her argument. She closed it without speaking. Moto could imagine the look the Queen must have leveled her with. At least, it was something, he thought.

"While it is my desire the Chosen should bond with a Shanees," Queen Shakti glanced behind her at Moto, "I am not willing to put aside our traditions to make it so. Nor is the matter of the heart a decision for this Council. With that said,"

Moto's attention sharpened on the Queens 'but' words.

"I can no longer ignore the current situation of our people, as you have so eloquently pointed out, Shanees Tanyu."

"Eloquently my ass," Moto muttered under his breath.

"Less and less of our young seek their talismans from Crystal Lake. Our people are losing the capacity to hear the call of the life giving energy that permeates Ki, and thus will not be able to harness the energy to develop their abilities. It saddens my heart to think of a day when none among us feel or touch the energy of our world. Your arguments have merit and will not be ignored. However, at this time the decision remains with Moto."

Moto should be relieved by the Queen's words. He wasn't.

"The day is wearing long. Please take respite in the guest huts provided to each of you and join us as honored guests for the evening repast." The Queen remained standing as each of the twelve Shanees stood from the half circle of benches arranged before the dais the throne sat upon. Each inclined their head to the Queen before heading down the aisle and out of the exit.

Moto impatiently watched and waited for them to file out of the throne room. When the last of the Shanees had left, Queen Shakti turned to face the four males and nodded once to dismiss the Chosen.

"A moment, Moto," Queen Shakti said.

Moto's heart sank to his stomach. He remained and waited for her to speak which wouldn't be until the other Chosen had exited the throne room.

The Queen descended the dais once they were alone. She sat on one of the benches the Shanees had occupied during the meeting. "Come join me." She held her hand towards Moto in invitation.

He inwardly cursed as he walked towards her. This cost him more precious time than he could afford. The dread and panic he'd felt before the meeting had intensified to unbearable proportions. "My Queen," he said when he stood before her.

She gave him a smile. A sad smile he'd seen far too many times of late. "Sit." She patted a place on the bench beside her.

Moto sat as instructed.

The Queen took his hand in hers and patted it like she would a small child.

Moto supposed that at 150 annual cycles, and one of the two oldest Kahoali, he would seem as a child to her.

"What do you think about Shanees Tanyu's offer?"

Moto opened his mouth to answer and then closed it. His first response an adamant and resounding no, not happening! That kind of answer wouldn't go over well with the Queen or put her in a good humor. He glanced at the floor to gather his thoughts and emotions. "While I am flattered by her offer," he stopped himself from adding 'made in public' to avoid disrespect towards the Queen. "I do not believe we would be a good match."

Queen Shakti nodded once. She studied him for a long while.

Moto began to wither under her scrutiny.

"You are five cycles past when you should have taken a mate."

Moto briefly closed his eyes. This he knew. Why would it matter? He still had time.

"What about Shanees Sari?" Queen Shakti asked.

Sari? No! Moto thought. They were close, but he just couldn't see himself with her for life. "Shanees Sari and I are close, but she is more like a sister to me than a potential mate."

"I see." Queen Shakti sighed.

Moto remained silent.

"I will allow you more time, but I suggest you reflect and decide soon whom you wish for a bonded mate. Strongly suggest." She gave him a piercing look which told him that her patience with him dwindled.

Moto knew without the words being spoken that she expected him to step in line and become the perfect example of what a Kahoali male should be. "As you wish, my Queen." Moto gave her a small bow of his head.

The Queen shook her head at him. "Go! Enjoy your freedom while you have it."

Moto nodded and turned to leave.

"Moto?"

He turned back to face her.

"I prefer your choice be a Shanees."

He inclined his head in acknowledgment.

The Queen waved her hand in his direction as way of dismissal.

Moto left as quickly as was acceptable. Once outside, he glanced at the sky to the fading light and cursed. The day was almost gone! He had yet to find the girl and sage the disquiet inside of him. He tried to console himself with Shimani's words that the girl was probably fine. Still, panic rose inside him that shouldn't exist. There was absolutely no reason for him to experience any kind of alarm, outside his trepidation from his night terrors. This panic felt different, foreign. He hated when things didn't make sense.

"Moto!"

He groaned inside. Why couldn't he catch a break? He reluctantly turned towards the one who'd called his name. "Sari?"

"Walk with me."

Moto glanced in the direction of his hut.

"Please."

Moto briefly closed his eyes and let out a sigh. "As you wish." He stepped beside Sari and kept pace with her stride as they made their way to the guest hut she always stayed in when at Center Village. He glanced sideways at her.

Sari gave him a smile similar to the one Queen Shakti had given him. "Why didn't you tell me that Tanyu was being so insistent on becoming your bonded mate?"

Moto took a deep breath. "It wasn't important."

"Seemed pretty important in the meeting back there." Sari waved a hand over her shoulder.

"Tanyu is a stupid child who can't take no for an answer." Moto took another deep breath to try and cool his rising temper.

Sari gave a short unamused laugh. "We are the same age, Tanyu and me."

"That's different." Moto interrupted whatever else Sari was about to add to her comment. He stepped in front of Sari's path and stopped, forcing her to stop as well. "Look, I mean no disrespect, but I have something I need to attend to."

Sari raised an eyebrow. "What?"

"None of your business." Moto closed his eyes a moment and took another deep breath. "Nothing important."

Sari tilted her head and narrowed her eyes. "Then you can finish walking me to my hut."

Moto ran a hand over his face. He glanced at the passing Villagers. Just to have a moment's peace and privacy! Apparently, both were too much to ask for, Moto thought. "Okay, nothing I wish to discuss. Look, I,"

Sari held up her hand for silence.

Moto had to admire how much she personified regality. Almost as regal as the Queen. "Sari, please,"

Sari shook her head. "You can either tell me what is going on with you or I'll get it out of Shimani."

"Good luck with that." Moto muttered.

Sari glared at him. "Rude!"

Moto inclined his head to her. "My apologies, Shanees Sari."

Sari sighed and shook her head. She pulled him to the side of the path and waited for other Villagers to pass them. "I am just worried about you, Moto. Your behavior lately is out of character, even for you. The Queen is not going to be so patient with you for much longer, despite how favored you are by her."

"I know." Moto said.

"Do you?"

Moto didn't answer.

Sari brushed her hand down his upper arm. "If you're not careful, you'll face punishment for the neglect of your responsibilities and for your attitude. Please, talk to me or Shimani about whatever is going on with you."

Moto's gaze shifted to the ground between them.

"I can talk to the Queen about you staying in my Village for a while."

Moto lifted his gaze to Sari. "I appreciate the offer, but no."

Sari opened her mouth.

"Please, Sari, let me finish."

Sari inclined her head to him.

"I may take you up on your offer just not now. I appreciate that you worry about me and care enough to say something. Really, I do. Right now, I just need space and time to myself. Please." His gaze locked with hers as he waited for her response.

"Fine." Sari answered after a long pause.

"Thank you." Moto turned away from her and made a hasty retreat to his hut. He didn't look back to see how his sudden departure was received. He couldn't ignore the discomfort inside him. He felt the kind of alarm that not even his night terrors had elicited. They'd brought an urgency to the surface of his emotions, but this full on panic was something altogether different and unfamiliar.

"Piss the Queen off?" Shimani asked with a great deal more amusement than Moto thought appropriate.

Any sense of relief Moto had momentarily felt upon seeing Shimani within his hut faded. He swept the chair out from under Shimani.

Shimani landed with a thud. He gained his feet with a few choice words directed at Moto. "I'll give you that one, for now," Shimani said. "But only because you're so out of sorts."

Moto refrained from comment. He didn't have time for banter with Shimani. Moto stepped forward and gazed down into the looking bowl on the table. He placed his hands flat on the table on each side of the bowl. He emptied his mind of unpleasant thoughts and focused his attention on the girl. Finding someone in the looking bowl could be a bit tricky. He had to know whom he sought and their general vicinity.

"Anything?"

Moto shook his head. He took several deep breaths. He again focused his thought on the cursed girl while he again attempted to empty his mind of any distractions. The girl was distraction enough.

Thankfully, Shimani remained silent.

He continued to take deep breaths. He forced his thoughts to focus on nothing but the girl. He tried every mental trick he knew to pull her image forward into the looking bowl. He succeeded in pulling the two locations he'd previously found her, which confirmed his effort to focus the conduit of Crystal Lake water was working, but still no girl. He hit the side of the bowl in frustration, sending it flying across the room. The bowl crashed against the wall and splintered into pieces, too many to fix.

"Well, that helped." Shimani backed up and out of Moto's reach.

Moto glared at him. "Door. You. GO!" He pointed first to the door, then to Shimani, and then to the door again.

Shimani was not easily intimidated. "What about going back to the last place you saw her?"

"I JUST TRIED THAT!" Moto pointed to the splinter remains of his looking bowl. He would have to make another one which would take too long. Making a looking bowl was not easy, and far different than making a regular wooden bowl.

"I meant physically," Shimani said, "or are you going to tell me you haven't been going to her world?"

Moto glared at Shimani.

Shimani stood his ground and waited.

Moto shook his head. "Fine." He wouldn't give Shimani the satisfaction of answering him. "Will you cover for me?"

Shimani shook his head. "No."

"What do you mean NO?" Moto cringed for not taking more care with his volume. While the Village huts were built with a respectable distance from each other, they were not far enough apart not to be overheard when speaking in loud tones. He didn't need to draw undue attention. No telling what the Queen would do if she ever learned of his excursions off world. Especially, for a girl he clearly obsessed far too much over.

"No." Shimani repeated. "I'm going with you."

"What?" Moto shook his head. "No. I need you to stay and cover for me. The cursed meeting went on for far too long and the evening repast will start soon." The evening repast was not the only or even main reason he didn't want Shimani tagging along while he located the girl. He liked Shimani, but what if they found the girl? He didn't want to share that particular moment with him. Or have a witness to his cowardly behavior around her. An unpleasant thought he pushed to the deepest, darkest recesses of his mind.

"I understand that you have your reasons for wanting to find this girl on your own, but you can't deny that you might require my expertise."

Moto glared at Shimani. "You learned everything you know from me."

Shimani shrugged. "Then consider it another lesson to bestow upon my unworthy head. Besides, we've missed other evening repasts. It would look less suspicious if we both were absent than if just you were."

"And you wouldn't have to cover for me?"

"Exactly!" Shimani said.

Moto crossed his arms over his chest. This repast wasn't like the others, but Shimani made sense, and he didn't like it. He really didn't want or need a shadow. He gave a small shake of his head. "Fine." Moto said. "Don't slow me down."

"Do I ever?" Shimani asked.

Moto didn't answer. Instead, he grabbed a dagger from his weapons wall, and slipped it into his boot. He headed out the door without a backwards glance at Shimani. He wouldn't get lucky enough to have Shimani change his mind and remain behind. He made his way to the edge of Center Village and into the forest, away from curious eyes.

Shimani followed close on his heels.

They stopped in a secluded area. Both glanced around. Moto's eyes locked with Shimani's.

Shimani nodded once.

Moto held up his hand and opened a portal to the Ancestral Gateway. He stepped into his portal first. He knew Shimani would follow. They both exited the portal at the Gateway.

Moto hurried to the large stone arch. He lifted his hand to open the Ancestral Gateway to the girl's world.

Shimani laid a hand on Moto's arm to stay his actions.

Moto looked at him and frowned.

"When you scanned for the girl, did you happen to notice if the vicinity of our destination was void of the worlds' Inhabitants?"

"No." Moto cursed his lapse in common sense due to his preoccupation of the girl.

"This should be fun." Shimani removed his hand from Moto's arm. He waited for Moto to activate the Gateway.

Moto placed his palm over the rune to the girl's world and quickly went through the steps to open the Gateway. He stepped through as soon as the shimmer indicated the path was open. He felt Shimani follow him. On the other side he hid behind the partial wall.

Shimani followed Moto's example.

The light of day faded on this world as it had on Ki. Moto cautiously peeked around the partial wall and frowned. It was unusual to see so many in that place. The panic he barely kept in check started pushing its way closer to the surface of his emotions. He sensed worry and sadness from those gathered in that place. He glanced from those congregated to Shimani. He expected to find Shimani beside him. Instead, he found him standing in front of the Gateway on this world.

Moto crept to where Shimani stood. "What are you doing?"

Shimani shrugged. "Nothing useful." He replied and pointed. "Are there often this many people here?"

Moto shook his head.

Shimani frowned. "Wanna head back?"

"No," Moto said. He kept his voice low. He was grateful Shimani had done the same. "Neither do I want to be discovered." Moto frowned and glanced over his shoulder towards the wall between them and the others gathered there. He couldn't see them, but he sensed them. The emotions pouring off them bothered him more than he cared to admit. Something was wrong, and he feared their concerns centered on the girl he wished to locate. He returned his focus to Shimani. "Open the Gateway, quietly."

"I am appalled at your lack of confidence in my abilities." Shimani opened the Gateway and stepped through before Moto could respond.

Moto followed. On the other side, he held his frustration in check as best as he could. Now what? He thought. He began to pace. He avoided speaking in case he might take his frustrations out on Shimani. More than he already had.

"What if we head to Crystal Lake and try scanning for her again?"

Moto stopped pacing and turned to Shimani who leaned carelessly against the Ancestral Gateway. "With what?" He all but yelled at Shimani. "In case you hadn't noticed, my looking bowl no longer works."

"With this." Shimani pulled a small wooden bowl from inside his vest pocket. The calmness in Shimani irritated Moto. He barely kept his ire to himself. He reminded himself that Shimani merely wanted to help. Although, he preferred less of Shimani's unwanted attempts at humor. "Guess you paid attention to that lesson." Moto opened a portal. He stepped aside to let Shimani enter first.

"I always pay attention," Shimani said, "for the most part," he added as he stepped into Moto's portal.

Moto shook his head and followed Shimani.

They exited the portal just this side of the path to Crystal Lake. They took the stationary portal to the meadow of Crystal Lake at the same time. Shimani handed Moto his looking bowl once they emerged.

"Thank you." They hurried to the edge of the Lake. Moto knelt and scooped up some of the water with the bowl. He cupped the bowl tightly with both hands and stared into it. He gathered energy and focused on the water.

Shimani knelt beside Moto and peered into the bowl.

Nothing appeared on the surface of the water. Moto tried to ignore the frustration growing stronger inside him.

"Concentrate, Moto."

"What do you think I'm doing?" Moto looked up and gave Shimani a fierce scowl.

"Letting your frustrations cloud your mind and diminish your concentration."

Moto's scowl intensified. He might have growled at Shimani as well. He wasn't certain. Either way, Moto felt a modicum of appreciation at Shimani's good sense to remain silent. He took a deep breath and forced his focus to concentrated on finding the girl. As he stared into the bowl, he thought the water shimmered a few times. Still, he couldn't make her image solidify. Moto slammed the bowl down on the ground after yet another failed attempt.

Shimani picked up the discarded bowl.

"What do you think you're doing?" Moto demanded.

Shimani shrugged. "Giving it a try."

"What makes you think you can succeed where I couldn't?" Moto's temper began to get the better of him. He kept from snatching the bowl out of Shimani's hand by sheer warrior's will power. How could Shimani have the audacity to think he might find her when he couldn't!

"There is no harm in me trying, Moto. You are not as calm as you need to be, and I paid attention to your lessons. What could it hurt for me to try?" Shimani looked pointedly at Moto.

"Fine!" Moto stood and walked away. He didn't have patience left to watch Shimani's foolish attempt he was certain would fail. He walked away from the Lake towards the forest. He moved back after gaining a bit of control over his temper.

Shimani didn't look up once at him.

Moto begrudgingly admitted to himself that Shimani appeared to have better focus than him at the moment. He walked back towards the meadow and back again towards Shimani. He found it too difficult to remain in one place. As he walked back towards the Lake and Shimani, his eyes focused on the misty waterfall. His mind and thoughts turned inward. He was being foolish, he knew. He should just leave it alone. She meant nothing to him. He shouldn't pry into her life. He had to let her go.

"Found her."

Moto ran back to Shimani. "How?" He should have been grateful, but he felt incredibly frustrated. Shimani had succeeded where he'd failed.

Concentrated," Shimani said. "I know where she is."

Moto accepted the bowl Shimani carefully handed him. He stared into the bowl and felt his mouth drop open before he could stop it. He shut his mouth and clenched his jaw. Her image shimmered in the water of the looking bowl. She stood in a place he'd not seen before and was not familiar to him. "Where is she?" His gaze locked with Shimani's.

Shimani smiled. "On Ki."

"How would she be on Ki?" Moto did growl at Shimani for certain that time. "She possesses no ability to touch what little energy that flows through her world, let alone open the Gateway." It was not possible. There was no way she was on Ki, his world. Impossible!

Shimani shrugged. "Do you want to know where?"

Moto glared at Shimani who grinned like a young boy who just landed his first blow on his opponent during training. "Wipe the grin off your face. Where?"

"One of the Agenors strongholds."

Moto's gaze drifted back to the image in the bowl. His eyes narrowed as he focused on her surroundings. "Are you certain?"

"Yes. Remember when you first told me about your night terrors, and I suggested we do some looking around on the Agenors Isle?"

"Yes." Moto frowned at Shimani. "I also remember we discarded that idea as being too dangerous."

"You discarded the idea. Anyway, she seems to be alone now. If we wait until she is asleep, she won't notice us."

Moto looked up at the sky. The last vestiges of daylight had faded. The dark had settled in. The evening repast would continue for a while longer than usual since all the Shanees attended. If he and Shimani hurried they would make the repast without being too late, and then he could visit the girl after. He emptied the bowl and handed it back to Shimani. "You know I don't want you to come with me, right?"

"Yes," Shimani said. "You wouldn't deny me after I found her, would you?"

"Yes."

"Seriously?"

Moto said nothing and looked a long while at Shimani. He obviously begged with the look on his face. Moto let out an exasperated breath. "Fine."

"Yes!"

"Don't make me regret giving in."

"Of course not." Shimani replied.

Moto rolled his eyes. He would regret taking Shimani with him. In reality, he didn't have a choice. It was a bad idea to open a portal to a location he'd never before been, especially in a closed building. "We need to make an appearance at the evening repast which will give her time to fall asleep."

"Agreed."

They took the stationary portal back to Center Village for the repast.

The repast was as political as he'd expected it to be. He'd spent most of the time avoiding Tanyu. Fortunately, Sari was really good at running interferences for him. He'd felt a surge of gratitude when Shimani pulled him aside.

"We should be good to go." Shimani said.

Moto glanced around the clearing by the Queen's hut where the repasts were held. He concurred with Shimani's conclusion. They could make their escape. "Agreed. Let's go."

They made their way to the cover of the surrounding forest.

Moto turned to Shimani. "Open a portal to where she is."

Shimani gave him a partial bow, bending at his waist.

Moto refrained from knocking Shimani to the ground for his insolence.

"See you on the other side." Shimani said and stepped into his portal.

Moto closed his eyes and sent up a silent prayer to the Universe for patience. He stepped into the portal. Once on the other side, Moto glanced around the room with a frown. He and Shimani stood in a room with a sparse amount of furniture and far too many books for the tiny space. He turned to Shimani. "She isn't here."

Shimani ran his hand over the surface of the desk as he walked around it. "She was."

"How do you know?" Moto demanded.

"Can't you feel her energy?" Shimani asked.

Moto didn't answer. She addled him too much that he couldn't feel anyone's energy lately, let alone hers.

"Look at this." Shimani called to Moto.

Moto turned towards him. Shimani held back a wall covering which exposed an open doorway. Moto frowned.

"Shall we see what's up there?" Shimani asked.

Moto groaned at the excitement lacing Shimani's tone. He should have left him at Center Village. He didn't think about just how helpful Shimani had been in locating the girl. He wasn't comfortable exploring a place that made him feel so uneasy. Something about the place didn't sit well with him, and he couldn't quite put a finger on the source of his unease. His gaze roamed around the room. His eyes landed on the closed door and back again to the open door way. Unfortunately, he couldn't rest until they located the girl. As much as he hated the idea of exploring this place, he had no choice.

"Guess it's as good as any other option." Moto finally replied. He stepped through the open doorway.

"That's the spirit," Shimani said. He followed Moto through the doorway and up the stairs, taking them two at a time.

"You could at least attempt some control." Moto shot Shimani a glare. "And keep quiet. We don't want to draw attention to our presence."

Shimani smiled, and silently followed Moto.

At the top of the stairs, Moto eased opened the door a crack and listened.

Silence.

It unnerved him to be in an oppressive building with no sounds. He preferred the wooden structure of his peoples' huts where muffled sounds drifted in from time to time.

He poked his head in and found a larger room. His eyes immediately gravitated to the bed. There was dark, blood red material draped over the top, like a canopy, and tied to each of the four posts. The material on the bed matched the other. Within the folds of the material, lay the girl he'd longed to find. How in the Universe had she gotten herself to Ki?

Shimani pushed his way around Moto and through the door.

Moto barely caught himself from sprawling forward and prevented a face plant on the floor. He glared in Shimani's direction.

Shimani crept closer to the bed. He turned back to Moto. "I see why you're obsessed with her."

Moto would have knocked him on his ass if he thought he could without waking the girl. Instead, he gave him a low warning hiss.

Shimani turned to face Moto and held up his hands.

Moto stepped up to the side of the bed. He stared down at the sleeping girl. He felt such an overwhelming relief at finding her, disturbingly so.

"Moto!" Shimani called in a loud whisper.

Moto turned to face Shimani, ready to lecture him on what quiet meant.

Shimani gestured for Moto to join him.

Moto walked with purpose towards the window Shimani stood in front of. "If you wake her, I swear," he stopped mid-sentence. His gaze locked on the sky and the world which loomed over them. He hadn't realized the cycle had begun. Living in the forest made it easy to forget that world existed.

"That confirms that. She's on Ki."

Moto glared at Shimani. "We already confirmed she's on Ki." He said as he pointed impatiently towards the bed with the sleeping girl.

"Just in case we weren't positive. I should probably get back."

"Yes, you should." Moto opened a portal.

Shimani inclined his head to Moto and stepped through the portal.

Moto glance again at the sky, and then shut the wooden shutters to the window. Why Shimani would show him their hated enemy's world, he had no idea, and didn't care. His concern was for the girl.

He turned back towards her. How had she gotten there? The how was probably the door in the room they had portaled to. He hadn't gotten a solid look at everything, but he'd seen enough to notice the runes on the arched doorway. They seemed, at a glance, to be similar to the runes on the Ancestral Gateway. Still, she couldn't have opened the Gateway. Yet, there was no other explanation. She clearly lay in the bed, on his world.

He walked to the bed and carefully sat on the edge. If he had any sense, he would take her back to her world, and forget he ever saw her. He knew he didn't possess any sense where she was concerned. A cruel twist of the Universe's sense of humor that he should be drawn to her in the first place. No stories existed of a Kahoali bonding with Inhabitants of other worlds. None! Only a true Kahoali bonding produced a proper mating and offspring. Which might have been some of the reason Kahoali remained separate from other Inhabitants of the Universe. Not the complete reason, he knew, but those other reasons were too dark to think upon now.

He brushed a stray strand of her dark auburn hair from her pale face. He liked the way her hair shone in the light of day, like dark bronze metal. "Ah, little one, I don't even know your name. What am I to do with you?" He spoke the words so softly they came out as barely a whisper. She tormented his very being by her existence.

Moto stood and scanned every corner of the room with his eyes while he contemplated what he should do about the girl. Should, was to take her back to her world, and forget she existed.

Wanted was an entirely different matter.

He couldn't bring himself to voice what he wanted to do with her, not even within his own mind. He couldn't do what he desired. The cost would be more than he was willing to pay. Still, he needed to understand why he was so drawn to her in the first place. And for that, he required time.

After making his mind up, he slowly walked back to the edge of the bed. He drank in every nuance and detail of her delicate features. In that one brief moment, he allowed himself to simply feel without thought or sensor.

He placed a light kiss on her forehead. "Forgive me, little one." He whispered.

It was enough to know she was on Ki, where he could find her at will. As long as she remained on his world, he would be able to locate her no matter where she went. Keeping her on Ki would give him the time he required.

Chapter Four

Kaily jolted upright in bed. Her eyes darted from one corner of the room to the other. Her breath caught in her throat. Her heart pounded hard against her chest. She leaned forward to see the other parts of the room she couldn't glimpse from her position on the bed. She leaned back uneasily against the headboard and hugged her knees to her chest. The room was as empty as when she first lain down the previous night. For the past week, she had startled awake, certain she was not alone. Yet, upon each waking, she found the room to be just as empty. It was enough to make a girl lose her mind.

It didn't help that none of the doors could be locked. Not even a crossbar to be found in the bedchamber. Who would build a damn castle without locking doors! The chairs were too heavy for her to push in front of any of them. She didn't feel safe. She knew that was part of the problem. Still, Kaily couldn't shake the feeling that someone had been in the room with her, despite what her eyes told her.

She might have blamed her paranoia on dreams, except she hadn't dreamt. Not once since arriving at that bleak place. Even her dark warrior dreams had abandoned her.

She ran a tired hand through her hair as she attempted to calm her beating heart.

Kaily spent countless hours this past week in the library searching for answers. It was the room she'd first found herself in when she'd been whisked away from her home. They had been uncomfortable hours. The gruesome tapestry, the tiny space, and her unease made it difficult for her to remain in the room for long. She endured as long as she could each day, pushing her discomfort aside. When she couldn't take the rising panic, she retreated to the bedchamber.

She hadn't gathered enough courage to venture beyond the bedchamber and the library. The rest of the time she spent staring at the flames in the hearth or out the window. The air outside was fresher than she would have expected in a castle. There was a strangeness about the place, both modern and medieval at the same time. But the strangeness went far deeper than structural or functional. The people moved from task to task without any sense of life within them. They existed without joy from what she had observed from her albeit limited vantage point. She hadn't spotted children either. Happiness did not exist in that place.

Her only contact had been Jaren and the two serving women who went about their tasks with minimal words spoken to her or each other. She'd fallen into a routine of sorts. Jaren entered the bedchamber first each morning to stoke the fire in the hearth. There seemed to be a constant fire going from roaring blaze to smoldering embers. She had no idea how he kept it going and didn't care. The fire kept the cold at bay. The women would follow shortly after with morning breakfast. They would set up the table with the morsels, and then gather clothing which they took into the bathing chambers where they would draw her bath. She would be left to her own devices for the remainder of the day. At night, Jaren would again stoke the fire, and the women would put out her night clothing and turn down the bed. She would simply watch the proceedings, contemplating how they could possibly have mistaken her for the 'Mistress' of that castle.

On the rare occasions when Jaren remained alone with her, she had tried to get answers from him about her circumstances. She kept feeling like he knew something and refused to communicate that knowledge to her. Not exactly refused. He would give her vague answers or change the subject. Still, she sensed him holding back.

Knowing how hopeless sleep was now, she threw back the covers and got out of bed. She opened the shutters to the window and perched on the ledge without opening the window. The mornings were too cold to endure. She usually waited until afternoon to get her dose of fresh air.

Her fears grew with each passing moment. According to Jaren, she had a week left before the rightful Mistress returned. She couldn't figure out how to return home.

She lifted tired eyes to the sky and moon, if it could be called such. A golden sheen surrounded the large globe. At times it looked more like a planet than a moon. The sight in the sky confirmed she no longer dwelled on Earth. Jaren had at least told her she was on Ki, but she didn't know if Ki referred to the planet or the castle. The uncertainty reminded her of her foster mother's lessons, languages were tricky. What one might assume to be one thing, to a native speaker might actually mean something else entirely. Language was all about perspective. She sighed in frustration as this really didn't matter, she was in a strange place and had no way to return to the certainty of her home.

Her attention snapped back to the bedchamber as the door opened. Even though she'd been staring at the sky, she'd not noticed the day getting brighter. Time was a funny thing. She never knew the exact time, ever. She only knew when one day ended and the next began. It was bizarre not to have a clock to tell time by. These people lived by the rising and setting of the proverbial sun. She had yet to actually see any kind of globe in the sky that would pass for a sun. If she had been braver, she might have taken time to explore the world, she wasn't, so she hadn't.

She watched Jaren go about his normal routine. She knew the serving women wouldn't be far behind in their routine.

The only brave thing she'd done was to try and repeat here what she'd done on Earth. At least, what she thought she'd done. She'd tried to find the exact rune she'd been looking at and touched it, many times, in many different ways. It'd all been for nothing, but at least she'd tried. She didn't consider herself courageous by nature. She stuck to safe. There was nothing there that made her feel secure.

She waited for Jaren and the serving women to leave the chambers before she uncurled herself from the window ledge. She closed the shutters.

She glanced at the bathing chamber's open door. She'd allowed herself a long soak each of the previous mornings. An indulgence she couldn't afford to allow this morning. She'd failed in her previous attempts to get home or at least find answers on the how of it. Kaily needed to come up with an alternative plan. If she couldn't get back to Earth, she needed to find someplace else to be, before the rightful occupant returned.

She walked over to the table in front of the hearth. She tore off a piece of bread and dipped it into the porridge like substance. She popped the moist piece into her mouth. The food wasn't bad tasting, but neither was it the best. She wasn't particularly hungry. She needed to keep up her strength, so she ate a few more pieces of porridge dipped bread.

When she'd finished eating what she could stomach, she grabbed a gown from the wardrobe. What she wouldn't give for her jeans and sweater. She made do with the gown, dressing as quickly as possible. She ran her fingers through her hair to get some of the tangles out. After she thought her appearance presentable enough, not that she would purposely come across anyone, but just in case she did, she took a deep breath to steady her nerves. She was, after all, portraying the Mistress of the castle, who she suspected seldom looked disheveled.

She made her way across the room to the stairs leading to the library. She intended to avoid Jaren and the serving women and anyone else she could avoid in her intended uncharacteristic exploration of the castle. Irrespective of how her situation had come about, she needed to find a way to deal with it and keep herself safe. Notwithstanding her lack of courage.

After several attempts, and several additional deep breaths, Kaily finally made it through the doorway and down the stairs. It was one thing to traverse to the library, and another to know she would move beyond the tiny room, with enough courage. She moved the tapestry aside just enough to slip through the opening. She stopped in her tracks, staring at the solid doorway. Trepidation encompassed her as memories of what happened last time, she walked through the stone arch flooded her mind. Her failed attempts to make the rune glow aside, fear paralyzed her. What would happen this time when she walked through the door.

Kaily took a deep breath and shook her head. Today, she needed to be courageous, damn the consequences. Whatever would happen, it had to be better than her current situation. She hoped. She crossed her fingers for good measure. With another deep breath, she opened the heavy wooden door.

She shouldn't have been surprised to find Jaren standing on the other side of the door. She was.

"Mistress," he said in his annoyingly calm manner. He bowed slightly at his waist.

She'd learned from Jaren's subtle and not so subtle hints that responding in her usual polite manner was not the way she should respond. Of course, he hadn't bothered to explain to her what was expected. Frustrating didn't quite describe her thoughts on the matter. She didn't know if he meant to be less than helpful on purpose. Sometimes his helpfulness was apparent, other times not so much. So, she did what worked best. She ignored him.

From her time staring out of the alcove window in the bedchamber, she'd discerned the room took up one of three possibly four towers. But her vantage point didn't give other details of the castle layout. She thought the battlement connected the towers but didn't find a door leading to them in the tower she occupied. To be fair, she hadn't spent as much time exploring as she should have.

Kaily glanced down both directions of the hallway. Without a clear indication of which direction would serve her purpose, she stood there, indecisive.

She glanced at Jaren.

He stared at the wall in front of them.

Figures! No help from that source.

She took a deep breath, picked a direction and headed down the hallway. She concluded that it didn't really matter which direction she explored first. She had no clue what she was looking for, not exactly. She wanted an escape plan in place. Other than that, she didn't know what she needed. So, she walked and took in her surroundings.

She heard the tapping footfalls behind her of Jaren. The sound grated on her nerves. She didn't like to be followed. She stopped and glanced back at him. He stopped each and every time she had. He maintained the exact same distance between them no matter how slow or fast she walked. She might have been amused by his actions, maybe even make a game of it, if she were in a better state of mind. She stopped again and glared at him before continuing her journey down the insanely long hallway.

Jaren wasn't fazed.

The direction she'd picked brought them to a busy part of the castle. She had no idea so many worked or resided within the castle. The number of people milling about grew as they traveled farther down the hallway. She noticed more knights similar in dress to Jaren, and more serving people. She thought they were such from their garb. She didn't make eye contact with any of them.

She stopped just short of a large opening in one side of the wall. She cautiously peered inside. Beyond the threshold lay a great hall. People entered and exited the room through the opening and the large double doors opposite her position. The aroma convinced her that breakfast was being served. Her stomach rolled at the smell. It wasn't the odor that affected her, but her fears.

She watched the crowd without focusing on any one person. Indecision of what her next move should be clouded her mind. She fought a strong desire to scurry back to the safety of the bedchamber. There were too many people for her liking to explore further. She needed to explore. She had to find a safe escape. But too many people. Their obvious avoidance of her perplexed and bothered her. She should have been happy about it. Her stoic, silent shadow didn't help.

She turned towards Jaren. "What?"

He ignored her. Didn't even bother to look at her. Instead, he nodded in greeting to two passing knights.

Kaily crossed her arms over her chest.

Jaren suddenly stepped uncomfortably close to Kaily. "Perhaps, Mistress, you would like to inspect the battlements?" His words sounded like a question, but his tone did not.

Her gaze locked with Jaren's. Her eyes narrowed as she contemplated if she actually had a choice.

Jaren remained silent.

Maybe she didn't want to be too hasty in refusing his suggestion, if she could call it such. He hadn't given her enough useful information over the past week. Maybe she would get something out of him if she agreed to the battlements. She had, after all, tried to find a way to them. She shrugged, more to herself and inner dialog. "Lead the way. I don't much care for being followed."

Jaren inclined his head. He glanced around them. She noticed that those who looked in their direction ducked their curious gazes and hurried away when his eyes landed on them one by one.

Kaily's temper rose with each step they took as she realized he led her back the exact way she'd come. All the way back up towards the bedchamber. "Jaren!" Kaily called after him. He walked faster than she could keep up with.

Jaren stopped and turned to face her.

Kaily hurried to catch up to where he waited. "Are you taking me back to the bedchamber?"

Jaren glanced at a few passing women.

Kaily stood in front of him and crossed her arms over her chest.

Jaren's attention drifted back to her.

Kaily opened her mouth to speak.

Jaren gave her a slight shake of his head. His eyes contained warning. He placed his forefinger in front of his lips for the briefest moment, and then made it look like he rubbed his chin. After the women walked out of sight, he turned and ran up the tower stairs two at a time.

Kaily narrowed her eyes at his retreating back and pressed her lips tightly together. What was with him not answering her? She muttered a few unflattering words under her breath as she ran up the stairs after him.

When she arrived at the top, Jaren ducked into a side door Kaily had failed to notice earlier. It was near the main bedchamber door but surprisingly hard to notice.

Kaily followed Jaren through the door to another spiraling staircase. "Figures!" Kaily grumbled as she followed a disappearing Jaren.

At the top of those stairs, Kaily struggled to catch her breath. Damn him for running up them. "Why didn't you answer me?" She demanded once she had enough breath to speak.

"Keep your voice down." Jaren hissed at her. He turned and pushed a stone on the wall before Kaily could reply.

She heard the grating sound first before seeing the stone wall move in, and then slide aside. The receding of the wall exposed an open doorway and more damn stairs. She hadn't thought the tower was so tall from her vantage point looking out of the window in the bedchamber she'd been staying in. Apparently, it was. She took a deep breath and ran up the stairs.

"We did pass the bedchamber, didn't we?" Kaily asked while taking his offered hand.

Jaren gently held her hand as he helped her through the narrow door at the top. "Aye, we passed the bedchamber." He closed the door.

The door they passed through hugged the high wall of what looked like the battlements. The inner wall, Kaily assumed was the inner wall, stood about waist high. The inner bailey, if she had her bearings, lay below. She spotted three other towers, all connected by a walkway. She moved closer to the lower wall and looked out into the inner bailey. They main gate stood a little off center from their position. She glanced around the area at the other buildings. Some she recognized as ones she'd seen from the bedchamber window, others she had not. The castle grounds were larger than she expected.

The wind chilled her. She stepped back towards the high wall to get some relief. She glanced at Jaren who leaned against the higher wall with his arms crossed over his chest. He watched her. She shifted from foot to foot and shifted her gaze back to the main gate.

The silence between them stretched and became uncomfortable. She didn't have to look in Jaren's direction to know he still watched her, intently. She thought in that moment that she preferred his indifference over his intense scrutiny. When she couldn't take it any longer, she gathered some of her courage and focused her attention on Jaren.

"You know I'm not the Mistress of this castle, don't you?" Her tone sounded more like a statement instead of a question.

"Aye," Jaren said.

"How long have you know?" Kaily could probably guess, but she wanted to know his truth.

Jaren didn't answer.

Kaily glared at him.

He still didn't answer.

She shook her head and returned her attention to the inner bailey and main gate. She didn't have enough courage to force an answer from him. Not that she could. She didn't have any kind of skill with a sword which might be what it would take. Assuming she could actually lift one. His looked quite heavy from the way it hung from his wide leather belt.

The silence continued. Kaily refused to give him the satisfaction of glancing again in his direction.

"Since the beginning," Jaren finally answered.

Kaily took several deep calming breaths before acknowledging his reply. His soft spoken words startled her. "I see." She said when she'd calmed enough. She turned towards him. Her eyes locked with his. "Do you know how to get me home?"

Jaren frowned and rubbed the bridge of his nose. "That is a bit more complicated. The short answer is nay. I don't know how to get you back from whence you came."

Kaily's eyes narrowed. "And the long answer?"

Jaren shrugged without comment.

"Perfect," Kaily said more to herself. She took a deep breath. "Is the true Mistress returning in a week?"

Jaren slowly nodded. His eyes did not leave hers.

"Am I right to believe that I don't want to meet her face to face?" Kaily forced herself to ask the question. She feared she knew the answer but wanted, needed confirmation. She'd thought about what it might be like to meet this Mistress person, and each time a stone dropped heavy into the pit of her stomach as paralyzing dread consumed her. The thought brought forth something familiar and terrifying within her mind, but not enough to completely surface as more than emotions.

Jaren again nodded.

Kaily turned away and went back to her contemplative staring. Now what? Alarm rose quickly inside her as the hopelessness of her situation settled around her. Her eyes began to burn as she struggled to hold in her emotions and panic. Not that she could keep either in check, still, she tried. Before she knew what happened, Jaren wrapped his arms around her, pulling her in close to his chest. She attempted to pull away. His relentless strength wouldn't budge.

"Shhh," he said. He held Kaily closer, tighter. "Shhh." He repeated.

"Stop shushing me!" Her tears slid from her eyes unchecked as she gave up her struggle to hold it all in.

Kaily didn't know how long she cried or how long she took comfort in Jaren's warm embrace. Long enough to soak his shirt. Finally, she wiped the remains of her tears as her sobs subsided. She pushed on his chest.

Jaren loosened his hold on her.

"Won't this all look out of place to the others?" Kaily asked as she moved fully out of his embrace.

Jaren dropped his arms to his sides and leaned against the wall. "Not as much as you might think."

Kaily couldn't decipher the emotions that passed through Jaren's eyes. There was pain, sadness, loathing, and something else she couldn't interpret. She couldn't decide if she should say more or not.

"People turn a blind eye to this part of the battlement," Jaren said at last.

Kaily frowned but didn't press further. The look in his eyes gave her the impression he wouldn't add more on the subject. So, she changed subjects. "Why do the others not question who I am?"

Jaren frowned and remained silent.

Kaily let the silence hang between them. She figured he would answer, or he wouldn't. She'd be damned if she begged for a reply.

"Because you look like her," he said. "Care to take a walk? The air will do you good, and you will be able to get a better view of the castle layout."

"Do I have a choice?" Kaily turned in the direction Jaren indicated with a gesture.

He shook his head.

Kaily concentrated on the hushed tone and words Jaren spoke as they walked along the battlement. He told her about the guards, where they were stationed and their schedule for changes. He told her about each of the buildings and their function. He told her when they held activity and when they were empty. He told her about his position as personal guard to the Mistress. She thought he might have left some details out as he gave far less detail about his duties to his Mistress than he had about everything else. She did learn that when the Mistress left the castle, she traveled alone without any guards. Kaily thought this strange but refrained from asking any questions. She really had no desire to learn more about her, not even her name.

Jaren grabbed her arm, abruptly stopping her just before the third tower.

"What is it?" She quietly asked as her eyes followed the path of Jaren's gaze.

"Trouble." With a firm hold on her upper arm, he hurried her back the way they'd just walked.

While Jaren yanked the door to the bedchamber tower open, Kaily's gaze drifted towards the dark figure striding through the main gate. He was garbed in a long, dark cloak. The garment gave her the impression of a deep, dark pit one could fall into and never escape. A cold shiver traveled down her spine. She shook her head to clear her mind of the disturbing image. She couldn't look away.

The stranger's face remained deep within the hood of the cloak. Although she couldn't make out his features, she observed the way others reacted to him. They gave the cloaked figure a wide berth and averted their gaze. Jaren yanked her down to a low crouching position.

"Take heed to my words. You do not want to come face to face with that man out there." Jaren pointed in the direction of the cloaked figure.

The shiver down Kaily's spine intensified to a painful cold spike sensation.

"Wait in the solar for me at the bottom of the tower. Do not venture out of that room. Not for any reason no matter what you hear. Do you understand?"

Kaily nodded. She tried to swallow the lump lodged in her throat.

"I will try to get rid of him." Jaren held open the door and helped her get back through it.

She grew apprehensive. His tone lacked confidence in his ability to get rid of the cloaked figure. "Who is he?"

"I'll explain later." Jaren opened the bedchamber door. "Use the private stairs."

Kaily hesitated going inside the bedchamber.

"GO! Hurry!" Jaren all but shoved her inside and slammed the door.

She stared for a moment at the closed door before making haste to the door of the private stairs. She fumbled to open the door. Finally, she managed to get it open. Panic gave her speed as she practically flew down the stairs to the sanctuary of the solar, if she could call the room such.

Kaily breathed a sigh of relief to find the room empty. She always found the room empty, but her luck never seemed to work in her favor. She rushed to the heavy wooden door and searched for a way to lock it. She noticed for the first time a slide lock on the door. She slid it firmly into place. She leaned against the door and tried to catch her breath. Her legs grew weak and rubbery as her adrenaline started to drain away. She was slowly sliding towards the floor when a loud, firm knock made her jump away from door.

She spun around to face the doorway and backed away from it. "Aye?" She called out in an unintentional harsh tone. Fear lodged in her soul and made it impossible to control her trembling.

"Mistress, Ener demands an audience," Jaren called through the door.

Kaily thought it sounded like he almost yelled. "I'm busy. Tell him to come back later." She spoke as loud as her trembling voice would allow. "In a week or so," she muttered under her breath. Her heart pounded in her chest. She held her breath as she waited. She couldn't make out what this Ener person said, but she could hear the tone of his words. A cold fear passed through her. She pressed her ear hard against the door and listened. She heard the sounds of heated words exchanged. She couldn't even make out what Jaren said, he'd lowered his voice.

Silence.

She strained to listen harder for any sound. If she could just figure out what transpired in the corridor.

Kaily screamed when Jaren touched her on the shoulder.

"Shhh! It's me." Jaren covered her mouth with his hand. He held her gaze for a moment before removing his hand.

"What happened?" She quietly asked.

"He's leaving," Jaren said, "for now."

"What do you mean for now?" Kaily didn't like the way he sounded.

"For now," Jaren repeated. "Ener is the kind of trouble that not even the Mistress likes to deal with."

"Great! Just great!" Kaily pushed past Jaren and ran up the stairs to the bedchamber. "Fantastic!" She paced the length of the room. "Now, what am I supposed to do, Jaren?" She asked when he entered the room. She watched him walk to the hearth and pace.

He shook his head. "I don't know."

Kaily wanted to tell him just how helpful he was NOT being. Never mind that he did get rid of Ener, for now, she thought. Fear took a firm hold in the pit of her stomach. She focused her efforts on keeping her heart within the confines of her chest. She took deep, even breaths to gain some semblance of calm. If she wasn't careful, she'd be debilitated by one massive panic attack. She was more afraid than she'd ever been in her life.

Jaren stepped into her path.

Kaily stopped and shook her head. Where had he come from? She thought glancing at the area in front of the hearth.

He placed his hands on her upper arms. He held her in place so she couldn't continue pacing.

Her panic grew. She reluctantly made eye contact when he remained silent.

"I don't know how yet, but I swear I will do everything in my power to prevent any harm from befalling you."

Kaily wished his promise made her feel better. It didn't. She'd heard the fear mingled in his words of reassurance. She couldn't ignore it. She nodded at Jaren. Words flowed through her mind that she wanted to say, but none of them would help the situation. She was afraid and trapped. Her words sparked by fear and frustration wouldn't change either of those emotions.

"Are you going to be okay if I leave?" Jaren asked.

Kaily nodded. She didn't want him to leave, but she figured he had reasons to leave her alone now.

"I'll check on you later. Try not to worry. Somehow we will figure something out." Jaren stopped at the main door and looked back at her.

Kaily nodded again. She watched Jaren walk through the door and close it behind him. She walked towards the hearth where she sat in one of the chairs. She sat there for the remainder of the day. The serving women brought food, and then took it away later, untouched. Jaren checked on her as promised. She nodded when he asked if she was alright. That night she crawled into bed. Her fears took a deeper hold. She was screwed and she knew it.

Chapter Five

Moto woke to a profound fear coursing through his veins. His heart raced in concert to his shallow breaths. If he didn't know better, he would swear he was having a panic attack.

Kahoali warriors did not have panic attacks!

He focused to separate his emotions from his awareness of the world around him. Clearing the intense emotions from his awareness helped center his mind enough to hear the sounds outside his hut. He slowly inhaled and exhaled as he focused his other senses to search his surrounding area.

Nothing unusual explained the disturbance which woke him.

He pushed himself to a sitting position on his sleeping pallet and rested his arms on his bent knees. He stared at nothingness as he continued to mentally scan outside his hut and the surrounding forest.

The fear lingered despite his efforts to quiet his emotions. He was accustomed to waking with such alarm. His night terrors often caused him to wake in like manner. Moto frowned and shook his head. This seemed different, more intense.

The past seven days he'd experienced an uncomfortable quiet fear for his sea-green eye with auburn hair girl that he'd left in the cursed stone building among the Agenors. He kept the fear under a semblance of control with nightly visits to confirm for himself that she remained safe. As safe as she could be among those barbarians.

He ignored the guilt gnawing at him for not yet taking her immediately back where she belonged. He blamed the lingering Council meetings for his inability to find the time to return her to her home world. There was a modicum of truth in his reasoning, but not fully. Too many of the weeklong meeting discussions had centered around him and his night terrors. Which is why a three-day meeting turned into seven.

Moto sighed. He ran a weary hand through his tiny, dark braids.

The girl's presence on his world gave him a measure of comfort and peace. Watching her sleep calmed him in ways he didn't bother to examine too closely. He had yet to make his nightly visit to her. He'd thought to rest for a short while before traveling to the Agenors stronghold. The previous day's meeting had been particularly intense with strong opinions about his night terrors being tossed about in a way that put him on the defensive. Kahoali did not have foresight, and that was what the Queen and most of the Shanees clung to instead of taking precautions. He didn't know why they had bothered with the discussions in the first place if they weren't going to take them seriously.

Maybe they would if he'd disclosed the truth about his abilities outside of the Kahoali norms. He hadn't. Sari and Shimani were the only two who knew the truth about his atypical abilities, and neither would betray his trust. He might be forced to expose all to Queen Shakti, one day. But until that day came, he intended to keep them to himself. Kahoali, as a people, did not react well to anything outside the norms.

He sensed the start of day was not far off. Since he couldn't pinpoint the source of the emotional distress, he might as well get the day started.

Moto stood and stretched. He rolled up his sleeping pallet to stow it in the corner. Next, he grabbed his trousers and vest, and took them to the shower room in his hut. He hoped the warm water would wash away the unpleasant emotion and clear his troubled thoughts about the girl. He should have been able to determine the source, being such a strong empath. One of the strongest among the Kahoali villagers. He shook his head. For whatever reason, he wasn't able to locate the origin of the fear that woke him.

He let out an exasperated breath. He would just have to wait and see what the day revealed.

Moto stood under the warm water, letting it run down the length of his body for a moment before he shut it off. He scooped out a portion of the cleansing paste and replaced the jar's lid. He took time to thoroughly lather his entire body and hair. The clean scent permeated the air. There was nothing like a good, clean scrub to clear way unpleasant remnants of the day or night.

He turned on the water to rinse off.

Blinding terror slammed into him so hard he grasped for the sides of the shower stall to keep from dropping to his knees. He had not experienced such heart wrenching terror in his life. Not even during the rare skirmishes against the Zaltys or waking from his own night terrors.

He concentrated to slow his frantically beating heart.

He forced slow, methodical intakes of breath into his lungs.

When he regained enough control, he finished rinsing off the lather from the cleansing paste and shut the water off. He made quick work of drying himself and dressing. He returned to the main room of his hut. Standing in the middle of the room, he inhaled deeply and exhaled just as deeply a few times. Enough to calm the emotions coursing through his being.

He closed his eyes and reached for the energy of Ki through his talisman. Despite his best efforts, the terror coursing through his veins threatened to rob his tenuous control. He forced the emotion to the back of his mind as he attempted to separate himself from the terror. Emotions would not serve him in finding the source of the fright. He was certain the emotion was not his, although, at that moment a part of him wondered if it were. The emotion seemed to emanate from within himself, and yet he knew it was not his.

He kept his eyes closed as he continued to draw in more energy from Ki. Only when the surrounding air pulsed with the energy, did he focus his mind and reached out for the origin of the fear. The image of the girl sprang into his mind, and became a sharp pain, stabbing the inside of his skull with hot, sharp knives. In that moment, he knew, beyond any doubt that the terror belonged to her.

A deep frown creased his brow.

He was a strong empath, but to feel her terror from so far away should have been impossible, even for him. He forced his angst over feeling her emotions at such a distance aside. She was in trouble, and he had no choice but to help her. If anything happened to the girl, it would be his fault for leaving her with the Agenors in the first place. He set aside his rising guilt for his actions and focused his mind and energy to the task at hand.

He narrowed his mind to determine her exact location. He only hoped he could open a portal close enough to help her. He didn't know why he sensed it, but he thought her life was in peril. Normally, he would have used a looking bowl to reveal her exact location but getting Shimani's would take precious time he didn't think she had to spare. Opening a portal this way held certain dangers.

He opened a portal when he grew certain he could do so safely, well, reasonably safe. He took a deep breath, and then stepped into his newly created portal while sending a prayer to the Universe.

It surprised him how close to the girl he'd opened his portal. He shook off his astonishment and scanned his surroundings. They stood outside, but within the confines of the stronghold. Men with swords drawn encircled them and closed in fast.

Moto pulled the girl against him. He held her close and placed a protective shield around them both.

The girl screamed and struggled.

"Be still," Moto commanded. "You're safe." He added the last part as an afterthought. He hoped she'd be safe with him. He held no coherent thought other than saving her life.

She shifted in his arms. It took him a moment to realize she meant to turn to face him. He loosened his hold on her only enough to allow her the movement. Her eyes collided with his. The terror in her eyes fell away as relief replaced it. Stunned, his shield almost faltered before he redoubled his efforts to keep it firmly in place.

The girl laid her forehead against his chest and covered the sides of her face with her hands as if to block out the scene playing out before them.

A warmth spread inside his chest in the vicinity of his heart. To be shown such trust. He cleared his throat to dislodge the sudden emotion threatening to choke him.

Moto shook his head and lifted his eyes. He didn't have much time before the armed men were upon them. He gathered more energy from Ki. He dropped his shield while simultaneously opening a portal. Before he stepped into it, a woman running towards them drew his attention. She looked almost identical to the girl in his arms. So similar they could be twins. The sight of her sent a shiver down his spine. His eyes narrowed. He hesitated.

"STOP THEM!" The woman shrieked.

Moto sprang into action as he lifted the unyielding girl into his arms and stepped into his portal before it was too late. The darkness pouring off the woman disturbed him on too many levels to comprehend in full. He didn't like the terror that woman sparked within the girl gently cradled in his arms. He didn't like the uncanny resemblance of the two. He pushed the disturbing thoughts to the back of his mind. Only one thing mattered in that moment, the girl in his arms. His eyes dropped to her face as his facial expression softened.

"You're safe." He reinforced his words with reassurance. He concentrated to slow his beating heart. He'd come too close to losing the girl all because he'd selfishly wanted to keep her close to him.

The girl lay motionless in his arms.

He frowned.

She lay so still that he couldn't tell if she still drew breath. He placed his hand on her chest and waited. He let out a sigh of relief as she drew in a shallow breath.

A soft smile touched his lips. He couldn't fault the girl for fainting. Her terror almost forced him to his knees, and he was a trained warrior. She was merely a slip of a girl. He carried her carefully to the corner where he kicked his sleeping pallet from its place to the middle of the room. He worked to lay it out without disturbing the girl. Not a feat he would care to repeat with anyone to witness his clumsiness.

When he had finally flattened out the pallet enough, he lowered the girl on top of it. He brushed back strands from her face. His fingers caressed the soft skin of her cheek. His eyes roamed the length of her, and his frown deepened with each moment. The heavy gown she wore would not work in the humid Kahoali forest. While the thought of removing her garment appealed to him, he kept his ironclad control in place. He squashed this unwanted desire taking hold inside him as much as possible and cursed the Universe for bringing the girl into his life. He should have returned her to her home world.

While he waited for her to wake, he lay down beside her. Not so close to intensify his desire for her, but close enough he could continue to caress her cheek and brush her hair with his fingers. "What am I going to do with you?" He whispered.

Over the past seven days, he'd considered going to the Queen to ask permission to bring the girl to Center Village. And discarded the thought just as many times. The last outsider permitted into Center Village cost many Kahoali lives. It was one of the most devastating moments in Kahoali history.

While he longed to keep her with him, he couldn't. The Queen would never allow it. She'd been one of the few survivors of the massacre, and one of the two only remaining after so long. One hundred forty annual cycles were not long enough for her or Baridi to forget.

Moto sighed. He needed some place to keep her safe and close. He wasn't willing to take her back to her world, not yet. Only he and Shimani knew where the girl came from, and he knew Shimani would not betray his trust. He would have to figure something out when the girl woke. He couldn't keep her hidden in his hut. He would have to decide where he could take her. For now, he would savor this time with her. He continued his caresses as he waited.

As the day grew longer, the girl did not stir. A deep frown took the place of Moto's soft smile. She should have awoken by now. Although, he'd not had experience himself with fainting spells, he was certain they should not last so long. He couldn't blame the portal as he'd transported Shimani a number of times before without a problem.

He sat up and knelt beside her. He gently shook her by the shoulders.

Nothing. She remained unconscious.

He shook her again with a little more force.

Still nothing.

He laid a finger against her neck to check for a pulse. The beat of her pulse thumped a slow, weak rhythm against his fingers. She still drew breath which comforted him, but laying so motionless, concerned him.

He patted the side of her face and continued to shake her.

She didn't respond.

He leaned close so his lips brushed her ear. "Wake up."

He shook her some more. "Wake up!"

Nothing.

Moto sat back on his heels. Everything inside him wanted to keep her safe. He uttered a number of choice curses as he stood. He ran his hands over his face and through his braids. He tied them at the nape of his neck. He needed to keep her safe and he needed to get her help. He couldn't do both. If he brought help, they would know he'd brought in an outsider. He shook his head.

Out of all his developed abilities, healing was not one of them.

He cursed again. He walked to his door, and then back to the girl. He knelt beside the girl and touched the side of her face. Her complexion seemed paler than it should have. Her skin had grown warm and sweaty to his touch. He didn't know how much of that was from the heavy gown she wore or the reason for her unconscious state.

He cupped the side of her face. "Forgive me, little one." He stood with resolution. He couldn't keep her safe and healthy. He feared one would be sacrificed for the other.

He walked to his door, with his hand on the handle he glanced one last time at the girl. A part of him hoped that she might wake

up in his hesitation. She hadn't. Kesho would know what
to do, but he would also know that Moto had broken
the unspoken rule about outsiders. Kesho would not keep
the information to himself. He cast one last look at the
unconscious girl, and then stormed out of his hut. She
required help, and only Kesho, their healer, could help her.

Moto returned with Kesho fast on his heels. He stopped
beside the girl on his sleeping pallet and looked expectantly
at Kesho.

One look at the girl, and Kesho stopped in his tracks.

Moto had been admittedly vague about the details of the
emergency.

Kesho glanced with a disapproving glare from the girl to
Moto.

Moto's eyes locked with Kesho's without flinching. He
refused to be intimidated by him, despite how many more
annual cycles he was than Moto. He'd made his choice in
bringing the girl to his Village. He refused to behave in a
shameful or guilty manner.

Kesho looked away first as his attention focused on the girl.
He moved to kneel beside the girl on the opposite side of
Moto.

Moto watched Kesho closely as he examined the girl. He
sensed him drawn in Ki's energy, and flow through his hands
as he examined the girl from head to toe. Kesho appeared to
pay particular attention to her head.

As the examination dragged on, Moto became impatient. He stood and began pacing as he waited for Kesho to finish his examination. He forced himself to remain silent.

"She'll live," Kesho said, after what felt like an eternity to Moto.

Moto stood face to face with Kesho. He waited for him to elaborate.

Kesho didn't.

Moto refused to give Kesho the satisfaction of asking for details. So, he waited for Kesho to leave. Once alone, he intended to take the girl somewhere, anywhere than the Village before anyone else became aware of her presence. He fully expected Kesho to go straight away to the Queen to advise her of the situation.

Kesho didn't move towards the door. Instead, he bent and lifted the girl into his arms.

Moto stepped forward. How dare he touch her! His silently uttered outburst remained in his mind alone, only by sheer will power. He was far more protective over her than he realized he would be. Anger rose fast and coursed through his veins before he recognized his temper flared.

Kesho glowered at him. "Control yourself! You are in enough trouble as it is."

Moto held his ground and tongue. He struggled to just stand by and let Kesho hold the girl so intimately in his arms. He silently scolded himself for not taking her back to her home world. Whatever happened to her now was his fault and his alone.

Kesho stepped up to the door. He waited for Moto to open it. "I'm taking her to the holding hut, and then we are going to advise Queen Shakti of the situation."

The last thing Moto wanted to do. He no longer had a choice. The moment he chose her health over her safety, he'd sacrificed his choice in the matter. He opened the door and followed Kesho outside.

"After you," Kesho said.

Moto's eyes narrowed for a moment. So much for keeping an eye on the girl. He inclined his head to Kesho and started moving towards the holding hut at the edge of the forest outside of the village common area.

They walked in silence. Once at the holding hut, Moto opened the door and waited outside while Kesho placed the girl on a too thin pallet within.

Kesho stepped outside and secured the door. "You first." He gestured with his hand for Moto to precede him to Queen Shakti's hut.

Moto had the distinct impression that Kesho didn't trust him.

On the way to the Queen's hut, Kesho stopped a young village girl. He whispered something in her ear. She turned startled eyes towards Moto and ran off.

Moto didn't need to hear what Kesho said to know the Queen would be informed of the situation long before they arrived at her hut. He refrained from commenting, barely. Any comment he might make would not bode well for him or the girl. This wasn't the first time; he'd found himself being escorted to stand before the Queen's judgment.

They made their way to the Queen's hut without incident and stood before the dais. Both clasped their hands behind their backs and waited.

The wait seemed to take far too long for Moto's peace of mind. He wanted answers from Kesho about why she remained unconscious. He needed to check on her. How could Kesho just leave her alone in the holding hut? What if she woke alone in the strange place? How scared would she feel then? Questions flowed through Moto's mind making it too difficult for him to remain still. He clamped down on his thoughts and forced himself to remain in position.

He almost sighed in relief when Shimani and Baridi entered the throne room and took up their positions on the dais behind the throne. The Queen arrived a few moments later. She took her place on the throne.

Moto didn't acknowledge Shimani's quizzical look directed at him.

Queen Shakti leveled Moto with a steely gaze. The look in her eyes spoke volumes of just how angry she was with him. "Am I to understand correctly that you brought an outside into the midst of Center Village?"

Baridi narrowed eyes on Moto. Shimani raised an eyebrow and curse him if he didn't appear just a little bit amused.

Moto ignored both.

"Yes, my Queen," Moto said as he lowered his eyes. Her anger vibrated the air surrounding them. It wouldn't be the first time Moto had angered the Queen, and probably not the last. He had a way of trying her abundant patience, although, he might have gone too far this time.

"Am I also to understand that she is not well? Kesho?" Queen Shakti's gaze shifted from Moto.

"Yes, my Queen," Kesho said with a slight nod of his head.

"What's wrong with her?"

"She is unconscious. From my examination she appears to have recently suffered a traumatic episode, my Queen."

"Explain."

"There is evidence of a strong fear response in her system, although I was not able to determine the exact cause of her unconscious state. Perhaps the traumatic situation which caused her fear." Kesho shrugged. "There is indication she will regain consciousness when her system calms down enough. She will require medicine to set her system in balance again and cure the headache her mind shows evidence of having when she wakes up."

"She will recover?"

Kesho nodded. "There is every indication that she will, my Queen."

Queen Shakti turned her fierce attention back to Moto. She drummed her fingertips on the arms of her throne as she regarded him in silence.

Moto caught himself before he started to shift from foot to foot.

"Shimani?" Queen Shakti's eyes did not leave Moto.

Shimani took the steps necessary to come around the throne and faced Queen Shakti.

She turned her gaze towards Shimani at that point. "Check on the girl. Bring her to me as soon as she wakes."

Shimani inclined his head in acknowledgment.

"Kesho, go with him and administer the medication she requires. Shimani, if she is well enough, remove the barriers necessary for her to understand our language. It may not help her to speak it, but at least she will know what is said to her when she is brought before me."

"Yes, my Queen," they replied in unison.

Queen Shakti watched as Shimani and Kesho left to do her bidding before her attention focused on Moto.

"Why, Moto?" Queen Shakti leaned forward to perch on the edge of her seat. "Why would you dare bring this outsider into our midst?"

"I feared for her life, my Queen."

Queen Shakti stood and stepped off the dais. She stopped an arm's length in front of Moto. "What I don't understand is how you came across her in the first place."

Moto opened his mouth to reply.

Queen Shakti held up her hand. "That was not a question." She turned back to face the dais. "Baridi, have the Shanees returned to their villages?"

"Most of them have, my Queen."

Queen Shakti nodded once. She glanced back at Moto, and then returned her attention to Baridi. "Send word to all Shanees who have not mated that Moto will be making his choice for bonded mate. Please discover who would be interested in being considered. We will hold a feast to give Moto the opportunity to choose which of the Shanees will have the honor of being his bonded mate."

"Yes, my Queen." Baridi bowed low to the Queen. He spared a disapproving glare towards Moto, and then left the throne room.

Moto held his tongue and focused his attention to not losing his temper.

Queen Shakti turned back to face Moto. "You left me no choice. Maybe your bonded mate can keep a tighter leash on you." She took several calming breaths.

Moto hoped he'd kept his anger from shining from his eyes. Leash? Never! Only one Shanees could he tolerate to bond with, and he couldn't bring himself to do that to her. Sari deserved a chance to find her forever love for her bonded mate. A secret desire she had confided to him long ago. Not that he hadn't taken the opportunity to tease her about it. He respected her heart's desire too much to take it from her.

"I'm at a loss, Moto. I have many questions, but I don't think you would give me a straight answer to any of them."

"I wouldn't lie to you, my Queen."

"No." Queen Shakti raised her eyebrows. "Neither would you disclose everything, would you, Moto?"

Moto remained silent.

Queen Shakti nodded to herself. She stepped back up on the dais and sat upon her throne. "You will maintain your distance from the girl. The others will see to her needs while I decide what her fate will be."

"Is she to be left in the holding hut?" Moto's anger got the better of him.

"I haven't decided." Queen Shakti shot an unfavorable glare at Moto. "As far as you're concerned, she does not exist. She is not yours to look after, nor will she ever be. Remember that, Moto!"

Moto held her glare, too long to be considered respectful.

Queen Shakti sat up straighter on her throne. Her gaze did not waver, and she did not blink.

Finally, Moto dropped his eyes, and bowed his head.

"Dismissed," Queen Shakti said with a wave of her hand towards Moto.

Moto bowed lower at the waist, straightened, and then left the throne room. He started walking towards his hut but stopped mid-stride. He didn't want to be cooped up. He let out a long breath and turned towards the direction of Crystal Lake. It was the one place he wouldn't be disturbed while he gave thought to his situation and what his next move should be. He cursed himself again for not taking her back to her home world, not that he intended to take her back now. He should, but he wouldn't.

Chapter Six

Kaily woke to a blinding headache. She patted the surface beneath her to find she lay on a kind of thin mat that did nothing to soften the ground underneath it. She attempted to open her eyes. The light intensified the stabbing pain in her head. She thought about moving, rolling over or even trying to sit up. She abandoned all thought of movement as a wave of nausea passed through her. She focused her efforts on opening her eyes. If nothing else, she needed to see where she was and what she might be dealing with.

She opened and closed her eyes in an effort to adjust to the light. This also gave her time to accustom herself to the sharp increase of pain with each attempt. She kept up her efforts while she examined her last memories. Her mind refused to work, much like her eyes.

When she could keep her eyes open long enough, albeit mere slits, she glimpsed her surroundings. The roof over her head appeared to be made of reddish-brown bamboo poles. She slowly turned her head. The wall matched the roof. The floor was hard packed dirt.

She closed her eyes against the bright light. With some effort, she managed to roll to her side. She cupped her head between her hands to keep it from exploding, not that it would. Tiny razor-sharp knives bore holes into the inside of her skull, at least that is what it felt like.

She took a deep breath. She struggled until she was able to sit up. She braced herself for the wave of nausea that overcame her. She focused her efforts on keeping the contents in her stomach from coming back up. She inched her way towards the wall to lean against something solid. The tiny hut like building didn't appear to be all that sturdy. She laid her head on her upturned knees and concentrated on making the pain in her head go away. She didn't handle pain well, and wishing it away never seemed to work for her, but she tried anyway. It wasn't like she could just pop into the bathroom for an aspirin.

She thought back to the last moments she could remember. She remembered Jaren telling her to run. The Mistress had returned earlier than expected. A full week earlier if her calculations were correct. She'd ran in the direction she thought Jaren instructed her to go. The direction which would lead her to a way out of the castle grounds without being noticed.

She took a deep breath and focused her thoughts. What happened next? She struggled to remember. If only she could clear the fog from her mind which hindered her ability to recall what transpired to bring her to where she was now.

Somehow, she must have gotten turned around, and ended up in the inner bailey instead of outside the gates as Jaren had intended. Everything had happened so fast. Armed guards chasing her. A vile woman, who looked just like her, shouting orders to those same armed guards. She would have shaken her head at the impossibility of it all, if the small movement wouldn't cause her excruciating pain.

Then what? She frowned. She turned her head on her knees and stared at the wall of the tiny room. She ignored just how tiny that room was and forced her mind on the task of remembering.

Her dark warrior? It seemed too much like a dream to be real. Yet, she remembered being pulled closer by her dark warrior. Very close. Heat rose in her checks at the brief glimpse of the memory. She frowned. If it was a memory and not a dream. She honestly couldn't say for certain. She gave a small shake of her head.

"Owww!" She closed her eyes tight, and gently massaged her temples. That was stupid, she thought to herself. Movement bad.

No matter how hard she tried, she couldn't remember what happened next. Her dream world seems to have collided with reality to make much sense of the images flowing through her mind. They couldn't be actual memories.

Kaily winced as the door she hadn't yet noticed unexpectedly opened. Two warriors strode into the already tiny room, which became incredibly smaller with their presence. They shut the door behind them. Her breathing grew more labored as she strived to catch her breath from her sudden fright. She had nowhere to run. She was trapped. These thoughts did nothing to help silence the fear coursing through her veins.

She pressed her back harder against the wall as if that small movement would provide ample space between herself and the two warriors staring down at her.

Her eyes widened when one of them approached her. He knelt on the dirt floor. Although within reach, he kept his hands to himself.

Her eyes narrowed. She concentrated on calming her breathing. She didn't bother with her racing heart. Nothing would calm it at this point.

The dark warrior glanced back at the other one. He was not her dark warrior, but similar in stature and looks. Similar enough, she had to reconsider her earlier thoughts on her dream world colliding with reality. Still, she remained cautious. The other warrior appeared to be older than the one who knelt before her. She didn't speak or attempt to communicate with either one of them. She wouldn't have had the voice or words to anyway.

The younger warrior said something to the older one. She couldn't even distinguish between the words. Her language skills usually allowed her to do at least that much. So much on communication, she thought. She had no hope of either being able to understand her, and she certainly couldn't understand them. But she tried to.

She focused on the words passing between the two warriors. The tone of the older one concerned her, especially since she couldn't understand their words. She guessed they conversed about her, but what were they saying?

Suddenly, the older one standing, approached her. He knelt beside the younger one. Kaily tried to pull away as he immediately grabbed her head. His palms rested firmly against her temples. Her heart lodged in her throat, and she struggled for breath, again. The panic surfacing threatened to engulf her. She closed her eyes and focused on her breathing. She would have rocked back and forth if his hold hadn't been so firm.

A high-pitched ringing pierced her ears.

She opened her eyes. Their eyes locked for a second before he let go and sat back on his heels.

The pain in her head flared for a moment to excruciating portions, and then settled back into the previous stabbing pain. Another wave of nausea made her cover her mouth and close her eyes. It was a miracle she hadn't yet lost her stomach's contents. Vomiting was one of the worst things in the world to her. She would do everything possible to prevent that from happening.

She forced her eyes open. Despite her discomfort, she had to remain aware of her situation, and the potential danger. Not that she could save herself! Too bad she couldn't just wish herself back home.

Her eyes narrowed, and her brow creased.

The younger one held a cup in his hand. He spoke to her and attempted to give her the cup.

She shook her head. No telling what the contents might be, and frankly she didn't trust her situation or them. She did, however, regret the movement as it amplified the pain, and caused a wave of dizziness. She didn't even want to think about the rolling and gurgling in her stomach.

"I thought you cleared the barrier." The younger one said to the other warrior.

Kaily's frown intensified. She glanced from one to the other.

"I did," the older warrior said. "Either she will do what you tell her to, or she won't." His eyes shifted to focus on her. "She understands." His attention returned to the younger warrior. "Bring her when she is well enough." He stood and backed towards the door. His eyes fixed on her, and his brows creased. "Don't be long about it. The Queen's patience has limits." He strode out the building and let the door slam behind him.

Her focus shifted back to the younger warrior.

"This will help your head feel better." He made a drinking motion with his hand.

Kaily slowly shook her head back and forth despite the pain the movement caused her. She covered her mouth with both hands for good measure.

"It will help." He again attempted to hand her the cup.

Kaily shook her head. She kept her hands protectively over her mouth. She didn't know where she was or who he was. There was no way she was going to drink whatever he offered her. Not that she wasn't somewhat tempted. Alleviating the fierce pain in her head, and the rolling of her stomach might be worth the risk.

He rested the cup on his thigh. "Here's the thing," he slowly began.

Kaily's eyes narrowed. His tone gave her the impression of speaking to a small child. She might have growled at him for his condescending attitude, if she had the courage.

"Kesho," he tilted his head towards the closed door, "indicated that your head is paining you to the point of nausea. This," he held up the cup, "will help. So, you can either drink this, and feel better or you can face the Queen as you are feeling now." He held the cup towards her and gave her a pointed look.

Kaily glared at him.

He didn't flinch or add further comment.

She suspected he could be quite stubborn. She removed her hands from her mouth. "How do I know it's not poisoned?"

He smiled. "You speak the language of the Agenors. Good to know. It's not." He took a drink and held it out to her.

"Maybe you have an immunity to the poison." Kaily said.

He kept the cup held towards her.

Kaily's eyes moved from his face, to the cup, and back again. She reluctantly took the cup. She eyed and sniffed the contents.

"It won't hurt you."

"Wanna bet?" She jumped when he laughed, nearly spilling the liquid on herself.

"My apologies." He said with a slight nod of his head.

Kaily kept her eyes locked with his as she took a sip. She winced. "Disgusting!"

"I didn't say it tasted good. I said it would help. Drink all of it."

Kaily drew in a deep inhale and held her breath while she downed the foul liquid. She glared at him over the rim of the cup. She gagged as she finished the last of the drink from whatever mix had settled in the last remnants. She handed back the empty cup.

"Thank you," he said. "I'm Shimani and you are?"

"Wondering where the hell I am."

"And I'm wondering what your name is."

Her eyes remained locked with his.

He didn't move or blink.

She let out a long sigh. "Kaily."

"Kaily," he said with a thoughtful look and nodded his head. "Is your head feeling better?" He spoke in the Agenors' language.

Kaily nodded. She relaxed enough to allow her back to rest against the wall without pain. She held no delusions about her precarious situation. She wasn't safe or at least, she didn't feel safe. He kept his distance and remained at her eye level. Perhaps as a way to set her at ease. Still, he was an obvious warrior, and a great deal bigger. She would be powerless if he had ill intents towards her.

"Good." Shimani smiled at her.

Kaily decided he definitely was trying to put her at ease. To be fair, his smiles seemed genuine. They at least reached his eyes. Regardless, she wanted to go home. She wouldn't feel safe in the foreign lands she'd lately found herself within. "Where am I?"

Shimani moved closer to her. "We don't have much time, so listen very carefully."

Kaily forced herself to not scoot back away from him. Not that the wall would have allowed her the room to put distance between them. It didn't escape her attention that he did not answer her question.

"Moto, the one who brought you here," he paused. His eyes narrowed as he regarded her.

She stopped listening. Moto? Her dark warrior did exist and now she knew his name. She yelped in surprise from the tap on the top of her head.

"Pay attention! This is valuable information. I know most of this is not going to make sense, and for that I apologize. You will begin to understand in time, if you pay attention." Shimani shifted his weight. "If given the time." Shimani muttered the last part under his breath.

Kaily remained focused. The mention of her dark warrior's name made her heart pound faster. Hope rose inside her at the confirmation of his existence. Still, she didn't want to give Shimani another reason to thump her on the head. Not that it hurt, it hadn't, just surprised her.

Shimani continued. "Moto shouldn't have brought you to Center Village. Strictly speaking, outsiders are not welcome among any of the Kahoali Villages, and most especially this one. The Queen is extremely unhappy and demanded that you be brought before her as soon as you are awake and well enough. Kesho made it possible for you to understand us, but you won't be able to speak our language. You can learn over time with what Kesho did, but I can make it possible for you to speak our language now, if you will permit me to open your mind."

"How?" Kaily frowned.

"The how doesn't matter," he said. "Do I have your permission?"

Kaily narrowed her eyes at him as she considered. The older male did something, she had no doubt. How else could she abruptly understand them? But it had been quite unpleasant, to say the least. Did she really need them to understand her?

Shimani waited patiently for an answer.

Kaily took a deep breath. "Aye." Any limitation in communication was never a good thing.

Shimani held his hands on either side of her head, similar to the position of the older warrior.

"Wait!" Kaily pulled away. She was surprised he let her. "Where am I? I know you said Center Village," she shook her head, "but where am I? What planet?"

Shimani tilted his head to the side. His eyes remained locked with hers. "Ki."

Kaily looked away. Ki. It's what Jaren had told her. Her hands trembled. She'd known she wasn't on Earth, but now, she had confirmation. "I was on Ki when," she hesitated. She took a deep breath. "I was on Ki when Moto rescued me?"

"Yes, with the Agenors." Shimani regarded her. "Kaily, we don't have time. We need to hurry. Please, trust me. The answers to your questions will come, I promise. Will you trust me?"

Kaily began to shake her head no. There was something in Shimani's eyes which prevented her from giving a firm no. She didn't trust, not easily. She could count on one hand how many people she actually trusted, and two of them were dead. She reluctantly nodded.

"Thank you." Shimani leaned in closer and placed his hands on either side of her head. He covered her temples with his palms.

A tingling sensation passed through her head, but no pain. The sensation dissipated as suddenly as it had begun.

"Give it a try." Shimani said, reverting back to his Kahoali language.

Kaily frowned. "How?"

"Like that." Shimani's smile broadened.

"That doesn't tell me how." She didn't think she'd spoken any differently than she had previously with him.

"It's more instinct based at first. In time, it will get easier to discern when you are speaking Kahoali, and when you are not."

Kaily opened her mouth to ask for clarification.

Shimani held up his hand.

Kaily sighed. "I know. Give it time."

Shimani nodded. His smile faded. "When you meet the Queen, limit your responses to head nods and shakes. It will prevent you from inadvertently speaking Kahoali better than you should right now. Let's keep what I've done for you between the two of us. Limit the extent of what you say in Kahoali in the beginning of your time with us. Over time they will accept you have picked up the language from being able to understand it."

"Alright." Kaily would trust his instructions, despite his lack of reasons. What he said made sense to her even without a clear understanding on her part. She would trust him, for now. "What makes you think I'll be allowed to stay?" Not that she wanted to stay, but if they couldn't get her back home, what choice did she have? She absolutely didn't want to return to the Agenors.

Shimani stood and held down his hand as an offer to help her to her feet. "Call it a feeling or wishful thinking, if you prefer." He shrugged. "I don't know what Queen Shakti intends to do with you, but I prefer to be hopeful. We are not a cruel people or without compassion, Kaily."

She took hold of Shimani's proffered hand and let him pull her up to stand. "Is that supposed to comfort me?"

Shimani shrugged again. "That's up to you."

Kaily shook her head at him. She let out a long sigh. She was not one to land on the side of hope, especially considering the past week she'd just had.

Shimani opened the door and held it for her. "After you."

"Where exactly?"

"To see the Queen, of course." Shimani shut the door behind him.

"That's so helpful." Kaily rolled her eyes.

"Don't be rude, Kaily." Shimani smiled despite his rebuke. "The Queen's hut and throne room are down this path. Moto will not be in attendance."

Kaily shrugged. "Is that supposed to matter to me?"

Shimani smirked. He extended his hand to show her the direction he wished her to walk towards.

Kaily started down the path he indicated.

Although, Shimani followed her, he guided he with small gestures and touches.

Kaily imagined from an outside perspective it appeared as if she might actually know the direction she should walk. She attempted to look around her surroundings, but the pace Shimani ushered her to keep was too fast to notice more than a cursory glance of the jungle forest surrounding them. She glimpsed bigger huts, although, she hadn't gotten a really good look at the one they'd just vacated to know how much larger. Both seemed strange, but again, she wasn't given time to absorb what she saw.

She held up the hem of her heavy gown to keep from tripping on the edges. She was not dressed for the humid heat of the jungle forest surrounding the village they traipsed towards or through. They seemed to be a fair distance from the Queen's hut. To make matters worse, sweat beaded all over her body and streamed down her back, and other places she didn't want to mention. The sensation of the beaded sweat drops made it feel as if tiny bugs crawled all over her skin. She gave an involuntary shudder.

"Are you okay?" Shimani asked.

Kaily glanced at him. "Just hot." She didn't elaborate. She felt sick to her stomach and overheated. She couldn't trust these people. The deeper into the village they walked, the more she noticed the looks. They moved quickly, but not so fast that she didn't notice the way the few villagers they came across stared. She saw Shimani give each village a head nod, and yet said nothing. An unexpected pang pierced her heart when she noticed some of the adults ushered their children inside as they drew near. She glanced at Shimani.

He smiled at her and pressed his hand on the small of her back with a tilt of his head.

She took a deep breath and hurried her pace. A large two-story hut loomed in the distance before them. The much bigger building than the surrounding ones reminded her of a cultivated mansion of sorts. If that mansion also appeared to be hut like in construction. Her pace slowed.

Shimani leaned in closer to her. "You'll have time to explore later."

Kaily looked up at him and nodded her head.

Shimani stopped her at the entrance to the two-story building, the Queen's hut. "Be respectful," he advised in a low tone. He opened the door for her and gestured for her to enter.

Kaily stopped just inside. The room she entered held a high ceiling with large fans. The welcome coolness hit her full on. It was almost as cool as an air-conditioned room. Benches were arranged in a semi-circle at the far side of the room just in front of a dais. A throne sat upon the raised platform. An older woman sat on the throne. She wouldn't say the woman appeared elderly, but something about her gave Kaily the impression she was older than she appeared. Behind the woman stood the one Shimani had called Kesho and another warrior. That other one displayed an obvious hostile expression directed solely in her direction.

She started moving from the pressure on her lower back, propelling her forward. She tried to swallow around the lump of fear lodged in the back of her throat. She focused her attention on the throne and the woman who sat upon it. The regal bearing of the woman, left no doubt in Kaily's mind that she was in charge, and that her own fate lay in the hands of that woman.

Shimani stopped Kaily a few feet in front of the dais. He gave the woman a low bow. "My Queen." He straightened. "Kaily is ready for questioning."

Kaily glanced at Shimani and frowned.

"Can you understand us?" The Queen asked.

Kaily nodded.

"Good." The Queen nodded. Her eyes roamed over Kaily. "Do you know where you are?"

Kaily glanced at Shimani. She shifted nervously from foot to foot.

"I've advised her that she is among the Kahoali on Ki, my Queen." Shimani answered.

The Queen's gaze shifted from Kaily. "Does that mean anything to her?"

"No, my Queen," Shimani said. "She speaks the language of the Agenors but doesn't seem to be one of them."

"I see." The Queen regarded Kaily for a long while.

Kaily became fidgety enough that Shimani touched her arm to get her attention and gave her a small shake of his head when she glanced at him. The coolness of the room evaporated. Sweat again beaded on her forehead. She didn't think the room had grown hot again, just her. The heavy gown became oppressive. She swayed with exhaustion she'd not previously noticed. All she wanted was to sink into one of those benches, if only for a minute.

"Do you know where you were when Moto found you?"

Shimani tapped her on the arm.

Kaily's gaze moved from the nearest bench back to the woman on the throne. She tried to focus. She shook her head. She caught something about knowing where she was. Her head swam with dizziness as she grew more lightheaded. She turned to Shimani. "I don't feel good." She hoped she'd spoken in Agenor and not Kahoali.

Shimani grabbed her arm and wrapped his other arm around her back before she crumpled to the ground.

Kaily maintained consciousness, but not without a great deal of effort. The room spun.

Shimani guided her to the closest bench and helped her sit.

"Baridi, get the girl some water," the Queen said.

Kaily didn't look to see the reaction of the one who left the dais to do his Queen's bidding. One hostile glare from that one was quite enough to endure.

"Apologies, my Queen." Shimani bowed his head. "The walk must have been too much for her in her heavy dress."

The Queen held up her hand. "No apology is necessary."

Baridi approached with a cup in his hand. "Much thanks." Shimani took the cup from him.

Baridi inclined his head towards Shimani, and then took his place back up on the dais.

Shimani handed Kaily the cup.

Kaily smiled at Shimani. "Thank you." She quietly replied. She downed the cool liquid.

"Better?" The Queen asked her.

Kaily nodded. Her eyes met the Queen's for a brief moment. She hated being in such a position. She didn't know what she could or should say. She didn't know how she should act. She still dealt with the fact she no longer stood on Earth, which was nearly impossible to wrap her head around.

The Queen turned her attention back to Shimani. "Where do you think Moto found her?"

Shimani didn't answer right away. He remained silent long enough that even Kaily frowned at him.

"Shimani?" The Queen prompted.

Shimani walked to his previous spot, leaving Kaily sitting on the bench. "My Queen, I would hesitate to give such an opinion." He gave the Queen a low bow.

"I see."

Kaily continued to frown. She looked from the Queen back to Shimani. Moto found her with the Agenors. Why would Shimani not say as much?

"I found her on Ki, with the Agenors." A baritone males voice answered from the back of the room.

Kaily's breath caught in her throat, and her heart skipped a beat or two. She knew the voice belonged to her dark warrior even before turning around to see who spoke. The room itself became charged with electricity or something along those lines. She didn't exactly know how to describe what she sensed. Her eyes followed him as he strode towards the Queen's throne. He commanded a presence. She wondered if others thought the same or if it was only her.

"You were not invited," the Queen said.

Kaily's eyes drifted towards her. The Queen glared at Moto, clearly not happy with his appearance there. Her tone reeked of displeasure, all directed at Moto. Her eyes moved back to her dark warrior. He was clearly unaffected by the Queen's tone or words.

Moto stopped beside Shimani in front of the dais.

Kaily felt a pang of disappointment as her dark warrior didn't bother to spare a glance in her direction.

Shimani did spare her a glance, and a minute tilt of his head in the direction of the throne. His eyebrows raised slightly.

Kaily got the impression that he wanted her eyes forward.

"I mean no disrespect, my Queen, but I found the girl." Moto inclined his head. "I am the one to provide the answers you seek."

Shimani shifted position, effectively blocking Moto from Kaily's view. She would almost swear he knew the perfect spot to keep her from having an eye full of her dark warrior. She took a deep breath and focused her attention on the Queen.

"Well," the Queen gestured with her hands, "by all means, explain how this girl came to be in our midst."

Kaily didn't know how Moto wasn't squirming under the Queen's harsh scrutiny. The Queen's tone alone, made her want to find a place out of sight to hide.

"I found her on Ki with the Agenors," Moto repeated. "I helped the girl escape when it became apparent the armed Agenors intended to harm her. I had nowhere else to bring her." Moto bowed his head towards the Queen. "I only thought of her safety when I brought her into our midst. I apologize for my rash actions."

Kaily frowned. She wouldn't say he lied to his Queen, but he didn't tell her the whole truth. He'd been on Earth more than once, if her glimpses of him were true. Questions of her own began to form in her own mind. How had he known she was with the Agenors in the first place?

"How did you happen upon her among the Agenors?" The Queen asked.

Exactly! Kaily thought to herself.

"By chance," Moto said.

"How?" The Queen reiterated.

Silence.

Kaily's eyes riveted to Moto, well, Shimani since he still blocked her view of her dark warrior.

The silence dragged on.

No one spoke.

Kaily could almost feel Moto taking a deep breath before he finally broke the silence.

"I woke early this day to an intense fear emotion that was not my own. I followed the sensation and found this girl to be the source."

The Queen leaned forward. She perched on the very edge of the throne. "Explain how you physically went to the Agenors Isle."

Shimani glanced back at Kaily and gave her a slight tilt of his head.

Kaily rolled her eyes but forced her attention back to the throne and Queen. The silence which followed made her both nervous and angry. She didn't know why. Something disturbed her about the whole exchange between the Queen and her dark warrior.

"I possess the ability to move from one place to another on Ki, much in the same way we use portal paths."

Kaily heard an audible intake of air from all assembled except Shimani. Her eyes narrowed as she glanced at Shimani.

Silence again dragged out. Again no one broke it. They all waited.

Kaily's gaze drifted from Shimani to the raised platform. She took in the expressions of the Queen and two males on the dais. It surprised her how the males' features showed little to no emotions. Even the hostile one had cleared his features of emotions. Of course, his attention was not being directed at her. Only the Queen's countenance showed any emotions at all, and she was clearly angry. She appeared to be attempting to control her temper. Kaily looked back at the spot Shimani, and Moto occupied.

"Kaily?"

The Queen's voice intruded on Kaily's silent speculations. Despite the Queen's obvious temper smoldering below the surface, her ability to maintain a level tone of voice impressed Kaily.

Kaily heeded Shimani's earlier instruction as she didn't verbalize anything near what she wanted to say. She merely turned her attention back to the throne and waited.

"Is Shimani correct when he said you are not of the Agenors?"

Kaily nodded.

"Do you know how you came to be among the Agenors?"

Kaily shook her head.

"Are you from this world?"

Kaily again shook her head.

"Do you know how to get back to your world?"

Kaily reluctantly shook her head. A sudden sadness welled up. What if she could never get back to Earth? She fought back the tears beginning to burn in the back of her eyes.

"I see." The Queen's scrutiny again fell on Moto. "You and I will converse about what you've disclosed here today." She turned her attention back to Kaily. "The question at hand is what to do with you. The problem, child, is that outsiders are not welcome among us for good reason, and yet it is not our way to knowingly cause harm to another. It seems that sending you back to the Agenors would cause you harm. You are not from this world. You have no idea how you came to be on Ki or how to get back to your world." The Queen leveled her gaze on Moto.

The burning sensation in the back of Kaily's eyes intensified. She struggled to keep her tears at bay.

"Baridi?" The Queen directed her attention back to Kaily.

The openly hostile one stepped forward so that he stood in the line of sight of the throne. "Yes, my Queen."

"Is it possible that she is Druid?"

Kaily noticed Kesho and Baridi glance at each other. She looked in the direction of Shimani and Moto. Since she only could see Shimani, mostly his back, she couldn't determine his reaction. She still couldn't see her dark warrior to know what his reaction might have been. She focused on the hostile one, even though she didn't want to.

Baridi walked to the edge of the dais and turned intense eyes on her.

Kaily would have taken several steps backwards if she hadn't already been sitting. She could not drag her eyes away from Baridi's. She felt pressure in the back of her mind build, and then disappear. A dull ache followed. The locked gaze broke. She closed her eyes and bowed her head. She rubbed her temples with her forefingers. She took a deep breath, opened her eyes, and focused her attention again on the dais.

"There is nothing in her mind to indicate that she is. She does have the coloring for it." He glanced back at her with narrowed eyes. "I haven't heard of any female Druid ever to exist. The energy of Ki does not flow within her." Baridi cleared his features of any hostile emotion as he redirected his attention to the Queen. "I don't believe she is Druid, my Queen." He stepped back behind the throne and took his place next to Kesho. He spared Kaily another glare, and then cleared his features of emotions.

Kaily did her best to ignore Baridi's hostility. Druid? She thought how strange the question. She would not have expected a term from Earth to be spoken on another planet. Not that she had anything to go by as far as expectations. Still, this was not Earth. The Queen asked the question as if Druids existed there.

"Kesho?" The Queen kept her gaze focused on Kaily.

"Yes, my Queen?" Kesho answered. He'd stepped forward and around the throne in the same manner Baridi had.

"Do you concur with Baridi's assessment?"

Kaily's frown deepened. Was she to be forced to endure more mind probes? She shook her head. She didn't know what to call them.

"Yes, my Queen."

Kesho's quick reply surprised Kaily. But then, again, he'd been in her mind already.

The Queen stood and turned towards Kesho and Baridi. "I thank you both for your assessment. It has been long since a Druid walked among us. You have my apologies for requiring you to relive such a painful memory in our history."

Both inclined their head, but neither gave away their emotions in their expressions or eyes.

Kaily remained more confused than ever at the bizarre exchange and words from the Queen.

The Queen turned towards Kaily. "What do you want?"

It took Kaily a moment to realize that the Queen addressed her in the Agenors' language. She glanced down at her clasped hands in her lap. She tried to keep the tears swimming in her eyes from falling. She failed. She lifted her head to look the Queen squarely in the eyes, in spite of the tears falling. "I want to go home, back to Earth." She tried to make sure she answered in the Agenors' language. She noticed the Queen's expression softened a little towards her.

"I wish I could give you a way to go back to your world, child. It's unfortunate that you found your way to this world. There are three Inhabitants of Ki. The Kahoali, Agenors and Zaltys. None are welcoming of outsiders, although we are not as harsh as the other two."

The Queen's eyes remained fixed on Kaily, although she didn't think the Queen saw her in that precise moment. Her eyes appeared lost in some faraway thought from Kaily's perspective.

The Queen's gaze shifted to Moto briefly before returning to Kaily. "I will allow you to stay, for now. I will not condemn you to death. The Zaltys would not hesitate to kill you, and so would the Agenors it would seem." She glanced at Moto and then back to Kaily. "It will not be easy for you here. You will not receive a warm welcome from most, but we will all do what we can to make certain it is not altogether unpleasant. Won't we?"

"Yes, my Queen," the four warriors replied in unison.

Kaily thought she should feel some kind of comfort in the Queen's words. She didn't. She was stuck in a place she didn't want to be, among a people who didn't want her there. More tears fell. She hastily brushed them away.

"Shimani will guide you in our ways. I suspect that as you acclimate to our way of life that the Kahoali Inhabitants will learn to accept you among them, to a point." The Queen gave her a small, sad smile. "Be at peace, Kaily. No harm will come to you within our Villages. Shimani, please show Kaily to one of the guest huts. Take her to the seamstress to obtain more appropriate attire. Give her something to eat and drink to hold her over until this evening's repast."

Shimani bowed low. "Yes, my Queen."

"Welcome, child, such as it is. Perhaps in time we will find a way to send you back to your home world." She glanced for a moment at Moto.

Kaily bowed her head as she observed the others do. "Thank you." She couldn't keep the tears from slipping out of the corners of her eyes as the weight of her situation settled upon her.

Shimani held out his hand to help her to her feet.

Kaily graciously accepted his assistance. She gathered up the hem of her long, heavy gown and followed Shimani towards the back of the throne room. They exited through the same door they'd entered. She kept her eyes trained on the floor, and then the ground outside to avoid eye contact with any of the villagers. She hated crying in front of others. It made her feel weak.

They stopped at a hut where Shimani had her wait outside. Kaily was appreciative that she didn't have to go inside. She heard voices but didn't bother to make out the words spoken. Her thoughts stayed focused on the fact that she would be with the Kahoali for a while it would seem. All this because she needed to know if her dark warrior existed, and she'd tried to find out that fateful day on Earth. He did exist, and now all she wanted was to return home.

Shimani exited the hut carrying a small bundle. He guided her to one of the smaller huts. Still larger than the one she'd woke up in, but smaller than most of the others. The guest hut stood just off of the main group of huts near the Queen's. Closer to the jungle forest line. The location suited her fine. It would provide her some semblance of privacy.

"It's not much, but it has all the necessities." Shimani opened the door and stepped aside for her to enter first. "The forest is not too dangerous, but it is easy to become disoriented, and we wouldn't want you to get lost."

"So, what you're saying is 'don't stray too far'?" Kaily stepped inside the hut and looked around.

Shimani followed her inside. "Something like that."

A dim glow lit the interior and grew brighter as she moved around inside, inspecting the interior. The light originated from the small, elongated windows at the top of the wall where it met the ceiling. She couldn't see any glass in the opening from her vantage point. The hut was much cooler than outside. She didn't see the kind of technology necessary for air conditioning, but the coolness seemed to indicate there must be something of a sort. The hut, itself, consisted of one large room divided into sections. One for sitting, another for sleeping, and another for eating. A door stood on the far side opposite the outside door. In the sleeping area lay a thicker mat than what she'd woken up on, but not as thick as her mattress at home.

She wiped at her tears and wet cheeks.

"Through that door is the shower room." Shimani walked to the door and opened it as he spoke.

Kaily followed and glanced inside. The room contained a shower stall, sink and a kind of toilet. It was large enough to take care of necessities, but not much more. She stepped back into the living space.

Shimani stepped into the shower room.

Kaily peered inside.

Shimani set the bundle on a cupboard in the room. He opened the cupboard and pulled out a jar and towel. "The jar contains scrubbing paste. It will help you freshen up. The dress within the pack is considerably thinner and should be more comfortable." He pointed to another jar on a shelf near the toilet. "This jar contains powder that you put in the bowl base after you, ummm,"

"Use the facility?" Kaily asked. She found it strange that she understood, and to a point spoke the Kahoali language with what Shimani had done. Yet, trying to think of the right wording just now seemed difficult or maybe it was Shimani's obvious embarrassment over explaining how to use the toilet.

Shimani frowned. "We'll go with that wording. Afterwards, pull this cord." He picked up a small cloth from a stack. "This," he frowned and paused.

"I get the idea, Shimani. I'm sure I'll figure it out." Kaily might have smiled if the circumstances were different. She no longer possessed a sense of humor. Although, she had to admit, there was something funny about explaining such a simple thing as using the bathroom and how very complicated it could be on another planet. Maybe not complicated exactly, just different enough to need explanation.

"I will bring you food and drink. There is enough time to freshen up and rest before this evening's repast."

"Thank you, Shimani." Kaily stood in the middle of the common room, unsure what to do with herself. "I appreciate the kindness you've shown me. What is the evening repast?"

"It's a time for the entire Village to share," he paused. His brow furrowed. "The Villagers gather near the Queen's hut to enjoy food and music while sharing conversations with each other."

Kaily closed her eyes as she partially turned away from Shimani. Great! She thought. Just what she needed. They could parade her around in front of the entire village.

Shimani moved to stand in front of Kaily. He tilted her chin up to force her to look him in the eyes. He produced a cloth and wiped her tears. After, he handed the cloth to her. "I promise it will be alright."

Kaily tried to give him a smile. It came out more of a grimace.

Shimani gave her a small smile. There was compassion in his eyes. "You'll see. For now, take time to clean up, change and rest. The sleep will help. You can stay here and hide a way for a while. No one will disturb you."

"Thank you, Shimani."

He nodded. "I'll leave the food and drink on the table over there." He indicated a small table with two chairs in the eating area. "The doors don't have locks. I understand if that makes you uncomfortable, but trust me, you are safe here, Kaily."

She nodded. Kaily watched Shimani walk to the door. She didn't like being forced to trust anyone. Still, there was something about Shimani that made her want to trust him, if only a little bit. Which bothered her. She didn't feel safe and didn't know if she ever truly would. Even in her home back on Earth, she didn't always feel safe. The brief moment in Moto's arms gave her a sense of security, but that too disappeared.

Shimani stopped at the door and looked back at her.

Kaily thought he might say something, but instead he smiled and left, quietly closing the door behind him.

———— *ele* ————

"Where do you think you're going?" Shimani pushed off the outside wall to the guest hut Kaily now resided within.

Moto glared at Shimani. "Checking on the girl. Not that it's any of your business."

Shimani stepped into Moto's path, stopping him from reaching her door. "The girl's name is Kaily, and she's fine. I just dropped off provisions for her."

Moto moved to step around Shimani.

Shimani again blocked his path.

"Move!"

Shimani stood his ground. "She needs time, Moto. She just found out that she is trapped among Inhabitants who don't want her in their midst. She doesn't know how to get home, and she doesn't understand what happened to bring her to Ki in the first place. She needs to come to terms with her circumstances, and for that, she requires time and rest. She is exhausted. Or do you intend to take her back to her home world?"

Moto stabbed a finger in the direction of the guest hut. "You saw the tears in her eyes!"

Shimani nodded. "I did, and that is why she needs peace. At least, for this night. If you are not going to take her back to her home world, then I am asking you to give her this night alone.

She's endured enough, Moto. Check on her in the morning. Please give her this night." Shimani crossed his arms over his chest. "Oh, and when you do check on her, be careful not to get caught. From what I hear, the Queen ordered you to keep your distance."

Moto stared at Shimani. He ran his hand over his face. "Fine! I'll wait until morning, and I am always careful, Shimani."

"Are you?" Shimani's tone held a hint of amusement. "I also heard that you're in life changing trouble with our Queen."

"Who told you that?" Moto took one long look towards the guest hut.

"Sari," Shimani said.

"Of course, she did."

"Even for you this blatant disregard for the Queen's authority is out of character."

Moto grumbled and mumbled some unintelligible words.

Shimani laughed and slapped Moto on the back. "Shall we see if we can get you back into the Queen's good graces?" Shimani gestured towards the direction the other Villagers walked.

"How is it you seem to always be in our Queen's good graces?" Moto asked with a fair amount of sarcasm.

"I don't get caught." Shimani turned Moto towards the Queen's hut and evening repast.

"Who's going to tell the Queen the girl isn't coming?"

"Me," Shimani said. "I am still in her good graces."

"Fine." Moto cast a last glance at the guest hut. He stopped resisting and walked with Shimani towards the evening repast. Their conversation became indistinguishable as they drifted farther away from the hut.

Kaily closed the door she'd cracked open to eavesdrop on the conversation. She leaned against the door and slid to the cool floor. She replayed the conversation in her mind. Moto could get her back home, but he didn't. Why? What did he want from her? What did he think he would accomplish by leaving her among his people who didn't want her there? Why?

She forgot about the sustenance Shimani had brought for her as tears slid unchecked from her eyes. She hated being at the mercy of others. She hated not understanding what they wanted from her. She wanted to go home. The one person who could make that happen seemed to not want to.

Music and laughter drifted in through the openings. Her tears flowed. She was okay with being alone as she had been for the past five years. The sounds of the evening repast mixed with the impossibility of her situation made her tears fall harder. Realization came to her that she would always be an outsider to the Kahoali. She wanted to go home.

Chapter Seven

"How's our guest this morning?" Shimani asked as he wiped the sweat from his brow.

"Fine." Moto finished wiping his sweat and hung his towel back on its hook. He accepted the water skin Shimani offered and took a long drink. He hung the water skin on a hook next to their towels.

"Fine?" Shimani asked. "That's all you have to say? Fine?" He grabbed his pole leaning against the tree and walked back to the center of the clearing they used for training.

Moto grabbed his pole, and joined Shimani, who appeared to be far too amused, leaning against his pole. "There's nothing more to say. She's sleeping." He took up a fighting stance.

Shimani continued to use his pole for a leaning post. "So, let me get this straight. You couldn't wait to see Kaily last evening, and this morning you're content with 'she's sleeping', 'she's fine', and nothing else? Seriously, didn't you even take the time to have a conversation with her, Moto?"

"She was sleeping!" Moto swept Shimani's feet out from under him as payment for his lack of focus on training instead of a certain girl who was none of his concern.

Shimani bounced back to his feet, unfazed. He took up a fighting stance. "You expect me to believe that Kaily could actually sleep? After all she's been through? I know I wouldn't have if I were in her circumstances."

Moto mirrored Shimani's stance. "You are not in her circumstances."

"Did you actually check on Kaily or cheat?" Shimani aggressively advanced.

Moto gave ground while deflecting each of Shimani's strikes. "Hard to cheat without a looking bowl." He ground out between clenched teeth. He focused his efforts on not losing his head.

Only when he'd been driven to the edge, did Shimani let up. "So, you checked in on her?"

"We're here to train!" Moto attacked Shimani with a vengeance to drive him back to the center of the training area. After all, fair was fair. In truth, they were well matched sparring partners. Shimani had learned well, and now made Moto work for his victories. Although, much to Moto's irritation, Shimani didn't have to work very hard this session. Moto tried to ignore the reason for his distracted state, which grew increasingly more difficult to ignore. Shimani wouldn't keep his eyes from straying to a particular nearby tree, where a certain green-eyed distraction hid behind. He suspected Shimani had recently become aware of her presence with his sudden incessant questions about her. Moto, on the other hand, had become aware of her presence the moment she drew near. Curse her for showing up shortly after they had started.

"Shall we talk about how slow you've become in your old age?"

Moto didn't communicate his displeasure with words of Shimani's inability to be silent. Instead, he attacked harder and faster, hoping to give Shimani little breath to waste on running his mouth. If he couldn't breathe, then he couldn't speak. His plan worked, for the most part. Moto found it increasingly difficult to keep his attention from straying to the girl. He tried to keep Shimani from making a fool of him in front of her. It was in one of his distracted moments that Shimani's pole caught him unawares. The pole caught him squarely in the chest and sent him flying. He landed a short distance away flat on his back. He struggled for breath.

"My apologies." Shimani hurried over and held his hand out to offer help.

Moto narrowed his eyes at Shimani. He couldn't help but notice the irritating twinkle of amusement in Shimani's eyes.

"I didn't realize your mind lay elsewhere." Shimani's eyes darted towards the tree.

Moto took Shimani's hand. He momentarily considered sending his wayward student flying. Instead, he allowed his help to stand. He bent over with his hands on his knees to allow himself time to catch his breath. When he could breathe again, Moto picked up his pole from the ground. He threw it at Shimani. "We're done here!"

Shimani caught the pole. He gave Moto a salute followed by a smirk.

Moto glared at Shimani. He wanted to wipe that smirk from his protege's face. Instead, he watched Shimani jog towards the exact tree his impossible distraction still used as a shield. She wasn't any good at being stealthy, not that it would do her any good if she were.

Moto gritted his teeth. Just as Shimani passed the tree, he turned and winked at the girl. Moto shook his head. He would have to teach his pupil a lesson in manners, but not this day. Not with her near enough to be a greater distraction than he could endure.

He walked back to the tree which held the water skin and towels. He slowly dried his face, bare chest, and arms before donning his vest. He took his time fastening each clasp, one by one by one. He could sense the girl's eyes on him. With a smile, he took a long drink. When he'd finished, he portaled the towels and water skin to his hut. He slowly turned towards the tree.

Moto glimpsed the girl duck back behind the tree. Warmth spread throughout his center at the sight of her. He couldn't deny the physical attraction between them. Despite, how much he wanted to. Nor could he deny the intense connection they seemed to share. The physical attraction bothered him, but not nearly as much as the other which kept drawing him to her did. He couldn't understand why it existed. She wasn't Kahoali. There shouldn't be any kind of pull between the two of them. It shouldn't have been possible, and yet the connection existed and drew him towards her. He didn't understand, but he needed to, which was why he'd chosen to keep her close, regardless of the consequences.

He hadn't gone into her hut that morning. Not even in the 'cheating' way. He'd wanted to. He told himself he merely wanted to be certain that she was alright. That she had endured her first night among the Kahoali. He hadn't for reasons he refused to acknowledge, not even to himself. Instead, he'd listened intently at her door for any indication that she might be awake. When he'd heard no sound, he'd convinced himself that she still slept. After all, it had been well before dawn. Apparently, he'd been mistaken. She must of been awake, and followed him to the clearing. It would be the only way she would have found it or him.

Of course, if he hadn't lost his temper, and shattered his looking bowl he could have cheated. He had, and he couldn't. Moto still hadn't found the opportunity to fashion another one. Finding the right piece of wood which hummed with the energy of Ki would take time. Eventually, he would need to make the time or risk more unexpected disturbances at inappropriate times.

Moto sauntered towards the tree and his unsuspecting disruption. He smiled to himself at her futile attempt to shield herself from him. He didn't require eyes to be aware of her precise location. Not with her on his world. Not with her in such close proximity. His awareness of her had little to do with his empathic abilities. A part of her moved inside himself, disturbingly so.

He absorbed her emotions which emanated from her as he approached. Even her emotions penetrated deeper inside him than anyone else had in his entire life. Excitement and fear stood out strongest amongst all the others. The excitement stirred him, but the fear unsettled him. He didn't want her to be afraid of him. One consolation was that her fear of him differed from her fear with the Agenors the day he rescued her. Perhaps in her current circumstance fear was understandable. Still, he didn't like it. She should have more courage than what she currently displayed!

He stopped and leaned his shoulder against the tree's smooth bark. He had to give her credit for picking one of the largest trees in the forest closest to his proximity. If his senses and core weren't so attuned to her energy, she might have somewhat succeeded in shielding herself from him. His empathic abilities would have prevented her from completely masking her presence.

Moto remained utterly still and listened. He heard her soft intake of breath. He heard the rapid beating of her heart. His smile grew, pleased he affected her as much as she him. He waited, counting her heart beats, or his, or both. He couldn't quite tell whose heart beat louder.

His patience paid off.

She bumped into him when she came around the tree. She squeaked and ducked back around the tree.

Moto moved fast as he followed her. He placed his hands on either side of her, effectively blocking her escape. If she had intended to escape. He didn't know for certain what her next move would have been.

He inhaled her sweet floral scent deep into his lungs. He found the combination of her fragrance mixed with the forest's spicy one intoxicating. He took a second, deeper inhale. He savored the exquisite moment. He slowly exhaled and slid the tips of his fingers from her temple down the edge of her cheek. He brushed back a stray strand of her hair and looped it behind her ear.

Her wide eyes remained locked with his. They were the most unusual sea-green eyes he'd yet seen. Her eyes hypnotized him. He feared he might lose himself within their depths if he stared too long. He forced his gaze elsewhere. He brushed back her hair on the other side while he gathered his wits.

Her fear lingered, but she held a bit of fire within her as well. He grew pleased at her show of courage as she continued to maintain eye contact.

Moto lightly traced the outline of her lips with his fingers. "You are supposed to be sleeping." He deliberately spoke to her in Kahoali. He knew from the previous night that she would understand him, since the Queen had given Kesho permission to open her mind. But it would take her time to learn to speak his language. He knew he probably should have had the decency to speak the Agenors' language. He hadn't. It would have let her know they could speak a common language and taken away his advantage over her.

He'd been surprised to hear her speak the Agenors' language when she was presented to the Queen. In truth, he knew so little about her, in spite of the time he'd spent observing her.

Her breath caught in her throat.

He smiled inwardly, pleased with her response to him. He had so much to learn about her. So much to learn about their connection. He could only hope he would be given the time he needed. The Queen had allowed her to stay, for now. He knew she could change her mind at any moment. Especially, if she ever learned that he knew where and how to take the girl back to her home world.

"Are you afraid of me?" Again, he spoke in Kahoali. He liked having an advantage over the girl, for now. She unbalanced him too much. It was time he unbalanced her.

She shook her head.

Moto smiled down at her. "Liar."

She crossed her arms over her chest and glared up at him.

He laughed. He pushed aside his sudden urge to kiss her senseless. Instead, he dropped his arms to his sides and took a small step backwards. He remained close enough he could prevent her from bolting. Part of him wanted to see if she would attempt to run, although, he would be disappointed if she did. He wanted to learn so much about her. What did she think about when no one was watching? What in life did she desire most? Would she run from him, if given the opportunity?

He let out a silent breath and took another step backwards. That one small step took more willpower than he would care to admit. He, a disciplined warrior with an ironclad willpower honed from years of training. It disturbed him just how much control this small, slip of a girl exerted over him and his waning willpower.

"Why did you lie to your Queen?"

Moto almost laughed at her audacity to pose such a question to him. He heard the increased speed in her heart beats. "I didn't." It took him a moment to realize that she spoke to him in Kahoali. His eyes briefly narrowed. He wasn't easily surprised.

"You did. You told her you found me with the Agenors, but we both know you found me on Earth." She took a deep breath.

Gathering her courage, Moto suspected.

"Why did you lie to her?"

"It's complicated." Moto crossed his arms over his chest, growing less amused by her fiery side. "How is it you speak my language?"

A smile spread across the girl's facial features. "It's complicated."

One of the things about being empathic, Moto knew when others were near and when they were not. At that moment, no one was nearby. He moved faster than the girl could respond. He pressed her hard against the smooth bark of the tree. The heat of her body burned his.

He cursed his careless action, and his own response to her nearness. He closed his eyes and took a deep breath. His fault. He would endure the consequences. His breath skimmed across her cheek while he whispered in her ear. "You can't even begin to imagine what complicated truly is." He took her sweet scent deep into his lungs. He feared that he would never get enough of her. He swallowed hard and forced himself to step back from her. "Do you remember the way back?" He gazed into her eyes as if he could memorize her every nuance.

The girl nodded.

"Good." He turned to leave when he felt a small hand grab his arm. The unexpected contact shocked him. He reacted on instinct. He turned sharply, breaking the light hold on him, and startling the girl.

Her hand dropped to her side. A wave of her fear washed over him.

He silently cursed. Remorse flooded him for having scared her. He locked down the sudden wave of emotions from the abrupt loss of contact. He resisted his desire to drag her into his arms to give her what comfort he could muster. Instead,

he stood perfectly still, and waited for her to speak. He had to
remain in control of his overpowering desires for this girl.

"Are you the reason I found myself at the Agenors' castle?"

He sensed the question was asked with some difficulty on the
girls part. She possessed courage, but not an abundance of it.
He frightened her, which angered him. He'd caused this new
wave of fear with his sudden reaction to her touch. He again
cursed his carelessness. He would have to be more careful with
her in the future. Part of his anger was in not knowing what
caused her to possess so little courage while still having a bit of
fire underneath the surface. He squashed his thoughts on the
matter and focused on the situation at hand.

He considered his response to her question. The answer was
complicated. He almost smiled as he imagined she might not
like such an answer to be given a second time. He thought
perhaps he might have been, but he didn't know for certain.
The Gateway didn't remain open long. He didn't think it would
have been open long enough for her to travel through. Not to
mention that she should have ended up at the Kahoali Gateway.
He didn't think the Agenors possessed a Gateway of their own,
but then there was no other explanation for how she traveled
from her world to his. He hadn't sensed any ability within her
to harness the Universal energy to open the Gateway herself, let
alone the knowledge. Yet, she stood on his world.

Moto didn't look away or give any outward indication the
emotional turmoil her question stirred within him. "I'm not

certain." He wanted to add more, to explore further how she might have come to be there. He couldn't. Another moved within the forest, heading their way. And it wasn't Shimani. Being seen with the outsider was the last thing he needed. He wasn't exactly on the best of terms with his Queen. He made a hasty retreat before the newcomer spotted them. He forced himself to keep moving away from the girl without looking back. Not an easy task considering the confusion his actions caused within her. Curse his empathic abilities. He kept moving away before his willpower completely failed him.

He knew she was not in danger from any of the villagers. They may not like outsiders in their midst, but none would defy the Queen. The girl was safe. The danger came from what lay between them. If he possessed any sense, he would take her straight back to her home world without another thought.

He couldn't let her go, not yet.

Kaily collapsed against the tree as she stared at her dark warrior's retreating back. She touched her lips where his fingertips had caressed them. Her cheeks flamed from their brief exchange.

"Damn!" She muttered under her breath. There were too many trees to watch him for long. The problem with being in a somewhat dense forest or jungle. She still had not decided which one the surrounding area reminded her of most. The trees were quite tall and thick. The leaves were flat and big, but thick like needles on a pine tree. The greenery appeared similar to Earth, yet different. Even the green coloring differed in minuscule ways.

The canopy hid the sky above, and yet, the surrounding area remained bright as a summer's day. Such a strange world she never expected to find herself. Not that she expected to be on any other world other than Earth. She'd never actually considered the possibility of traveling to another world. In truth, she'd never given much thought to life on other worlds.

She turned away from the direction her warrior had retreated. She ran her palm down the smooth bark of the tree she'd used for a shield. All the good it had done her. She had wanted to observe from a far without being noticed.

She turned around and slid to the soft mossy ground. She knew she should probably have made her way back to the hut they'd given her. She didn't want the confining space to take away the moment.

She leaned her head back, savoring the interaction with her dark warrior.

She could hardly breathe, pressed up between her warrior and the unforgiving tree. He hadn't hurt her, but neither had he given her space to escape. A smile crossed her lips. Not that she had any intention of escaping, not yet. Something lay between them, something far beyond a physical attraction. There definitely was an attraction, but something more.

She sighed.

She'd never much put stock in the belief of love at first sight or soulmates. Then again, she hadn't met anyone like her dark warrior.

With him so close to her, she'd struggled to hold a coherent thought in her head. She had questions for him to answer. All she had to do was ask them. Not that it would matter. He hadn't exactly answered the couple she'd succeeded in asking. She didn't consider his answers to be adequate. It's complicated, she mimicked. She had a feeling he could complicate a great many things. Not to mention his hasty exit. Why had he left so suddenly?

She shook her head.

She had a feeling he knew far more than he'd shared. She thought he might even be the solution to getting back to Earth. If her suspicions were true, what was the purpose in bring her to his village? His people didn't want her there. His actions had obviously pissed off his Queen. So why risk it?

She sighed. Kaily knew she wouldn't obtain answers just sitting there, mooning over her elusive warrior. Somehow, she had to corner him again, and keep cornering him until he gave her satisfactory answers to her questions. All while trying to blend in to avoid drawing unwanted attention to herself. This should be fun, she thought.

She pushed herself to a standing position, using the tree for support. He affected her in so many ways. It took a moment to gain her balance. She couldn't ignore the attraction between them. Maybe he couldn't either. She took a deep breath and pushed off the tree. It was past time she found her way back to the hut.

Kaily kept her head down as she passed a few of the villagers. It was unsettling to be among strange people who weren't exactly open and welcoming. They weren't outwardly hostile either, just indifferent. She wasn't positive if such indifference was better or not. Either way, she made it back to the hut without incident.

"Did you have a nice conversation?"

Kaily squealed in surprise. She hadn't expected anyone to be inside the hut. Her hand instinctively covered her rapidly beating heart. She didn't know how much more her heart or nerves could take.

"My apologies, Kaily." Shimani gave her a slight bow. "I didn't intend to startle you."

Kaily finished shutting the door. "It's okay. I just wasn't expecting anyone to be in here."

"I thought you might be hungry."

Kaily glanced at the table and the little feast laid out upon it. "Thank you, Shimani." She didn't feel hungry, but she wasn't going to say as much.

Shimani held out a chair for her.

Kaily sat and watched as he filled the plate in front of her. He then sat opposite her and filled a second plate. She smiled at him.

She had thought she wanted to be alone. It surprised her to find she was mildly pleased he intended to eat with her.

"Did you?"

"Did I what?" Kaily asked as a frown slightly creased her brow.

"Have a nice conversation?"

Kaily blushed. "Umm."

Shimani nodded. "Ah."

"Ah, what?" Kaily's frown intensified.

"Nothing." Shimani shook his head. "Just ah."

"It was a nice conversation." Kaily wouldn't have actually described her exchange with her warrior as nice or a conversation, but she wasn't going to tell Shimani what she would have called it.

"I'm sure it was, and probably interesting." Shimani took a bite of his food. "Thirsty?" He poured liquid in a cup without waiting for an answer.

Kaily took the drink he offered her. She took a sip of the liquid. She had no idea what it was or what most of the items on her plate were. The food seemed somewhat similar to foods she'd have eaten on Earth, but not quite the same. Tastes and textures didn't exactly align with what the item appeared to be like. They all tasted pleasant, even the drink, just different.

They ate in silence for a bit.

Kaily contemplated what her day might be like there. To say she felt lost, didn't cover how out of place she actually felt. She had a routine back home on Earth. She'd lost any semblance of

such the moment she'd fallen into her current bizarre dream
like situation. She still had a difficult time believing that she
was on another planet, and yet she couldn't deny it either.
There were too many differences to account for any other
explanation. So, she forced herself to accept that somehow
that stupid doorway had brought her there.

She finished her drink and placed the cup on the table.
"What does a normal day look like for you?"

Shimani shrugged. "Depends on the day. We do what needs
to be done when it needs to be done." Shimani pointed at her
half empty plate. "How do you like the food?"

"It's tasty." Kaily's nerves made it hard to eat. She'd
consumed what she could safely keep on her nervous
stomach. She had to admit, the food was far better than
she'd been given during her time with the Agenors. Still, she
possessed little appetite. Stress affected her that way.

Shimani put his empty plate aside and took her hands in
his.

Kaily was too surprised by his sudden action to react. She
forced herself not to pull away.

"Give yourself time to adjust. I promise you, it will be better
in time." He let her hands go and sat back. "Would you like
a tour of Center Village and the surrounding area?"

Kaily's instinct screamed no. She was not an adventurous sort
of person. Instead, she smiled at him. "That would be nice.
Thank you, Shimani." She compelled herself to say. Sneaking

around on her own was bound to get her into trouble, and she needed to get her bearings.

"I'll clean up when you're finished, and then we can get started."

Kaily glanced at her plate. She wasn't going to get any more down. Shame, she thought. It would have been nice to eat a little more. She picked her plate up and handed it to Shimani. "I'm finished."

Shimani nodded and took the plate from her.

She watched him carefully wrap the remaining food items, and then placed them in a cupboard.

"This is a cooling cupboard. The food will keep for when you get hungry later."

Kaily smiled. "Thank you." The cupboard appeared to her like any other cupboard. Definitely different than her fridge at home. She hadn't taken time to explore the hut yet, and from what she'd observed while he cleaned up, there wasn't much to it. She wasn't positive if the lack of things was because none lived in it or because the people led minimal lives. They certainly seemed to live simpler than she was used to. And that was saying something, considering she lived a rather simple life on Earth, compared to so many others.

"Ready?" Shimani asked after he finished cleaning up.

Kaily nodded. She really wasn't, but she would convince herself to be.

Shimani held the door open for her.

Kaily stepped outside and waited for him to shut the door. She'd found it disconcerting that there weren't any locks on the hut. She didn't have the courage to see if other huts had secured doors. She'd never lived in a place without the security of a locked door.

"This way."

She followed Shimani to the edge of the village and into the forest-jungle.

He slowed his pace so that he walked more beside her. "As I've said before, the forest isn't necessarily dangerous, but you probably shouldn't wander around it by yourself."

Kaily ignored the pointed look he gave her, instead, she smiled up at him. "I'll keep that in mind." She thought they should have passed the clearing she'd followed her dark warrior to by now, considering how far they seemed to have walked, but they hadn't. To her surprise, they came upon a group of villagers who were clearing away debris and trimming the trees. Some carried baskets of something that appeared similar to what Shimani had given her for breakfast. The food items had tasted more like vegetables, but considering they were harvesting them from trees they could be fruit. She honestly didn't know what to make of the differences on this planet.

"What are they doing?" She asked Shimani.

"Cultivating what we use." Shimani pointed to various areas as he explained. "Most of the food we eat come from the trees, some from bushes. I don't know what you would call them on

Earth. The Villagers over there are cutting the leaves we use to make our boots."

The leaves appeared to sprout from the ground in substantial sheets. Kaily would have sworn the low cut boots she'd been given to wear felt like suede leather. She'd been given a light dress as well that felt like silk. She couldn't imagine what the material might actually be made from. "May I touch one of the leaves?"

Shimani smiled at her. "Of course." He guided her to a stand of leaves that none of the villagers were harvesting.

She smiled at him in return, grateful he'd taken her to a spot away from the others. She touched the leaf, and then yanked her hand back. "Ouch." The leaf pricked her finger. She frowned at Shimani.

"There is a process which softens the flesh of the leaf." He took her hand in his, and gently touched the pricked fingers.

Her fingers instantly stopped stinging. "How did you do that?"

"Majik." He said with a twinkle in his eyes.

She shook her head at him. She didn't quite know what to make of him yet.

"There is more to see."

She nodded and followed him.

He took her to other areas of the forest where other villagers were hard at work. He showed her the plants that provided the fibers they used to weave the cloth for their clothing. She listened, and cautiously touched the things he showed her, considering her first experience. She ran her hand over the dress she wore. She grew more amazed at the difference in texture from the raw material to the finished product. "This is astonishing. You utilize so much from the forest. How do you process the raw materials?"

"The tradesman amongst us fashion the plants into various items, depending on their expertise and interest."

Kaily looked up at Shimani. "Tell me about the Kahoali people."

Shimani led her to a secluded area. He helped her sit back against a sizable boulder. "It's,"

"Don't say complicated." Kaily said, interrupting him.

Shimani smirked and shook his head. "There are a great many complications in life, Kaily. You can't escape that fact."

"Wanna bet."

"How do you feel about the word difficult?"

"About the same as complicated."

Shimani laughed. "I see. It is difficult to describe the Kahoali people in a way that you would understand without more time among us."

Kaily narrowed her eyes at him. "Try."

"Don't say that I didn't warn you. You have seen only a small part of Village life. Tell me what you make of it so far."

Kaily frowned and shook her head. "What do you mean?" She didn't think he referred to the actions she saw before her.

"How would you describe the Kahoali people?"

Kaily glanced out over the villagers. "I don't know. It has only been a day, less than that in reality." Simple she wanted to say but kept her observation to herself.

Shimani gave her a smile she couldn't quite decipher. He looked out over the villagers. "As you can see, everyone works together. Even our children pitch in where they can to complete day to day tasks. We each have our special interests and abilities. That's where each devotes their improvement of skills. Everything we do and dedicate our lives to is for the sole purpose of benefiting everyone in the Villages."

"Doesn't seem that complicated, Shimani."

He glanced at her for a moment before continuing. "Perhaps not. Is it so different from life on your world?"

Kaily looked at the villagers again. Laughing and working. There was a camaraderie there. Perhaps somewhat similar in her own village back in Scotland, but the atmosphere wasn't the same. The camaraderie at the pub might be somewhat similar. She smiled. The gossiping ones had a certain amount of camaraderie. She glanced back at Shimani. "Life is not like this on my world. On my world life is so,"

"Complicated?" Shimani offered.

Kaily shook her head in annoyance at him but smiled. "Not what I was going to say." She glanced at those nearby. "They don't seem to have a care in the world. No stress, just life." There was a certain amount of wistfulness in her tone she couldn't

squash. She looked back at Shimani. "I feel out of place here."
She didn't understand what made her confess such to him.

"Why?"

Kaily shrugged. "Maybe because I'm not on Earth in my
familiar surroundings. I am still having trouble wrapping my
head around the fact that I am on another planet."

"Did you honestly believe that life only existed on your world,
and no others in the entirety of the Universe?" Amusement
thick in his tone.

"No." Kaily lied.

Shimani laughed.

Kaily could tell from the way he laughed he didn't believe her.

Shimani stood and pulled her to her feet. He kept her hand in
his. "Follow me."

"Should I be concerned?" Kaily half-jokingly asked.

"No, Kaily." Shimani laid a reassuring hand on her shoulder.
You are safe among the Kahoali, and especially with me. I want
to take you some place where I can give you answers to questions
you are afraid to ask."

"I'm not afraid to ask questions. I've asked many questions."

Shimani stopped their progress. He turned to stand face to
face with her. He crossed his arms over his chest and raised an
eyebrow. "You have asked questions, but are they the questions
that you truly want the answers to?"

"Yes." Kaily tried to swallow the lump suddenly in the back of
her throat.

Shimani narrowed his eyes at her, ever so slightly. "In truth?"

"Yes." She stubbornly stuck to her first answer.

"So, you don't want to learn how Moto brought you here?"

Kaily shook her head. Heat crept up her neck. She did want to learn, but dammit all. She was not going to admit it to him.

"Really?"

Kaily crossed her arms, mirroring Shimani's stance.

"It was a portal." Shimani said.

She didn't much care for the amusement in his tone. She frowned. Portal? What was this nonsense? Granted she couldn't explain what had happened. One minute she was in her dark warrior's arms, the next she woke up in a hut. How was she to understand how that happened? Did she honestly want to? Probably not. If she possessed any sense at all, she would cover her ears, and hum a tune to drown out Shimani's words to follow if he intended to explain it to her.

"You asked me to tell you about my people."

"I changed my mind."

"Too late." Shimani's eyes shone bright with humor.

Kaily glared at him.

"It will help to understand a little more about us. Some of us possess abilities. The best way to describe them to you, I think, is as elemental abilities. It's more,"

"Complicated?" Kaily asked without any humor in her tone. This was stuff of fiction.

Shimani smiled. "Exactly. The abilities align with a natural part of Ki. We learn to harness energy that manifests in different types of skills which may be easier to show you." He rubbed the deep crease between her brows. "Back to how Moto brought you to Center Village. He has the ability to open a doorway from one place to another. We call them portals. There are different types, but I think that might confuse you more."

"You think?" Kaily couldn't help the sarcasm. What the crap was he talking about? People did not have 'magical abilities' of any kind. At least, not in reality. Doorway my ass! It wasn't possible. Yet, she couldn't explain how she traveled from Earth to Ki, other than that damn stone doorway. She took a deep breath.

"Hmm." Shimani regarded her with a slight frown.

Kaily felt a sudden gust of wind stir the air around her. She rubbed her arms, chilled.

"You felt that?"

"So?" Kaily shook her head.

He held up his hand.

Another gust of chilled wind hit her face. Her vision blurred. She found it hard to breathe.

"Sit," Shimani gently pushed her to the ground, "before you fall over."

"Sorry." She stammered. She closed her eyes, and focused on taking deep, even breaths. "Why are you telling me all this?"

Shimani sat next to her. "You're no longer on your world, and the Universe just got a whole lot bigger for you." He let out a long sigh.

"No kidding."

"There are a great many wonders in the Universe, Kaily. Now that you're on Ki, it's important for you to begin to understand what has changed for you. Understanding it all could lesson your desire to return to Earth."

Kaily looked down at the ground between her knees. "You think my understanding these so called abilities you have will help me? In truth?"

"They are not so called. They are real, and the sooner you accept what might be possible, the better it will be for you. Possibly less," Shimani paused, "complicated." He added with far too much amusement.

Kaily spared him a long glare.

Shimani laughed. "Not all Kahoali possess abilities. The majority of the Villagers don't."

"Why?"

Shimani shrugged. "A variety of reasons. Are you ready to head back to your hut?"

"Yes." Kaily took his hand and allowed him to help her stand up. "I think I've had enough touring for one day."

"I imagine you have." Shimani said. "If you are up to it, I think it would be good for you to join the evening repast."

"Why?" Kaily frowned. She didn't exactly comprehend what he wanted her to attend. She was certain she wasn't ready to find out.

"You have no idea what I'm inviting you to. Do you?"

Kaily didn't reply.

"The evening repast is where the Villagers gather after dark to eat and enjoy each other's company to end the day."

"I see." She took a deep breath. "You seriously want me to present myself to the whole village when no one wants me around?"

"Yes. It will do you good to mingle with the people, Kaily. It will do them good too. They need the opportunity to get to know you. They need to become used to you being around. And," Shimani gave her a pointed look, "some of us want you here."

"I prefer to hide away for a while."

"Really?" Shimani stopped and turned her to face him. "You really want to hide? Aren't you curious enough about us to attend?"

She was curious about the Kahoali or at least a certain someone. She sighed. "I am curious. I am also apprehensive, Shimani."

"All this new world and new people stuff can be scary. It is a lot to take in."

"And unwelcoming." Kaily added.

Shimani raised his eyebrows. "Are we that unwelcoming, in truth?"

Kaily drew in a deep breath. She glanced around the area and the villagers she could see. "They ignore my presence, Shimani. I don't call that welcoming."

"What about me?"

Kaily shook her head. "No, you have not ignored me."

"But not welcomed?"

"No, you have been," Kaily paused looking for the right word, "kind." He had been more than kind, in truth. But still, she shook her head. She didn't feel comfortable there.

"Give them a chance, Kaily, please. It takes time to become comfortable enough for everyone to take a chance on getting to know each other."

Kaily nodded.

"Thank you." Shimani turned and led her in silence towards her hut.

She begrudgingly had to admit the wisdom in his words. She still didn't want to go.

Shimani opened the door to her hut. "I will escort you to the evening repast."

"No choice?"

Shimani shook his head. "No."

"Fine." Kaily replied.

Shimani smiled.

"Thank you for the tour, Shimani." Kaily stepped inside, and closed the door before he decided to come in. She needed to be alone. The evening repast? It was the last thing she wanted to attend. Still, Shimani was right. It would take time for the villagers to get used to her, and she them. Shimani had been more than kind. She decided she would not ruin their blossoming friendship. She couldn't help but wonder if her dark warrior would be in attendance as well.

Chapter Eight

Moto glanced up from the blade he sharpened. He frowned as he heard another knock on his door. He hung up the blade on the weapon wall where it belonged before seeing who had the nerve to disturb his solitude. Of course, it was Shimani. "Since when do you knock?" No one else possessed the audacity to disturb him unless they had official business from the Queen.

"Since now." Shimani stepped inside without being invited. "Don't get used to it."

"Of course not." Moto shut the door, and then turned to face his bothersome pupil. He crossed his arms over his chest.

"I thought you should know, I'm bringing Kaily to the evening repast."

Moto shook his head. "No."

"I wasn't asking permission."

Moto narrowed his eyes. "Bring her another night. This is not the best time for her to be at the evening repast." Not that there would be any acceptable time. There were too many prying eyes.

Shimani grinned. "Since some of the Shanees will be there?"

Moto glared in response. His stern looks should have been enough to squash Shimani's unwanted antics. They weren't. For some reason, he couldn't seem to intimidate Shimani the way he did others.

"Kaily needs to get out among the Villagers if they are ever to accept her."

"They can learn to accept her at the next repast."

"Does it matter, Moto?"

"Yes."

Shimani walked over to the weapons wall. He fingered one of the blades. "You brought her here."

Moto groaned. "Leave the blade alone, Shimani."

"It's better than leaving her alone to wander at will." Shimani turned to face Moto. "Who knows where she might end up if left to her own devices? The repast will help her acclimate to the layout of Center Village."

Moto shook his head. "No." He knew Shimani goaded him, simply to get his way. "Why is this repast the one she needs to be at?"

"Sari wants to meet her."

"She can meet the girl another evening."

"Sari will be here this evening. She is not going to take no for an answer. She wants to meet Kaily, this evening."

"Of course, she does." Moto didn't like it. He didn't know how many of the Shanees would be in attendance, not that it mattered. They would be there for one reason, and one reason only, him. The situation would be intolerable enough without adding the girl to the mix.

Moto shook his head again. "No, Sari can meet her another time." He'd have his hands full, especially if Tanyu showed up, which she would. He wouldn't be lucky enough to avoid her. She had made it quite clear that she wanted him for her bonded mate. She would stop at nothing to make him hers. It wasn't the Kahoali way, but she didn't seem to care about traditions.

"This really isn't up to you, Moto."

"Did you obtain the Queen's permission?" Moto knew he was grasping at straws. The girl was an outsider. Shimani would have to get permission before bringing her to such an event.

Shimani laughed. "Yes. I came here as a courtesy. Kaily will be at the evening repast."

A stone sank in the pit of Moto's stomach. He clenched his teeth. If Queen Shakti had given permission, she would expect the girl to attend. He couldn't do anything to stop it. He couldn't keep her isolated. "You should know better than to bring her to this one, Shimani." How was he to keep the truth from her?

"Be reasonable. What could possibly go wrong?" Shimani asked with a shrug.

Everything, Moto thought to himself. What was Sari thinking, wanting the girl there as well? Why would she want to meet her? Moto shook his head. He hoped it had nothing to do with their conversation earlier in the day. Sari informed him that she wanted him to choose her as his bonded mate. She gave him several logical reasons why mating with her would be the best choice. Except the one reason that counted. He suspected she had something planned, otherwise she wouldn't have suggested it. She often kept him out of trouble, and he figured this time was no different. They had been interrupted before he got the real reason out of her. Without knowing why, he couldn't bring himself to choose her. Once a Kahoali pair bonded there was no going back. They only bonded once in their lifetime. He wouldn't be responsible for taking Sari's chance at finding her true mate away from her. He knew that she longed to find her forever love. He wouldn't risk taking that from her. Somehow, he would have to figure a way out of his predicament.

"Moto?"

"Fine. Bring her." He wasn't surprised Shimani would accommodate Sari's wish to see the girl. He had given into Sari on more than one occasion. Maybe she just wanted to meet the one who caused him to defy their Queen and the rules about outsiders. "Keep her occupied, Shimani, and make sure she does not find out the purpose for this evening's gathering." If he possessed a smidgen of sense, he would take the girl back to her home world before everything went sideways. He blatantly ignored the stab of pain to his heart that option caused him.

"Glad you came to see it my way." Shimani gave Moto a friendly slap on the back. "See you there, my friend. And the girl's name is Kaily. Try to remember that." He added as he left Moto's hut.

Moto glared after him. It did not escape his attention that Shimani hadn't acknowledges his request to keep the girl occupied. He closed his eyes and sent a silent prayer out to the Universe that the evening repast would not be the complete disaster he expected it to be.

❧

Kaily impatiently waited for Shimani to escort her to the evening repast as he promised. Despite, her misgivings about going, she was surprisingly looking forward to the evening. Maybe because of the potential in again seeing her dark warrior. She no longer wondered if he were a dream, although, he might as well be. He remained as elusive as an illusion. They had yet to have any meaningful sit-down conversation. The forest exchange didn't count.

She heard the villagers outside. She'd been hearing the commotion for a while, which added to her impatient pacing. She figured they were gathering for the evening repast, while she was stuck in her hut, waiting to be escorted.

Earlier, Shimani showed her the clearing just outside the Queen's hut utilized for the evening repasts. He showed her the nearby kitchen where the nightly feasts were prepared. It wasn't like any kitchen she'd seen. He'd also given her an overview of the leadership structure. Apparently, there were thirteen villages in total with Center Village responsible for them all. The other twelve villages were governed by a Shanees, some of which would be in attendance at this evening's repast. He didn't elaborate on why, and she didn't ask. She didn't comprehend enough about Kahoali society or structure to understand if their attendance was as unusual as he made it sound. He'd given her enough information to almost make her change her mind about going. Her desire to lay eyes on her dark warrior overrode her desire to hide in the face of so many people, especially considering her status as the outsider.

She had mixed feelings about staying or trying to get back home. She wanted to learn more about the Kahoali and the inner workings of their society. She also wanted to return to the familiarity of her home. She was fairly certain her dark warrior possessed the ability to take her back. The fact that he hadn't yet done so, made her curious, and a little bit angry.

Curiosity overrode her anger. She wanted to learn more. The more she learned about his people, the more she learned about him. Still, she'd never been comfortable around so many, especially after her foster parents' untimely deaths. She'd worked hard to build a comfortable, secluded life, to recover from the sorrow of their loss. With one unfortunate stumble, that life had dissolved into chaos and uncertainty.

She stopped her pacing and glared at the door. What the hell was keeping Shimani? She thought he should have been there by now. She had even tried to draw out the process of getting ready. Including taking a long, hot shower. The cleansing paste the Kahoali used worked surprisingly well as both a shampoo and body wash. She'd been in the shower longer than intended, it had been so soothing.

Adding to that, the time she took to choose the right dress from the additional garments Shimani had brought her. She chose one that matched her green eyes. She still couldn't believe how soft and silky the material was to her touch. Nor could she accept that the cloth came from leaves. She shook her head in disbelief. Shimani had shown her, but still, it amazed her.

Then there was the time she took on her hair. She spent longer brushing it than she normally did to get it as straight as possible. A difficult feat in a humid climate. Usually, she had hair product at home to tame the frizzy mess. Once her hair dried, she'd been mildly surprised that it wasn't as frizzy as she expected it would be. She guessed it would do. Not that she cared about her appearance. Well, usually, she didn't care. She had no use for other people's opinions. She blamed her dark warrior for her sudden worry about how she looked.

She tapped her foot as she stared at the door. She probably could locate the place of gathering on her own. All she really had to do was follow the others. If she possessed the courage to step out among so many strangers. She didn't. She'd poked her head out the door a few times to confirm that it was indeed after dark, and past time Shimani should have been there. To make matters worse, she sensed it getting dark by the minute. Plus, the sounds floating her way didn't help her vanishing patience. She thought the repast might already be well underway, which by her reasoning meant they were late.

It would have been simpler if Shimani had given her a specific time. From what she had observed thus far, these people didn't have an accurate time keeping system. Not even the Agenors had anything resembling clocks. Tasks appeared to be completed by the rising and setting of the sun. Not that she'd seen one of those in either location. All of it was too bizarre to contemplate for long.

Kaily jumped, startled from the sudden loud rapping on her door.

Shimani poked his head in. "Are you ready?"

"If you are." Kaily replied as if it didn't matter to her. At least, she tried to make it sound like she hadn't been impatiently pacing.

Shimani smiled at her in a way that made her think she had not succeeded. Although, she gave him brownie points for keeping his comments to himself. She walked past him as he held open the door for her and waited while he secured it behind him. Not that he locked it, since there wasn't any. She still couldn't understand how these people could possibly feel safe without locks on their doors.

"Are you always in such a happy mood?" Kaily asked. She was not skilled at small talk. Neither was she comfortable with awkward silence.

"Not always." Shimani said with a wink.

Kaily glanced at the villagers. Almost all of the women wore headdresses. She subconsciously touched her unclothed head.

Shimani pulled her hand away from her hair. "You look beautiful, Kaily. This is a special night with guests, so the women have dressed up a bit. Most nights they are less formal without a reason to impress."

Kaily tried to take comfort in his words, but how was she supposed to fit in if no one told her these things? Not that she would have had the first clue how to put one on. They appeared a bit complicated for cloth coverings. "The males don't appear to be concerned about impressing?" The males' tan and brown garbs were quite plain in comparison to the brightly colored dresses the women wore.

"We're not." Shimani smiled and winked again.

Kaily smiled and shook her head at him. She tried to think of something else to say or ask to keep the conversation going. Nothing came to her mind. Shimani seemed okay with walking in silence, so she gave up. Instead, she glanced around to absorb the sights and sounds as she followed him to the gathering place. In truth, she was a bundle of nerves. They encountered far more villagers than she thought lived there. Similar to her other outing, the villagers paid little attention to her. She didn't like to be the center of attention and should have been more grateful for the lack of interest. After all, it was better than the first day when they ushered their children inside as she passed.

She experienced a slight pang of disappointment when Shimani guided her to a bench on the edge of the festivities. The bench was close enough to be a part of the gathering, but far enough to not be at the same time. She tried to push her disappointment aside, unsure why she felt that way. She didn't like crowds. She supposed he meant nothing by it, but he had been the one to insist she get out among the villagers. She took a deep breath. Then to sit her on the outskirts! She let out a small, silent sigh. He must have a good reason. Not that she would know. What did she actually know about Shimani? Only that he had been kind to her in an impossible situation, she reminded herself.

At least, she could observe everything. The bench did offer an adequate vantage point to take it in all of the activity without being in the middle of the commotion. From her location, she was able to spot drums of various sizes. She smiled. She enjoyed music. She grew curious to hear what kind of music the Kahoali would play. She also spied a long table filled with all kinds of delectable foods. Even on the fringes, the mouthwatering aromas wafted her way.

"Would you like me to bring you a plate or would you prefer to pick out your own repast?" Shimani asked.

Kaily glanced at the villagers gathered near and around the long table. "Whatever you bring me will be fine." To say she felt awkward, didn't quite cover it.

"I'll bring you the tastiest bites." Shimani inclined his head.

Kaily smiled. Her eyes followed him. He talked to several individuals along the way. She envied his ease with people. She didn't mind being a loner at home. For some reason, it had started to bother her among the Kahoali. She didn't understand why. She wished for once in her life that she fit in better. The people were so open and friendly, with each other.

Her eyes continued to roam over those at the repast. They'd split into a variety of different groups. She spotted the Queen near the center of the gathering with her own plate of food in her lap, and mug by her side. She talked and laughed with the villagers as they passed by or joined her. The ease with which she interacted with everyone was informal, and far different from what Kaily detected in the throne room. The children appeared quite taken with the Queen as several of them gathered around to eat their meals with her instead of their parents.

Kaily glanced down and sighed. A happiness permeated the atmosphere and sparked a deep yearning inside her to belong. She suddenly found herself wishing that she was not an outsider. It was a strange sensation to want to be included.

She looked back to the children gathered around the Queen and smiled.

The Queen glanced in Kaily's direction. She inclined her head, to a slight extent.

Kaily nodded back. Being a loner had been how she kept people at arm's length. She'd never regretted her need to be by herself, until now. Sorrow began surfacing inside her. She glanced around as she contemplated disappearing back to the hut. She would feel better in solitude where she could remember why she preferred to be alone.

When she glanced up, Shimani stood in front of her. Too late! She couldn't leave now. She accepted the full plate and mug he handed her. An exquisite woman came to stand beside him. She didn't wear a headdress like the other women. Not that she needed to. She would stand out in any crowd garbed in the plainest of garments. She radiated beauty. Kaily felt quite plain next to her darker sun-kissed complexion, similar to the other Kahoali. She wore her hair in tiny braids like her dark warrior did. She had the same athletic body type. As a people, they were in annoyingly great shape.

"Kaily, this is Shanees Sari." Shimani waited for Sari to settle in next to her on the bench. "Sari, this is Kaily." He handed Sari her plate.

Kaily narrowed her gaze at Shimani.

He smiled from ear to ear at her.

How was she supposed to hide the fact that she could speak Kahoali, thanks to his doing? Especially since he advised her to hide the fact for a while. Not only had he sat the most beautiful woman she'd laid eyes on next to her, but a Shanees, no less. She turned to Shanees Sari, smiled, and nodded her head. She glanced back at Shimani and frowned. He didn't have a plate or mug of his own. She gave him a pointed look she hoped he would interpret as 'don't you dare leave me alone with her'.

"Not so formal, Shimani." Sari focused her attention on Kaily. "Call me Sari."

"I will leave you two to get acquainted." Shimani left before Kaily could call him back.

Traitor, she thought to herself. She thought for a moment she might have heard him laugh but shook her head against the thought. He didn't appear to be laughing as he walked away, and she couldn't actually discern the sound specifically from him. She took a deep breath and focused her attention on Sari. She smiled at her again. This was going to be just perfect without the ability to communicate.

"Shimani tells me that you picked up Kahoali quite well."
"Something like that."

Sari smiled. She leaned in close to Kaily. "It's okay," she whispered. "I am aware of the truth, and Shimani sat us far enough away so we can converse without drawing too much attention." She straightened and winked at Kaily.

Kaily regarded Sari. Being Shanees would make her a leader of one of the twelve villages. What could they possibly have in common to talk about? She drew in a deep breath. "I'm not very good at these types of settings." She glanced around the gathering. In truth, she wasn't adept at one on one get togethers either. She kept that part to herself.

Sari touched Kaily's arm, drawing her attention. She smiled in the same good-natured way Shimani always managed. "I suspect you'll figure it all out soon enough."

Kaily shrugged. She didn't have the same confidence in her ability to figure anything out.

"What do you think of our feast?"

Kaily glanced down the plate in her lap. "Everything looks delicious." She found it curious that from what she could tell, the Kahoali didn't eat anything that looked or tasted like meat.

Sari pointed to a particular section on Kaily's plate of thinly sliced strips. "Those are pahini. One of my favorites."

Kaily picked up a slice. It had the same texture and consistency as an apple but smelled like walnut cheese. She took a tiny bite. "Mmmm. That is delicious."

Sari nodded. "I thought you might like that one." She pointed to another item on Kaily's plate. "I told Shimani not to give you any of that. It's a bitter root that has the same flavor as dirt. For some strange reason, Shimani loves it."

Kaily picked a piece up and sniffed it. She placed it back on her plate with a disgusted expression. "That doesn't even smell yummy. Shimani loves this?"

Sari nodded. "Oh yes. Shimani has no sense of what actually tastes good."

Kaily genuinely smiled at Sari. "I'll keep that in mind."

"You would be wise to do so." Sari smiled. "I also made sure Shimani gave you nectar of brey instead of actual brey."

"That bad?"

"On the contrary, brey's quite enjoyable, but intoxicating. The nectar is milder, and mostly for the children. I figured you could work your way up to the brey. The nectar is brey mixed with a specific fruit which negates the intoxicating affects, for the most part." She added with a shrug. "We wouldn't want you to forget your first repast, now, would we?"

"Ah, no." Kaily accepted back her mug from Sari that she had set aside.

Sari tapped her mug against the side of Kaily's, and then took a drink.

Kaily smiled at her and took a hesitant sip. Sari had been right. The nectar of brey was flavorful. It was sweet like juice, but not sickeningly sweet. She found the liquid to be quite refreshing. "Delicious." She liked the woman beside her.

"I'm happy you like it." Sari set her mug aside. She focused her attention of on the food on her plate.

Kaily ate more of the pahini. She tried several other items Shimani had given her, making sure to avoid the pungent root one. She finished the last of the pahini. "This is delicious." She said, looking longingly at the empty spot on her plate. "I understand why it is your favorite."

"I'll have Shimani keep you amply supplied."

"Yes, please." Kaily said with a small laugh. She peered at the different groups. She wanted to absorb everything about these people. She was an outsider and didn't want to be. She needed to understand the Kahoali people if she were ever going to fit in with them. They were her dark warrior's people. She glanced at Sari, who also looked around the gathering. She liked that Sari appeared okay with the silence. Kaily returned to her perusal of the groups. She still was conflicted about staying any length of time. She wanted to, and at the same time she didn't. She missed her home.

She peered back at her plate. She picked up one last bite, and then set her plate aside. She'd eaten more than she expected to. Sari had already finished her own plate and set it aside.

Kaily attempted to nonchalantly search the faces of those gathered. She had not yet spotted her dark warrior. A frown creased her brows. She was about to give up when her eyes landed on the object of her exploration. Her dark warrior stood next to Shimani. A small group of villagers, including young children gathered around them. She couldn't help but notice the inordinate number of women surrounding her dark warrior. In truth, one would be too many.

She focused her attention on Shimani as he entertained the children with the same abilities he'd demonstrated to her earlier in the day. Keeping her attention on him gave her time to get the sudden spark of jealousy under some semblance of control. It was an emotion she was not familiar or comfortable with. It also gave her time to behold more of the strange abilities that up until her time on Ki, she would never have thought possible. She couldn't squash just how unnerving watching such a display was to her.

Despite her unease, Kaily couldn't help smiling at the fun the children obviously were having with Shimani. The ease with which he entertained them astounded her. Her dark warrior by comparison, stood aloof and statue like amongst his admirers. Shimani looked out of place next to him or any of the other males gathered at the repast. The Kahoali males appeared reserved, and emotionally withdrawn, while Shimani freely displayed emotional responses towards the children, and her for that matter. Even with his back towards her and ramrod straight, she knew her dark warrior's features were void of any emotions. He was the epitome of an immovable statue. What Kaily didn't grasp was if he disliked evening repasts or the incessant women vying for his attention. She hoped it was the later.

"See something you like?"

Sari's sudden question startled Kaily. She forced her attention and gaze back to Sari, who glanced in the direction she herself had been keenly focused moments before. "Shimani is good with the children, isn't he?" She couldn't prevent the heat from rising to her cheeks or the blush that followed.

Sari smiled at her with a fair amount of amusement. "He is, but I doubt he was the center of your unwavering focus."

Kaily's blush intensified. She looked away.

Sari laughed. She returned her gaze in the direction of the two males and leaned in close to Kaily. "Moto is a fine enough specimen, and worthy of any woman's steadfast attention. He certainly knows how to mesmerize without even trying."

Kaily frowned. She didn't like Sari's comment. She didn't like how all those women competing for her dark warrior's attention sparked a jealousy inside her. She knew that she didn't have a right to be envious, but there it was anyway. Neither did she like how he ignored her. His aloofness towards her hurt more than she cared to admit.

"I'm teasing you."

Kaily tried to give Sari a warm, reassuring smile.

"It's understandable that you would be attracted to him. Moto draws a fair amount of attention."

"So, I've noticed," Kaily said before she could stop herself as, yet another woman joined the group.

Sari rubbed her back in a soothing way. "You have nothing to worry about." She leaned in close and added in a hushed tone. "Moto has eyes only for you."

Kaily's frown intensified. "I'm not so sure." In the forest, there had definitely been sparks between them. She sighed.

"Trust me, Kaily. Moto's eyes are set on you, and only you. No one has ever drawn his interest the way you have." Sari said. "Ever." She added, looking at the group.

Kaily's gazed shifted to Sari. "How do you know?"

"You're here."

Kaily shook her head. "That answer tells me nothing of the sort."

"On the contrary, Kaily, it tells you beyond a shadow of a doubt."

Kaily gazed down at her remaining contents in her mug. She wasn't convinced. She lifted her mug to finish its contents. As she did, her gaze focused on her dark warrior. With a soft sigh, she set her empty mug next to her discarded plate. She allowed herself to drift on the waves of the music and background noise of the gathering. She emptied her mind of her unpleasant contemplations. The children laughed, played and lived worry free. The adults appeared to have a similar, albeit more reserved, carefree life. The village certainly was peaceful, and to a point, comfortable, despite her not exactly being welcomed among them. She and Sari sat on the edge of the activities. No one else spoke to her, but still, there was a comfortableness to the evening she didn't expect to experience. "Sari?"

"Yes?" Sari turned her gaze towards Kaily.

"I see the women and children sitting, and eating, but I haven't seen any of the males doing the same. Did they eat already?"

Sari shook her head. "No, our society is matriarchal."

"Shimani ate with me earlier this morning."

"The men will eat with the women and children for earlier repasts in the day, but the evening repast is a bit more structured. The women and children's needs are seen to first." Sari pointed to a group of males gathering up the empty plates and refilling mugs. "They will make sure everyone has had their fill, before settling in for the night, and partaking of the sustenance." She indicated the Queen's group where two males were performing the same duties. They were the same two who had stood on the dais the day she'd been presented to the Queen. "The Chosen see to the Queen's needs. Tonight, they will also take care of the Shanees as well. At least, those who remained seated with Queen Shakti."

Kaily frowned. There was something in the way Sari added the last part the made her take a second look back. She let it drop, instead of asking for clarification. She had so much to learn about these people. She shifted her attention back to Sari. "I also noticed that many of the women filled their own plates."

Sari nodded. "Many of us prefer it that way. Easier to get what we actually like." She said with a wink.

Kaily smiled. She glanced at Shimani as he handed something to a toddler and whispered in her ear. The child appeared to be about three, give or take. She glanced back at Sari. "I didn't notice Shimani serving anyone else." She hadn't detected her dark warrior serving anyone either, but she kept her observation to herself.

"Shimani is looking after us." She smiled at Kaily. "Moto has been excused for this evening's duties."

Kaily nodded. "So, the males are servants?"

Sari choked on the drink she'd just taken.

"I'm so sorry." Kaily patted her back.

Sari shook her head. "No apology necessary." She replied, once she stopped coughing. "I would not say such within Moto's earshot." She gave a small laugh. "No, the men are not our servants. Everyone has daily duties and responsibilities they must perform. Shimani has been assigned to you, so his responsibilities fall on the others. Moto's reassignment of duties was for other reasons."

"Reasons you're not willing to share with me?"

"No. They are not for me to share. While the men eat after, they do grab bites here and there. We each have a place and purpose within the Villages, but we are not so strict as to make anyone suffer. Such ceremonial observances are ways we honor our responsibilities to each other, and our places within our society."

Kaily squeaked, startled by a small child running up to them. It was the same toddler Shimani had given something to earlier.

"This is Niele." Sari said as she put a loving hand on the girl's head. "Did you bring a gift for our guest?" She asked the child.

Niele giggled and nodded. She dropped the item in Kaily's lap. Niele looked expectantly at her.

Sari leaned close and whispered to Kaily. "She wants you to take a taste of the fruit."

Kaily smiled at the toddler as she picked up the fruit. Its texture was similar to a plum, but bright, white with tiny brown specks. She took a bite as the eager child watched. Kaily's eyes watered, and her face puckered from the extremely sour fruit. Unwanted juice dripped down her chin. She attempted to catch the drippings with her hands without dropping the offending fruit. She didn't want to hurt the girl's feelings.

Niele giggled and ran in the direction of Shimani who had been watching with a big smile on his face.

"Shimani has a mischievous streak." Kaily set the fruit on her plate. She glanced sideways at Sari. "So do you."

Sari handed her a damp cloth. She nodded. "We do. I'll make it up to you. May I?" She pointed to the discarded fruit.

"By all means," Kaily said, "have at it." She had no intention of trying that particular piece of food again.

Sari picked up the fruit. She cut it in half.

Kaily hadn't seen where she'd come by the knife or cloth. She would have sworn Sari didn't have either one with her when she sat down.

"This is called maka'nakua." Sari held up the two halves, one in each hand. She handed Kaily the half with the bite she'd taken.

Kaily shook her head, trying to refuse.

Sari laughed. "It will be worth it. I promise." She placed the half firmly in Kaily's hand. "Trust me."

Kaily glanced at her half. Sari obviously wasn't going to take no for an answer. "You ask for trust, but you didn't warn me about how sour it was."

"Yes." Sari nodded. "Maka'nakua's a rare delicacy. There are only a few bushes which grow this delicacy. They are ripe for a short period of time, and only once per annual cycle."

Kaily gave her a dubious look. She glanced down at the fruit. The center was quite dark, surrounded by white plum texture. From that angle, it resembled an eyeball. She glanced back to Sari.

"The secret to utter enjoyment of this treat, is to take a bite of the darker center with the outer layer."

Kaily gave Sari a skeptical look.

Sari smiled and shook her head at her. "Like this." She took a bite of her half.

Kaily monitored for signs of any adverse reaction. She didn't see one. She took a deep breath and mimic the bite Sari had taken. Her eyes widened in surprise. "Wow that is good." The flavor wasn't like anything she'd ever tasted on Earth.

"Glad you trusted me?" Sari took another bite.

Kaily nodded. "Only because it tastes so good."

Sari laughed. She focused on finishing her half.

Kaily did the same.

"It's ready." Shimani announced as he joined them. He gathered up their discarded dishes. He winked at Kaily as he left them.

"What's ready?" Kaily asked.

"Come." Sari stood. She held down her hand to help Kaily stand.

"I don't think I should." Kaily shook her head. "You and Shimani are not to be trusted." She smiled at Sari so she would see she meant her comment as a joke, sort of. In truth, it bothered her just how much she thought she could trust them. She didn't trust easily, ever. Yet, despite their show of a mischievous side, she thought they were trustworthy.

"Have I steered you wrong so far?"

Kaily gave her a look.

Sari smiled. "It's rude to refuse a request from a Shanees."

"You're not like the other Shanees." Kaily replied. She took Sari's hand and stood. She very much liked Sari. She was easy to converse with, and she felt welcomed in her presence the same as she did with Shimani. Although she hadn't met any of the other Shanees, she could tell, even from a distance that

Sari was different. Assuming the women around the Queen and Moto were mostly Shanees. She thought so in the way the other villagers acted around them. There was a slight deference given to certain women at the gathering.

"What makes you say so?" Sari linked her arm with Kaily's. She started walking closer to the activities of the evening repast.

"For one, you're not wearing a headdress which tells me you don't see the need to impress. You welcomed me in a way that the others have not." Kaily gave a slight nod of her head in the direction of the women gathered by the Queen. "How many of them are Shanees?"

"With the Queen or with Moto?"

Kaily glanced at Sari, and blushed.

Sari smiled at her. "Six are with Moto and two are with the Queen. The other women around both are from other Villages."

"Do the other villagers often come to this repast?"

Sari shrugged. "Each of the Villages have their own repasts, but sometimes others will come to Center Village. It can be easier to have a moment with Queen Shakti than requesting a formal audience. As for the impressing part, you're right, I don't. I have a very different range of attire I prefer that I wear in my Village."

Kaily frowned at Sari. "Which is?"

"Pants." Sari winked at her. "Kahoali women wear dresses, and a Shanees must be an example to others."

Kaily gave a short laugh. "Figures! I would love to get a pair of pants instead of these dresses."

"I'll see what I can do about that. Here we are."

Sari guided Kaily to a spot closer to the musicians. A shiny, satin like sheet lay spread out on the ground. On top were two oversized, pillow like cushion chairs. They reminded Kaily of huge bean bag shaped chairs. A low table stood between the two seats. Two large filled mugs had been placed on top of the table. She sat at Sari's silent invitation. "Oh my, that's comfortable." Kaily sighed and closed her eyes. "I could fall asleep right here."

"I won't be offended if you do. The evening repasts are about winding down the day's activities with good food, time with family and friends, and pleasant music." Sari handed Kaily one of the mugs.

Kaily accepted with a smile. She glanced around the area. Other such seating places had been set up. Theirs, while near the activities, was still positioned closer to the outskirts of the other groups.

"Thank you for passing a pleasant evening with me, Kaily. I have enjoyed getting to know you better." Sari lifted her mug as if in a salute.

Kaily held up her mug, mimicking Sari's gesture. She took a sip. "Wow that is not nectar of brey." Her eyes watered a bit.

Sari smiled. "No, Shimani watered it down for you, but definitely not nectar of brey. Drink it slowly. Even watered down, the affects have a way of sneaking up on a person."

Kaily nodded. "This is quite good." The flavor was distinct, and not quite describable. The liquid slid down her throat entirely too easy, once she got past the initial shock. She could easily drink way more than she should without even noticing until it was too late. "Thank you, Sari. I have enjoyed getting to know you as well."

Sari nodded and smiled at her. "Sit back, and enjoy the night, Kaily."

"Sounds like a perfect plan." Kaily returned Sari's smile. She settled deep into her cushioned seat. She let the melody of the flute like sounds drift over her. The melody was mixed with a soft background beat of drums. She could get used to this kind of life, quite easily.

Sari settled back into her own chair.

Kaily sighed. Undeniably, this was a life to hold on to. Her eyes drifted to her dark warrior. Even though his group had changed locations, she found him with less effort than the first time. The gaggle of women still vied for his attention. She tried to suppress a flare of annoyance at the women. As she kept on eye on the group, her eyes narrowed. It wasn't simply the women making a fuss over him that irritated her. It was his uncanny ability to keep his back firmly towards her, despite their respective position change.

She settled deeper into her cushion and sipped on the brey in her mug. What did it matter who her dark warrior talked to? She shook her head and let out a heavy sigh. It didn't. Regardless of how she thought of him, he wasn't hers. She closed her eyes. She took a long drink of her watered down brey. She allowed the soothing musical sounds to sweep over her as she tried to empty her mind of her irksome thoughts.

—— *ele* ——

Kaily realized she'd fallen asleep only when she woke up to Shimani gently shaking her. Someone had taken her mug from her hands and placed it on the table. "I'm sorry. I must have dozed off." She suppressed a yawn. Less people remained in the clearing. A number of villagers were in the process of leaving.

"No need to apologize." Shimani helped her stand. "I'll walk you back to your hut."

"Thank you." Kaily's attention shifted to her dark warrior. He walked around the side of the Queen's hut with Sari beside him. His hand rested on her lower back. She didn't want to feel pangs of jealousy towards Sari, but the unfortunate emotion sprang to life inside her. She liked Sari which made the emotion more uncomfortable. Why would Sari be leaving with him? Why would he be touching her like that?

Shimani guided Kaily with his hand at the small of her back. "Moto is just seeing Sari back to her Village. They are childhood friends." His words were spoken in hushed tones. Kaily caught them all the same.

Her eyes met his. She wanted to reply in some way to show that it didn't matter to her. The words refused to come out.

His words didn't give her the comfort she suspected he intended them to. If anything, his words intensified the pangs of jealousy she attempted to suppress.

Shimani gave her a reassuring smile.

Kaily walked with him in silence.

Shimani opened the door to her hut.

"Thank you."

"My pleasure," Shimani replied.

Kaily stepped inside. The interior lit up the moment she walked over the door's threshold.

Shimani followed her inside. "Did you enjoy the evening repast?"

Kaily nodded. "More than I thought I would, to be honest. Thank you for taking me, Shimani." She'd been embarrassed that she'd fallen asleep. She wished she could have said good night to Sari, or her dark warrior. He appeared content to pretend she didn't exist.

"I'm glad. Sari enjoyed your presence, as did I. Sleep well, Kaily."

"Thank you, Shimani. You as well."

Shimani gave her a slight nod. He closed the door as he left her hut.

Once alone, Kaily looked around. It had been a pleasant evening. Better than she'd anticipated.

She yawned.

She suspected the brey was responsible for how tired she was. It could be the lack of a restful night's sleep or both. So much had happened to her in such a short period of time. The events felt like a lifetime ago since she'd arrived on Ki. The Agenors and Kahoali had such a different life than she had back on Earth. So different, it gave the impression of being dream like. A part of her waited for herself to wake up.

She set to getting ready for bed as her mind sifted through the evening's events. She thought back to the conversations. The sights, the sounds. She smiled to herself. A part of her envied the easy-going life the Kahoali had built for themselves. Another part of her longed to return to the familiarity of her life.

She sighed as she laid down on the sleeping mat. It was not nearly as thick as her mattress at home, but it was comfortable enough. She stifled another yawn and curled up in the blanket. It wasn't cold enough to be so bundled up, but she liked the comfort of her makeshift cocoon. It provided her a sense of security. She latched on to the sensation, even if it were nothing more than an illusion.

Her mind strayed to her dark warrior. She really should stop thinking of him so, but she couldn't help it. Thinking of him as hers felt natural. She hoped the attention he had received that evening was not the norm. She couldn't shake the feeling that there was more to it all. Although, to be fair, she didn't understand what the norms were for him or any of the villagers. She knew what she'd learned from Shimani, but honestly, what did she know? She was an outsider. She couldn't avoid that fact. It was nice that Shimani and Sari didn't treat her like the outsider she was. She still had so much to learn about the Kahoali and her dark warrior.

She took several deep, cleansing breaths. In. Out. In. Out. She would take the time the Queen allowed her to learn everything she could. Right after a sound night's sleep. She needed rest, if she wanted to be coherent enough to find answers to the questions swimming around her mind. Tomorrow was another day. She closed her eyes and let herself be carried away into the blissfulness of slumber.

Chapter Nine

Moto stood by the edge of Crystal Lake, gazing out over the water. The soft night's glow gleamed off the surface. A cool breeze stirred the spicy-floral aroma of the surrounding forest.

He took a deep breath, taking the scent deep into his lungs. He closed his eyes as he listened to the lapping of the water hitting the edge. The calmness washed over him in slow waves, replacing the evening's frustrations. The choice forced upon him, proved to be a heavy burden. The earlier conversation with Sari hadn't helped. It made the weight on him heavier to bear. Not even the calm of his favorite place could completely lighten his load or his mood.

He shook his head.

The Queen had been adamant. He must choose a bonded mate. Choosing a mate was the price he was obliged to pay for bringing the girl to Center Village. Not exactly how Queen Shakti had worded it, but the result ended up being the same.

If he hadn't brought the girl to his Village, he wouldn't have to make this choice, at least, not yet. He took another deep breath.

Crystal Lake was the one place where he could let his guard down. He could allow his emotions to run free without judgment or ridicule from his peers. He was far too emotional for a Kahoali male, and he always had been. At times, he wondered if no other male possessed the depth of emotions he did. If they did, how did they keep them so suppressed all the time?

Moto shook his head and took another calming breath. He would not spoil this peaceful moment with useless pondering. These moments were becoming too rare. He needed this place where he had no duties or responsibilities to anyone but himself. In this meadow he was free for a time. Although, it wouldn't last. He put those troubling thoughts out of his mind. He had it now. It would have to be enough.

He took off his vest and folded it so he could utilize it for a pillow. He took off his boots and dipped a toe into the water. It was just cool enough to be refreshing. He took off his trousers and folded them in like manner to his vest. He placed both items in a neat pile. The light breeze caressed his body. Goose bumps prickled his bare skin. The meadow was cooler than in the Villages and provided the perfect elements to cool his temper. He let the events of this particular day slide away as he had so many times on other previously difficult days.

He stepped off the edge and sank into the depths of Crystal Lake. He surfaced only when the need for air became stronger than his need to sink into the endless tranquility of the water. He needed only a few strokes to break through the surface. The Lake awed him in its uniqueness. He never understood why others didn't spend more time there. For him, the meadow and Lake were like a sanctuary from life's troubles. Most Kahoali only took to the water when they answered the call to retrieve their talisman, and even then, too few heard such a call now. Most avoided the meadow except when they couldn't for special occasions, forced by tradition or the Queen's orders. Their avoidance bothered him, although he welcomed the solitude.

A welcome embraced him each and every time he stepped out of the stationary portals. The place gave him what he needed most when he required it. That was part of the uniqueness that astonished him. The Lake, in part, gave the impression of being a living entity. It always gave him what he needed, but hardly ever what he thought he wanted. It was a mystery he still couldn't entirely piece together. He'd learned over the years to allow his wants to align with his needs, as provided by Crystal Lake.

He smiled. Either way he usually found peace to unburden his core.

What he required this night was a long, hard swim. He knew from past experience that the Lake could be big or small depending on need. This night, the Lake was so large that he couldn't swim fast or hard enough to reach the other side. When he'd expended enough energy to feel somewhat at peace, he flipped to his back, and floated under the canopy of the night.

Moto's mind sifted through the events of the evening repast. It had been a very long evening. He spent time talking to each of the Shanees, and the ones who were not. Each had requested to be considered for his bonded mate. The Queen stated that she preferred his choice to be Shanees. Why the others had presented their request was beyond his comprehension. Fortunately, Shimani had provided some distraction, and kept conversations on track. He'd been grateful for the assistance, even though he was not happy about him bringing the girl to the repast. Still, he would have floundered with Shimani. He'd found keeping his mind on the conversation difficult more than once. Ignoring the girl's constant gaze boring into his back proved to be nearly impossible. She was the only one there he desired to spend any time speaking with and was also the one person he had to ignore. The staring was bad enough, but the emotions pouring out of her had been grueling to endure.

Sari had managed to keep her away from the unpleasantness of the evening, and somewhat occupied. Although, her spending the entire evening in the girl's presence didn't sit well with him either. While he had forbidden Shimani from giving the girl brey, he refrained from saying anything when he provided her with a watered-down version. The resulting slumber helped diminished her scrutiny, which allowed him enough focus to finalize his conversations with each of his suitors. At least the evening hadn't been a complete disaster. Something to thank the Universe for, he supposed.

He still had to provide Queen Shakti with his decision. She would be expecting one, and of course, he couldn't provide her with what she wanted. Reconciling his temper with being forced to choose a mate sparked a rebellious streak in him. One he should contain. The Queen was cross enough with him.

Moto swam to the edge of the Lake and pulled himself out. Water slid down his sleek body, and dripped from his tiny, dark braids. He could have used his abilities to portal a towel from his hut but chose not to. Even in the cool air, he would dry soon enough. He lay on his back. The soft, moss carpet of the meadow supplied a comfortable enough spot for a quiet moment. His head rested on his folded clothes. He didn't bother dressing. No one would disturb him, and he savored his carefree time.

He stared up at the night sky. At least, the part that wasn't obscured by the forest canopy. He loved the densely, star sprinkled night sky, when a certain world wasn't visible. Thankfully, that cursed world wasn't visible from Crystal Lake. Since the Villages were within the cover of the deep forest, he caught sight of the world so little, sometimes he forgot about its existence. For some obscure reason, he could sense its presence this cycle. He wanted to blame the reason on catching sight of the cursed world when he found the girl with the Agenors but, he didn't entirely believe that was the true cause.

He let out a long sigh and closed his eyes. He rubbed the space between his brows. He had other matters to think about other than a world he would rather forget existed.

Sari for one. She'd made a formal request to be considered as his bonded mate to Queen Shakti. He'd been against the idea before hearing why she made the request. Now, after hearing more, he shook his head. He still had misgivings about her plan. Admittedly, it was an intriguing idea, but also dangerous. The possible consequences were incomprehensible should their subterfuge be discovered. To his knowledge, no one had ever faked a bonding in the Kahoali's entire history. Such a thing was too egregious to consider. Yet, they were considering it.

The Queen would have no choice but to banish them if their deception were ascertained. Banishment was beyond fathoming. He couldn't even imagine what life would be like without his people. To never see another Kahoali ever again. To never spend the night beneath the canopy at Crystal Lake. To never again step foot upon the soil of Ki. All of those consequences and more were too unthinkable to contemplate.

Sari laid out a good argument. But how could he allow her to take the risk? He shook his head. He couldn't, regardless how unbearable the alternative might be. Sari argued that no one would suspect since it'd never been attempted. And how would anyone prove it? He didn't have a counterargument to give her.

Neither did he delight in tempting fate. The Universe could be an unforgiving place where maintaining balance was concerned.

From Sari's perspective, faking a bond would allow him time, and the sanctuary of her Village, where he would not be under the watchful eye of the Queen and the other two Chosen, Baridi and Kesho. She said he needed time and space to determine who his true bonded mate should be.

Moto harshly laughed.

They both knew he wanted to choose the girl as his bonded mate, but he couldn't. She wasn't Kahoali. He didn't think it was possible to have a true bond with her. Neither could he ignore the pull she had on him. A connection existed between the girl and himself that he couldn't deny or ignore. There was no rational explanation. Sari had been right. He required time to understand what existed between them, and why. How was a connection even possible?

Just as he couldn't ignore the pull the girl had on him, he couldn't disregard the potential consequences to Sari. She'd tried to convince him that even if their ruse were discovered, she wouldn't suffer any repercussions. She had a reason but wasn't prepared to disclose it to him. They had known each other for a long time. Getting anything out of Sari before she was ready to share always proved ineffectual. She would share with him when she was good and ready, and not a moment before.

Even if he were allowed to choose the girl as his bonded mate, she wasn't Kahoali. She lacked the understanding of what bonding with a Kahoali truly meant, and the ramifications to herself, and her life moving forward. How could he make her understand? Explaining in words was one thing, true understanding was another. As a Kahoali, comprehending the connection between bonded mates was as natural to them as breathing. No one required explanation to understand. The comprehension existed as innate knowledge that could never be properly explained to an outsider.

A sharp pain pierced his heart. The girl was an outsider, no matter how many ways he turned it over in his mind. She would never understand. He was faced with an impossible choice and future.

Sari impressed upon him to make a choice, before the Queen decided for him. He absolutely did not want to leave the selection up to Queen Shakti. No telling who she might make him bond with. He couldn't risk the choice being Tanyu. All the prospects filled him with dread, but Tanyu would be beyond intolerable. Sari and he could have a decent life as bonded mates, albeit an odd one. She was more like a sister to him, which would make actually bonding with her awkward.

He shook his head again. An impossible choice, indeed.

He wasn't fool enough to believe Queen Shakti wasn't aware of his attraction towards the girl. All Kahoali had some level of empathic abilities, the Queen was no exception. Not even his acting as if the girl didn't exist would convince her otherwise. The pull was too strong. Even if his people weren't empathic, he'd brought the girl to his Village which was telltale sign enough. He skirted the rules often, not outright defiance, until now.

Moto abruptly sat up.

What he didn't understand was why Queen Shakti was forcing him to take a mate. He figured the girl had sparked the situation, plus Tanyu, but still, why would the Queen force him? Nothing in their history gave precedence to forced pairing. Their traditions allowed each male to choose their bonded mate in their own time. Okay, so he was five annual cycles past the usual age, but still, it shouldn't have been enough to result in being forced. He hadn't felt any connection with anyone, until the girl. Was it possible? Could she and he create a true bond between them? Was that why the Queen forced the issue?

He rubbed his hands over his face in irritation. Even if it were possible, she would never be accepted among his people. Despite, Sari and Shimani's obvious optimism. They liked the girl.

How could the Universe make him choose between his people and her?

Her status as an outsider was the root of the issue. If he chose her, he would most assuredly become an outcast. Where would they go? Would his bond with the girl be enough? Could he give up his connection to his people? Could he give up his world for hers without becoming bitter about what he'd lost? Would she eventually resent him when she began to understand the depth of connection the bond would forge between them? Impossible questions that he had no true answers. There were entirely too many uncertainties. He was not used to being so indecisive in his life. There wasn't a viable choice that would not require some kind of sacrifice. The Universe, he thought, had turned brutal in this regard.

He lay back and closed his eyes. He begged the Universe for a sign. There had to be a way to keep the girl and remain among his people without having to sacrifice anything. He just couldn't see the solution yet. There had to be a way. He couldn't accept there wasn't.

Chapter Ten

K aily woke with a thin layer of sweat covering her entire body. Her hair lay damp against her head. The intensity of the dream was far more potent than her past dreams of her dark warrior. Her dreams of him often sparked an aroused response, but this night was more intense. She would have touched herself to offer some relief if she thought it would help. The few times she had tried, proved it wouldn't. She was better off leaving well enough alone, especially since discovering her dark warrior was a real flesh and blood man.

She threw off her blanket and sat up. A soft glow sprang to life at her first movement. The light's source remained a mystery to her, and frankly she didn't care right then. She looked around the hut without any idea what she expected to find. She stood, and walked around the small, confining space. The room grew more oppressive with each step she took. In spite of the coolness within the hut, sweat continued to seep from her pores. Her night gown hung damp against her bare skin. She peeled it off and used a towel to dry off the moisture clinging to her body. She put on the dress she wore to the evening repast.

She stared at the door while she ran her fingers through her damp hair. She bent over and ruffled her hair to dislodge it from her itchy scalp. She stood upright, not entirely happy with her disheveled hair. Her gaze fixated on the door. The hut had become far too tiny to remain within, but what was the alternative? She chewed on her lower lip.

"Stop being a coward." She muttered to herself. She resolutely stomped to the door and yanked it open. She stepped outside before she changed her mind. She glanced around her surroundings, taking in as much as possible. The night had not yet given way to daytime. Thankfully, no one was up yet. Although, the eerie quiet of the village almost sent her scrambling for the safety of her hut. Regardless of how the one room hut bothered her. She wasn't able to determine how long she'd slept. The inconvenience of no clocks. If she had to hazard a guess, she would say it was barely before predawn or earlier. In other words, practically the middle of the night.

She took a deep breath and started to take a step in the direction of the training area she had previously found Shimani and her dark warrior. Her first waking thought had been to find him. She needed answers that only he could provide. She needed something else from him too, but she would settle for answers. She wasn't brave or aroused enough to initiate the other, close though.

She shook her head as painful memories of how he'd so completely ignored her at the evening repast sprang to the forefront of her thoughts. She tried to push aside the hurt his actions caused her. She hadn't expected such treatment from him, not after their brief encounter earlier in the forest. Truth was, she didn't know him, so how could she expect a certain type of behavior from him?

She took several calming breaths. In all likelihood, she wouldn't get what she needed anyway, so her destination didn't matter. Plus, he probably still slept like every other person in the village from all appearances. The village remained entirely too quiet. She took another calming, deep breath. She'd hated how fear consumed her existence. If she had just a little bit more courage, maybe her isolated existence on Earth wouldn't be her shelter from the storm of life.

"You can do this." She told herself.

She refused to remain cooped up inside the hut any longer this night. She turned a full circle several times, before choosing a direction. She took her first step to nowhere in particular. The unknown would be her guide. An early, not quite morning walk would do her good, she hoped.

She ended up walking to the main parts of the village, and the clearing the Kahoali utilized for repasts. She realized as she drew near that no one stood guard outside the Queen's hut.

Kaily frowned.

She couldn't imagine a place being so peaceful that the leader didn't require some sort of protective watchman. True she had the four Chosen, as Shimani had explained to her, but still, the emptiness of the clearing startled, and confused her.

A shiver ran down her spine.

She thought a walk would be a good idea, but now, she shook her head.

The dark, dense forest surrounding the village didn't offer much comfort. She was a stranger on a strange world. Her courage rapidly evaporating, she turned to hightail it back to her hut, when the sound of trickling water caught her attention. Mesmerized, her sudden spark of fear forgotten, she moved in the direction of the sound.

The soft noise took her closer towards the Queen's hut, and around the side. She didn't recall hearing anything similar during the repast. When she rounded the back of the building, she half expected to find some sort of water source. Only the forest greeted her. She stood still. She strained to pinpoint the direction of the soft trickling noise. An image of a waterfall formed in her mind. A frown deepened the crease between her brows.

After a few steps into the forest, a momentary shift of the ground unbalanced her movement. Not enough to make her fall, but enough she stumbled. A cold bubble encompassed her, followed by a wave of dizziness. Both sensations passed so fast she thought she might have imagined them. The nausea, however, remained. She rested her hands on her knees with her eyes closed and drew in deep breaths until the queasiness eased. Thankfully, the sensation dissipated.

She stood up straight and opened her eyes. Her backside hit the soft, moss-covered ground. She no longer stood within the forest, but a meadow. The same meadow she had dreamt about so many times before setting foot on Ki. This was the location of every single dark warrior dream she'd had. The lake, the waterfall, even the surrounding forest were all the same. Her dreams had always been so vivid, sight, sound, smell, all of it was so real. But to be there in reality, brought so many emotions to the surface. How could this be possible?

A person laying by the edge of the lake caught her attention. Her eyes narrowed. Her heart skipped a beat. She recognized him as her dark warrior, even though she could not clearly see who the individual was. She'd dreamt this exact moment so many times, she pinched herself to be certain she was not actually asleep. She knew she wasn't.

She cautiously rose to her feet. Her eyes remained locked on the sleeping figure. As she drew near, she realized he lay on his back, naked for the world to see. Her feet kept moving forward of their own validity. The figure loomed closer. She couldn't alter her advancing momentum. Finally, she regained control, and halted her progress.

She scanned for signs of his potential wakefulness. She found none. She carefully crouched where she stopped. Her attention remained focused on him. She interpreted his lack of movement as a sign that he indeed remained asleep. How soundly asleep, she had no idea. She moved as quietly as possible to prevent disturbing him. She inched a little bit closer. She held her breath and let it out slowly. She moved to where she was within reach of touching him, if she had the courage to do so, which she didn't.

She glanced over her shoulder, momentarily considering escaping before her dark warrior became aware of her presence. Her heart wrenched at the thought. She chided herself. She'd wanted to see him, and there he lay. She reminded herself to be brave. She forced her gaze to return to the figure laying within reach. She inched her way forward to get just a little bit closer. She stopped and watched for any movement. She told herself she was being cautious, not cowardice.

She didn't detect any indication he'd woken up. She closed her eyes and took, silent deep breaths to calm her racing heart. She settled in beside him, when she convinced herself that he was not awake. She clasped her hands in her lap, careful not to touch him. Her bravery only went so far. With her eyes, she inspected every inch of him. She had to agree with Sari, he certainly was a fine specimen of a man. There was not an ounce of flab on his body, anywhere. Even in his state of rest, he was impressive, or maybe it was her state of arousal.

"Like the view?"

Kaily squeaked. Her eyes locked with his. Heat flooded her cheeks. She tried to scramble backwards. Somehow, she ended up pinned underneath him, back pressed against the ground. He moved faster than she thought feasible. "Get off me!" She pushed at his immovable, bare chest.

"No." Amusement shone in the depths of his eyes and echoed in his tone.

She pushed harder on his chest. He didn't budge, not even the slightest bit. Kaily frowned up at him. She would have crossed her arms if it were possible. "At least, put your clothes on." She tried to ignore a part of him wedged firmly against her thigh.

"No." Something more resonated in his tone in addition to amusement.

"You were supposed to be sleeping."

"So were you."

Kaily glared at him. "Something woke me up."

"Someone's staring woke me up."

"I wasn't staring."

His finger caressed the side of her cheek. "You were."

Kaily closed her eyes. A sigh escaped before she had a chance to stop it.

"Look at me."

Kaily shook her head in defiance. She squeezed her closed eyes tighter.

Soft laughter drifted to her ears. His breath caressed the side of her neck. "Look at me." His voice held a velvety, seductive vibration.

Her breathing grew shallower. Her heart raced. She took a deep breath, and slowly opened her eyes. They collided with his silver webbed ones. His strange hazel eyes held her enthralled in a spell she couldn't break. He wasn't ignoring her now.

"Better." He brushed her hair back from her face. His finger traced the thin line of her lips.

Her eyes drifted shut of their own accord.

"Open your eyes." His words, while spoken with tenderness, held a note of authority.

Kaily didn't defy him.

He smiled at her, a true smile that reached the depths of his eyes. He placed a chaste kiss on the side of her neck.

Moisture pooled between her legs.

His hand slowly traveled down the length of her body, igniting flames in its wake. His tense stare remained fastened with hers.

She couldn't advert her gaze, even if she wanted to.

His fingertips pulled at the skirt of her dress until his hand caressed bare skin. He raised the edge of her dress up the length of her body.

She remained immobile for fear of breaking the spell between them.

Her heart skipped a beat when his hand slid down the inside of her thigh.

His fingers fondled her swollen nub. "You did like the view." His voice became somewhat hoarse.

Kaily blushed. She turned her head to look away.

He cupped the side of her face and turned her head back to face him. "Don't be embarrassed by your arousal." He traced his moist finger along the bottom of her lip. She tried to turn away, but his lips claimed hers. His tongue traced the path his finger created, tasting the evidence of her desire.

She closed her eyes, and slightly parted her lips.

His tongue teased the inside of her mouth as he playfully deepened their kiss.

She sighed or he did, maybe both. She couldn't exactly determine for sure.

He rested his forehead against hers. "See? Nothing to be embarrassed by."

Kaily nervously laughed, still blushing.

His hand returned to the apex of her thighs. He slowly slid a finger inside her.

Her expression sobered, and her breath caught in her throat.

She lifted her hips to press harder into his hand.

"Deeper?" He teasingly asked.

Kaily nodded, unable to speak the words.

He pushed his finger deeper inside her.

Kaily groaned in protest as he withdrew it.

He laughed. "Tell me what you want."

"I don't know," she said, breathless. "More."

He slid two fingers excruciatingly slow inside.

She lifted her hips higher. Her eyes flew open and locked with his when his forward progress stopped.

He smiled down at her. "Deeper?"

"Yes." She lifted her hips higher, trying to force his compliance. It didn't do any good. She couldn't deny in the slightest that he controlled this particular exchange between them. "Please!" She begged.

His soft laughter enveloped her as he pushed his fingers deeper.

She rode the increasing waves of pleasure as he plunged them in and out. Her hand slid down the length of his abdomen.

He withdrew his fingers and grasped her wayward hand. He held it firmly against his chest. A frown creased his brow.

"What's wrong?" Kaily asked.

He leaned in close, and tenderly kissed her. "Nothing." His smile was mixed with sorrow.

"I don't understand."

He took a deep breath. "I know."

Her confusion grew. She couldn't for the life of her understand what happened. "What can I do?"

He gave a harsh laugh. He took a deep breath and released it with a sigh. "I can't give you what you want."

"How do you know what I want?"

He gave her a pointed look.

She turned her head away.

He laid a finger on the side of her face and forced her gaze back to his. "I explored parts of your home world enough to know we have different viewpoints about intimacy."

"Seems like we had similar viewpoints moments ago." Kaily couldn't keep her frustration from echoing in her words.

He growled in response, and abruptly sat up. "We are not so free with our bodies."

Kaily sat up and yanked the hem of her dress down. "Not all of us are 'free with our bodies' on my world."

He turned startled eyes towards her.

"Oh, don't look so surprised. You don't know me."

"And you don't know me."

She looked at her clasp hands in her lap. He spoke true.

He pulled her back underneath him. "It would be so easy to take you here and now." He pressed the evidence of his own desire against her thigh.

"I want you to." She tried to move to cradle him between her legs.

A sudden burst of words assaulted her ears that she had no translation for in her mind.

"What's wrong? Please, tell me."

"Nothing." He growled. "Nothing." He repeated in a softer, gentler voice. He rolled to his back, taking her with him. He settled her so she lay halfway on him.

She brushed back his braids. "Please tell me what I did wrong." Tears began to sting the back of her eyes. "Moto, please, explain it to me." It was the first time she'd spoken his name aloud.

"It's not you." He closed his eyes, and gently pushed her head to rest on his shoulder.

A painful silence settled between them.

Kaily had no idea what she'd done wrong. Despite, his reassurance, she couldn't shake the feeling she had. "I'm sorry," she whispered.

"There is nothing to apologize for, little one." He patted her back as if to comfort her. "I will give you release to ease your arousal if you wish."

Kaily shook her head. She couldn't speak for the burning in her eyes and throat.

He responded with a sigh of frustration.

Kaily tried to hold back the tears that threatened to fall. The last thing she wanted, was to cry in front of this man. She lost the battle. The tears fell, and she lacked the strength to stop them.

He sat up and pulled her onto his lap. "Please don't cry, little one."

She didn't reply.

"There is so much you don't understand, and I'm not sure how to explain it to you." He patted her back, and he rocked her back and forth. "Please don't cry."

She wrapped her arms around his neck and buried her face in the crook of it.

He rocked her back and forth while intermittently rubbing and patting her back.

She was grateful he'd stopped trying to comfort her with words. She let the tears fall and took what comfort he offered her. Finally, she spoke when the tears ceased. "Take me home."

The rocking stopped, and his hand stilled on her back. "I can't."

She turned a tear-streaked face towards him. "Can't or won't?"

He had the decency to not say 'can't' again. "Do you truly want to go home?"

She let out an exasperated breath. "Yes. You don't really want me here." She shook her head. "Although, for the life of me I don't understand why you brought me here in the first place." She looked away, breaking eye contact.

"You have no idea what I really want."

Kaily turned angry eyes on him as a fire sparked in the depths of her soul. "You don't acknowledge my existence in front of others. And now this!" She waved a hand in the air.

He shook his head and rubbed a hand across his face. He opened his mouth and closed it several times.

Kaily stood.

He let her.

"You're right." She paced to the edge of the lake. She didn't bother looking at him. "I don't understand, and I'm not going to if you don't at least try to explain things to me." In her anger, she failed to notice that he also stood, and moved with her.

He wrapped his arms around her. "You're right, little one. I have not explained anything to you, and for that, I apologize. But I am not going to apologize for bringing you to my Village instead of taking you back to your world."

Kaily turned in his arms and looked up at him. She saw pain in the depths of her dark warrior's eyes that made her heart sink. "Tell me what you want from me." She kept her eyes locked with his. "Please."

He pressed her head against his bare chest.

She gave him credit for at least putting on his pants.

"I can't."

She would have smacked him for that answer, if he hadn't been holding her so tight.

"If you absolutely want to go back to your home world," he drew in a deep breath, "I'll take you."

She pulled back enough to glimpse the emotions in his eyes. Giving her that option cost him.

"But I am asking that you have patience with me and stay. Please, Kaily. Stay."

She opened her mouth to reply, but then shook her head, and closed it.

He stood with his arms loosely holding her. He remained silent.

She glanced out over the lake, and then back up at him. "Tell me why you don't speak to me when others are around."

Moto closed his eyes.

"You owe me that much." Kaily said when she thought he wouldn't answer her.

He opened his eyes and took a deep breath. "I broke a law in bringing you to Center Village. The Queen was adamant that I keep my distance from you."

Kaily opened her mouth.

He laid a finger against her lips and shook his head. "I'll admit, I've taken it to an extreme. I only do it to protect you. There are consequences at play right now that I'm not prepared to discuss with you. Please, trust that I have a good reason for all my actions where you're concerned. They are not meant to hurt you. The last thing I ever want to do is cause you pain, Kaily."

She laid her head against his chest. She stared at the lake, and the waterfall which fed into it. A part of her still wanted to go home. Home was safe. It was a known factor, but it also was not an entirely happy place. Not like it was before her foster parents' death. She took a deep breath. "I'll stay."

"Thank you."

Kaily heard relief in his tone.

Moto kissed the top of her head and held her closer.

She didn't resist.

He rested his chin on her head.

She wanted to stay in his arms for all times. She wanted the peace of his embrace, and the lake to always wash away her sorrows. She wasn't convinced staying would be the right decision for her. She couldn't bring herself to leave him either, not yet. She owed it to herself to give him a chance. She needed to see what was between them or could be.

He cupped the back of her head in his palm, and again kissed the top of her head.

Kaily stared into the depths of the lake, content in his embrace. She watched the lapping of the water against the shore where the carpeted meadow gave way to sand.

Moto lifted his head and gave her one last squeeze. "It's getting light out. We should head back." He pulled away from her and retrieved his vest.

She felt the loss of his touch. She didn't want to go back to the village quite yet. She sighed. She turned her attention away from the lake to Moto. She watched him secure the clasps on his vest.

He smiled at her.

She returned his smile.

He turned to start back up the path.

She started to follow, but then stopped. She peered one more time at the lake. The sand sparkled, and her gaze followed it deeper into the depths of the water. Gem like stones lay at the bottom of the crystal-clear lake. She moved closer to the edge of the water without conscious thought. She forgot about Moto, and the need to get back before the villagers started their daily activities. The sand winked invitingly at her. She took a step forward to feel the wet granules between her toes. She wanted to touch the gem like stones, gleaming in the morning light just below the surface of the water.

Without warning, Kaily fell into the lake. She rapidly sank. She struggled to break free of the water's surface. She saw it scarcely out of reach. No matter how hard she kicked, and paddled, the surface remained out of reach. Panic set in. She was a fairly good swimmer, but it didn't matter. She just couldn't break through. She ceased her efforts and stopped struggling. She sank deeper. As the last breath left her lungs, she was thrown onto the moss carpet of the meadow. She lay on her side and coughed. She struggled to expel water from her lungs and replace the liquid with the air she desperately required.

Moto pounded on her back as he held her steady on her side. He uttered several Kahoali curses.

When she'd coughed up enough water, she drew in a steady, shaky breath.

Moto helped her sit upright while supporting her back with his upturned knee. "What did you do that for? What were you thinking? Do you have any idea what could have happened to you?"

Kaily held up her hand as if the action would stay his anger, and questions. "I didn't do it on purpose!" She tried to yell back while struggling for breath. Her throat was raw from coughing, and her lungs burned from lack of air. "I wanted to stand on the sand."

"What sand?"

"That sand!" Kaily pointed at the ground. She frowned when she saw no sand. The carpeted moss of the meadow went all the way to the water's edge. "But," she turned bewildered eyes to Moto.

His scolding words stopped. His expression softened. He stood and helped her gain her feet. "Here," he said as he wrapped a towel around her shoulders. He took several calming breaths before he spoke again. "Crystal Lake is," he paused, and glanced out over the Lake. With a small shrug, he turned his attention back to Kaily. "Tricky. You have to be careful around the Lake, and don't ever, and I mean ever, go into it again. Ever."

The last part came out rather harsh.

Kaily almost smiled when he took more calming breaths. She maintained a serious expression by looking towards the lake.

He pulled her roughly into his arms.

"I didn't mean to fall in," she said.

"I know." Moto stepped back and looked at her with a fierce frown. "How did you get here in the first place?"

Kaily rolled her eyes. "I walked." She tried to pull out of his arms. Did he have to be so annoying?

"I mean, how did you get here, to Crystal Lake?"

"I walked!"

Moto let out an exasperated breath. "Never mind!"

Kaily shook her head. She inhaled, and slowly exhaled. "Thank you for the towel," she said, instead of what she really wanted to say. He didn't have the right to be irritated, she did. And she was not going to ask about the towel thing. She'd seen it materialize in his hand, but she couldn't bring herself to believe what she'd witnessed. The strange impossibly new displays drove her perilously close to overload. She turned and started walking in the direction she thought she had come from. She stopped and turned in a circle. Everything looked the same. She couldn't determine where the path lay. She turned irritably towards Moto. "Which way?"

Moto pointed in the opposite direction she had chosen.

Kaily suspected that he suppressed a smile. She glared at him.

A wide grin spread across his face.

Damn him, she thought. She crossed her arms over her chest.

Still grinning, Moto turned, and started walking the direction he'd indicated.

She followed him in silence. When they came near the edge of the forest, she experienced the same intense cold sensation, and shifting ground followed by a brief dizzy spell that she had the first time. She hurried to catch up with Moto, intending to question him about what she just encountered. His grin had vanished and was replaced with a fierce frown. His focus was directed elsewhere. She took a deep breath and maintained their uncomfortable silence. She kept her eyes on the ground as they made their way along the path back to the village.

Moto cursed under his breath as they rounded the corner of the Queen's hut.

Kaily glanced from him to her surroundings to determine what might have upset him this time. Some of the villagers were already partaking of the morning repast laid out on a table outside the kitchens. The morning repast didn't consist of the kind of feast the evening one had, but ample enough to feed the village. She frowned, unsure what inspired the source of his foul mood, until her gaze landed on the Queen. She glanced up at Moto. He no longer wore a frown. His features were completely void of any emotions. She continued to frown and glanced back at the Queen.

The Queen signaled to Moto, a silent invitation to join her. Kaily's gaze shifted to him.

Moto inclined his head towards the Queen. While his head was bowed, he whispered to Kaily under his breath, so quiet, she almost didn't hear him. "Go back to your hut. I'll send Shimani as soon as I can." He left her side without a single glance at her, and walked toward the Queen, his back ramrod straight.

Kaily stared after Moto, his words barely registering. The Queen didn't appear particularly happy, but neither did she give the impression of being overly angry. Certainly not to the level his reaction indicated. Questions flowed through her mind, but she would have to save them for later. She struggled to grasp his words recently spoken, and rapidly fading into nothingness.

GO!

Moto's silent command startled her. She would have sworn his voice sounded as if he stood right next to her. She clearly saw him moving closer to the Queen. She shook her head.

Now, Kaily! GO!

She turned towards the direction of her hut. She continued to shake her head. She had to be imagining him silently ordering her around. There was no way she actually heard his voice in her mind. She shook her head again and pushed the weird sensation aside. Whatever was happening, she'd be better off in her hut, away from anyone's unwanted scrutiny.

Chapter Eleven

Relief flooded Moto when he caught sight of Shimani near the kitchen hut. He discretely signaled to him, asking if he would check on Kaily. After Shimani indicated he would, he focused his attention solely on Queen Shakti. He and Shimani had developed a silent communication method for their off-world explorations. He never expected to need it on his own world. But then, he never expected to bring an outsider to his world either. Shimani could take care of Kaily, while he attended to the Queen.

"My Queen," Moto said, once he stood in front of her. He bowed informally to her. Since he expected their conversation would be an informal reprimand, he responded in kind.

Queen Shakti pointedly looked him up and down, taking in his entire wet self. She turned her stern gaze in the direction of Kaily's retreating back. Anger practically poured off of her in waves. She set her recently filled plate on the table. "Walk with me."

Moto silently cursed his carelessness as he followed the Queen around the back of her hut. He ignored the sideways glances from the other Villagers. She took the opposite direction of the way to Crystal Lake. Moto silently sighed. He, unfortunately, could deduce where they were headed. Conversations didn't go well, when the Queen wanted privacy.

She stopped at her special, secluded spot she often spent the early morning. "Sit!" Her tone strained with anger.

Moto sat on the bench she pointed to without comment. He struggled to maintain the facade of emotional detachment.

She paced back and forth in front of him.

Her pacing was a sign of just how angry she was with him. Normally, she was a fairly even-tempered woman, so much so that he frequently admired her skill of maintaining emotional control. He didn't intend to stretch her patience beyond her endurance. It just happened that way on too many occasions. It appeared this would be one of those instances. He kept silent and waited. Nothing he said would help now.

Finally, Queen Shakti stopped her pacing. She turned to face him. "Why would you take the outsider to Crystal Lake?"

"I didn't." He forced himself to remain in control of his emotions.

"Don't insult my intelligence, Moto." Fire burned in the depths of her eyes. "There is not the remotest possibility she just happened to discover the stationary portal behind my hut, and she just happened to know how to use it to gain access to our most sacred site!"

"My Queen, I swear, I did not take her to Crystal Lake," Moto said in as neutral a tone as he could muster. He'd learned a long time ago that conversations with his Queen went so much better if he didn't allow his emotions to get away from him. A difficulty in the best of circumstances, which these were not.

"Then how did she get there?"

Moto shook his head. "I don't know."

The Queen walked a small distance away. She stood with her back towards him.

Despite the difficulty, Moto remained seated, and silent. He couldn't provide acceptable answers to the Queen when he didn't understand how Kaily came to be there in the first place.

"How did you two get wet?" Queen Shakti turned back to face him.

"She fell in, and I went in after her."

The Queen closed her eyes and took several deep breaths. She opened her eyes and pinned him with a fierce scowl. "Here's the thing, Moto, the outsider should never have gotten close enough to fall into the Lake. Assuming you are telling the truth." She held her hand up.

Moto closed his mouth.

"The moment you discovered her at Crystal Lake, you should have escorted her back to her hut. You should not have let her get close enough to fall into the Lake." Queen Shakti took another deep breath, and slowly exhaled. "It is becoming apparent you lack the ability to do the right thing where this outsider is concerned."

His temper rose to the surface. He remained silent, barely. He struggled for control.

"Who do you choose as your bonded mate?"

The abruptness of her question caught Moto off guard. He stammered, in his attempt to give a proper response. He wanted Kaily but knew better than to voice his inner most desires to the Queen. Plus, she wasn't Kahoali. A true bonding would be impossible between them. His mind understood this fact, his heart did not. He shook his head in response to his inner thoughts.

"You're out of time." Queen Shakti said when he failed to give her a coherent answer. "Choose or I will choose for you."

A mired of emotions washed over Moto, and his control slipped. "Why?" He demanded. By sheer force, he remained seated. "Is it because of the girl that you're forcing this choice on me?"

"Yes."

"Why? She isn't a threat! She's not Kahoali and would never be a candidate for a bonded mate to any of our people. Why force a choice on me that I'm not prepared to make? Compelling me to make this choice is against our traditions!" Moto stood. Too many emotions coursed through his veins. He was trapped in his own skin. He struggled to escape the confines that bound him, not physically, but emotionally. "Or is she?"

The Queen flinched at his hastily asked question.

He hadn't meant to give voice to his ludicrous thought sparked by her reactions. It just slipped out. His eyes narrowed. He took a step closer to the Queen. "Is it possible? Could she bond with me?"

Queen Shakti sat heavily on the bench. She patted the spot next to her. "Sit!"

Moto took a deep breath. He rotated his neck, cracking it in the process. Sitting was the last thing he wanted to do. He struggled against her command, and the expected obedience. With some effort, he forced himself to sit as ordered. He stared into the forest to collect his thoughts while he tried to regain a semblance of control over his emotions. "Is it possible?" He turned his gaze to the Queen.

Queen Shakti sighed. She maintained eye contact. "I don't know." She shook her head.

"But you believe it might be?"

Queen Shakti shrugged. She shook her head, and then shrugged again. "I don't know. Maybe." She looked away and stared in the direction of the forest.

Moto sensed some of her anger slip away. He suspected her focused attention resided somewhere other than the forest her gaze penetrated. He remained silent and forced an observance of patience as he waited.

"I was very young when I pulled my talisman from Crystal Lake. Far younger than anyone else in our Village or history." Her voice seemed as far away as her gaze. "I almost drowned." She glanced at Moto, and then returned her gaze to the forest.

Moto hadn't noticed how aged the Queen appeared until this very moment. He suddenly spotted silver threads sprinkled throughout her dark braids. "What happened?" He asked.

"A man I'd never seen before, pulled me from the Lake. I haven't laid eyes on him since that day." Queen Shakti smiled at the memory. Sadness penetrated her words. She took a deep breath and returned her attention to Moto. "He wore the cloak of the Druids, but his appearance was unmistakably Kahoali, but not entirely. He seemed to encompass both somehow." She shook her head. "I don't know. I was only six at the time, and maybe I saw something that wasn't quite real. But, even now, his image is crystal clear in my mind. I believe I saw someone who was both, Druid and Kahoali." She shook her head again. "There is nothing in our history to indicate that our two peoples have ever been anything but enemies."

Moto frowned and shook his head. "Impossible."

"Maybe." She glanced at the forest, and then back at Moto. "His existence, if real, says otherwise."

Everyone knew, Kahoali bonded with Kahoali. It was the only way to create a true bonding necessary for offspring. Moto started to stand.

Queen Shakti put her hand on his arm to stop him. "That day he told me that I would be Queen at a very young age, and in the face of a great sorrow for the Kahoali people."

"The massacre of Center Village," Moto quietly said. He settled back on the bench.

Queen Shakti nodded. "He said that I would not see him again until the day of my death." Her gaze penetrated his. "And I haven't."

Moto closed his eyes and attempted to gather his thoughts.

Queen Shakti laid her hand over his. "Moto?"

He opened his eyes and met the Queen's gaze.

"I see the struggle within you, and it scares me."

Moto let out a sigh. "Why?"

"I would be blind not to sense the connection between you and the girl. I feel the pain this struggle causes you. If she were Kahoali,"

"You would give your blessing," Moto said, interrupting her. He couldn't keep the bitterness out of his words.

Queen Shakti shook her head. "No, I would not. This connection between you two concerns me, and not because she is not Kahoali. It's not unusual for there to be some kind of connection between a pair before the bonding takes place, but this connection," she shook her head, "I see between you and her," she sighed. "The link between you two is like nothing I have seen before, not even between bonded mates. It frightens me."

Moto glanced down at the ground. What could he say? He felt the link, and it scared him. For it to be so strong that even the Queen could sense it in such a brief period of time, frightened him even more. He looked back at the Queen.

Queen Shakti nodded. "Good. You understand what I'm saying."

"I do," Moto said. "Is it really so bad? Isn't it possible that the Universe brought us together, and we are meant to be bonded mates?"

The sadness in the Queen's eyes grew deeper. She shook her head. "No, Moto, it is not."

Moto opened his mouth to protest.

The Queen held up her hand. "Think about it, Moto. If I am correct, and that man who saved me was Kahoali and Druid, it would mean the girl's Druid."

"NO!" Moto abruptly stood. "No, she is not!" He paced away from the Queen.

Queen Shakti stood as well. "If there is the slightest possibility that she is Druid, I can't allow you to bond with her. I can't risk an accidental bond between the two of you."

"She's not!" Moto adamantly shook his head. "Druids are male, not female."

"Are you certain?" Queen Shakti asked. "We know so little about them. Can you honestly say for certain that she is not?"

Moto stopped pacing and turned to face his Queen. "She's not!" He would stand his ground on that point. Everything he'd seen about the girl, did not for a moment give him any indication she was one of them! He would stake his life on his certainty. "Yes, I am positive beyond a shadow of a doubt that she is not Druid."

"I'm not," Queen Shakti said. "Why are you so certain?"

Moto struggled to answer. Did he dare disclose the full truth? Would the Queen demand he sends the girl back to her home world, if she learned the fact of the matter? He already knew the answer to both questions. There were so many possible consequences of disclosing the full truth to his Queen, but it was the possibility of losing the girl that solidified his determination to remain silent about how she came to be in his life. But he had to give the Queen something. "Because she told us herself that her home world is Earth."

Queen Shakti scrutinized Moto for so long, he struggled to remain still. "So, you are reasoning that since she is not from Celtan that she can't be Druid?"

"Yes, my Queen."

"I'm not convinced." Queen Shakti held her gaze firmly locked with Moto's. "I'm also not convinced that she is a threat, since she hasn't displayed any ability to touch the energy of Ki."

Moto opened his mouth to speak.

"She's not a threat to the Kahoali people!" Queen Shakti interrupted. "You are another matter."

"She's not Druid!"

The Queen gave him a sharp shake of her head. "The time for discussion is finished. Now, you listen."

Moto bowed his head. He clasped his hands behind his back. He clenched his jaw shut to keep himself from adding more fuel to the fire of his damnation, so to speak.

Queen Shakti nodded in response. "I don't know how she obtained access to Crystal Lake, but I doubt it was on her own. When I find out who did it," her glare intensified. She took a deep breath, and slowly exhaled. "That is another matter I will deal with when the truth is made apparent. She is as much a victim of these circumstances as any of us. Until we know how to take her back to her home world, we have no choice but to allow her to stay. I will not send her out to a worst fate among the other Inhabitants of Ki than she must endure among us. Hear me, Moto, and hear me well. I will not permit you to bond with this outsider. If you don't want me to change my mind about sending her away, you will choose a mate."

"In other words, I choose a mate, or you will banish the girl?" Moto's tone was strained, and he felt his control slipping.

"Yes, Moto, I will."

With some effort, he remained silent. His gaze drifted past the Queen to the surrounding forest. It wasn't fair of the Queen to make such a proclamation. He knew she didn't make idle ultimatums that she would not carry out if pushed too far. Forgive me, Sari, he silently uttered in his mind. "Then I choose

Sari." He didn't like it, but the Queen had left him little choice. He would protect Kaily anyway he could.

"Accepted," Queen Shakti said. "I will make the arrangements and inform you when the ceremony will take place. Until then, don't do anything foolish." The Queen gave Moto a piercing glare.

"Yes, my Queen." Moto bowed low, in a formal way.

"Dismissed." Queen Shakti waved of her hand as she sat on her bench.

Moto bowed again, before taking his leave. He walked back to his hut without speaking to anyone. Too many emotions coursed through his veins. Jumbled thoughts clouded his mind. He stepped inside his hut but couldn't stop pacing. He had too much pent-up energy. He considered opening a portal to Kaily's hut but discarded the thought almost as soon as it formed. He didn't want to put the girl in undo jeopardy, more than he already had. So, he opened a portal which would take him to the one person who might understand, Sari. He adamantly hoped her plan would work out. The last thing he wanted to do was hurt Sari in the process of protecting the girl. He would never forgive himself if this plan hurt Sari's chances to find happiness with her true bonded mate, whoever he turned out to be.

Chapter Twelve

Kaily sat on the edge of Crystal Lake and dangled her feet in the water. She wasn't fooled by the sand illusion a second time. There was no beach leading up to the water, despite appearances. The edge was a sheer drop off, like one would expect to find in a deep-water swimming pool. With her eyes closed, she could almost feel the cool, wetness of the tiny granules against her palms. With her eyes open, her hands rested on top of a sandy beach apparition. As she began to understand more about this place, she was amazed and truly frightened of its oddity.

She noticed this time around that the waterfall held the same illusive quality as the sand. The mist at the top and bottom obscured details to both. Even the rock face behind the falling water shimmered in and out of existence. In her dreams, and her first visit, she thought she could differentiate these details that now refused to solidify for her. She shook her head. Truly amazed and terrified at the same time.

The meadow was no exception. At first glance, it appeared quite large. She walked the parameter, searching for the stationary portals about which Shimani educated her. She discovered the space was far smaller than its appearance. The only thing she hadn't imagined was the temperature changes associated with them.

Portals? She shook her head. She would never have in a million years thought about such things as if they truly existed, which apparently, they did.

During her walk around the meadow, she had been careful not to enter any of them. Shimani had explained the portals to her, but he had not indicated where each led. Frankly, what he had shared, frightened her enough, she didn't want to know more about portals and such things. He also must have thought it prudent to impress upon her dangers associated with Crystal Lake, although, his details were rather lacking. Maybe he intended to frighten her enough to keep her from coming back. Which worked, for a while. She took three days to gather enough courage to try coming back.

Part of the reason had been her dark warrior. She sighed. Moto, she mentally corrected. She needed to start using his name, even in her own mind.

Moto had been true to his word and sent Shimani to her. However, he was nowhere to be found. She hadn't laid eyes on him since their time at the lake. He wasn't even at the repasts Shimani had forced her to attend. Not exactly forced, at least, not the first night. She had eagerly attended the night she and Moto returned from the lake, hoping she might glimpse him. But she hadn't. The night grew more uncomfortable since Sari hadn't been there either. Kaily grew reluctant to partake in the subsequent evening repasts. Her status as an outsider became more prevalent with each passing day. Being around the Kahoali people was not helping them get used to her as Shimani said it would.

She wiped away a stray tear.

In addition, her mental stability grew more precarious with each passing day. There were times she would swear that she heard Moto's voice as if he stood right next to her. Each time she turned to look; he wasn't there. In fact, no one was. These episodes occurred mainly when she was alone in her hut. Honestly, everything was becoming too much to endure.

She blinked her eyes to keep more tears from falling. She took a deep breath and exhaled. She pushed the unpleasant thoughts out of her mind and focused on the gemstones under the water. They gave the impression of being just below the surface. Yet, she couldn't reach in and grab one. She'd tried. She realized to grasp one she would have to swim for it. After her previous experience, she was reluctant to actually get into the water. She was a decent enough swimmer, but she'd come too close to drowning. The event was enough to make any one wary of risking another brush with death.

She glanced at the meadow behind her for the umpteenth time. She kept hoping she'd encounter Moto there. She let out a heavy sigh. Obviously, it was too much to wish for. She secretly hoped he might be able to somehow sense how desperately she needed him.

She closed her eyes and rubbed her temples. Never in all her life, did she ever want to be so close to a male the way she wanted to be near him. A magnetism existed between them that she'd never before come across. She couldn't explain it. Perhaps, nobody could. How would anyone make sense of something so intangible?

The gemstones continued to taunt her. The longer she stared at them, the clearer they became. The shapes, like large opals or maybe small river rocks. If river rocks shown with such vibrant hues. There was every variation she thought possible under the rainbow. Each one glimmered in its own way. But one in particular stood out among all the others, like a beacon, calling to her.

She shook her head and closed her eyes. She searched as she opened her eyes. Her gaze locked with the gemstone. She stood without awareness of her actions. Her gaze did not waver from the one which drew her. She dropped her dress and under clothes to the meadow floor, not far from her discarded boots. Her hypnotic like state tugged her closer to the lake's lip.

Kaily?

She rubbed sweat damp hands over her thighs. She licked her lips. As she stared at the stone, it appeared to rise closer to the surface. There was a part of her that thought she might be able to grasp it, simply by reaching out her hand into the water.

Kaily? Answer me!

Her reluctance to dive into the water slipped away, heartbeat by heartbeat. Her fear began to evaporate, barely noticeable. A part of her logical mind screamed at her. She experienced a strange sensation as her impulsive control disintegrated.

Kaily!

Her focus narrowed to only the stone. Everything else fell away. A peace stilled over her as the last remnants of her resistance, and impulse control shattered, leaving nothing but her desperate need to hold that gemstone in her hands.

KAILY! ANSWER ME!

She frowned. Fragments of Moto's voice echoed within her mind so strongly, she took an involuntary step backwards from the lip of Crystal Lake. *What?* She involuntarily responded to the imaginings in the own mind.

What are you doing?

Nothing. She shook her head at her own stupidity of talking to herself. Seriously? How deranged had she become? She shook her head to clear the imagined voice from her mind. She took a step closer to the lake. She was not going to let imagined fear hold her back. The stone called to her. She lifted her hands above her head, in dive position.

KAILY!

She ignored the imaginary voice. She pushed off the side, and dove headfirst into Crystal Lake.

NO!

She dove deeper and deeper. Still, the stone remained out of reach. No closer, and no further away than when she stood on the shore, staring at it. She broke through the surface as she exhaled the last remains of air in her lungs. She took deep breaths to feed her starved lungs much needed oxygen. She swam to the edge and held herself aloft as she glanced around the lake. She shook her head to clear the fog which had settled within her mind. Her eyes immediately located the gemstone she strived to retrieve. She kept the stone firmly centered in her mind, and field of vision.

Several Kahoali curses, for which she had no direct translation, echoed in her mind.

Kaily dived under the water. She swam towards the stone for as long as she could. There was a brief moment where she thought she might have gotten within reach of it. She stayed under longer than she should have. She had too, the damn thing was so close, practically within her reach. She turned back when she had no choice. Finally, she broke through the surface. She sputtered and spat out what water she hadn't accidentally swallowed. She wiped at her eyes to clear the water from them.

She yelped as rough arms hauled her to the edge. She immediately sensed that the arms belonged to Moto. "Let go of me!"

Moto turned her around to face him and held her at arm's length without relinquishing his firm hold on her. He took several deep breaths. He scowled at her.

She glared back.

"What," he said between clenched teeth, "do you think you are doing?" Moto took several deeper breaths.

"Nothing."

"Nothing? NOTHING?" Moto clenched his jaw.

She waited as he appeared to need more air. She might have found the situation comical, if she weren't so mad at him for interrupting her.

"You were told NOT to go into that water ever again. Instead of listening, I find you HERE TRYING TO KILL YOURSELF!" Moto closed his eyes. He pulled her closer to the side of the lake.

She grabbed on to the edge.

He dropped one of his hands and rubbed the bridge of his nose.

Kaily could almost hear him silently counting.

He opened his eyes. Heat radiated from their depths. He opened his mouth, and then closed it several times. He shook his head. Finally, he lifted her out of the water and set her on the side. He positioned his hands to pull himself out next to her.

Kaily swiftly hurled herself back into the water. She didn't make it very far.

Moto grabbed her, and practically threw her out of the lake. He scrambled out after her, and roughly grabbed her arms. He hauled her to her feet as he stood with her firmly in his grasp. "DO YOU HAVE A DEATH WISH?"

"NO!" She tried to kick him, which was no small feat, as he appeared to be quite adept at avoiding her attempts. "LET GO OF ME!" She struggled to break free of his hold on her. Another futile endeavor.

"STOP STRUGGLING, KAILY!" Moto tightened his hold.

Kaily ceased her struggles. Her efforts weren't getting her anywhere anyway. She took a deep breath. "Put. Me. Down." She ground out each word between clenched teeth.

"Promise me that you will NOT jump back into Crystal Lake!" Moto kept an unyielding hold on her.

"No." Kaily shook her head for emphasis.

"Why? What are you doing?" He didn't quite yell at her, but his tone remained harsh, and demanding.

She looked away from him. She was embarrassed enough without giving voice to her foolishness.

He forced her to look up at him.

Kaily didn't resist. She could tell he attempted to be as gentle as his temper would allow.

"Answer me. What are you doing?"

She glared at him and let out an exasperated sigh. "I just want to see one up close. Okay?" She would have crossed her arms over her chest if he weren't holding her so tightly.

Moto frowned. "See what up close?"

"The gemstones!" Kaily pointed at the lake, as much as she could, all things considered.

Moto's frown deepened as he looked to where she indicated. "Sand?" He whispered.

"You see it?"

He nodded and loosened his grip on her.

She smacked him on the chest. "I told you I saw sand the last time we were here!"

Moto turned her halfway around and gave her a swat on her backside. "That's for hitting me."

Kaily frowned and rubbed her offended butt cheek. "Jerk!" She pulled completely out of his hold.

He let her and turned away from her.

Kaily ran and dived back into the lake before he could stop her.

Moto uttered several curses and ran to the edge where he stopped. His eyes searched the water. He took a nosedive in to the Lake, after locating her. With his arm locked around her waist, he swam to the edge, and grabbed onto it.

"Dammit!" Kaily's attention remained squarely fixated on the stone.

"I don't know if I should just kill you myself and be done with it or let you continue to do the deed yourself." He stretched his neck and unclenched his jaw.

"Don't be rude." She didn't spare him a glance.

Moto shook her. "Look at me!"

Kaily narrowed her eyes on him.

"Why are you trying so hard to get a stone? You're not even Kahoali!"

Kaily huffed at him. "I don't need you reminding me that I am an outsider. I feel it every minute of every day since coming to this cursed place! I just want to see one up close. Why is that so wrong?"

"Because you're not Kahoali!"

"I wasn't going to keep it!"

Moto took a deep breath. "That's not the point, Kaily."

"Then what is? Why are you so angry with me?" Hot, angry tears burned the backs of her eyes.

"I'm not angry at you."

Despite, his obvious attempts to calm his temper, it still remained very close to the surface. She took a deep breath herself, attempting to calm her own frustration. "Are you sure about that?" Her eyebrows rose as she asked the question.

"Fine, I am." Moto closed his eyes. He rubbed his hand over his damp face.

"Moto." Kaily touched the side of his face and moved closer to him as they clung to the side of the lake. "Talk to me. Why are you so angry with me?"

His gaze met hers. He took her hand in his and placed a chaste kiss in the middle of her palm. "You scared me, Kaily."

"I didn't mean to."

"I know." Moto pulled her into his arms. "I know."

Kaily wrapped an arm around his neck. "Please talk to me. What am I failing to understand?"

Moto caressed the side of her face. "Everything." He tightened his hold on her. "Don't pull away from me."

"I don't want to, but you have to start giving me some answers. You asked me to stay, to be patient with you, and then you disappear on me. Where the hell have you been for the past three days?"

Moto remained silent.

"Seriously?" Kaily sighed. "This is exactly what I'm talking about. I need answers, Moto."

"I know." Moto took a deep breath. "You're not Kahoali."

Kaily opened her mouth.

Moto shook his head. "Let me finish." He laid a finger across her lips. "You have to be willing to hear me out."

"Fine! Get on with it."

Moto rubbed the crease between her brows. "Patience, little one."

Kaily glared at him.

Moto half smiled. "What you are missing IS that you are not Kahoali. You shouldn't be able to see the stones, as you call them, in the first place. They are our talismans. In reality, you shouldn't even be able to enter this meadow let alone dive into Crystal Lake."

"But there's portals to travel here."

"And you shouldn't be able to activate one."

Kaily frowned. "I don't understand."

Moto laughed, harshly. "I know!"

Kaily sensed and heard his frustration.

"I know." He repeated. "I can't explain it, because I don't understand myself how this is even possible."

Kaily opened her mouth to reply, but then shut it. She laid her forehead on his chest with a heavy sigh.

"Your world is not like Ki. How am I supposed to explain concepts to you that don't exist where you're from?"

Kaily shrugged and shook her head.

Moto cupped the back of her head.

"Where have you been, Moto?" She didn't look up at him.

Moto kissed the top of her head. He lifted her chin to force her to look at him. "Can you still see the talisman that caught your attention?"

Kaily peered into the water and nodded.

Moto took a deep breath. "I must be losing my mind." He muttered.

Kaily smiled up at him.

Moto shook his head. "Don't smile. The hard part is just beginning." He kissed her hard on the mouth. "Don't kill yourself or I'll make sure you don't sit for a very long time."

"You can't if I'm dead."

Moto's hand came down surprisingly hard on her rear end, even under the water.

Kaily yelped. "Got it! No killing self."

"You are going to be a handful, aren't you?"

Kaily smiled in response.

Moto shook his head with a small smile. "The secret is to bring the talisman to you with your mind." Moto held up his hand. A smooth stone with strong reddish hues materialized in his palm.

Kaily reached out to touch it, but it vanished as quickly as it appeared. "Show off."

Moto's smile widened. "It is a bit harder than that, but the concept is the same. Visualize the talisman in your mind's eye as you dive under the water. See it in your hand."

"Got it." Her eyes focused on the stone.

"Kaily?"

Her eyes locked with his.

"Be careful."

Kaily solemnly nodded. She placed a chaste kiss on his lips. "Thank you."

Moto nodded once.

Kaily took a couple deep breaths, held the last one, and then plunged under the water.

Moto pulled himself out of the water to sit on the side. He stared into the depths of the Lake. *Kaily?*

I'm busy.

Moto smiled at her churlish tone. *Stop messing around and collect the talisman!*

What do you think I am doing?

Killing yourself, which I forbade. Remember?

Stop bothering me!

Hurry up! You don't want me coming in after you.

Some choice words passed through Kaily's mind.

I dare you to repeat that to my face.

"No!" Kaily said as she came out of the water.

"Coward," Moto said.

"I do have some sense of self preservation. Besides, it's not like you understood what I said."

"Are you sure about that?"

Kaily's eyes narrowed. She regarded him before answering. "No," she said. "My apologies." She inclined her head as she observed Shimani do on occasion.

Moto laughed and tousled her hair. "You learn fast. Are you ready to give up?"

"No." Kaily shook her head. "Besides, I got it." She held her hand out with the stone in the palm of her hand for him to behold her triumph.

Moto peered, opened mouth, at the talisman.

Golden threads spread throughout the stone as they both gazed upon it.

"I have never seen a talisman such as this." Moto picked it up. "And I have never seen a talisman change once it's been retrieved." Silver threads spread throughout it at his touch. "Strange." He handed the talisman back to Kaily.

The silver and gold threads remained. She reverently caressed the stone. She let out a heavy sigh. "I'll put it back." The last thing she wanted was to let go of the stone, but as Moto had pointed out, she was not Kahoali. She would not offend his people by keeping something that didn't belong to her or wasn't freely given.

Moto closed her hand around the talisman. "It's yours to keep, Kaily. The talisman belongs to the one who retrieves it for all time. But keep it hidden. Don't tell anyone about it, not even Shimani. Do you understand?"

"I can put it back, Moto. I don't want to cause any trouble for you."

Moto smiled at her. "The Lake would not have given you a talisman, if it wasn't yours to keep."

Kaily frowned. "Are you sure?"

Moto smiled and kissed her lightly on the forehead. "Yes. Do you understand why you must keep it hidden?"

Kaily nodded. "Because I'm not Kahoali." She couldn't keep the bitterness out of her spoken words.

"That's my girl." He stood and pulled two towels out of thin air.

Following his movements made her realize that he was naked. She glanced down at her own naked self. "Shit." She muttered as she glimpsed their discarded clothes. She blushed as she hurriedly grabbed for the towel, he handed to her.

Moto smirked as he dried himself off. He dropped his towel when he finished, his eyes on Kaily.

She hastily turned around.

He laughed and pulled her hard against himself.

Kaily grasped the towel in front of her. Her blush intensified with her back firmly pressed against his front, and his member wedged against her lower back.

Moto lowered his head and brushed his lips against her ear. "The last time we were here you were ready to give yourself to me."

Kaily shivered. An involuntary groan escaped her lips.

"There may come a day I take you up on your offer and bury myself so deep inside you that you tremble with need for days."

Kaily's breath caught in her throat.

Moto stepped back from her. He reached down for her clothes and handed them to her.

She clutched them close as she handed him the towel.

He picked up the other towel, holding both in his hand.

Kaily's eyes widened as the towels disappeared. She shook her head. She seriously didn't like witnessing unfathomable happenings. She scrambled into her under clothes, and then her dress.

Moto smiled at her as he donned his own discarded clothes. "Can you find your way back?"

"If you point me in the right direction."

Moto shook his head at her. "The portal is that way." He pointed. "Can I trust you not to dive back into the Lake?"

"Yes."

He narrowed his eyes at her. "In truth?"

"Yes." She repeated. "I have what I wanted." She clutched the stone close to her heart. "Can't we stay longer?"

Moto stepped in close to her, and tenderly kissed her. "No, but I do want to speak to you after this evening's repast."

"We can talk now." Kaily touched his chest.

Moto shook his head. "I have duties to attend to. Try not to be seen when you go back."

Kaily frowned but nodded. She watched him walk to the portal.

He glanced back at her.

She observed an assortment of emotions pass over his features. The intensity of her frown increased. She took a step towards him.

His customary blank stone mask fell into place, and then he turned away from her. He stepped into the portal without a backwards glance.

She sighed. Her gaze drifted towards the lake. The illusionary sand was no longer visible. She walked to the edge of the lake and gazed into the water. She could no longer catch sight of the stones at the bottom. She sat cross legged beside the lake, clenching her stone tight. She would think about going back to the village in a bit. For now, her heart swelled with joy at the prospect of having a moment with her dark warrior later that night.

Chapter Thirteen

Moto succeeded in gaining the safety of his hut without incident. When he left Kaily at Crystal Lake, he considered going back to Sari's Village, where he'd spent the past three days. He stayed away from Center Village mainly to avoid the Queen, but also to keep from adding to the girl's precarious situation. He'd been a fool bringing her to his Village, not that any other would have been any better. The Kahoali were a secluded people, even on their own world. If he'd just taken her back home, she would be better off. He hadn't wanted to risk losing track of her again. But now, she was in more danger, since pulling a talisman from the Lake.

Moto shook his head.

Taking her back home was no longer an option. Despite Kesho's earlier examination, and subsequent confirmation that Kaily could not touch the energy of Ki, she obviously could. Pulling a talisman from Crystal Lake meant she somehow touched the energy without conscious thought. Her actions changed everything. Now that she possessed a talisman, it was only a matter of time before her abilities manifested. He had to remain with in her proximity without raising the Queen's suspicious of his motives towards the girl. Queen Shakti was already concerned about a possible bonding between them. If she found out what Kaily had done, Moto closed his eyes and rubbed his temples, no telling what would happen to the girl

He had to protect her. Her current circumstances were entirely his fault.

He paced the confines of his hut.

How was he supposed to protect Kaily, while keeping up the ruse of his bonding with Sari? The situation was becoming more complicated by the day. He should have taken her home, he scolded himself. He couldn't now. She needed to be around people who would understand what was going to happen to her, and who might be able to help her learn to control her abilities, when they did manifest. Which presented more problems. When would they present? What kind of abilities would be revealed?

Her talisman was like nothing any Kahoali possessed. No shade dominated, so he had no idea which element she would be drawn towards. The element predisposition determined the nature of abilities. Her talisman held all the colors possible in equal, swirling portions. To make matters worse, the intensity of the tones indicated an abundance of power, beyond even the Queen's capability. And then the threads, he didn't know what to make of those. He'd be lying if he said it didn't scare him, even a little bit.

He cast his eyes upwards towards the rafters of the roof. He'd never felt so conflicted in his life. The ceremony between Sari and himself had been set for the following evening repast. Talking to Kaily before then was imperative. He intended to explain to her what was going to happen, and what it meant for them, or at least try to. He hoped he would be able to make her understand. He should have stayed with her at Crystal Lake and had the conversation. At the time, he didn't know what he was going to say or if he would fully disclose the charade he and Sari attempted to pull off. It wasn't that he didn't trust Kaily to keep the information to herself, but rather he didn't trust her ability to completely grasp the complexities of a Kahoali bonding, and the purpose of the ceremony.

In all honesty, her obtaining a talisman, and everything which transpired between them, stunned him so much. He wanted time to consider the ramifications. Not that there wouldn't be consequences if she found out about the ceremony before he talked to her. He weighed the risk and decided to wait. The Villagers would keep to themselves during the repast, and Shimani wouldn't dare overstep his boundary in this matter. Especially since Moto made it clear to him, he would be the one to tell her. Shimani gave his word that he wouldn't. There was a small chance she might overhear the evening conversations which undoubtedly the impending ceremony would dominate. He would still risk it.

Moto uttered some choice curses. He considered the forced ceremony a gross violation of his personal rights within their society.

He'd been raised, as all were, to believe Kahoali bonded with Kahoali. Any other bonding would not be true, which meant no children would result from the bond. His conversation with the Queen, and his undeniable link with Kaily suggested otherwise. The longer they were in close proximity, the stronger the pull became. If he had any doubt about their connection, it wholly dissolved the moment he realized they could communicate telepathically. Telepathy was not unheard of, but extremely rare. Every so often, bonded mates would develop the ability with enough time. Certainly not as fast as it had between them, and that was without bonding with her.

All of this angered him more about the forced ceremony. He consoled his temper with the fact it wouldn't be real.

A part of him wondered if the bonding process had somehow begun between him and Kaily. He shook his head in denial. There was no possibility. Bondings did not begin without consummation between the two involved. If spite of wanting to, he'd remained strong enough to walk away from his uncontrollable desire to make her his for all time. He'd walked away this time, he corrected. He didn't know for how long he would remain strong.

Moto cursed. How much easier all this would be if Kaily were Kahoali! He gave a long, heavy sigh. She wouldn't be his Kaily if she were. She might understand better. He shook his head. She wouldn't be who she is. He honestly didn't know what he wanted to do about or with her. His mind told him one thing, and his heart another. He'd be an outcast if he chose her over his people. He refused to leave his people vulnerable.

His night terrors did not bode well for the future of his people. As long as the Queen, and Shanees refused to consider the possibility his night terrors might be visions of what's to come, he had to remain with the Kahoali. He had to choose his people over his desire to make Kaily his.

He also had to figure out what to do with her. He would keep her talisman secret from the Queen, but to do that he would have to secret her away somewhere. He had no clue where. He had to do something soon, before her abilities manifested. Once that happened, he wouldn't be able to keep her actions from the Queen. And he wouldn't be able to save her from the repercussions.

With resolve, Moto reached for the door. He needed to find Sari and speak with her about what's happened with Kaily. She might have ideas he had not yet considered. If nothing else, he would have someone with whom to share burden of knowledge.

Before he reached his door, a knock resounded. He opened the door to find Kesho on the other side. The emotions pouring from Kesho swept over him. Moto knew instantly that something was very wrong. "Enter." Moto stepped aside to allow Kesho to cross his threshold.

Kesho remained where he stood outside the hut. "The Queen has summoned you, and I am to escort you straightaway to the throne room."

Moto frowned before he caught himself. "Did our Queen indicate what this is about?" His heart sank.

Kesho's eyes locked with his. "The Queen will disclose her reasons for the summons in her own time." He stepped inside and laid a hand on Moto's shoulder. "I strongly advise that you maintain control of yourself when she does. You don't want to make things worse than they are already."

Dread washed over Moto. "What's happened, Kesho?" He didn't like where his thoughts took him.

Kesho didn't reply. He stepped back outside and waited for Moto to comply with the Queen's orders.

Moto took a deep breath. He removed all signs of emotions from his features before stepping outside. He shut the door to his hut. "Lead the way," he said.

Kesho turned and started walking towards the Queen's hut.

Moto walked in silence slightly behind and to the side of Kesho. His mind raced as he considered the possible reasons he'd been summoned in this fashion. There was only one thing which made sense, and he didn't want to accept it.

Kesho and Moto entered the throne room from the main entrance instead of the back door which led to the dais as was customary for the Chosen.

Moto stopped in his tracks.

All the Shanees were seated in their traditional circular benches. A number of Villagers were also present. A single Villager caught his attention. He stood on the dais to the side of the Queen. It was beyond rare for any male, not a Chosen, to observe formal proceedings such as this one.

Kesho glanced back at Moto. He motioned impatiently for him to proceed forward toward the dais.

Moto silently cursed his misstep. He consciously moved forward. His eyes scanned the room, searching for any clue that would confirm his dreaded suspicion. His eyes landed on Sari as he approached. The look in her eyes sent his heart plummeting into the depths of despair. He didn't know for certain, but enough he sent a silent query to Kaily.

Yes? Kaily replied.

Momentary relief washed over Moto. *Where are you?* His query held a harsh, demanding tone, even to him. He didn't want to alarm Kaily, but the myriad of emotions permeating the throne room, made it difficult to keep his own trepidations from bleeding through his telepathic communication with her.

Why? What's wrong?

Moto sensed panic rising inside Kaily. He tried to calm his thoughts. He didn't have time to explain, and he couldn't afford to divide his attention for long. Sometime in the near future he would explain to her the importance of just answering his questions. *Make your way back to your hut. I'll explain later.*

Why?

Just do as I say, Kaily, please! Moto pleaded. *Remember your promise to tell no one about your talisman. And for the love of the Universe, keep it hidden.* He didn't wait for her reply. He closed his mind. He would apologize later for shutting her out. He forced his full attention on the events beginning to play out in the throne room.

"Sari, step forward, and join your soon to be mate." Queen Shakti said. "This concerns you as well."

Moto concentrated on keeping his features void of any emotional reaction. He must remain in control. The Shanees in attendance boded ill, but a non-Chosen male meant something monumental had happened. He noticed Kesho had taken up his customary place on the dais with the other two Chosen, Baridi and Shimani.

"As you wish, my Queen." Sari stood and moved from her place with the other Shanees to stand beside Moto.

Moto glanced briefly at Sari, and then returned his focus to the Queen. This would be so much easier if he could speak telepathically with Sari the way he did with Kaily.

"Koa," Queen Shakti held her hand out to indicate the Villager who stood beside her, "witnessed Kaily at Crystal Lake."

Moto's eyes closed. He gave a minute shake of his head and forced his eyes open. He fixed his gaze on the dais.

"He advised me she is in possession of a talisman," Queen Shakti said.

A stone formed in the pit of Moto's stomach. A multitude of emotions warred inside of him. He struggled to maintain emotional restraint. He hadn't sensed anyone at Crystal Lake with Kaily and himself. He didn't know if it was because no one was there or because he'd been so absorbed with her, he hadn't sensed anyone. His first concern had been Kaily's safety, and then events just took a life of their own from there. He didn't expect anybody to be there until the next morning when preparations would be made for the ceremony later in the evening.

Queen Shakti continued; her attention focused solely on Moto. "Koa stated she was there alone. So, no punishment will be doled out at this time."

Moto maintained his silence. If the Universe saw fit to give him this gift, he would not reject it by advising the truth of the matter.

"While it remains unclear how she obtained one of our most sacred objects, we must decisively deal with this egregious affront to our traditions." Her focus did not waver from Moto.

He continued to wrestle with his emotional control under her scrutiny. He grew more desperate to whisk Kaily away from the reach of his people, before something devastatingly bad transpired.

"Baridi." Queen Shakti motioned for him to step forward.

"Yes, my Queen." Baridi inclined his head.

Moto was surprised he didn't spare him a disapproving glare as he often did in disciplinary situations Moto found himself the recipient of far too many times.

The Queen shifted her gaze towards Baridi. "Find the outsider and keep her confined to the guest hut." She returned her glare to Moto. "Chances are she still remains at Crystal Lake. Start there." She raised a quizzical eyebrow towards Moto.

He remained silent and attempted not to flinch.

"The bonding ceremony between Moto and Sari will take place at this evening's repast." Queen Shakti turned her attention to those assembled. "The Shanees will direct the preparations. Baridi, you will make the girl presentable, and bring her to the ceremony." She spared Moto a glance, and then turned her attention back to Baridi. "It is my wish she observes the bonding."

Baridi bowed low. "As you wish, my Queen."

Queen Shakti waited for Baridi to leave to do her bidding. Her gaze fell on Moto before she continued. "In the morning, the outsider will be sent to Celtan."

An audible gasp, and hushed murmurs exploded in the throne room as her words sank into the minds of those assembled.

Moto flinched at those words. A rush of anger burst to the surface. He didn't know if it was the sudden awareness that the Queen possessed a way to traverse to Celtan that caused the surprised response, or her implied accusation directed at Kaily.

Sari laid a restraining hand on his arm.

He didn't spare her a glance. His worst fears manifested right in front of him. His eyes remained locked with the Queen's. Moto reached out to Kaily. *Hear me, little one. Baridi is coming to escort you to your hut. Don't fight him, and don't let him find your talisman.*

Should I put it back?

No, just don't let him find it. I apologize, Kaily. He closed his mind again. The Queen continued speaking, but Moto stopped paying attention. His eyes scanned those assembled. Nothing spoken sunk into his racing mind as he considered options.

Sari laced her fingers with Moto's.

Her actions barely registered as his mind continued to sift through possible course of actions. He cursed himself several times for putting Kaily in such danger. Not that he possessed foresight about her retrieval of a talisman. She kept asking him if she should put it back, and he kept saying no, as if it would even be possible. The Lake would not gift a talisman to anyone who was not meant to have it. He seriously doubted the Lake would allow her to return the gift. Perhaps he should have let her try.

Sari guided Moto out of the throne room.

Moto moved with her; his mind still turned inward. He wanted to reach out to Kaily, but he didn't dare. There was far too much turmoil inside himself. He didn't want to heighten Kaily's fear. The remnants of her fear from his last telepathic communication beat at him.

"Focus on me!"

Sari's words scarcely punctured his awareness.

"Moto! Focus!"

Her stern tone began to make a hole in Moto's distant contemplations. He attempted to bring his mind back to the present.

She stood nose to nose with him and grabbed his head between her hands.

Moto's vision began to clear as he forced his attention to focus on Sari.

"Better," Sari said. "We will figure this out together. Whatever happens we won't let any harm come to Kaily. Do you hear me?"

Moto reluctantly nodded.

"Good." Sari dropped her hands to her side. "You must hold yourself together for a while longer. Understood?"

Moto again nodded.

"I promise I will do everything in my power to keep her safe."

Moto pulled Sari into a rough embrace. "Thank you." He could hardly speak the words through the marsh of emotions plaguing him. The gratitude he experienced for having her support in this moment was immense. Somehow, they had to prevent Kaily's exile to Celtan. He would keep her safe at all costs, even if it meant taking her back to Earth. It would be a small price to pay to keep her out of the clutches of the Druids.

Chapter Fourteen

Kaily stood near the stationary portal which led back to Center Village. Moto's voice stopped her from entering. She clutched the stone tightly in her hand. His last message froze her in place. Indecision clouded her mind. His words echoed through her brain, over and over again. She couldn't stop the replay reverberating inside her head. She shouldn't let fear paralyze her. She had to do something.

She stepped back from the opening of the portal and turned towards one of the others. She took a few steps forward. Moto had told her to go back to her hut, but something inside her said to run. Impending danger drew near. She could sense it. Still, taking any of the other portals was against his instructions. Make up your mind, she told herself.

Cold prickled the back of her neck. The portal behind her was about to open. Kaily reached under her dress and secured the stone in the one place she vehemently hoped would not be searched. She should have dropped it back into the lake, but she couldn't bring herself to part with the stone. Now, it was too late. She finished securing her stone in her safe place and smoothed the skirt of her dress down. She turned to face the opening portal.

Whatever danger headed her way, she would face it head on. She preferred to run, but she took a deep breath, running wasn't an option. Fear coursed through her veins. She took a steadying, deep breath.

A formidable figured stepped out of the portal.

Baridi, Kaily thought to herself. She remembered him from her first day among the Kahoali, when she was presented to the Queen. Fear gripped her, and cold fingers ran down her spine. She reached for Moto within her mind. She encountered silence. She glanced in the direction of the closest portal.

"Don't!" Baridi ordered.

Kaily glanced back at him. She frowned. He stood too close for her to make a run for it anyway. She couldn't risk the stone falling out of its hiding spot. It had slipped in far easier than she expected, and she feared it might just as easily slide out. If it weren't for the warm pulse she detected, she wouldn't even know it was there. She took a deep breath in an attempt to calm her racing heart. It didn't help.

"Show me the talisman." Harshness radiated from Baridi.

Kaily opened her mouth to reply.

Baridi stepped closer.

So close, his hot breath struck Kaily's face.

"Don't lie to me by acting like you don't know what I'm demanding to see. Show me the talisman!"

Kaily resisted her immediate, instinctive response to turn, and run for her life. She swallowed hard. To make matters worse, she had to lie to his face. She wasn't adept at lying, but she couldn't admit the truth either. "I told Moto I would put it back." His reaction made her instantly regret her words. She realized too late that she shouldn't have mentioned Moto. She kept silent, afraid she might make things worse.

Baridi's eyes narrowed as he regarded her. "Did you?"

His eyes remained locked with hers long enough, sweat beaded on her forehead, and trickled down her back. She didn't know if his question referred to the stone or Moto. Nor did she ask for clarification.

Baridi's angry glare perused her up and down. "Show me the talisman!"

Kaily held her hands out towards him, palms up. "I have nothing to show you."

His eyes twitched. "I don't believe you."

Kaily stretched her arms out from her sides. "Search me." She slowly turned a complete circle. Her false bravado increased the tempo of her pulse. She only hoped Baridi wouldn't test her bravery beyond what she could muster. She stopped to face him and dropped her arms to her side. "I said I would return it."

Baridi regarded her a moment longer, before speaking. "By the command of Queen Shakti, you will be confined to the guest hut the remainder of your time among us. You will not leave the hut without permission or an escort, which will be provided."

Kaily tried to swallow the lump in the back of her throat that threatened to choke her. Tears burned her eyes.

"This evening, I will escort you to the ceremony the Queen commanded you attend. Afterwards, I will escort you back to the guest hut. You will not converse with anyone at the ceremony. Understood?"

Kaily nodded. She fought to keep the tears from falling. She had been demoted from outsider to prisoner. *Moto?* She attempted to reach out to her only ally. Silence answered her plea. Why would the Queen want her at a ceremony, but otherwise hold her confined to the hut?

"After you." Baridi held out his hand towards the stationary portal he'd exited.

Kaily complied. She sensed him follow close behind her. She'd tried a couple more times to reach Moto within her mind. Only silence answered her. She didn't know if it was because he purposely ignored her, or she wasn't doing something right.

On the other side of the portal, she waited for Baridi to emerge. Thoughts of running, surfaced in her mind, but she didn't have a clue where she would be safe. She didn't know enough about this planet or its population to determine which way would be ideal for an actual escape. Plus, the abilities these people possessed was so far beyond her understanding. How could she avoid capture? And that assumed she could escape the village in the first place. Ultimately, there was only one option, Moto. He could take her safely back to Earth. She would have to trust him, despite her misgivings about relying on anyone. For some bizarre reason, she trusted him. She shook her head, amazed at her capacity to put her safety in a stranger's care, and on a strange world to boot.

Baridi exited the portal. He pinned her with a steely glare and signaled for her to follow him. He set a brisk pace through the Village.

Kaily kept her eyes averted from everyone they passed. *Moto! Where are you? Why won't you answer me?* She silently demanded. She didn't exactly know how to project. When Moto had communicated with her telepathically, it seemed so easy. Why was it so difficult now?

"Wait here." Baridi pointed to a spot just outside a hut where he'd stopped.

Kaily was so focused inward that if he hadn't spoken when he did, she would have run into him. She kept her eyes downcast, and obediently waited. The last thing she wanted was to draw undue attention to herself. She certainly didn't want to further anger Baridi. She should have put the damn stone back. No, she thought to herself. She should have stayed away from Crystal Lake in the first place.

When Baridi emerged from the hut, he shoved a bundle into her unprepared arms.

Kaily fumbled the load, but somehow kept from dropping it.

Baridi didn't help or wait for her.

She scrambled to catch up with him, awkwardly carrying the bundle. Thankfully, the stone remained in place. It seemed to be secure enough without much effort on her part, surprisingly.

Once at the guest hut, Baridi opened the door. He held it open for her to enter, and then followed her inside.

Kaily placed the bundle on the table and turned to face him. She would have preferred to find a suitable hiding place, but that was not a recourse available to her. She concentrated on holding her tears inside. She refused to break down in front of this man. She declined to give him the satisfaction of breaking her.

Baridi pointed to the bundle. "You will wear that dress to the ceremony this evening. Eat what's in the cupboards here. You won't be allowed to partake in the feast afterwards. Remember, do not speak to anyone. You are there to observe only, and only because the Queen has ordered it. Understood?"

Kaily solemnly nodded. She did not make eye contact. She stood in one spot and waited for him to leave. Of course, she understood. She was no longer welcomed among the Kahoali people. Dammit to hell! She should have put the stone back into the lake.

Baridi left without a backwards glance, or another word spoken.

Apparently, she wasn't worth it. Once the door closed, she sank into the nearest chair at the table. She put her face in her hands. Tears, she'd held in, fell unchecked. *Moto? Please, answer me?*

No response.

She began to wonder if they really had conversed telepathically. She cradled her head in her arms on the table, and let her despair drain from her eyes.

After her tears ceased, she decided to get ready for the evening. A bit earlier than perhaps necessary, but it would give her time in the shower to clean up and wash away the day. Not that it would help but maybe she'd feel just a little bit better. At least, for a little while.

She stripped off her clothing on her way to the shower room. Once inside the shower stall, she turned on the water, and then retrieved the stone from its hiding place. She frowned as it fell out quite easily. She rinsed the stone off in the warm water. The curious pulsing rhythm inside the stone comforted her. She didn't understand, and maybe it didn't matter. She would accept comfort from whatever source provided such to her.

She'd finished getting ready far too early. She'd attempted resting, which didn't work out. She'd opened the cupboard to eat something. Nothing appealed to her. She couldn't reach Moto. She half expected Shimani to show up at some point. He didn't. She couldn't help but feel disappointed. He had to have his reasons, and no telling what was transpiring outside the tiny confines of her prison.

She'd poked her head out once, only to find two guards stationed outside the door. The look they gave her sent her scurrying back inside for cover. She didn't make that mistake a second time. Instead, she ended up pacing from one end to the other of the tiny hut. Her mind sifted through various thoughts, theories, and other useless ponderings as she paced. Suffice it to say, she was lost in contemplation when a knock on the door startled her.

Kaily hastily put the stone back in its hiding spot and stepped towards the door to open it.

Baridi opened the door and stepped inside before she'd taken more than a couple of steps.

Why bother knocking? She wasn't fool enough to utter her sentiment aloud.

"Why are you not wearing the headdress?" Baridi held up the scarf like cloth she had left on the table.

"I didn't know how to put it on." Kaily mumbled without making eye contact. There was too much anger and hatred in his voice for her to endure. She didn't want to see it mirrored in his eyes.

"Speak up woman! What did you say?" Baridi stepped menacingly towards her.

Kaily took a step back. "I didn't know how to put it on." She spoke louder than the first time, but not by much. If someone had shown her how, she would have. But no one had bothered.

"Turn around." He ordered.

Kaily obeyed.

Baridi grabbed the cloth. He then gathered her hair in his large hand. He deftly twisted and wrapped until the headdress was securely in place.

Kaily winced at his heavy-handedness.

He finished in short order, and then walked to the door without a word.

She wished she'd had a mirror to see what the headdress looked like. From the look Baridi leveled on her, she wasn't going to get the chance. She followed his impatient self out the door. She steeled her resolve and told herself that she would not give into her tumultuous emotions. One way or another, she would make it through this night. Then, she would find Moto, and beg him to take her home.

Baridi took her to the portal, and through it to Crystal Lake.

Kaily's senses became overwhelmed when she exited the portal. The meadow had been transformed into a copious assortment of brightly colored pavilions. Flowering vines tied to the posts. Blankets laid out with cushioned chairs situated under each of the coverings. Delectable aromas saturated the air. Her stomach grumbled in protest. In one of the pavilions, a table loaded with so much food caught her attention. She even recognized some of the Shanees.

Baridi testily snapped his fingers at her.

Kaily sighed and focused her attention on her ill-tempered keeper. She followed Baridi to a blanket that had been laid out underneath a nearby tree. It was close to the portal they exited, but on the edge of the festivities. She didn't have to be told in words, that her presence was not entirely wanted. Again, she questioned, in her mind, why she was there. It didn't make any sense to her.

"Don't move from this spot."

Kaily nodded, and obediently sat in the place he pointed.

He left without another word.

Her eyes followed him to a tent where the Queen and other Chosen, including Moto, were seated. Sari sat between the Queen and Moto. Shimani was the only one who glanced in her direction. A frown furrowed Kaily's brow.

She tried to give him a smile but grimaced instead.

He looked at her a moment longer, then turned his attention to the Queen.

Sadness swelled inside Kaily. She let out a long sigh. She diverted her attention to the others in attendance of this ceremony. Everyone, including the males, were attired in brightly colored outfits. Not one woman's head was uncovered. Her eyes drifted back to the main tent. Even Sari, wore a headdress. She regarded the throng of people in attendance. Everyone spoke in hushed, excited tones.

Kaily's frown intensified as she took a closer perusal of those gathered. Everyone's attire appeared quite formal. But what caught her attention most, was Moto and Sari's matching outfits. Not only did they match, but also far more ornate than anyone's present, including the Queen's. Her eyes drifted to the tent at the edge of the lake, and the table underneath it. Two goblets, a pitcher, and braided cord had been placed in the center.

Apprehension settled in the pit of her stomach. She glanced back at the Queen who talked with Moto and Sari. Kaily didn't like what this ceremony appeared to be. Her uneasiness increased as she watched the Queen stand, followed by Moto and Sari.

The crowd instantly quieted. All eyes riveted on the three.

They entered the pavilion by the lake. The Queen stood in front of the items on the table. Moto and Sari stopped in front of her and faced each other. Moto tenderly took Sari's hands in his. Their eyes locked.

"No." Kaily whispered. Tears surfaced in her eyes. She fought to hold them back.

The Queen began to speak.

The words were barely audible from where Kaily had been deposited. She strained to hear. Slowly, the words punctured the silence of the meadow. She lost the battle as her tears freely rolled down her cheeks. The words differed, but the intent remained the same. The so-called ceremony the Queen wanted her to witness was Moto and Sari's marriage. She shook her head, and hastily wiped at her tears. She failed to stop the outpouring of her sorrow. As the ceremony continued, her sadness battled her anger. Anger that Moto hadn't told her. Anger that he had led her to believe, she shook her head, unable to complete the thought.

Why had Moto brought her there?

She stood.

Why would he subject her to such humiliation?

She backed up.

Why hadn't he taken her back to her home when he rescued her? Nothing of his actions made sense.

She took another backwards step. Her back hit the tree. Her eyes found Shimani's. Sympathy crossed his facial features.

Her anger grew.

She didn't want his pity.

Kaily glanced towards the portal. Her eyes darted back to the events in the main tent. More tears slid down her face. She was helpless to stop them. Her eyes drifted to Shimani.

He gave a slight shake of his head.

The motion was enough she understood his intended message, but not enough to draw attention to himself. She closed her eyes for a moment and bowed her head.

She couldn't stay. She inched her way towards the portal. She never had a chance with Moto. Damn him for making her believe she might. She stepped close to the portal, almost within reach.

Baridi turned his head. His eyes collided with hers.

Kaily didn't wait for him to move or respond. She spun around and ran through the portal's opening with all due haste.

Once on the other side, she continued to run. She blindly ran into the forest.

Tears streamed from down her face.

She ran for all she was worth, without direction or thought. At some point, she tore the headdress from her head, and flung it aside.

WHY? She mentally demanded.

Silence answered her.

Kaily didn't know how long she ran. She just ran without care or clue of direction. Tears burned her eyes and blurred her vision. Excruciating pain enclosed her heart and soul. She stopped running when she had no choice. Her lungs burned. Her legs refused to carry her further. She looked around and screamed when she realized she stood in the center of the clearing she'd found Moto and Shimani sparring her first morning with these damn people.

She fell to her knees and covered her face with her hands. She bent forward so that her forehead rested on the ground. She didn't bother stemming the flow of her tears. She sobbed and poured her soul out onto the soil of Ki. Her weeping racked her body for a long time. There didn't seem to be an end to her sorrow. Questions raged through her mind.

How could he do this to her?

What had she been thinking?

She shook her head, although, she didn't bother lifting her forehead off the ground. She didn't have the will or strength.

Of course, he belonged to someone else. But did it have to be Sari? She liked Sari. She hated the anger and jealous which sprung up towards the woman who claimed her dark warrior as hers.

She was an outsider. Kaily had been a fool to hope she'd be allowed to be with him. She should have known better than to allow herself to get caught up in this, she snorted. She shook her head.

What had been the point in asking her to stay? In asking her to be patient with him?

Anger rose, swallowing her sorrow. Her fury bubbled up from the center of her soul. Warmth spread throughout her entire body. Her tears slowly began to subside. She pushed herself off the ground. The warmth intensified until it ran white-hot in her veins. The heat consumed her sorrow. She wiped the last remnants of her sadness from her eyes. There was a hum and vibration in the air. She scanned the surrounding forest.

Night had settled.

Her anger continued to grow as if it possessed a life of its own. She stood. She'd been a fool. He'd made a fool of her. The three of them made a fool of her, she corrected. Shimani and Sari, so welcoming, she bitterly thought.

She closed her eyes and turned in a circle.

She vowed that she would never let anyone make a fool of her again. She would keep everyone at arm's length, like she should have done in the first place. She knew better than to let anyone get close to her. She knew better than to trust, anyone. Curse them all to hell and back.

Kaily ceased her circular turning. She opened her eyes and stared into the darkness. She stood still for a long time in the center of the training clearing.

Time passed unnoticed. Time no longer meant anything to her. She stared out into the forest but focused on nothing. She no longer saw her surroundings. All she could see was her life in turmoil. She burned from the inside out. Anger, her only companion, turned to rage. The heat of her rage consumed her, and she didn't care. She welcomed it.

Kaily held her arms out from her sides. Everything, all the events which had happened since she first set foot on Ki, welled up inside her. They boiled and bubbled until she could no longer contain the emotions.

She screamed. She continued to scream without ceasing. The rage burning in her veins flowed outward. She was aware of the exact moment the rage broke free from deep inside her, becoming a blazing beast she had absolutely no control over.

And then nothing. Blackness consumed her. She collapsed in a heap on the ground.

Chapter Fifteen

Moto tried to settle back in the two-person cushioned seat he shared with Sari. The officiating part of the ceremony had finished, and evening feasting had commenced. Unlike the usual evening repasts, these types of celebrations tended to last well into the night. As the honored guests, Sari and he would be expected to remain for far longer than Moto wanted. Their place of honor put them front and center for all to see. They had been provided with enough food and drink on two low tables to last the night. He wasn't hungry or in a celebratory mood, so hadn't even made a small dent. Sari ate here and there, but mostly entertained the toddler in her lap.

Sari adjusted the energetic child.

Niele smiled up at Moto.

He returned her smile.

She was a happy girl. She and Sari shared a mutual fondness for each other. From the outside, you wouldn't know this child wasn't hers. The two of them were inseparable, except when Sari was away from her Village. Even in her absence, the child didn't lack for attention. The entire Village took part in showering her with love. It's what happens from being an only child in a community of many. Fortunately, the Villagers were birthing children again, but it was slow going. The Kahoali needed to birth the next generation or risk fading away into extinction. One of the reasons, he didn't want risking bonding with anyone who might jeopardize the possibility of offspring.

He gazed lovingly at the child. He was grateful for the small distraction. He adored children, but especially this one. She had a way of wiggling into hearts. He handed Niele a slice of fruit. She happily accepted with so much delight, you'd think he'd given her the world. He ruffled her tiny braids. She settled back down on Sari's lap and indulged in the treat given to her.

His gaze drifted to those gathered and strayed to the tree they'd placed Kaily under. He hadn't sensed when she left. He'd kept his mind closed to her, and focused on blocking the bombardment of her emotions, and presence. He'd reasoned it was to protect her, but perhaps his reasons had been more selfish, and not something he desired to examine too closely. He couldn't afford to react to her in any way, which was also true. His reactions could worsen her situation with the Queen. He wasn't certain how, but he didn't want to risk it. He suffered too many regrets already where she was concerned. Looking back, he should have made different, better decisions for her own good, and safety.

"You're frowning again," Sari whispered in his ear.

Moto struggled to smile at her. He relaxed his facial expression as best as possible, given the circumstances.

Niele jumped from Sari's lap to his. She reached up and smoothed the deep crease between his brows with tiny fingers.

Moto let out a sigh. He gave the child a hug. She was too perceptive for her own good, even at her tender age of three. "Do you think, you could find us one of those fruits Sari likes so much?" He asked as he set the child on the ground.

Niele nodded and dashed off towards the food tent.

"It won't be much longer before we can leave without too much protest." Sari squeezed his hand.

"I wish," Moto started. He didn't finish his statement. Wishes were pointless now.

"I understand." Sari gave him a sad smile.

Moto leaned in closer to her, grateful for the small amount of privacy space surrounding them. Well, private enough for whispered conversation. "I need to find her." His voice contained an ache he wasn't able to hide, even in a whisper. He needed to speak with Kaily, to explain. He cursed himself for not taking the time earlier with her.

"Patience." Sari rubbed the furrow between his brows in the same way Niele had. She handed him a goblet of brey. "This will help."

Moto accepted the offering from Sari. He took a deep, long drink, and handed the goblet back to her. He ignored the frown she gave him. He refrained from comment as more Villagers came by to congratulate them. Telling them how they'd been expecting this for a while now, and so on. He tuned most of what was said out, and let Sari handle the well-wishers. Sari was very good at conversing with them, making them feel important, and then dismissing them before they realized what happened. Her skill certainly wasn't something he'd acquired.

Moto's gaze strayed to the tree. Shimani advised him, that Kaily left shortly after the ceremony began, and Baridi let her. That was something, even more so as he didn't pursue her once the Queen completed the officiating part. Shimani thought it might have been because the Queen's point she wanted, had been made. Moto had to concur with Shimani's assessment. They appeared content to leave her alone, until morning, which suited Moto just fine. It would give him privacy to correct his grave error where Kaily was concerned.

Sari had tried to assure him Kaily would be fine, and they would look for her once they left. He didn't correct her assumption of Kaily's wellbeing on the fact that she understood their bonding was a charade. It wouldn't help to have Sari, and soon after Shimani upset with him. They both were quite fond of the girl.

Moto cursed his carelessness in the handling of her. He should have prepared her. No, he silently corrected. He should have taken her home when he found her. He knew he should reach out to her telepathically, but he couldn't bring himself too.

He feared her emotional state. She, like him, was an emotional creature. He knew himself well enough to know, he wouldn't be able to endure her pain when he couldn't comfort her in person. He wouldn't be able to placidly remain seated, waiting for an end to his current misery.

Moto startled. He barely caught Niele as she jumped into his lap. She held the prized fruit in her tiny, sticky hands, he'd sent her off to find. He recovered and settled the child on his lap. "Well done." He smiled as he accepted the prize from her.

"Thank you," he said to Sari, and took the knife she handed him. He cut the fruit in half. He gave the bigger half to Sari and the other to Niele. From her sticky hands, he suspected someone else had already shared one with her. "Take part of the darker area too, when you bite into it."

Niele giggled. "I know."

Moto smiled and shook his head at her.

Niele giggled harder.

Moto held Niele while she ate her portion. He smiled at Sari as she bit into her half with her eyes half closed. He didn't much care for the fruit, but these two loved it.

Sari smiled back at him. She ruffled Niele's tiny braids. "You're going to make a great father someday."

Moto continued to smile at her but didn't reply. If he became a father, he thought to himself. The only one he wanted as his bonded mate was Kaily, he wasn't convinced there could be a true bonding. Which ultimately didn't matter as he intended to take her home. Maybe her abilities wouldn't manifest on her world. The Inhabitants, he'd observed, didn't appear to have energy related abilities. Plus, her world, except at the Gateway, didn't possess much of an energy flow, not like it should have. No one else sparked his interest. He would most likely end up mateless. Probably just as well. The Queen nor his people would ever accept his bond with an outsider.

When Niele was finished, he wiped off her fingers, face, and settled her more comfortably on his lap. He traced patterns in the palm of her hand and watched the others in the meadow. They celebrated what they thought was a joyous event. It would have been if Sari were bonding with her forever love. A part of him was grateful to Sari for her momentary sacrifice. He hoped it would be short lived. Another part of him was filled with guilt for placing her in this position, possibly jeopardizing her chance for a true bond.

"She's asleep," Sari said, drawing his attention from the happy revelers, and his inner ponderings.

He glanced down at the child. "So, she is," Moto said. "Do you want to take her?"

"Let's take her back to her parents," Sari replied. "I think we can make our escape without offending too many."

"Finally!"

Sari smiled and shook her head at him.

Moto ignored her amusement, and repositioned Niele to make it easier for him to stand without waking her. It'd been a long night for the child, and for him, to be honest. He'd been surprised, she'd remained awake as long as she had. He cradled her in his arms as he prepared to stand. A force passed through him, robbing him of his breath and pushed him back into the cushioned seat. He glanced around to determine if anyone else had experienced the same thing.

No one seemed fazed. They all continued to enjoy the festivities. He turned a frown towards Sari.

"What is it?"

Moto shook his head. "I can't explain it. I felt," he struggled for the right word. He shook his head again. "Something. I don't know. We need to get out of here. I have an extremely bad feeling." There was a sense of urgency that descended upon him. A keen sense. He had to find Kaily, and fast. He started to open his mind to her but stopped. He couldn't allow himself to be distracted more than he already was. Too much was at risk. He stood with the sleeping child. He moved to hand her off to Sari.

Sari shook her head. "You take Niele back to her parents. I'll take our leave of the Queen."

Moto hesitated for a moment, and then nodded. He took a deep breath. Sari was the levelheaded one.

Sari turned.

Moto reached out and gave her arm a brief squeeze. "Thank you."

Sari turned back, nodded, and smiled. She tenderly touched the side of his face, and then turned away. She quickly walked towards the Queen's tent, where she sat with several of the Shanees.

Moto made his way to Niele's parents as quickly as prudent. Once there, they thanked him for entertaining their daughter as he passed her to her mother. He touched the top of her head. After, he turned to see where Sari stood. With a quick good-bye, he walked to Sari who was by the portal which led to her Village.

He opened his mind to Kaily as he made his way to Sari. Icy fingers of fear crept up his spine. *Kaily?* Moto reached out telepathically to her. Where he normally perceived her mind, he sensed nothing. Not even the slightest hint of her presence within his own mind. He cursed his carelessness for not reaching out to her sooner.

When he finally reached Sari, she kissed him full on the mouth. After, she took his hand, and opened the portal.

Their exit was followed by a loud uproar of cheers.

Once they exited the portal, Sari faced Moto. "My apologies," she said with a slight bow of her head. "I wanted to leave a certain impression, if you catch my meaning."

Moto nodded. "I do. No apologies are necessary." He glanced around, not certain what he searched for or expected to find.

"Tell me what sensation you experienced."

Moto began to shake his head, still frowning. "I felt," he paused, "something. Like a force physically pushed be into the chair, yet no one else appeared to notice anything. Did you?"

Sari shook her head. "No, not really."

"What do you mean by 'not really'?"

"I thought I discerned a disturbance of some sort, but nothing I could pinpoint, and the sensation was so swift, I thought I might have imagined it. Did you reach out telepathically to Kaily?"

"I tried, but I can't reach her," Moto said. Realization hit him of the oddity of Sari's question. "How are you aware that I can?" He hadn't shared with her or Shimani that they could speak mind to mind.

"Shimani said he suspected you two might have a telepathic connection." Sari shrugged.

"Why would he suspect that?"

Sari smiled. She reached up and rubbed between Moto's brows. "You should relax."

Moto impatiently pushed her hand away and waited for an answer.

Sari dropped her hand, unfazed by his impatience. "Kaily asked Shimani about Kahoali being telepathic, and no she didn't indicate your ability with each other. He deduced the reason behind her question by how she asked and grilled him a bit too much. We all sense a connection between you and Kaily, a rather strong one it would appear. Now back to the problem at hand. Can you sense where she is?"

Moto looked around. His gaze shifted back to Sari. He shook his head.

Sari frowned.

Moto's attention drifted to the surrounding area. Agitation made him fidgety, and he found it difficult to stand in one place.

"Look at me, Moto."

"I can't sense her. I don't know where she is or why she won't respond." Desperation saturated his words. He glanced at Sari, before looking away. He hated the show of weakness, his distress communicated to Sari. He didn't have the focus to bother controlling his emotions. His heart pounded and sweat broke out on his forehead. If something happened to her, he would not forgive himself.

"We'll find her, but I need you to focus," Sari said. "Close your eyes and empty your mind of all emotions."

Moto frowned at her.

Sari raised her eyebrows and waited for him to cooperate.

Moto locked gazes with her. He took a deep breath and reluctantly closed his eyes. Fear and urgency were uppermost within his mind. Pushing his emotions aside proved to be quite difficult.

"When you have calmed the emotions inside yourself," Sari said. "I want you to think of Kaily. Say the first place that comes to your mind. Don't think about it, just speak the place. Do you understand?"

Moto nodded. He didn't understand how that would work in finding Kaily, but he didn't have any other ideas to try.

Sari placed her palm in the middle of his chest. Calm began to spread from her point of contact.

Moto took a deep breath and slowly let it out. Heat radiated against his chest from Sari's palm, filling him with tranquility, and focus he would not otherwise be able to obtain. He took comfort in her touch, and assistance. He took another deep breath and let it out. The sense of calm pushed back the fear and urgency uppermost in his mind. Somehow that calm force created a barrier between his ability to focus, and his fears. He took another deep breath and slowly exhaled as he reached his mind out towards Kaily's.

"Don't reach for her!" Sari said. "Only think about her. Build a picture of her in your mind. Concentrate on the details. Focus on what she looks like, and feels like to you, but stay within your own mind. When you have a clear picture built, when you sense her within you, then and only then think about where she is, without reaching for her."

Moto growled in frustration.

Sari thumped him on his chest. "Focus!"

Moto pulled his mind back and forced his mind to focus on Kaily in the manner Sari instructed. Resisting the urge to reach for Kaily was hard. He had to force himself not to reach for her, to do everything possible to bring her to him. He pushed back his impatience of how long this way would take. He forced his iron-clad will to focus on the task at hand. He took another deep breath.

He thought about the first time he laid eyes on Kaily, and the first time he'd touched her. He thought about her scent that permeated his every sense. He could smell it even now. He thought about how it felt to hold her for the first time in his arms. Their first kiss. As he thought about their time together, an image began to form within his mind, and solidified. *Where are you?* He sent out his query before stopping himself. He sensed Sari's disapproval.

Fear beat at the edge of his conscious thought, despite the calm trying to keep it at bay. He took more deep breaths, and slowly exhaled each one. He focused on the solid image of Kaily within his mind, and only her image. The task pushed him to his limits of focused control, but he maintained his avoidance of his emotions. The turmoil inside him would only hinder his ability to locate her, assuming Sari's method worked.

He allowed the emotions she inspired in him to seep into his mind as he concentrated on her image. She was everything to him, regardless of his efforts to keep her at arm's length. She permeated his entire life, his very being. In that moment of clarity, he realized he would do anything for her. His Kaily needed him to be strong, and focused. For her, he would be. He kept himself from reaching out to her.

When his Kaily, and all she was to him filled his mind, he thought about what her current surroundings would look like. He allowed the place to form in his mind, surrounding her image.

"The training clearing." Moto announced after what felt like an eternity. He opened his eyes and turned his attention to Sari.

It took far longer than he would have preferred. "She's in the clearing that Shimani and I use for training." He knew it to be true as he said it, but it didn't make sense. How would he be so aware of her whereabouts with such confidence?

Sari nodded. "I'll find Shimani and meet you there."

"How are you going to do that?" Moto asked.

"I have my ways. Go. If Kaily isn't answering your telepathic query, she may be unconscious." Sari waited for Moto to leave first.

His eyes narrowed.

"Just open the portal, Moto."

"You know?"

"Go." Sari shooed him with her hand.

"Thank you." Moto inclined his head towards her. He opened and stepped through his portal. He arrived in the clearing not far from where Kaily lay sprawled out on the ground. His heart stopped for a split moment at the spectacle which greeted him. The sight that stopped his heart was not Kaily on the ground. The clearing and nearby forest had been absolutely destroyed, creating a charred circle around her. The ground was scorched as if a white-hot fire swiftly blasted outward, only to suddenly stop. The blasted trees lay flat on the ground as if pushed over with no effort at all. The exposed side burnt crisp, while the underside remained green.

He swallowed hard and pushed aside his fear. He rushed to her side.

His heart raced, and despite his efforts, fear crept to the surface inside him. Thoughts and questions surfaced as well. He tried to push those to the back of his mind. He didn't want to think about what had happened to cause such devastation where once his training clearing stood. When his abilities first manifested, and he was learning to control them, he'd destroyed things here and there. All Kahoali new to their abilities had at one point or another, but not like this destruction in front of him.

He cursed himself for letting her obtain a talisman. He didn't want to believe his Kaily had been the one responsible for what he saw, but he couldn't deny the evidence. He pushed his troubling thoughts to the dark recesses of his mind. The strength of his fear could not be denied or dismissed so easily. For Kaily's sake, he had to.

He rolled Kaily on to her back with care. He patted her from top to bottom, front to back checking for injury, and was grateful to find none. He didn't find her talisman either. "Kaily?" He grasped her by the shoulders and gave her a shake.

No response.

He patted the side of her face. "Kaily?" He spoke her name louder.

Still no response.

Panic crept in with the fear that coursed through his veins. "Please, little one, wake up!" Moto glanced up as two portals opened.

Shimani stepped from one, which didn't surprise him. Although, Shimani didn't open portals in front of him, and always asked him to open them, he suspected Shimani possessed the ability. The second portal was a different matter altogether as Sari stepped from that one. She'd always been reluctant to use her abilities in front of him, which they'd argued about from time to time. He knew she possessed abilities from her possession of a talisman. He'd thought he and Shimani were the unusual ones, where Kahoali abilities were concerned. Guess not.

Shimani and Sari hurried over to him.

"Moto, I need you to step back." Sari knelt beside Kaily on the opposite side he occupied. "You too, Shimani," she said, when he moved to kneel beside her.

Shimani stood and stepped back.

"I'm not leaving her side."

Sari's gaze locked full force with Moto's. "You will obey me," she said. "Now!"

A fire shown in the depths of her eyes, and something else Moto had never before seen. He sat back on his heels in shock. Sari's eyes always held the hazel coloring that came with her ability to harness the energy, as with all Kahoali who could. Her being Shanees made the haze hue deeper, but not like her eyes appeared at that very moment. Sari's eyes were the deepest fiery hazel he'd seen. They glowed with amber light. Not even the Queen's eyes held the depth hers did. But what shocked him the most were the silver flecks within the depths of her fiery hazel-amber eyes. The gift and telltale sign bestowed on the one destined to be the next Kahoali Queen.

"You think her eyes are something, you should see her talisman," Shimani said. Amusement infused his tone.

Both Moto and Sari spared him a stern scowl.

Shimani held up his hands in surrender.

"Moto, I need room to examine Kaily," Sari said with a measure of restrained patience. "Did you find her talisman?"

Moto shook his head. He reluctantly stood and took a step back. Not quite as far back as Shimani had. "Why?" He could sense urgency growing in Sari, and it troubled him. She was not easily rattled, not quite as laid back as Shimani, but close.

"Because of this," Sari said. She waved her hand to indicate the charred clearing.

"Kaily didn't do this." Moto adamantly denied the truth of Sari's words. He knew a part of him believed she did, even feared she had, but he didn't want it to be true. He needed it to not be true. Not many other Inhabitants he came across in his travels off world could harness the kind of energy required to do such damage. Only one came to mind, and that thought he immediately rejected.

Sari didn't reply. Her focus remained on Kaily. She laid a hand, palm down on Kaily's forehead and another on Kaily's abdomen. She closed her eyes. Lines of concentration creased her forehead.

Shimani moved to stand next to Moto. "Kaily will be okay." He placed a hand on Moto's shoulder.

Sari shushed him without opening her eyes.

Moto didn't reply.

Shimani dropped his hand.

Moto's eyes remained glued to Kaily and Sari. He sensed the intake of energy as Sari drew in energy from Ki. He thought he saw a faint glow radiating from her hands. He frowned and filed away what he witnessed Sari do for later contemplation. They would have words about her hiding the extent of her abilities, and predestined position from him later. Right this moment, his entire being focused on Kaily, and needing her to be okay. He wouldn't accept anything less, and he wouldn't forgive himself if she weren't. It was his fault she was in her current condition. Yet, another failure at protecting her.

Moto paced as time passed.

Shimani stepped aside to give him room.

What was taking so long? Moto thought more than once. He didn't ask the question, as he didn't want to interrupt Sari.

Impatiently, he turned his attention to the destruction. If his Kaily did this, what was he going to do with her? How could he help her control so much power? He'd trained Shimani, but he didn't possess this kind of ability. Neither did the Queen. He seriously doubted any Kahoali did.

Sari cursed aloud.

Moto stopped pacing and turned to face her. He hadn't heard the like from Sari, not even when he made her particularly angry from time to time. He knelt beside Kaily and looked at Sari. "What?"

Sari's eyes met his. "I need to separate her from her talisman."

"So, what's the problem?" Moto attempted to hold back his rising alarm. Sari wouldn't have cursed or panicked for such a simple task. All she had to do was locate the talisman and take it from Kaily.

"I detect her talisman here." Sari glanced down at her hand hovering at the apex of Kaily's center between her hips.

Moto frowned. "I didn't find the talisman anywhere on her."

"I think," Sari took a deep breath, "it's inside her."

"What!" Moto and Shimani uttered in unison. Shimani knelt beside Sari. "Are you absolutely certain?"

Moto glanced from Shimani to Sari. "How can her talisman be inside her?"

Sari raised an eyebrow at him. "Do I really need to answer that question?"

Moto looked away. "No."

"Guess that was one way to keep it hidden." Shimani said.

Sari and Moto glared at him.

Sari returned her attention back to Moto. "I don't have time to give a full explanation. Please understand that I must separate Kaily from her talisman, the sooner the better. And it is not going to be pleasant," Sari said. "To say the least," she muttered under her breath.

"Can't I just reach in, and grab it?" Moto asked with a frown. He didn't see what the problem was other than Kaily putting it there in the first place. What had she been thinking?

Sari shook her head. "I need you to hold her down, both of you." Sari held out her hand. A cloth and pouch appeared in her palm. I need one of you to brace her head and upper body, and the other to hold her legs."

Moto continued to frown, but moved to hold down Kaily's shoulders, and braced her head between his knees. He nodded once to Shimani, who accepted the task of holding down her legs.

"Hold her steady." Sari instructed them both as she glanced from Shimani to Moto.

Both nodded their comprehension.

"No matter what happens, don't let go of her." Sari fixed her eyes on Moto. "I need to do this fast enough that she won't have time to retaliate."

Moto's frown deepened, but he nodded again, and took a firmer hold. He could sense from Sari's tone he wouldn't like what she was about to do to his girl. He wasn't certain what Sari meant by retaliate. What could Kaily do? She was unconscious. Moto closed his eyes for a brief moment and took a deep breath. He opened his eyes and braced himself.

Sari pulled up the hem of Kaily's dress enough so she could position her hand right outside her opening and spread Kaily's thighs apart.

Moto suspected Sari must have removed Kaily's underclothes considering that she was exposed. Moto was not happy about it, but he refrained from comment. He did, however, spare Shimani a warning glare. An air of seriousness replaced Shimani's usual life centered amusement, giving Moto a measure of solace.

Shimani positioned himself so he could hold her legs in the spread position Sari placed them, while he stayed out of her way.

"Ready?" Sari asked both.

"Yes."

Sari draped the cloth over her hand and focused on her task.

Moto detected a sharp intake of energy.

Sari took a deep breath. "Forgive me," she said.

Before Moto could ask her what she meant by her words, he sensed a rapid release of energy, followed by Kaily's bloodcurdling scream.

Kaily thrashed about and fought to break free of their hold on her.

Moto sensed a brief intake of energy, and knew it came from Kaily.

"Hold her!" Sari ordered without looking at either one of them.

Both were hard pressed to hold Kaily down.

Sari sat back on her heels after obtaining the talisman. She quickly covered it up and set it on the ground.

But not before Moto saw the blood and tissue covering it.

Before Kaily could release the small amount of energy she was able to draw in, Sari placed her hands on Kaily's forehead and chest. Power emanated from Sari's hands. "Sleep," Sari commanded Kaily.

A wave of relief washed over Moto when Kaily succumbed and was once again unconscious. He would not have expected to be grateful Kaily was not awake. How, in all that was sacred in the Universe, had Kaily learned to draw in the energy of Ki? Moto's frown deepened. How had Sari put her to sleep?

He sensed Sari drain off the energy Kaily gathered. He grew more impressed by Sari's command of power and control. They would definitely talk about all she'd kept hidden from him in the near future. He'd known Sari since she was a child, they were friends. He was with her when she retrieved her talisman from Crystal Lake. He was with her when she started training to use her powers. He was with her when the Queen appointed her as Shanees. In all that time, he never once suspected the depths of her abilities.

Sari moved her hands further down Kaily's body, and the creases in her forehead deepened with concentration. Sweat broke out.

Moto and Shimani loosened their grip on Kaily but remained where they were.

Again, a faint glow emanated from Sari's hands.

After what seemed an eternity to Moto, Sari let the energy of Ki flow back into the ground. He didn't know how much time actually passed since locating Kaily.

Sari sat back on her heels and picked up Kaily's talisman. She carefully held it in her hands with the cloth.

Moto watched, noticing she didn't allow herself to touch the talisman. Transparent fire, unlike anything he'd seen before, surrounded the talisman. The fire cleansed away the blood and tissue.

Sari put the talisman in the pouch and handed it to Moto. "Keep this safe for Kaily. Don't give it back to her until," Sari glanced around the clearing, and then back at Moto, "until she learns control." She finished with a heavy sigh.

Moto nodded without comment. What could he say? At that moment, he had no intention of ever giving Kaily back her talisman. He had half a mind to drop it back into Crystal Lake. He placed the pouch in the inside pocket of his vest. "Now, what do I do?" Moto asked, looking down at Kaily. He brushed a strand of her hair away from her face. "I can't take her back to her home world, can I?"

"No," Sari shook her head, "you can't. Now that her abilities have awakened, you will need to train her. She can't be left untrained, Moto." Sari and Shimani exchanged a look.

Moto ignored it. He focused his attention on Kaily. "I don't have any safe place to take her."

"I do," Shimani said. "I found some caves a while back that will work. There are some pools nearby to help her heal. One part of the caves was converted to a living space, and the other will make a good training room. It's been shielded."

"Why didn't you tell me about these earlier?" It would have saved Kaily and him a lot of trouble if he'd known about the caves, before he brought her to Center Village.

Shimani shrugged. "It didn't occur to me earlier."

Moto opened his mouth to admonish Shimani.

"Shimani, take Moto and Kaily to the caves." Sari interrupted. "I will gather some supplies to hold you over until we can bring more to you." Sari shifted her attention back to Shimani. "Once they are settled, portal to my hut. You can help bring the supplies and show me the caves." She glanced at Moto. "Kaily is going to need time to rest and heal and quiet to do both."

Moto nodded. He knew Sari's interruption was her way of telling him to let it go with Shimani. It didn't matter. What was done, was done. He hadn't consulted anyone before bringing Kaily to Center Village. That was on him. He carefully picked up Kaily and cradled her in his arms. He moved her so her head rested against his chest, close to his heart. "When do you think she'll wake?"

Sari laid a hand on Kaily's head and held Moto's gaze. "She will sleep through the night, I hope. I will bring you salve to apply where her talisman fused and will give her another healing session. I believe we found her early enough she'll make a full recovery."

"Thank you," Moto said. "My apologies for putting you in this position." He inclined his head towards Sari. "My absence from your side is bound to raise questions."

Sari laid a finger across his lips. "No apologies necessary."

"She's the future Queen." Shimani chimed in. "What can they do to her?"

Sari gave Shimani as shove. "Go, before you get yourself in trouble with the future Queen." She returned her attention to Moto. "I'm aware that you have questions. We will talk more in the coming days. Right now, Kaily needs your undivided attention to keep her safe while she properly heals."

"Agreed," Moto said. "Thank you for helping."

Sari nodded.

Shimani opened a portal and waited for Moto to step through with Kaily. Before stepping through, Moto turned back to Sari. "We will talk."

Sari inclined her head.

Moto stepped through the portal with Kaily cradled in his arms. He did not witness Sari and Shimani bow their heads to a cloaked figure, who stood within the shadows, where the trees remained standing on the edge of the charred circle.

—ele—

Moto found himself in a tiny clearing just outside the mouth of
a cave. There were large boulders on the edge of the clearing that
created a small half circle wall. Behind those boulders stood tall
trees similar to those which surrounded the Villages, but slightly
different. Moto could tell from the way the trees stood; he was
on a plateau.

Shimani arrived shortly after and closed the portal behind
him. "To the right of the cave is a small path that leads to the
pools." Shimani pointed to what barely passed for a narrow
walkway.

Moto followed Shimani through the mouth of the cave.

Once inside, Shimani threw three consecutive energy balls
at three fist sized stones, embedded in the walls. The stones
absorbed the energy and sprang to life. Each gave off a brilliant,
blue tinted light. The cave came to life with the bright light
but was not harsh on the eyes. Next, Shimani opened an ornate
wooden chest set in a nook on the far side opposite the entrance.
He pulled out a pallet and blankets from within. He placed
them near a fire pit set further back in the cave. After, he neatly
stacked wood in the pit. He threw a fireball at the wood, setting a
roaring fire a blaze. A stone ring surrounded the pit, and a metal
tripod was set up so food could be cooked over a fire.

Moto admired the efficiency with which Shimani went about
setting up the area for Kaily and himself.

Next, Shimani moved back to the chest, and pulled out two pots. He concentrated first on one, and then the other. One he placed on a flat stone near the fire, and the other he placed on the hook of the tripod.

Moto saw that liquid filled both.

Shimani drew a heavy covering across the entrance attached to the side. "It gets cold up here at night. Let me help you put Kaily on the sleeping pallet."

"I'll do it," Moto said. He regretted his harsh tone with Shimani, but not enough to apologize for it.

Shimani wasn't disturbed by Moto's harshness.

Moto laid Kaily on the pallet and accepted the blanket from Shimani. He covered Kaily and sat next to her. He accepted the second blanket Shimani handed him.

"I'll be back soon."

Moto nodded to him.

Shimani inclined his head and left the cave.

Kaily shivered, drawing Moto's attention. He covered her with the second blanket, and softly caressed the side of her face. Recent events began to replay in his mind. "What am I going to do with you? Why did you hide your talisman there?" He didn't expect an answer to either of his questions. Leave it to his Kaily to put her talisman in the worst possible spot. If he'd just let her drop it back into Crystal Lake, none of this would have happened.

Moto pulled out the pouch with Kaily's talisman from his vest pocket. He opened the pouch and peered inside. He hesitated, but only a moment. He reached inside and pulled out her talisman. The stone was cool to the touch. He held it up and examined every inch of the talisman. It appeared the same with the silver and gold threads spread throughout.

He glanced at Kaily laying motionless on the pallet. He laid a hand over her heart. He closed his eyes and focused on the beating of her heart against the palm of his hand. He didn't want to ever lose her, but life was not that simple. There were consequences to every choice made, some good, some bad.

As Moto sat, absorbed in the moment, Kaily's talisman thrummed in his hand. His eyes opened wide and focused on it. A dim glow shown from within the stone. With a frown, he dropped it back inside the pouch. He secured the pouch inside the pocket of his vest. He again placed his hand over her heart. He leaned down and placed a gentle kiss on her lips. "You are going to be the death of me."

"My apologies for taking so long," Shimani said as he followed Sari into the cave, carrying two large bags, and a smaller one slung across his back. He placed the bags by the chest. He pulled out some items from the smaller bag before setting it on top of the others. He made his way to the fire and peered into the pot hanging over it. "Good thing I only put water in there," he said as he glared at Moto.

"Wasn't my priority." Moto glanced back at Kaily.

"How's she doing?" Sari asked as she sat on her knees beside him.

"Sleeping."

"Rest will help her recover faster." Sari laid her hand over his. "We brought some medicine to help. Shimani will give you the instructions for them while I give Kaily another healing session."

Moto wanted to protest but held his tongue. Sari could help Kaily far more than he could, so it would seem. He stood and moved to see what Shimani was doing by the fire.

Shimani handed him a cup with a packet inside. "When she wakes, mix the contents with warm water. Make certain she drinks all of it. It will help with the aftereffects of," Shimani stopped. "It will help."

Moto suspected it was the look he gave Shimani that halted his words. He silently chided himself for the lack of control over his emotions, and his inability to keep from showing them.

Shimani handed him a small jar. "This is salve for her injury." Shimani glanced from the jar, back to Moto. "You can figure out what to do with that." He deposited a cloth in Moto's hand on top of the jar.

Moto almost smiled at Shimani's obvious embarrassment, almost.

"I put some more water in the pot." Shimani pointed to the one he took off the hook and placed next to the other one on the flat stone flab. "I mixed some porridge in the smaller one that should be ready when you wake. It shouldn't upset Kaily's stomach. Make sure she eats something after drinking my concoction."

Moto nodded. He set the cup next to the bowls placed on a flat rock top that passed for a small table near the fire pit. Not the same one the pots sat on top of. A larger flat rock was also nearby with cushion set around it. Moto hadn't seen Shimani place the cushions, but his attention had been focused elsewhere.

"This is for you." Shimani handed him a cup with warm liquid in it.

Moto accepted and sipped the contents. The taste wasn't unpalatable. He suspected that Shimani had put something in it. He wasn't certain for what purpose, and neither was he in the mood to ask.

Shimani set up another pallet, and blanket near Kaily's. He set a few other things up, that Moto didn't quite pay attention to. After, Shimani joined him near the fire. "Back there," Shimani said, pointing to an opening in the back corner, "is a room for training Kaily to control her abilities."

"What makes you think I'm going to train her?" Moto couldn't keep the anger out of his tone. He was angry at himself, Kaily, everyone. A part of him knew his anger was irrational.

"You have no choice." Sari sat on the other side of Shimani. She accepted the cup he handed her.

Moto glanced at Kaily. "I wouldn't know where to begin." He turned his attention back to Shimani and Sari. "If she destroyed the clearing, she is more powerful than I am or have ever seen. How am I supposed to teach her to control that much power?"

"You only need to teach her control," Sari said. "As long as you keep her talisman, and it remains inside the pouch, she can't access it to pull energy from Ki. She shouldn't be able to hold much within her being, at least, not yet." Sari glanced at Shimani.

Moto narrowed his eyes on the two of them. "Why do I suspect you both know more than you are sharing with me?"

"Because we do," Shimani said. "Ow!"

Sari zapped and leveled him with a glare. She pulled out her talisman and handed it to Moto.

He turned it over in his hand. The multiple hues swirling inside gathered in equal portions similar to Kaily's, and there was silver webbing overlaying her talisman. He turned startled eyes to Sari as he handed it back. "I was with you when you pulled your talisman from Crystal Lake, and it did not look like that."

Sari smiled. "No, it did not. Things changed since that time."

"So, I see," Moto said. He waited. He tried to push down his anger.

"After you were named a Chosen, and left our Village, I was called back to Crystal Lake. I won't bore you with the details, suffice it to say that I entered the Lake again, and when I emerged my talisman looked like this." Sari held her talisman up to the light.

"And your eyes?"

Sari nodded. "And my eyes changed at that time as well."

"Why haven't you come forward?"

Sari glanced at Shimani, and then back to Moto.

"I wish you two would stop doing that." Moto glared at both. "Or tell me why knowing looks keep passing between you two."

"It isn't time," Sari said.

"Time to tell me or time to claim your destiny?" Anger and frustration sharpened his tone.

"Both. Please understand, Moto. There are events in motion that go beyond our own small existence in the Villages. Trust me as you always have. I will reveal my destiny when the time is right, but until then, you must keep my secret."

Moto looked away. He shook his head.

"Moto?" Sari said, drawing his attention back to her.

"When will you clue me in to the details?" Moto leveled both with a fierce scowl. "You know, the things that have you two exchanging looks?"

"When it is time." Sari repeated. "Please, I need to know you'll keep my secret."

"Fine! I'll keep your secret." Moto glanced from Shimani to Sari. "So, have I been training Shimani or him me?" There was disdain in his tone. He didn't like being made a fool of, and he felt the fool. He didn't let anyone get close to him, except the two sitting in front of him. He loved and trusted them, and now he thought that he didn't really know them. They were the only two who saw a side of him no one else did, ever.

Sari smiled.

It was a smile that held a measure of something Moto could not quite decipher. Nor could he make sense of the emotions emanating from her.

"Both. This one," Sari thumped Shimani on the side of the head, "is still too impetuous."

Shimani shrugged. "What can I say? I'm young."

Sari shook her head at him. "Moto, are you still having your night terrors?"

"Not since Kaily came to Ki. Why?"

"Curiosity," Sari said.

"Curiosity?" Moto raised an eyebrow. "That's all you're going to say?"

Sari's smile widened. "Fine. It's more than that. I was curious if Kaily coming to our world changed," she paused as if searching for the right words.

"Future events?" Moto asked.

"That's the thing," Sari said. "We don't know if your night terrors are visions of the future."

"We?" Moto asked.

"We're going to leave you in peace," she said instead of answering his question. She stood and tapped Shimani on the back.

Shimani stood.

"It will be light out soon, and you need to get some rest before Kaily wakes. Don't forget to use the salve before you go to sleep, and again when you wake. More applications will depend on how she responds to the healing." Sari turned to leave, and then turned back to Moto. "And this time, tell Kaily about our bonding being a farce." She gave him a stern glare. "And don't consummate the bonding with her until she completely heals."

"What makes you think I've decided to bond with her?"

Sari tilted her head to the side and smiled. "You have, you just don't know it yet. We'll be back late afternoon. Come," she said to Shimani as she gave him a push towards the cave entrance.

Moto stared at the entrance for a moment after they left. He sighed and glanced around the cave. The stones and boulders inside had been placed in such a way that it did appear someone lived there at one point. He stood and walked around the interior of the cave. He spotted alcoves that were hidden. At first glance, the cave appeared to be one large room, but on closer inspection, there were hidden places.

One of those hidden places held a shower and facilities. Another held supplies of sorts, nothing perishable like food, but wood for fire, and metal tools. Odd looking ones. More blankets were inside the chest. Moto grabbed a couple. The cold had begun to seep into his bones. He also grabbed a poker, and more wood to fuel the fire. The last thing he needed was for Kaily to get sick from the cold.

He moved his pallet up next to Kaily's and covered her with another blanket. He spread a second blanket out on his pallet. Satisfied she would be warm, he walked over to the first stone light. Frowning, he held his hand over it, and thought about how Sari withdrew energy from Kaily. He tried to do the same.

The light dimmed.

He checked the covering over the entrance and secured the edges on the hooks at the bottom and sides. Next, he dimmed the other two stone lights. Once he was satisfied there was nothing else to see to, he lay down next to Kaily. He carefully pulled her into his arms and covered them both.

The cold in the cave was the kind that seeped in, penetrated the very core of a person, and made him wonder if he would be warm again.

Moto remembered about the salve as he got comfortable. Irritably, he stood and retrieved the jar with the cloth. He scooped out what looked like a decent amount. He pushed his fingers carefully inside Kaily and gingerly searched for the damaged area.

Kaily stirred when his fingers found the spot, but she remained asleep.

He coated the injured area with the salve. Once finished, he wiped his fingers on the cloth, and then put both items aside.

Moto drew Kaily close into his embrace. He kissed the top of her head. He rolled to his back, pulling her with him, and settled into a comfortable position. Sari's words replayed in his mind.

How could he bond with Kaily? Hadn't he caused her enough trouble?

He stared up at the ceiling. He didn't have answers, and he was tired. He closed his eyes. He took a deep breath and exhaled. He cleared his mind of any thought and gave into his exhaustion. He'd consider his options another day.

Chapter Sixteen

Kaily woke to excruciating pain. Pressure pushed on her skull from the inside out, making her think it just might explode. She took shallow breaths, trying to will the pain to subside. Her head rested on a shoulder. She instinctively knew it belonged to Moto. The warmth of his arms held her close, and firmly in place. His masculine, forest scent permeated her senses. Both kept the frigid coldness slithering deep inside her somewhat at bay. As awareness crept into her blissful unconsciousness, her pain increased. She concentrated on remaining utterly motionless. A whimper escaped from between her tightly pressed lips.

Moto stirred beneath her.

"Please don't move," she managed to whisper. She pressed her feeble hand against his massive chest as if she might stay his movement.

He kissed the top of her head. "I have something that will help." He scooted out from under her with as much care as the action would allow.

Kaily winced. A sharp pain shot through her head just behind her eyes. She rolled to her back, holding her pounding head between her hands.

"Shimani gave me something to help ease your pain."

She heard Moto rummaging around nearby in whatever location they occupied. The resounding noise echoed more than it would have in a hut. The cold bit deeper than the forest surrounding the village she'd been in. If her head weren't killing her right that moment, she would have opened her eyes to sage her curiosity. The light seeping through her shut eyelids didn't help. The rolling in her stomach almost kept her from becoming aware of an insanely, intense burning sensation in a place she didn't want to mention to Moto, almost.

Kaily whimpered again.

"I need you to sit up." Moto pulled back the blankets covering her.

She tried to grab for them, without success. "No." Kaily whimpered. She was dying. There was no other explanation for her condition.

"You have no choice, Kaily." Moto placed his hand under her back and grabbed her hands with his other one.

She was in no condition to protest. She winced with each increment movement as he slowly maneuvered her to a sitting position.

Moto sat so she could lean against his bent knee, but still face her, for the most part.

She might have been impressed by his thoughtful gesture if she weren't dying.

"Drink this." Moto placed the cup in her hands but kept a hold of it.

The cup warmed her frigid fingers. Moisture seeped from between her closed eyelids. "You should just let me die in peace."

"You are not dying." He wiped at her tears. "Drink." He guided the cup to her lips.

Kaily took a sip, and then tried to pull away. "No."

"Drink!" He ordered. "I promise, little one, the warm liquid will help with the pain you're experiencing."

"Tyrant," she muttered. She obediently drank the foul liquid. Not even holding her breath helped get past the awful taste.

"Tyrant, hmm?" Amusement infused his response.

Kaily finished as quickly as her stomach would allow. "Done." She turned her head away and pushed the cup away from her.

Moto looked inside the cup. "You drank most, but not all."

Kaily gave a small shake of her head.

"Guess it'll have to be close enough." He set the cup aside. He brushed her hair back and caressed the side of her face. He continued to wipe at her tears.

She didn't know from where all the tears came. She couldn't seem to stop them. She let herself rest back against Moto's knee. The pain had eased up a bit. "Shimani's concoction?"

"You've had the pleasure before, I see." He laughed.

"Don't move," Kaily said

"My apologies."

"Once before, yes. Horrible taste, but fast working," she answered.

"Better?"

"Starting to be."

"Enough to open your eyes?" Moto asked.

"No." Kaily giggled. "Oww." She grabbed her head.

"Serves you right." Moto placed a chaste kiss on her temple.

"For what?"

"For being stubborn."

"Hmph." The pressure behind her eyes continued to diminish. "You make a comfortable chair."

"Glad to be of service."

Kaily smiled.

"Ready to talk about what happened?"

"No." Aside from the pain, she didn't want to open her eyes to avoid reality crashing in on their peaceful moment. She didn't remember everything about what happened, but enough to make the memory painful. He belonged to another. She wanted, if only for a brief time, to pretend otherwise. Selfish as it was, she would take his comfort and attention for a while longer.

"Kaily?"

"Hush." She brought her hand up, intending to place it across his mouth for good measure.

Moto captured her hand and placed a kiss in the center of her palm.

She reluctantly opened her eyes.

His eyes locked with hers.

She loved his strange, silver webbed, hazel eyes. Gentleness radiated from their depths. She sighed. She shifted to sit up better and winced from the pain in her uncomfortable lower regions.

"I need you to lie back down," Moto told her.

Kaily frowned. "Why?"

"You were," Moto glanced uncomfortably around the cave. His eyes shifted back to Kaily. He took a deep breath. "You were injured."

Kaily narrowed her eyes at him. "Injured how?"

"You didn't want to talk about what happened." Moto reminded her. He hovered over her, and pushed her back to the pallet, forcing her to lie down.

She kept her gaze locked with his.

Moto grabbed a jar and cloth.

"Where?" Kaily asked, suspiciously eying the contents in his hand. There was only one place that she felt the kind of pain that might require whatever was in that jar.

Moto opened his mouth to say something, and then shut it. He took a deep breath. "Spread your legs, please."

Her gaze narrowed. "Why?"

"Do you remember anything about last night?" Moto forced her knees apart.

Notwithstanding his obvious attempt at gentleness, he gave her no choice. She didn't resist. She looked away without answering Moto's question.

Moto sighed. He scooped out a solid amount of the salve. He inserted his fingers inside as gently as possible.

"Owww!" Kaily arched her back. She tried to move away from his ministrations. "What the hell!"

"Be still!" Moto held her firmly in place. "You're the one who put your talisman there!"

The moment Moto withdrew his fingers, Kaily pushed on his arm, and fought to scoot away.

Moto let her. He wiped his fingers on the cloth, and then set both aside.

Kaily sat up. She brought her knees to her chest and wrapped her arms around them. She glared at Moto. She was more than aware he let her up, and she didn't like being at anyone's mercy, not even his. The burning pain began to subside.

Moto picked up the cup and sat it on the low table. He stirred the contents in the small pot on the slab near the fire.

"Why would the stone do that to me?" She demanded.

He glanced at her. "Do you remember anything about last night's events?" Moto again asked her.

"Oh, you mean your marriage ceremony?" Kaily angrily replied. Tears burned her eyes. She fought to keep them from running down her cheeks. She failed.

Moto visibly winced. "After that," he prompted.

Kaily looked away. "No."

She wasn't quite truthful in her answer. She remembered leaving the ceremony and running. She remembered stopping in the training clearing because her lungs burned, and her legs would not carry her any further. She remembered the emotional onslaught. She didn't remember much other. And especially didn't remember how she ended up in this cave with him. The cave didn't appear to be unlivable, but certainly a down grade from her hut.

Moto carried two bowls back to where she sat on a pallet. He held one down to her. "You need to eat."

Kaily stared at the bowl in his hand. Her eyes met his. She saw resolve in the depths of his eyes. He was not going to give her a choice. "What is it?" She asked, taking the offered bowl.

"Porridge," Moto said.

Kaily suspiciously eyed the contents. They didn't quite appear like anything she would call porridge, but it didn't have a terrible aroma either. Her anger simmered beneath the surface. There was also a deep sense of loss inside her, she'd only experienced once before in her life. Which was when her foster parents died.

She fought to contain her emotions. The feeling of loss part confused her. She didn't even know the man in front of her, to feel such towards him. Yet, she did, and that angered her too.

Moto sat down across from her on the pallet. He lifted her face and waited for her gaze to shift from the contents in her bowl to him.

Kaily unwillingly looked at Moto.

"You were unconscious when we found you in the training clearing." He waited.

Kaily remained silent.

"Your talisman was fused inside you. Do you remember anything, Kaily? Anything at all?"

Kaily frowned. She sensed something in his tone when he asked his questions that frightened her. She sighed and shook her head.

Moto nodded once. He remained where he sat and started eating his porridge. "Eat! It will help you feel better."

Kaily regarded him a moment longer, before picking up her spoon, and digging into her own bowl. She licked her lips. The porridge tasted quite good for a fire side meal.

"As for the marriage ceremony, as you called it,"

Kaily adamantly shook her head. "I don't want to talk about it."

Moto regarded her with a heavy sigh.

She could tell he clearly was not happy.

"It was a Kahoali bonding ceremony,"

Kaily clenched her jaw and shifted her gaze. Great! She thought to herself. That sounded so much worse than a marriage ceremony.

"Look at me, Kaily!"

"Why?"

"Because you need to understand what I'm trying to tell you."

"Fine!" Kaily's gaze collided with his. She set aside her bowl with a clatter.

Moto shook his head at her. "Do you remember when we were at Crystal Lake, and I said I needed to talk to you about something?"

Kaily crossed her arms over her chest.

Moto heaved a long sigh. "The Queen demanded that I take a bonded mate."

Kaily glared at him.

"Sari agreed so the Queen wouldn't choose someone else for me. Kaily, it means nothing. It doesn't change anything between the two of us."

Kaily shook her head. She looked away. More angry tears slipped out. Why would he say it meant nothing? She was certain it meant something to Sari! What female would be okay with meaning nothing to her mate! She certainly wouldn't! He was gravely mistaken if he thought it changed nothing between them. He belonged to another; she wouldn't interfere with that. And she absolutely would not be the other woman, ever!

Moto handed her back her bowl. "Eat."

Kaily took it, and started eating, if only to end this conversation.

He finished eating his.

She sensed him watching her, even though his gaze seemed fixed on his bowl. She finished her porridge and handed him her empty bowl.

Moto took it, stood, and set both on the low table. He returned and held his hands down to her. "I have something to show you."

She allowed him to help her stand and followed him outside the cave. Not that she had a choice. She tried to find the emotional numb place she once found from the shock of her foster parents' sudden deaths. She needed that kind of detachment from him. She fought to grasp it.

"There are pools down this path."

Kaily suspiciously eyed the narrow so-called path. "That is way too narrow to be traversable." Although she couldn't see a drop off edge from her vantage point, she suspected there was one.

Moto laughed. "It is, and you'll be fine with me."

She disagreed but allowed him to guide her down it.

"They should help with your healing."

Theme of the day! Yeah right! She thought. Nothing would help ease her pain inside. Maybe her physical, but not her emotional hurt.

Moto stopped as they stepped into a clearing and scanned the area.

The view was breathtaking. She'd not seen anything like it. She looked up at the bright, unobstructed sky. She'd not had a clear view of the sky since being brought to the Kahoali village. The planet she'd seen from the Agenors' castle hung humongous in view. Seeing it now, there was no mistaking it for a moon as she had first thought. The planet was more vibrant than before, and much larger. It practically filled the sky.

Kaily glanced at Moto. His eyes were not turned skyward. In fact, he seemed to be doing his best to ignore the planet. She frowned and gazed back up at the planet. For a brief moment, she considered saying something to him. She disregarded her impulse.

"Shall we?" He caressed the side of her face, drawing her attention to focus on him.

Kaily shrugged. She fought against the momentary pleasure his touch caused her. She attempted to remain detached as she watched him move closer to the pool. He stopped at the edge and removed his clothes. All his clothes! Her mouth dropped open, and she blushed. She promptly closed it. Warmth spread from her center outward. She hated how responsive her body was at the sight of him.

Moto dived into the pool. "Coming?" He asked, after surfacing.

Kaily glanced back up the path.

"The water will warm you."

She glanced back at him and moved closer to the pool. The water appeared inviting. She could use a good soak.

Moto turned his back, and slowly swam to the other side.

Kaily walked to the edge. Steam rose from the surface. She imagined the soak would be divine. She started slipping off her dress from her shoulders.

Moto glanced over his shoulder.

She glared at him.

He smiled but turned his head back around.

She stared at his back, as she slipped the rest of the way out of her dress. Somehow, she wasn't wearing her underclothes. She was not comfortable with her own nakedness without anyone around, let alone in front of him. She took a deep breath and sat on the edge to ease herself into the pool. It was strange to be so embarrassed in front of this man, and yet, desire his touch, unbearably so. Her feet barely touched the bottom, and only if she allowed the water to cover her head. Tiny bubbles tingled against her skin. The water was a welcoming warmth surrounding her sore body. What Shimani's concoction hadn't erased, the water did. She sighed.

Moto turned around.

While she clung to the edge, he obviously had no trouble touching the bottom.

Kaily's eyes remained locked with his. She thought he might be able to see the indecisiveness in her eyes.

He remained where he was without speaking.

She got the distinct impression that he was giving her a moment to make up her mind. The problem was, she didn't think he was waiting for her to just make up her mind about swimming to him.

Moto reclined against the opposite side as he regarded Kaily.

She closed her eyes and savored the warm bubbles bursting against her skin. The water almost felt like a seltzer bath. For the moment, she allowed her anger to slip away. She focused on the soothing water. She didn't want to feel anything. She didn't want to think about the ceremony or after. She wanted to hold onto a measure of peace, for as long as she was capable. What did it matter anyway? Once she convinced Moto to take her home, none of it would matter. He would be out of her life for good, and she could return to her quiet, uncomplicated existence. Everything she'd experienced would be nothing more than a dream, after a time.

Her gaze locked onto his. She had to play nice if she wanted to get back home. Regardless what it cost emotionally, she needed him. He was the only one who could take her home. Making up her mind, she swam to where he reclined. Her eyes did not leave his. When she was within reach, she grabbed the edge beside him, careful not to actually touch him in the process. For a second, she thought she might have seen a slight crease between his brows. It disappeared too quickly to be certain. "Thank you," Kaily said. "The pool is helping."

"You're welcome." Moto raised his hand.

She thought he might touch her. She moved slightly away.

He pointed to the pools below. "There seems to be a cascade of pools, but I don't see a path to get back up to the top."

Kaily glanced over the edge. There were a number of lower pools, one after the other in a stair step type formation. Each pool's water shimmered with a slightly different hue. A kind of rainbow of colors. "It's beautiful here." She glanced at Moto. There was an uncomfortable space between them, and not just physically. They were close enough to touch but didn't. She told herself that she was happy he kept his hands to himself. She thought he might be struggling too. Both wanting to touch the other, but neither one making the first move. She rested her chin on her hands clinging to the side and closed her eyes. She slowly moved her legs back and forth. A sigh of frustration escaped her before she could stop it. Damn him anyway! She thought.

"What can I do?" Moto whispered in her ear. "How can I help you?"

Kaily startled. She hadn't noticed him move to press against her. "Moto, please." She shook her head. What could she say? He kept telling her she wasn't Kahoali, and she wouldn't understand. As it turned out, he'd been right. She wasn't, and she didn't. They were from two different worlds, literally. She refused to be a side thing for him. His bond with Sari might not matter in his world, but it mattered to her. "I've been through a lot." She turned around to face him, and placed a restraining hand on his chest, all the good it would do her. "I need to breathe."

Moto frowned, and then cursed. He leaned close to her ear. "We will finish this conversation later."

Kaily frowned. What was there to finish? She opened her mouth to say as much, but he'd dived under the water, before she could utter a word. She watched in bewilderment as he pulled himself from the pool and grabbed his clothes.

Moto turned back to face Kaily. "I trust you won't drown yourself?"

Kaily stuck her tongue out at him. She thought he might be attempting humor. She was not amused. She turned her back on him. When she glanced over her shoulder, he had dressed, and was headed back up the path to the cave. With a sigh, she turned back around, and rested her chin on her hands. She let go of all her pent-up emotions. Her eyes burned with unshed tears. She let them go too. Damn him! She wanted him. It scared her to know just how tempted she was to say, screw it all. She would take whatever part of himself he was willing to give her.

She angrily brushed at her tears. He wasn't worth it, she chided herself. She swam back to the other edge. She pulled herself out, and hastily put her dress on over her damp skin. She didn't care. She sat by the edge with her chin resting on her upturned knees. The clearing, with the open sky, was not as cold as the cave. She would let her clothes dry and give herself time before facing him again.

She closed her eyes and worked to find a semblance of peace. "Moto said he talked to you about the bonding ceremony."

Kaily startled and glanced over her shoulder. She frowned at Sari. "Yes." She turned her head away. She was not prepared to speak to this woman about anything, and certainly not him.

Sari sat beside her. "You don't look like you're feeling the way I would expect you to feel."

Kaily glanced at her. "How should I feel, Sari." She was surprised to see a clearly puzzled look on Sari's face. "From my perspective, you two are married." She glanced at the path. "Moto, well, he is being," she shook her head. What could she say to Sari? She took a deep breath. "This bonding thing may not be a big deal to you two, but it is to me. As far as I'm concerned, you're married. End of story."

Sari's frown deepened, and a smile spread across her facial features. Amusement beamed from her eyes. She raised an eyebrow. "Um, marriage, as you call it, is a big deal here. A Kahoali bonding is for life, and only with one person, ever. There is no other once a bonding begins, and only deepens when the final ritual of bonding is completed. The bonding between two individuals cannot be undone."

Oh god! Kaily thought. It was worse than she previously realized. Marriage was a serious decision, but it was not something that couldn't be undone if the two so decided. "Then why is he acting like it isn't? I don't understand!"

Sari let out an exasperated sigh. "Moto was supposed to talk to you before the ceremony took place. He was supposed to advise you about the ceremony, and the reason behind it. He was supposed to explain that it was for appearances, to convince everyone he and I were bonded mates, so the Queen wouldn't choose someone else. I now know he didn't talk to you before, but he said he did today."

Kaily shook her head and shrugged. "He did and said it didn't matter." She would have explained further, but Sari was practically doubled over with laughter. "This is not funny."

Sari held up her hand. "My apologies. I'm not laughing at you, Kaily. I should have known that Moto wouldn't explain it right."

"Neither have you," Kaily said, anger straining her words. "Are you two married, bonded or whatever you want to call it or not?"

"Not," Sari said. "We are not. Our agreement to be bonded, the ceremony, all if it was done, to give the appearance of our bond, so the Queen, and everyone would think Moto was no longer available to bond with anyone else." Sari tilted her head. "So, he wasn't available to bond with you."

"Why?" Kaily still didn't see where it made any difference.

"To give him time and freedom to work through his feelings for you."

"Why?" Kaily pressed. Nothing about the whole situation between Sari and Moto made sense, and it was pissing her off.

Sari touched Kaily's arm. "I know this is all hard to understand. The Queen is never going to accept Moto bonding with an outsider. Moto needs time to come to terms with the consequences of what has happened between you and him, and what that means for his future. It is better for all of us if everyone thinks he and I are the bonded mates. It would have been easier on you if he'd talked to you beforehand." She shrugged. "He didn't. You should make peace with what has happened, and please try and understand."

Kaily shifted her gaze away from Sari. She really hated being an outsider.

"Kaily?"

She looked back at Sari and shook her head. "I don't fully understand this bonding thing. Why would anyone care if he was available to bond with me, assuming he wanted to? We don't even know each other!"

"Okay, first, I'll try to explain what it means to be bonded in the Kahoali way. There is something which brings two individuals together. It starts with a connection of some sort. It can be a physical connection, a spiritual connection, or enough similarities to forge a bond. In those cases, the two make the decision, and choose to become bonded mates. In some rare cases, like with you and Moto,"

Kaily shook her head and opened her mouth to disagree.

"Let me finish." Sari leveled her with a stern look. "In those rare cases, like you and Moto, there is a connection that is so deep that the two start the bonding process well before either one of them makes a conscious decision to become bonded mates."

Kaily shook her head.

Sari nodded. "Yes, you and Moto are one of those rare ones."

Kaily's eyes narrowed at Sari, and she frowned. She couldn't deny there was something between them. A type of magnetism pulling on them both. Something more than mere physical attraction. The physical attraction was undeniable, but there was more. He made her way too emotional. She hadn't yet decided if what drew them together was a good or bad thing. "How do you know that we are one of those rare cases?"

"Anyone with eyes can see that you are," Sari said.

There was way too much amusement in her tone for Kaily's liking.

She sobered and held Kaily's gaze. "Moto's out of character behavior around you, his defiance towards our Queen, the telepathic communication you two share,"

Kaily began to shake her head.

"Are you denying it?" Sari asked with a raised eyebrow. "You don't have a telepathic connection?"

Kaily held her denial. "Maybe. I have thought at times that I could hear Moto in my mind," she said, "but, Sari, all this?" She waved her hand in the air. "All this, I don't know what to call it. In my world we would say magic. All this is so far beyond my comprehension of what is real, and what is illusion, that it is hard for me to wrap my head around it, let alone accept this as reality without true understanding. This isn't real to me." She couldn't help her rambling.

"I can't imagine growing up not knowing about the energy of Ki, and the abilities that come to those who embrace their powers." Sari smiled.

Kaily gave a short laugh and shook her head. "Two different worlds."

Sari gave her a side hug. "You have no idea. All I can say is to have an open mind and be prepared for anything. And I mean anything. Above all else, be very patient with Moto while he comes to terms with his bonding with you. Trust me. It's not that he doesn't want to take you as his bonded mate, because he most certainly does. He is Kahoali through and through. His people are very important to him, and he believes that by bonding with you, he will have to sacrifice being a part of the Kahoali world."

"I don't want him to give up his world for me, Sari."

Sari gave her a sad smile. "He may not have a choice."

Kaily glanced away. She wanted to deny that he would have to give up his people, but she couldn't. The way they acted towards her, an outsider, she shook her head. What would they do with someone that chose an outsider over them? She couldn't bear to think about it. She returned her focus to Sari. "What do I do?"

"Be patient with him and follow your heart."

Kaily didn't add further comment. What should she say to that? There were too many times she didn't know what her heart wanted to do. She looked up at the planet above, seeking comfort. She glanced sideways at Sari, who also gazed up at the planet. "What is that world called?"

"Celtan," Sari said. She focused on Kaily. "It's the home world of the Druids, although it is not a topic you should bring up around Moto."

"I noticed that he avoided looking at it when he first brought me here."

Sari nodded. "Most Kahoali avoid looking at it. In the Villages it's easy to ignore since the sky is obscured from view by the forest canopy. It is a painful memory of a time when a bad choice cost so many their lives within Center Village. It was a long time ago, but not long enough to fade from memory or hearts. There hasn't been enough time for the bitterness to dwindle from the Kahoali people."

"Why don't you seem bitter about it?"

Sari shrugged. "Different perspective."

Kaily nodded. She tried to absorb everything Sari shared with her.

"I can't stress enough. To be patient with Moto."

Kaily glanced at her and smiled. "I'll try."

"He will come around, but he is stubborn. It takes him time to work things out for himself. Right now, he is trying to hold on to his world, and you, at the same time."

"How do you know he will come around?" A little bitterness tainted her question. To Kaily it was so simple. He wanted her, she wanted him. What was the big deal? Aside from sacrificing everything he has ever known. She sighed and glanced out over the pool. Selfishly, she wanted him to make the sacrifice for her, but she also understood what losing everything meant, and felt. She wouldn't wish that kind of pain on anyone. It wasn't like she wasn't giving up everything too. She wanted to go back to her life, but she sensed she wouldn't be able to. She couldn't imagine him in her world, any more than he could her in his, from what she could tell. In a sense, they both would be giving up their worlds for each other.

"I know Moto. He will come around, and he will make the right choice." She tilted her head. "Eventually. On a different topic, and let's keep this conversation between us. Do you remember what happened at the training clearing?"

"Why does everyone keep asking me that? No, I don't!"

"Everyone?"

"Okay, you and Moto."

"I see." Sari smiled.

Kaily glanced down. When she looked back up, Sari's smile was gone. "What's the matter?"

"We found you at the center of the training clearing. It had been destroyed. The ground of the entire clearing and some distance beyond was burnt to a crisp. The trees were blasted over, and you remember how big those trees were, don't you?"

Kaily nodded.

"You know your talisman was fused in the place you hid it, right?"

Kaily again nodded.

"That only happens when too much energy passes through the talisman, and the destruction comes from strong, uncontrolled emotions. To lose such control," Sari shook her head. "It is clear to me that you have great abilities, Kaily, more than you are aware of, and more than you can accept at the moment."

"Do you blame me for doubting? This falls in the realm of unbelievable for me."

"I know. You must put your doubt aside for both your and Moto's sake. You have to accept that you do have abilities that are beyond your comprehension at this time. You must believe that you are not imagining any of what has happened to you or what you have observed so far. It is real. It is your reality. You will learn the truth of my words in time, Kaily, but I'm afraid that your journey is not going to be an easy one. You will need to take a great deal on faith, until you come to know the truth for yourself. Moto will attempt to train you."

"Attempt?"

Sari glanced up at the planet.

"You don't think he can, do you?"

Sari looked back at Kaily. "Trust Moto. He is your anchor. He will keep you grounded, and as hard as it may become, know that it will all work out in the end, if you both trust each other."

Kaily gave a short laugh. "Trust?" She shook her head, and then focused her attention on Sari. "How do you know it will all work out?"

Sari smiled. "I know Moto, and I know enough about you. Together, you two can overcome anything." Sari glanced up at the sky. "It'll be dark soon. We should see what Shimani, and Moto are up to." She stood. "If I know them, and I do," she said, glancing down at Kaily. "They are wondering where we are."

Kaily stood up. She glanced up at the planet. She sighed and gazed at Sari. "Ready when you are."

"Then let's get back." Sari led the way up the path.

Kaily still would not call that narrow piece of dirt clinging to the rock side of an obvious mountain, a path. She kept her hand along the rock face as she made her way back.

When they entered the cave, they found Moto and Shimani bickering over what they were fixing for the evening repast. Shimani stirred something in the pot over the fire, and Moto set out edibles that Kaily could identify only a few of the food items. She startled when Sari walked over to Moto and smacked him on the back of his head.

"That's for not talking to Kaily about the ceremony, before the ceremony!" She punched him in the arm.

"What was that one for?" He asked, rubbing the back of his head, and then his arm.

"Just because," Sari said.

"Oh, so Sari gets away with hitting you?" Kaily's question slipped out before she thought better of it.

Sari turned narrowed eyes on Moto. "You didn't!" Sari made an inarticulate sound and zapped his ass with a small dose of energy, before he had time to answer her.

"Oww." Moto glared at Sari and rubbed where he'd been energy shocked.

"What was that for?" Shimani asked from where he stirred the pot.

"Nothing!" All three said in unison.

Sari glared at Shimani and held eye contact for a moment longer before turning her attention to Kaily.

Shimani smirked and focused his attention back to the pot over the fire.

"Let's see if we can find something warmer for you to change into. It feels a bit colder up here than in the Villages, don't you think?"

"Yes." Kaily rubbed her chilled arms. She followed Sari to a chest, and bags near it. She watched with curiosity as Sari rummaged through the bags until she found what she searched for.

"Here you go." Sari handed her pants, and a long-sleeved pullover.

It was not as bulky as her beloved sweaters back home, but close enough. The material was soft and warm to her touch. "Thank you." She gave Sari a bright, happy smile. "Where do I change?"

Sari glared at Moto and held up her hand as if she prepared to give him another zap.

Moto held up his hands in surrender. "She didn't need the room earlier."

Sari shook her head and took Kaily by the hand. "The shower room is over here, where you can change, and attend other needs."

Kaily looked inside. "Wow, impressive." She found a fully functional bathroom, similar to the shower room in her guest hut.

"Shimani found this cave a while back." Sari turned her attention towards Shimani. "Was this room here when you found it, or did you install it?"

"It was here. It might have been someone's home at one point, but no one has been back to claim it." Shimani set the pot on the stone table where Moto placed the uncooked food items.

Moto glanced up as he finished his portion of the preparations.

"I'll hurry," Kaily said.

"The repast will keep," Sari said. "Take your time." She handed her a small bundle, and turned her towards the shower entrance, practically pushing her inside.

Kaily pulled the curtain across the entrance. From a cursory view, the cave appeared to be just any ordinary cave like she might find back on Earth. There were differences between the worlds, but similarities too. She could almost forget that she was on another planet. She glanced around the bathroom. Almost. She hung up the pants and top and laid the bundle on a ledge. She stripped off her dress and hung it on one of the hooks.

From her conversation with Sari, she would be hard pressed to convince Moto to take her home. And from the looks of this room, and what she'd seen in the cave, and the abundance of items in the bags, she just might be there longer than expected. She had some thinking of her own to do about everything. She couldn't deny their connection, but what did it really mean? Could they make it work between them? She shook her head. She had no answers. Her desires were in conflict. She sighed. Thoughts for later.

She examined the small bundle first. She silently sent a thank you as they turned out to be underclothes. She quickly dressed and left the shower room.

When she rejoined the others, she found Sari sitting at the table with Shimani and Moto. The closeness between the three of them was apparent in the way they talked and laughed with each other. It was the most relaxed she'd witnessed Moto around anyone. She smiled to herself as she made her way to the empty place, they'd left for her.

"Pants, Sari?" Moto chided.

"They'll keep her warm."

"I like them," Kaily chimed in as she settled on a cushion next to Moto.

"So do I."

"Eyes to yourself, Shimani," Moto said.

Sari laughed.

Shimani smiled.

Kaily turned her attention to the spread on the table. The aroma hitting her nose made her stomach rumble. She suddenly felt ravenous.

Shimani dished up a bowl for each of them. Moto filled a small plate of the other items for each as well.

Kaily smiled, when she realized her, and Sari's plates were piled higher with pahini than anything else. Apparently, Moto was either more observant than she expected, or Sari had given him instructions before she sat down. She wanted to believe the former. "Thank you." Her eyes met his.

"What about me?" Shimani asked. "I cooked the stew."

Kaily smiled at Shimani. "Thank you as well. It smells delicious."

"She likes my cooking," Shimani told Moto.

"She hasn't tasted it yet." Moto countered.

Sari and Kaily shook their heads at them both.

Kaily glanced around the table at each of them. She liked this camaraderie between friends. She could get used to it. She allowed herself to relax, and simply enjoy the moment. They talked, of nothing important. They laughed and joked as they consumed their food.

Every time her gaze strayed to Moto, her eyes locked with his, and he would smile at her. She didn't know if it was because he never stopped watching her or if it was because he sensed her eyes drifting towards him. She didn't know if Sari or Shimani perceived how often their gazes found each other's or if they politely ignored it. The conversation flowed naturally, as if normal, and maybe it was.

As each finished, they pushed their plates and bowls towards the center of the table.

"Everything was wonderful." Kaily said. "Thank you both."

Shimani inclined his head.

Moto and Shimani cleared away the dishes and cleaned up. Kaily and Sari moved the cushions closer to the fire. Once they both were settled back on their perspective cushions, Moto handed them a warm cup, filled almost to the rim. How he kept from spilling any, she had no idea. Moto and Shimani settled on their cushions, holding a cup of their own.

"What's this?" Kaily asked.

"Yours is nectar of brey," Moto answered before Shimani did.

Shimani leaned forward, and closer to Kaily. "He wouldn't let me give you the real stuff, not even watered-down."

Kaily smirked. "Probably for the best. If I remember correctly, I fell asleep the one and only time you gave me the watered-down version of brey."

"You did," Moto said.

"Did you show Kaily the training room at the back of the cave?" Shimani took a drink from his cup.

Moto's eyes narrowed at him. "No."

"What kind of training room?" Kaily asked.

"Nothing to worry about tonight. "Moto answered, interrupting Shimani's explanation. "We can explore it tomorrow."

"We could now," Shimani said. He moved as if to stand.

Sari placed a restraining hand on Shimani's arm. "Finish your brey. They have plenty of time to explore the caves and talk about training later."

Kaily glanced from Shimani to Sari to Moto. She sensed tension in Moto that hadn't been there moments before now. Clearly, the thought of training her upset him for some reason. She frowned and sipped her nectar.

Silence descended on the group.

After a while of silence, Moto downed his brey. "It's a shame it's getting so late, and you two have to be going."

Kaily glanced at Moto. Apparently, he didn't like the silence. She'd drank about half her nectar.

Sari set her cup aside and stood. She took Shimani's cup from him, and prompted him to stand as well, who clearly was not happy at being thrown out.

Kaily smiled into her cup.

Sari moved to stand near Kaily.

She put her cup aside and stood to accept a hug from Sari.

"Patience," Sari whispered in her ear, and smiled at her when she pulled back. Sari glanced at Moto, and then back to Kaily. She inclined her head.

Kaily returned Sari's smiled and inclined her head in return. "Thank you," she paused, "for our conversation earlier." She watched Moto walk the two to the cave entrance and say his good-byes. She was relieved Sari and Moto were not bonded in truth, but she didn't know what that meant for them. She couldn't imagine it would be an easy road ahead, however it all worked out.

Moto secured the covering over the entrance and turned towards Kaily.

"It's been a day," she said.

Moto smiled. "Yes, it has." He slowly made his way towards her.

His slowness gave Kaily the impression that he was reluctant to be near her. She waited. When he finally stood in front of her, she laid her hands on his chest. "I'm sorry, Moto. I didn't understand what you were trying to tell me earlier."

Moto enfolded her in his warm embrace. "No, I should be the one to apologize. I should have stayed with you at Crystal Lake and had a conversation about the ceremony before it took place. It might have been easier to understand the explanation before witnessing it. My apologies, little one." He inclined his head towards her.

"We need to do something about this communication gap between us." She rested her forehead on his chest. She could hear his heart beating a steady rhythm.

"Agreed." He kissed the top of her head. "You do look beautiful in pants."

Kaily laughed. "But you prefer dresses?"

"Yes," he said.

"I see." She lifted her head and looked into his eyes. "Guess you'll just have to get used to not getting everything you want."

Moto stared down at her. "I can see I have let you spend far too much time in Sari's presence."

"Let?"

Moto shrugged.

"So, did Sari actually know what you did in retaliation when I hit you?"

Moto glanced away.

"You're blushing," Kaily said. "She does, doesn't she? How is that?"

Moto moved to turn away.

Kaily grabbed onto his vest with both her fists and shook her head. "You owe me an explanation." She squeaked when Moto swung her up into his arms and carried her to the pallets.

He carefully lay her down with her back against the soft mat. He stretched out beside her, reclining on his side. He brushed back her hair from her face. His eyes locked with hers. His body slid the length of her as he slid her pants down her legs. He pulled them off and dropped them to the side. "I owe you some attention," he said.

Kaily's pulse jumped, and her breath caught in her chest.

Moto reached for the jar and cloth.

"Ah." Kaily gave a nervous laugh. Her cheeks flamed red, and a heated blush crept up her neck.

"Not what you had in mind?" He smirked.

She opened her legs when his hand traveled up the inside of her thighs, gently coaxing her to relax for him. Her eyes remained locked with his as his mouth followed his hand's path.

Moto's tongue flicked her clit. "Tell me if this hurts you."

Kaily swallowed hard. Her eyes drifted shut from the warmth of his mouth gently suckling her.

Moto lifted his head. "Look at me, Kaily."

She forced her eyes open. Their gazes locked.

Moto smiled at her. He opened the jar and scooped out some of the salve. He pushed her thighs wider apart. He broke their eye contact and glanced down to insert his salve covered fingers inside her.

Kaily arched her back at his touch. Her breath caught in her throat.

His eyes found hers. "Does it hurt?"

Kaily shook her head. Her eyes watered.

Moto smirked. "Liar." He focused his attention of applying the salve to her injury.

Kaily tried not to wince. The spot pained her still, although not as much as when she first woke. The salve helped, but not fast enough. He'd ignited a slow burn inside her that she wanted to sage.

Moto wiped his fingers off on the cloth when he finished. He put the jar and cloth aside. He bent down and kissed the inside of her thighs.

Kaily softly moaned.

Moto stretched his full length beside her. "You like this?" He asked as his finger rubbed her clit in slow circles.

"Yes," she breathlessly replied.

His head slowly lowered towards hers. Their eyes remained locked until the last possible moment just before his mouth covered hers.

His kiss intensified her burning desire. He rubbed her clit faster and harder.

Kaily couldn't help but respond. She moaned and squirmed as she sought more.

"Give yourself to me, Kaily." Moto whispered against her ear.

She pushed against his touch as she tried to obey and let herself go. She wanted nothing more than to feel this moment they shared without thought or any other part of her interfering brain. She wanted to simply let her heart lead her into a moment of bliss.

"That's it," he said. He licked and teased her neck and the line of her jaw.

Ecstatic tremors shook her body as her release drew nigh. She tried to let the blissful euphoria come to her without forcing it.

Moto uttered encouraging words into her ear as he drove her closer to the precipice.

His mouth covered hers at the last moment when she finally tipped over and found release.

Kaily closed her eyes and allowed herself to ride the waves of pleasure.

Moto propped up his head on his hand and traced patterns on the inside of her thigh. "Thank you, little one."

Kaily opened her eyes and smiled at him. She brushed a finger down the side of his cheek. "I should be thanking you."

Moto smiled at her and shook his head.

Tears slipped out of the corners of Kaily's eyes. She didn't wipe at them in hopes that he might not notice, since she lay on her back.

Moto frowned down at her. He brushed the corners of her eyes with his thumbs. "Why are you crying?"

Kaily shrugged and shook her head. She didn't have a satisfactory answer to give him. "As stupid as this sounds, I don't know."

"Did you not enjoy what I did?"

"I did." Kaily touched the side of his face, attempting to offer him comfort. "I just," she shook her head. "I just feel like something is left unfinished." She gave a nervous laugh as the tears continued to slip from her eyes. "I really did enjoy you touching me, truly."

Moto shook his head and placed a finger across her lips. "I understand. It's not the same as me being inside you, claiming you."

Kaily turned her head to the side.

"Look at me."

Kaily hastily brushed away more tears. Her gaze found his.

"I want to claim you more than anything I have ever wanted in my life." He pulled her hand down his abdomen and further to briefly cover the evidence of his own desire for her. He pulled her hand back up, placed a kiss in her palm, and rested it on his chest.

"But?"

"Right now, you need time to heal, and I need to know that you understand what being claimed by me actually means."

Kaily opened her mouth.

Moto laid a finger across her lips. "I'm guessing Sari talked to you about the Kahoali bonding?"

Kaily nodded.

"Consummating seals the bond. There is no going back. Once I make you my bonded mate you are tied to me for the rest of your life and mine. No matter what obstacles we face in the future, we must face them together. You will have to remain by my side, no matter what."

"Sari said a bond can't be undone. I know what it means."

Moto smiled and half laughed. "Knowing and understanding are not the same thing. I need you to understand. Your life will not be the same."

"Neither will yours."

Moto brushed back a strand of her hair. "You have definitely impacted my life. But it's more than you can imagine, I think. For example, do you know the Kahoali live two hundred annual cycles, give or take a few."

Kaily sat up. She frowned. "You're telling me you will live to be two hundred years old?"

Moto nodded.

"How old are you now?"

Moto rolled onto his back and pulled her down to lay halfway on him. "Fifty-five."

"Looking good." She remarked with a bit of sarcasm in her voice.

Moto shook his head at her. "That is what I'm talking about. I'm still quite young among my people."

"Aren't you curious about my age?"

"No." Moto shook his head.

"Twenty-three," she said anyway.

Moto's hand came down hard on her butt. "I said no."

Kaily yelped and laughed.

Moto flipped her to her back and covered her body with his. "You have spent too much time with Shimani too." He caressed the side of her face. His tone turned serious. "When I claim you,

I need to know you fully understand the implications to your life, and mine. Truly understand what it means to be my bonded mate. I won't claim you until that time."

Kaily reached up and cupped the side of his face. "I'm never going to fully understand in the way that you want me to. There is so much about your world that is foreign to me right now. It will take time, but I'll get there, Moto. Some things I have to experience to gain the understanding. For example," her tone echoed what his had been, "twenty-three and fifty-five are very different life stages, and yet when I look at you, I would have said we were in the same life stage."

Moto closed his eyes and took a deep breath.

"Hey, look at me." She tapped his forehead. "What I do know, is that I don't want to be without you." She frowned. The words rang true the moment they left her lips, strange as they were. She still wanted her life back home, but she wanted him too. "I may not understand this bonded mate thing, but I understand that much. I want you in a way that I have never wanted anyone in my life. It hurts me in here," she pointed to her heart, "to think of life without you. It hurt me so much when I thought Sari and you were married." She held up her hand. "I know marriage and bonding are not exactly the same thing. I just know I want you more than you may know, especially after experiencing what I did when I thought I could never have you."

"What if it's not enough, Kaily?" There was a catch in his voice.

"We trust that it is." Her hand traveled down the length of his chest and abdomen. She stopped at the waist band of his pants. "Give yourself to me the way you asked me to." Her eyes remained locked with his as she waited. Conflict flickered in the depths of his eyes, and she didn't understand. Still, she waited.

Moto kept his eyes locked with hers and pushed himself to a standing position. He unclasped his vest and tossed it aside. Next, he removed his boots and dropped them to the side, one by one. Slowly, he slid his trousers down.

Kaily smiled.

Moto shook his head at her. He finished removing his trousers and dropped them with his other discarded clothes. "You understand, I won't claim you this day."

Kaily moved to sit on her knees in front of him. "I know."

"You still need time to properly heal."

Kaily nodded.

"You need time to understand."

Kaily smiled up at him. "I know."

Moto's eyes narrowed as he regarded her.

Kaily inched closer to Moto while still on her knees. She tentatively wrapped her hand at the base of his hard cock. She experimentally licked the tip. Swirling her tongue around the ridge.

Moto groaned. He clutched a handful of her hair at the back of her head. "Open your mouth."

Kaily released him and obeyed.

He pushed past her open lips.

A flicker of fear passed through her as he continued to push his cock deeper into her mouth.

I won't hurt you, little one. His words caressed the inside of her mind.

Kaily's eyes jumped to his. She willed herself to relax and trust him.

That's it. Moto slowly pushed deeper until his tip hit the back of her throat.

Kaily gagged. Her eyes watered.

Moto pulled back enough to stop her reflexive gagging. He caressed the side of her face. *Trust me.*

I'm trying to.

He smiled down at her and cocked his head to the side. *It pleases me that you have not been with another.* He set a slow rhythmic tempo, moving in small increments.

How do you know I haven't been?

Moto gave a small laugh. He shook his head at her. *I know.*

Kaily's eyes glanced away from his. *What about you?*

Moto tsked at her. *You already know the answer. Our society does not work that way.*

Not even for this.

Not even for this. Moto confirmed. *That's not to say that I haven't pleasured myself from time to time.*

Kaily's eyes found his.

Give me your hand.

She complied.

He wrapped her hand around the base of his cock. He covered her hand with his. *Allow your hand to slide with your mouth.* He increased the tempo.

Kaily gagged when he hit the back of her throat. *I'm sorry.*

He caressed the side of her face. *Nothing to be apologetic about. Close your eyes. Open your mind and clear your thoughts. Feel the pleasure you're giving me.*

Kaily's eyes drifted close.

Don't think about the mechanics of it all. Just feel the pleasure. Allow yourself to get lost in the moment.

I trust you, Kaily silently replied.

Moto smiled down at her. He closed his eyes and set a faster tempo. He tried to not hit the back of her throat too often. He increased the pace as his climax built. *That's it. Follow the rhythm.* He gripped her hair tighter with both hands and held her head steady as he moved faster in and out of her moist mouth.

She placed her hand against her lips when his pace was too fast for her to match. She tasted droplets of his essence on her tongue. She moaned at the intimacy of the act. She had no idea it could be like this with a man, but then, he wasn't just any man. She sensed him pulling out of her mouth. She wrapped her free hand around his thigh. Her eyes found his. *Please, don't pull away.*

I'm about to cum, little one.

Please give me all of you.

Moto hesitated for a moment. His eyes searched hers. He nodded once. He moved in and out a couple more times, and then plunged deep into her mouth. He sprayed cum down the back of her throat as he sought release.

Kaily's eyes widened. Her eyes watered. She gagged on the quantity of liquid hitting the back of her throat. She tried to swallow. More slipped out than down.

Moto smiled down at her. "I tried warning you." He massaged the back of her scalp. He gently pulled out of her mouth and handed her a cloth.

Kaily gave a nod. "You did." She laughed. "Sorry." She wiped up the mess she made.

He shook his head. "No apology necessary." He called the waterskin to him and held the tip to her mouth. "This will help."

Kaily took a long drink while Moto held the waterskin for her. She didn't dislike the taste of him, but she wasn't certain she would ever get used to the strange sensation of him cumming in her mouth. "Thank you."

Moto drank his fill and portaled it back to its hook. He pulled Kaily to her feet. "Thank you," he said with a smile and glimmer in his eyes. He pulled her top over her head and tossed it aside with their other garments.

Kaily shivered. She crossed her arms over her chest.

Moto shook his head at her. *Don't be embarrassed with me.* He pulled her arms away from her breasts. He bent, and he gently suckled and kissed each one. *You are beautiful to me.*

She frowned and nodded. A blush crept up her neck to settle in her cheeks.

He lifted her easily into his arms.

She wrapped her arms around his neck.

He kissed her, and then carried her to the shower room. He set her on her feet in the shower stall as he stepped inside. He turned the water on.

Kaily regarded him with a smile.

Moto turned off the water once they both were sufficiently wet. He scooped out some of the scrubbing paste and lathered her up from head to toe. He might have paid a little extra attention to a certain region.

She squirmed and giggled.

When he finished rinsing her off. She scooped out the same amount of scrubbing paste and lathered him up from top to bottom, paying close attention to a certain region in the same way that he had her.

Moto pulled her hand up after he couldn't take any more. "You are going to be the death of me."

Kaily laughed. "I was following your example."

"Hmmm." Moto rinsed off and shut the water off.

"I think you'll survive."

He stepped out of the stall first and grabbed a towel.

Kaily stepped out of the stall. She held her arms up as Moto stepped in close with the towel to dry her off. He wrapped the towel around her and grabbed a second one.

He dried himself off in a quick, aggressive manner. After, he wrapped the towel around his waist. He picked Kaily up to carry her.

"I can walk."

"I can change that." He made his way back to the sleeping pallets where he set Kaily on her feet.

She shivered despite the fire burning in the pit.

"You're cold." He traded her towel for a blanket.

She sat on the pallet.

Moto draped a second blanket around her. "Lay down."

"You know, I have noticed that your world is ruled by females. What is with all these orders?"

He thumped her on the top of her head. "You are not from my world."

She rubbed her head and laughed. "Maybe I should spend more time with Sari to learn how it's done."

Moto squatted in front of her. "Maybe you should just follow my lead."

Kaily smiled at him.

He cleaned up around their sleeping pallets and added more wood to the fire. He waited while the additional logs caught, and the blaze grew bigger. He checked the fastenings of the cover over the cave entrance.

"Shouldn't we get dressed?" Kaily asked when he returned to her.

"No." Moto lay down and pulled her into his arms. He covered them both with additional blankets.

She smiled against his chest and burrowed deeper into his warm embrace. She drew in a deep breath, taking his scent deep into her lungs. "So, how did Sari know?"

Moto groaned. "Aren't you tired?"

"I want to know." She traced patterns on his chest. He remained silent long enough she didn't think he would answer her. Her eyes drifted shut. She would eventually get the story out of him.

"Sari is ten cycles younger, and we used to live in the same Village."

"You've known her a long time." There was a catch in Kaily's voice she didn't want to be there. She couldn't help the spark of jealousy for the time Sari had with Moto. She was jealous of the way Sari knew him. She didn't want to feel that way, but she did.

Moto forced Kaily to look at him. "We have known each other a long time. She is like a sister to me. You have nothing to be jealous about."

Kaily looked away and rested her head back on his chest.

He kissed the top of her head. "As you learn our ways, you'll come to understand there is no one more important to me than you and never will be."

Her head lifted and searched his eyes. Sincerity shown out of their depths. She nodded once and resumed her former position. "What happened? How does she know?"

"Growing up, Sari was always hitting me. As she got older, she got worse about it. Once she came into her powers; she went from smacking to zapping me. She thought it was the funniest thing to do. She was about fourteen when I hit my limit. I can't even remember what started it that day, but we were at Crystal Lake. She zapped me particularly hard. I spun her around and gave her a sound spanking."

"Oh my. What did she do?"

"Honestly, I probably stung her pride more than her bottom that day. She stormed from Crystal Lake and didn't talk to me for a very long time, which was something considering we lived in the same Village."

Kaily snickered. "Wow. Did she stop hitting and zapping you?"

"Oh yes." Moto nodded with a smile. "It's funny now, but not at that time, but she learned the lesson that day. Now, she does it when I deserve it, for the most part."

Kaily shook her head. "Do you often deserve it?" She teased.

Moto flipped Kaily to her back and hovered over her. She searched his eyes as his expression sobered.

"You have turned my world upside down, little one."

"Same for me."

I know. If it means keeping you in my life, I wouldn't change a thing.

Neither would I. Kaily frowned. "Well, except maybe I would find a different hiding place for my stone."

"Talisman, Kaily, not stone." Moto shook his head. "I don't know what possessed you to put your talisman there." He rolled onto his back, taking her with him.

She settled back in her comfortable reclining position. "I won't make that mistake again."

"I would hope not." He slid his fingers up and down her spine. "Thank you for staying."

"You're welcome." She kissed his chin. "Good night, Moto."

"Good night, little one." He reached his hand out towards the lights.

Kaily watched him with fascination as he pulled the energy from each, darkening the interior of the cave. She might not believe, but there was a part of her that wished she did have these powers. She sighed and settled deeper into his arms, content. She closed her eyes and allowed his alluring scent and presence to lull her to sleep.

Chapter Seventeen

Moto woke before Kaily. He eased her off him, careful not to wake her. She'd been through so much and required rest from her recent ordeal. He blamed himself for everything she'd endured since arriving on Ki. All of it would have been avoided, if he'd taken her back the moment he found her with the Agenors. But then, she would not be with him now, on the verge of becoming his bonded mate.

He closed his eyes and rubbed them.

He still didn't know if he was making a mistake. Sari was right. He intended to claim Kaily, even if it meant the bond would not be true, and they couldn't produce offspring. She was a part of him more than he thought possible for anyone, let alone an outsider.

A part of him wished he could go back and somehow handle everything differently. Deep down, he knew, he'd probably make the same choices and the same mistakes.

He also didn't know how he was going to help his people and have her as his bonded mate. He couldn't choose between the two. He wanted both. He needed both.

He glanced at Kaily. He didn't know what it was about her, and it didn't matter. There was an undeniable connection between them. He wouldn't let her go. Strange how before he laid eyes on her, his life didn't feel like there was anything missing. He hadn't been drawn to any Kahoali women in any of the Villages, and he'd made peace with being alone for his life. He never wanted to take a bonded mate just for the sake of taking one. Not that he would have been allowed such a choice.

The Queen would have eventually forced the issue, and he would probably have been forced at some point to take a bonded mate. His people were dwindling into nothingness. He would have been expected to do his duty to avoid such an eventuality.

He moved the embers around and added more wood to the fire. After, he walked to the shower room.

His other issue was the night terrors. True, they had stopped since Kaily arrived, but he couldn't shake the feeling something devastating was coming for his people. He just couldn't figure out what his night terrors were trying to communicate to him. He didn't know what threatened his people. The only threat they faced in the past was from the Druids.

Not even the Queen believed they would attack after so many annual cycles. She and Baridi were the only ones left who were present and survived the Center Village massacre one hundred forty annual cycles ago.

He let the warm water run down his shoulders.

The Zaltys attacked the Outer Villages from time to time, but they didn't have the ability to cause the devastation his night terrors showed him. The Druids did.

He shook his head. All he had was speculation. Without knowing what to expect, he remained lost in how to help prepare his people.

He lathered up and rinsed off.

Until the Queen and Shanees took his night terrors seriously, there was nothing he could really do. The helplessness and uncertainty drove his sanity to the brinks of despair. He was a warrior of action and decisive decisions, usually.

He dried off and dressed. He grabbed more logs to place by the fire pit. He stopped at the sleeping pallets and gazed down at his Kaily.

She was a whole other matter. The destruction at the clearing indicated a great deal of power. Power he could use in defense of his people if he could train her.

He went back to the storage area where he grabbed a pot and supplies for porridge. He stirred water into the pot with the other ingredients and set it on the tripod over the fire.

Training Kaily, he shook his head. He honestly didn't know if he could. He made his way to the back of the cave and entered the domed training room. He closed the door with a wave of his hand. Shimani had conveyed what he'd learned about the room.

He walked the parameter. He brushed his hand along the dark, glass-like, polished surface of the curved wall. The walls shone an obsidian black and in stark contrast to the dull grey walls of the rest of the cave. Moto wondered if the process to shield the room was what caused the walls to look that way. He would love to learn far more than he knew. He'd always suspected there was so much more their powers could do, but no one had ever developed beyond their primary, elemental ability, almost no one. He was an exception.

The walls tingled with energy and hummed with life. The craftsmanship was exquisite.

After a full rotation of the parameter, he moved to the wall opposite the door and leaned against it. He braced a leg against the wall and crossed his arms over his chest. He regarded the room.

Shimani said the room was protected from portals. He couldn't get over what had been created in that room and the cave, for that matter. Truly incredible.

He glanced up at the domed roof. He slid to sit on the floor. In that moment, the magnitude of knowledge lost to his people weighed heavy. He sighed as his mind drifted back to his reason for being in the room. His current dilemma, all wrapped up in a small, feminine, annoyingly stubborn package. His Kaily.

He smiled to himself. What was he going to do with her? If he were honest with himself, he feared her potential. She was emotional, and she doubted herself. Neither were helpful in learning control. How could he teach her control over something she didn't believe in?

He shook his head and sighed.

He stood and walked to the door. He opened it with a wave of his hand.

An intense urgency within Kaily hit him. He frowned. He took a deep breath and focused his mind, resisting the urge to rush into the room. He gave himself a moment to gain control of his emotions. If he couldn't gain control of himself and stop panicking in response to her emotions, he had no business training her.

Moto calmed his fear and reached for her mind to determine what the problem was. It was getting easier to touch her mind and to hear her thoughts the longer they spent in close proximity. He listened to her thoughts.

She searched for something.

His frown deepened as he tried to determine what she so frantically needed.

What she wanted, had not yet fully formed within her thoughts. He stopped himself from reaching out to her telepathically. Whatever she sought, agitated her. The thought of asking him about it embarrassed her.

He smiled and shook his head. He stepped just outside the entrance of the training room. He leaned against the wall in the shadows and watched her. She was a sight to behold, clutching the blanket wrapped around her. Rummaging through stuff while trying to keep herself covered. His smile widened. When he'd seen enough, he stepped into the cave. "Good morning."

Kaily glanced over her shoulder. "Morning." She went back to rummaging through the bags by the chest.

"Can I help you find something?" Moto sauntered to where she tossed items out onto the cave floor. He glanced around at the mess. He refrained from smiling, too much.

"No." Kaily didn't bother looking at him again.

He stopped just behind her. "Are you positive that I can't help you?"

"No, dammit!" Kaily stood up, put a hand on her hip and glared at him. She glanced past him and scanned the cave with her eyes.

Her frustration beat at him. He kept his mind locked with hers, still trying to decipher what had her so irritated. Finally, he was able to determine what she searched for as her mind and eyes kept searching. He casually stepped around Kaily. "I almost forgot. Sari left a bag for you." He grabbed a small bag from a shelf near where she'd searched but out of sight.

Kaily turned to face him. She wore a fierce frown.

"Sari said it contained items you might need and more clothing. Pants, if I know her." A slight, teasing, disapproval tone laced his words.

Kaily shook her head at him. There was a smile almost breaking through at the corner of her lips.

He held the bag towards her.

She accepted it. She set it on the chest and looked inside. Relief flooded her mind and eased her tension and frustration.

Moto nodded to himself.

Kaily walked over to him and stood on tippy toes. "Thank you." She kissed him on the cheek or as close as she could reach.

He pulled her into his arms and kissed her full on the mouth.

She melted into him.

Warmth spread quickly through him at her responsiveness. "Good morning." He repeated as he released her from his embrace.

She blushed, still clutching the blanket to her. "Good morning."

"You can use the shower room while I finish setting out the morning repast." He ran a finger down the side of her face. He turned her towards the shower room and gave her a swat on her butt.

She squeaked and smiled at him over her shoulder.

He waited for her to enter the shower room, and then turned his attention to getting them both food. He stirred the porridge and removed the pot from the fire. He set bowls and cups on the table. His eyes landed on the jar of salve. He frowned. He wasn't certain she would let him put more on her injury considering her current condition. She still required the healing the medicine would provide. He sighed. He picked up the jar and cloth and made his way to the shower room.

Kaily exited the shower stall as he entered the room.

Her eyes landed on the jar and cloth in his hand. She shook her head and backed away. "No!"

Moto stopped in front of her.

She stopped backing up only because her back hit a wall. Heat infused her cheeks and grew hotter with each moment.

"We can do this the easy or hard way." Moto's tone brokered no room for argument. He hoped his tone convinced her how futile fighting him was where her health was concerned.

"Please, no, you don't understand." Kaily looked away.

Moto placed two fingers under her chin and forced her to look at him. *There is nothing you can hide from me.* He silently communicated with her to drive his point home. "You need to heal, little one. This salve will help you do just that."

Kaily heaved a heavy sigh and reluctantly nodded.

"I can make this pleasurable and less embarrassing for you, Kaily, if you let me."

Kaily shook her head. "Just get it over with."

He handed her the jar and cloth. "You could make it more pleasurable for me." His eyes locked with hers as he sent the image of her on her knees in front of him into her mind.

She smacked his chest with the flat of her hand. "No."

Moto smiled down at her. He leaned in close, pressing her firmly against the wall. He placed his hands on each of her hips and pulled her hard against him. "Sari is not here to protect you, little one," he seductively whispered into her ear.

She drew in a sudden intake of breath. "You wouldn't!" She tried to push him with her hands on his chest.

He didn't budge. "Are you sure about that?" He slowly hunkered down. His eyes remained locked with hers. He picked up one of her legs and draped it over his shoulder. He smiled at her.

Her pulse quickened. Her breath caught in her throat.

He caressed the inside of her thigh.

A sigh escaped her lips.

"Jar, please," Moto said as he held out his hand. He waited for her to place the jar in the center of his palm.

His eyes remained on her as he took the lid off and scooped out some of the salve. He replaced the lid and handed the jar back to her. She clearly had issues taking a steady breath. He smiled, pleased. He pressed his thumb against her clit and inserted his salve covered fingers inside her.

Kaily moaned.

He glanced up at her.

Her head rested against the wall with her eyes closed.

His smile widened. He focused on administering the medicine to her injury while giving her pleasure. He didn't stop until he felt the tremors in her body as she climaxed. It wasn't enough to cum hard, but enough to ease the moment between them. He wiped his fingers on the cloth and then wiped her.

Her eyes met his. Her blush deepened.

There is no reason to be embarrassed with me, little one. Not about this or anything.

I can't help it, Kaily said. She ran her fingers through his tiny braids.

How does it feel this morning? He asked instead. Her embarrassment would be something they would work on. Ultimately, she had to come to terms with these moments in her own mind. Other than reassuring her, there was little he could actually do to convince her.

Not as tender as yesterday.

Good. I thought as much. You didn't flinch like last time.

He put the cloth aside. Took the jar from Kaily and set it aside. He put her other leg over his shoulder.

She squealed and grabbed a hold of his braids.

Moto laughed. *Easy, little one. I prefer to keep those attached to my head.* He blew on her sensitive place.

Stop, please.

Moto hesitated and gazed into her eyes. He sensed her mortified embarrassment as the image of what he wanted passed through her mind. "I can be patient." Her womanly cycle was too much for her to handle with him, for now. He placed her feet back on the ground and stood.

She snorted. "Never going to happen." She slapped his chest as if making a point.

Moto shook his head at her. He spun her around and gave her two firm swats. He rubbed both cheeks to lessen the sting.

"Oww!" Kaily raised her hand.

"Do not!" He grabbed her hand. "I have warned you about hitting me," he said, his tone seriously harsh. He held her hand until he sensed the fight from her draining. He dropped her hand and wrapped a towel around her. "I don't like to be hit and there are consequences should you persist in ignoring my warnings."

Kaily bent her head. "I'm sorry."

Moto lifted her chin.

Tears swam in her eyes.

He stamped down his own emotional response at causing her emotional pain. "The correct phrasing is my apologies, as you have shown on occasion that you are aware. Please apologize properly when in the wrong. For the record, I have not spanked you for real, but I will if you persist in pushing me. Understood?"

Kaily nodded. "My apologies."

He wrapped his arms around her and drew her close. "Apology accepted." He rubbed her back.

I don't know why I keep doing that. I didn't mean any harm by it.

Moto glanced up at the ceiling. He hated hurting her, physically or emotionally. *I just need you to understand that such actions are disrespectful. I know you haven't been among us,* he paused and sighed, *around me enough to understand the Kahoali or my way.* He pulled back just enough from her to kiss her. He wiped away her stray tears from her cheeks. He knew his swat didn't hurt her enough to make her cry, but he embarrassed her, again. "Get dressed, then we'll eat. The porridge is ready." He left the shower room to give her privacy.

He dished out the porridge and filled the cups while he waited for Kaily to dress. There were times she seemed so fragile. She'd been so dejected by his actions. He knew her hurt emotions came from a lack of understanding and was a prime example of why he was reluctant to bond with her. She didn't understand their ways.

Kaily quietly entered the room and sat at the table.

He didn't know if he could adequately explain their ways to her, but he had to try. "You know," he began as he sat next to her, "it's not one sided."

Kaily picked up her spoon and scooped out a bite of the porridge. "What's not one sided?"

"Punishment." He took a bite of his porridge.

How so?

"Mild punishment," he refrained from saying 'like what I just gave you,' "is handled within the family unit. More egregious offenses are handled through the leadership of the Villages and if severe enough, the Queen.

Kaily made a disdainful sound. "So, you abuse your children."

Moto gave her a stern glare. "No."

Her eyes remained locked with his.

"Spankings are given sparingly and only when they fit the offense. If a parent were found to be overly harsh with their children, it would be considered a crime, and they would be duly punished in like manner."

She frowned. "Spanked? Really?"

Moto nodded. "In a manner of speaking."

Kaily shook her head. Her frown deepened. "A bit barbaric, don't you think?"

Moto took a deep breath. "How are offenses punished on your world?"

"A trial to determine guilt, and jail time if found guilty," she said with a shrug.

As she spoke, he discerned images from her mind of metal cages. "This jail is a cage? You put your people in tiny cages?"

She nodded.

"You call that civilized?"

Kaily looked down at her porridge. "Not the way you say it."

Moto let the conversation drop and finished his morning repast.

She finished hers. "Thank you. That was delicious." She handed him her bowl.

"You like my cooking better than Shimani's, right?" He accepted the bowl and put both aside. He much preferred the teasing.

Kaily's eyes jumped to his and narrowed. "There is not a great way to answer that."

Moto laughed. "The correct answer is, yes, yes I do."

Kaily shook her head. "And then you tell him, and I don't hear the end of it."

"Good point." He started cleaning up.

She stared into her cup. "You spank your adults? In truth?"

He heard curiosity and morbidity in her words. He could tell she was not going to be appeased by a short and simple explanation. He sat back down by her when he finished putting everything away from morning repast. "Seldom, but yes with a special strap."

"Does the number of hits depend on the crime?" She tilted her head.

"No, it's about the process of accepting responsibility for one's actions, being repentant, and letting go. You really want to talk about this?" He took her hands in his.

"Not if you don't."

He sensed disappointment in her at the thought of not getting answers. He took a deep breath. "It isn't a pleasant subject to delve into, but it is important for you to learn everything about being Kahoali."

She caressed the side of his face. "It is important. I want to understand, but only if you're okay talking about it."

He leaned forward and kissed her. "If it is within the family unit, the spanking is with the hand, and only occasionally with a strap. The number of times depends on the necessity to make a point about the egregious behavior, but never out of anger. If the punishment is administered at the direction of the Shanees or the Queen it is always with a strap, and always until the individual is repentant and let's go of any stubbornness they might be harboring. Kahoali are natural empaths, so we can sense when the individual being punished has truly accepted their responsibility and are repentant for what they did. It ensures that offenses are not repeated." He rubbed the deep crease between her brows. *Peace, little one, there is a purpose behind the process of administering punishment.*

"If you say so," Kaily said. "I just don't see what it could be."

He tilted his head to the side. "How high would you say crime is on your world?"

"High." Kaily glanced at Moto as she answered. "I didn't see anything like a jail in your village, other than the hut I woke up in. Is that what it's for?"

Moto shook his head. "It's a holding hut, but not for anything long term. We don't have anything like these jails of yours. Individuals make mistakes." He shrugged. "We punish them and let it go. They get on with their lives without any of it being held against them. Each person is an important part of our lives within each Village."

"What about those that cause severe harm to others?"

Moto winced at the images passing through her mind. He closed his eyes and pulled her onto his lap. "No Kahoali would ever consider doing any of those things in your mind to one another."

"I can't imagine a place that doesn't have someone somewhere causing harm to others. Small towns have less, but still some." She shook her head.

"And you want to go back to that world?" He rubbed his hand up and down her back.

It's my home.

His hand stilled on her back as he caught a brief note of longing. *I understand.* Home she knew. He couldn't imagine living in her kind of world, but he understood the longing for home and what was familiar.

Have you ever been, she hesitated. Even telepathically she couldn't give voice to her question.

"It's time to begin your training." Moto set her off his lap and stood. He helped her to her feet.

"Have you?" She touched his arm to stay his movement. A frown crossed her features.

Moto nodded.

"When? Why?"

Moto winced. *It doesn't matter, little one.*

Kaily stared into his eyes for a long time. Her frown deepened. *Was it recent? I can see it in your mind.*

Silence settled between them.

She continued to gaze into his eyes as if she saw to the center of his being.

He looked away. Shame infused his emotions that she might see the truth in his mind.

Because of me, she quietly said. "I am so sorry." She laid a hand on his chest.

He took her hand and brought it to his mouth. He placed a kiss on her palm. He pulled her close, unable to meet her compassionate gaze. The need to hold her close to his heart overwhelmed him. *It doesn't matter.*

It was during those three days you shut me out of your mind, wasn't it? She persisted.

Moto shook his head. *The day of the ceremony.*

Because I mentioned you by name to Baridi. She touched his face. "Oh, Moto, I,"

He shook his head. "Please, let it go."

"That's why you don't like to be smacked," she said.

Part of it, he said. He hated facing this with her. He demanded she overcome her embarrassment with him. He could do no less with her. *I was quite the unruly child growing up. This time was different.* He wanted to explain but couldn't find the right words.

Kaily tilted her head and held his gaze. "It's okay. I don't need a full explanation. I am so sorry. I would never want to be the cause of such pain for you."

Moto shook his head. "You are not to blame for what happened, Kaily. Please don't ever blame yourself for my actions. I never wanted you to know about this."

"Come here," she said, pulling or trying to pull his head towards her.

He smiled and gave her what she wanted.

She kissed him full on the mouth.

He tightened his arms around her and deepened their kiss. How could he have lived without her for so long? He set her on her feet and rested his forehead against hers. "Let's see if we can get you trained."

"I'm not feeling that great." She placed a hand on her lower abdomen.

He frowned. "Where's the bag Sari brought you?"

"I left it in the shower room. Why?"

"If I know Sari, she thought of what you would need for," he didn't finish his thought. His Kaily was getting redder with each word he spoke. "Sit, I'll be right back."

She sat on a cushion at the table. Her gaze followed him.

He returned with a small pouch in his hand. He handed it to her. "Put one of those under your tongue to dissolve. It works fairly fast for Sari. Take one as needed but not more than four in a single day."

Kaily opened the pouch and peered inside. She pulled out what looked to her like a small cocoa bean. She held it up with a frown. "What does it taste like?"

He laughed and shrugged. "How would I know? I don't need those, and I never asked Sari."

With a frown, she licked it. "Not great, that's what it tastes like."

"Probably why it goes under the tongue and not on it." Moto kept from laughing, but he wasn't able to prevent amusement from infusing his words.

Kaily stuck her tongue out at him. She put the offensive object under her tongue.

He helped her to her feet. "I can find a better use for your tongue, little one."

She blushed.

Moto smiled. He kept her hand in his and walked her to the back of the cave. He sensed her reluctance. He stopped at the entrance of the hallway that led to the training room. He turned to face Kaily. "Don't worry. We're going to take it easy."

Kaily smiled at him but remained silent.

He led her to the training room. He sensed panic rising inside her. He frowned. Once inside he closed the door with a wave of his hand. *It's okay, little one. Relax.* He sent waves of reassurance into her mind. He stopped in the middle of the room and pulled her into his arms. "It's okay," he repeated aloud.

Kaily closed her eyes and rested her head against his chest.

Moto rubbed her back and continued to push reassurances into her mind. He tried soothing her with reassuring words.

Her breathing became short intakes of breath. A cloud of panic rose within her mind.

He couldn't push back her growing fear.

Her heart thumped faster. She lifted terror filled eyes to his. She shook her head back and forth. "I'm sorry, Moto. I can't do this." She turned in his arms towards where the door should have been. "Where's the opening?"

He turned her back around to face him. "Kaily, look at me! You're safe with me."

Kaily continued to shake her head. "No, no, no, no, no." Her words became a mantra within her own mind.

He sensed her mind closing off to him.

She struggled to pull out of his arms.

He let her go, only to keep her from hurting herself. He tried to stay in her mind. With each passing moment, more of her mind closed off to him. He sensed panic and something else in her mind he couldn't quite decipher. He caught vague images passing through her thoughts. Then, her mind slammed shut.

Her eyes closed, she repeated one word, no.

He opened the entrance with a wave of his hand. He fought to push back his own rising panic. He helplessly watched her. She stood stock still in the middle of the room. Neither aware of his presence or the open doorway. He reached out to touch her but stopped midair. A warning of some sort registered in the back of his mind, telling him not to touch her. "Kaily!" He called her name to get her attention.

She turned towards his voice. Her eyes seemed clouded, unfocused.

"The door is open, Kaily." He moved closer to her but refrained from touching her. "Look at the door! It's open!"

She started shaking her head again and repeating no.

Moto cursed. He grabbed Kaily, despite the warning in the back of his mind. "Look at me!"

She shook her head. Her eyes closed shut. "Open your eyes!"

She shook her head. She would have dropped to the floor, if not for his firm hold on her.

"Kaily! Look at me! Please, Kaily, look at me!" He lowered her to the floor and sat beside her. He kept his hand on her back.

She curled into a tight ball and covered her head with her arms. "No," she begged, "please don't hurt me."

Moto's heart broke at the anguish in her voice. He cursed again. He struggled to pick her up. "Kaily, please," he pleaded, "open your eyes and look at me." When he finally cradled her in his arms, he carried her out of the room. He regarded the pallets as he fought to keep a hold of her. She still held tight to her curled ball form. He discarded the pallets. He needed something that would shock her out of her own mind. He hurried outside the cave with her. "KAILY!" He yelled. "Open your eyes! You're safe. I promise, you're safe." Helplessness overwhelmed him. He sat heavily on the ground, cradling her as best as he could. He rocked her back and forth.

She stirred in his arms.

"That's it, little one. Look around. You're outside," he said in as gentle a voice as his emotions would allow. He came close to being too overwhelmed by his own fear and panic.

She lifted her head and opened her eyes. She glanced around. A sob escaped her. She turned in his arms and wrapped her arms around his neck. She buried her face in the crook of his neck and wept.

He continued to rock her in his arms as sobs wracked her body. He'd never heard such pain wrenching sounds in his life. Her pain brought tears to his own eyes. He let them fall unchecked.

Finally, her tears lessened and became hiccups.

Moto wiped his tears away. He lifted her face from where she'd buried it. Their gazes locked. "I would never hurt you, Kaily."

She tried to look away.

He shook his head and held her face firmly towards his. "Don't, please, don't pull away from me. What happened?"

She shrugged. "I don't like closed in places."

Moto shook his head. "That was not just about closed in places, Kaily. What happened?"

She shook her head. "I don't know. I just," she shrugged, "I don't know what happened."

Moto sighed and let her lay her head back on his shoulder. "It's alright." He gently rubbed her back, attempting to soothe her. "We'll go back later."

Kaily lifted her head and adamantly shook it.

"The room is the best place for training."

She shook her head more vigorously.

"Peace, little one," Moto said. "We won't start there."

Relief emanated from her. "Okay."

Moto pressed her head back down. He rubbed her back as he considered his options. The room was the best place to train her, but if she couldn't stand to be in the room? He sighed. "We will use the clearing by the pool for training. Maybe starting there with defense training first will help you learn control." He nodded as he said it. He needed her trust and what control he could teach her.

Kaily nodded her agreement.

Moto uttered several curses as he stood in the middle of the clearing, clenching his fists. "Get up!" He ordered for the third time.

"NO!" Kaily lay on her back at the edge of the clearing by the pools.

Moto glared. He stretched his neck, staring at his unwilling pupil.

She'd plopped herself where she lay, not long after their training sessions started that morning. He'd worked with her for a full seven days and she still responded to his advances as if she'd learned nothing! She possessed absolutely no control over her emotional outbursts. He couldn't reach into her mind as easily anymore. A cloud descended within her mind in the training room that day that he still couldn't break through.

"GET UP!" He advanced on her. She was gaining her feet rather she wanted to or not. He reached down to haul her up himself.

Kaily pushed her hands out in front of her as if she wanted to push him away.

Moto's feet left the ground as he flew backwards away from her. He landed with a hard thud on the far end of the clearing and precariously close to the edge of the cliff. He cursed and worked to gain control of his own anger. Responding in kind wouldn't help either one of them. He struggled to ignore the rising fear inside him. His worst fears manifesting right before his eyes. Her abilities were surfacing before she learned any kind of control.

He stood and dusted himself off. He took several calming breaths. "Get up, Kaily." He kept his tone quiet, less harsh. His temper was not as well contained as he would have preferred. Not even Shimani tested his patience the way she did.

Kaily sat up. "I'm tired."

"We just began." Moto moved towards her.

Kaily stood. She put her hands on her hips. "I. Said. I'm. TIRED!"

Moto was sent flying a second time with greater force than the first. He grabbed the nearest tree with his own power to keep from going over the edge. When he gained solid ground, he erected a shield to absorb her energy and kept it in place, in case she attempted to throw him a third time. What frightened him most was he hadn't sensed her gathering any energy let alone what it would take to toss him around like she had.

His hand strayed to his inside pocket vest where the pouch with her talisman was located. Sari assured him as long as the talisman remained secured inside, Kaily wouldn't be able to access the energy of Ki. He didn't sense any energy surrounding the pouch or the talisman inside. The pouch barely allowed him to sense the presence of her talisman, so, he knew the damping properties of the pouch was working.

"ENOUGH!" Moto rushed towards her fast in an attempt to reach her before she could react.

Kaily's hands pushed at him.

Energy hit him, but he was prepared. He focused his thoughts and drained the energy from her while pushing on her with the energy of his shield. He used enough force to drive her to her knees. When the energy drained from her, he knelt beside her and clasped her hands in his. "I said enough." He only barely managed to keep his tone even.

"I'm tired, Moto." Kaily raised defeated eyes towards him.

Moto closed his eyes. "I know." He sat next to he and pulled her reluctant self into his lap. "Obviously, this," he glanced around the clearing and waved his hand for emphasis, "isn't working." He pushed her head down to rest on his shoulder. He rubbed her back. He sighed. "I'm out of ideas." He relaxed when he sensed her resistance fade.

"I'm tired, Moto," she said again. "I don't understand what's happening to me and I don't like the way it's making me feel."

"What's happening to you is nothing to fear, Kaily."

"I didn't say I was afraid."

He lifted her face, so her eyes gazed into his. He wiped the corners of her eyes. "I feel fear emanating from you, little one. You are afraid of what you are becoming and that is part of the problem. Your fear is making you fight it and me. Your fear is hindering your ability to learn control over what is happening to you."

Kaily shook her head. "It feels like it is consuming me. I was not meant to have these abilities or power or whatever else you want to call it. Can't you take them away?"

The pain in her plea pierced his heart. Moto shook his head. "No, little one. I cannot. I can help you learn control if you'll let me. Control will help you feel less consumed by your powers. But you have to trust me as you once did."

"I trust you."

"No, you don't. You stopped trusting me," he shook his head, "actually, I don't know when. You once showed me blind trust on the day I rescued you from the Agenors, but it is gone now."

Kaily lay her head back on his shoulder and stared at the pool.

Moto gently rocked her back and forth as much to soothe her as himself. He pondered what to do with her. He wasn't concerned with her hearing his thoughts. She no longer reached for his mind, and he couldn't connect with hers enough to communicate telepathically. It was as if something blocked their connection, but he couldn't discern the source. He had to find a way to reach her, and somehow gain the trust he required from her.

With her abilities surfacing, he had no choice. He had to take her back to the training room. She was too dangerous to train out in the open. He didn't know how he was going to make that happen.

Kaily pulled out of his arms and lap.

He let her. Moto had intended to consummate their bonding when her womanly cycle ended, but she no longer wanted him touching her intimately. He would not force his will on her, not in that way. For her health and safety, he absolutely would force his will on her. But for the bonding, she had to come to him willing as a true bonded mate would. Something changed in that training room. He didn't know what.

He glanced unwillingly up at the world looming over their heads. He caught her eyes drifting to the world too many times for his own comfort. The fading cycle had begun which meant the world would dim from sight soon. Unfortunately, he felt its pull and an emotion almost like sorrow as it faded. Never in all his cycles of life had he ever experienced such emotions towards that cursed world.

He pulled her back towards him and rested his chin on top of her head. "If only you were Kahoali," he said aloud.

"I wish you would stop saying that." She turned her head to look him in the eyes.

"It's true, little one. I wish you were. It would make everything so much easier. You would have grown up understanding what was happening to you. None of this would be necessary. You would have learned control long before your abilities emerged."

Kaily shook her head and glanced away. "If you would stop treating me like I'm not Kahoali, maybe I would understand and then maybe all this," she stood and waved her hand around the clearing, "would have been easier." She glared down at him.

He stood and loomed over her. "You want to be treated like a Kahoali woman?"

"Yes!"

"Fine!" He picked her up and tossed her in the pool clothes and all.

She surfaced sputtering and spitting out water. "What was that for?"

"That was for throwing me the first time." He stood at the edge of the pool; fists clenched.

She splashed water at him. "Jerk!"

He watched as she tried to pull herself out of the pool. The water-logged clothes and boots, plus her exhaustion made the task nearly impossible. Guilt warred with his amusement. He shook his head. "Here let me help you out." Moto held out his hand towards her.

Kaily glared up at him. She slowly took his hand.

He sensed too late the surge of energy.

She pulled hard on his hand and gave him an energy push.

Moto was sent sprawling into the pool. He surfaced ready to retaliate.

She clung to the side of the pool, laughing.

A smile crossed his lips. He closed the distance between them. "Better control. I'll give you that one as a reward." He brushed her wet hair back from her face. "What am I going to do with you?"

"Love me," she said. "I'm scared, Moto."

Her words caught him off guard. He drew her into his arms. "Kaily, I feel so much more than mere love for you."

"Then make love to me." Her hands moved to the clasp of his trousers. "Please."

Moto stayed her efforts. "You're not ready to be my bonded mate, and I'm at the end of my control over my desires to make you so and curse the consequences. So, I propose we get dried off, have a repast and pass an enjoyable day in each other's company."

She gave him a sad smile and nodded.

Moto helped her out of the pool, and then pulled himself out. They walked back to the cave, each lost in their own thoughts.

Chapter Eighteen

Kaily woke from another night fraught with nightmares. Ever since entering that damn training room with Moto, she'd been plagued with nightmares. If those weren't bad enough, Moto did his damnedest to pound her into the ground. She sighed. She knew he was only trying to help her, although how drilling her to extinction was going to help, she had no idea. She took a deep breath.

She turned on her side, moving slowly to keep from waking Moto. She thought he had woken earlier, so she was surprised to find him still on the sleeping pallets with her. She smiled to herself as she watched him sleep. She resisted touching him. Her mind turned inward.

This was the first morning she remembered her nightmare. The other mornings, the details faded too quickly for her to comprehend the content. She didn't know why this one stuck. It certainly wasn't by her choice. She would just as well have it fade like the others. The nightmare terrified her and perhaps she couldn't remember more of them because of the terror.

She'd tried reaching for Moto in her mind, but his mind remained closed to her. She didn't know what to do to reach him. She needed him in her mind for comfort, but mentally he felt out of reach. Their telepathic abilities weren't working now, although she hesitated to talk to him about it. If he didn't want her in his mind, she was not going to force the issue. He must have his reasons for keeping her out. She sighed and wiped away a stray tear. She didn't know what she did to make him shut her out.

She rolled to her back and stared up at the ceiling. The nightmare, she shook her head. The events seemed so real. She couldn't remember a time when a nightmare impacted her so concretely as this one. She was a small child, huddled in a tight ball, begging for mercy from a cloaked figure standing over her. He just kept hitting her with, she shook her head again. In the nightmare, she was not only that small child but also the observer. From the observer's perspective, he threw blue energy balls at the child, hitting repeatedly. His mouth moved, but even awake, she couldn't bring his words to the forefront of her mind enough to understand what he uttered.

The harder the child cried and begged for him to stop, the harder he hit her. Kaily wiped at her tears. She couldn't help that poor child. She kept telling herself it was just a dream. It wasn't real.

She sat up. She glanced at Moto.

She needed him to finish whatever would seal the bond between them. He refused. He kept pushing her away. True, she kept him at a distance while on her monthly cycle, but she thought when it was over, he might finish what they'd started. She wiped more tears away.

She reached her hand out and stopped. She shook her head and reached her hand out again. She brushed his braids back from his face. She moved to lay next to him with her head on his shoulder. It was how they fell asleep each night. He gathered her in his arms every night, so why couldn't he finish bonding? She thought maybe if they bonded, the telepathy would come back. Maybe she would not feel so alone and lost.

She traced patterns on his chest. Her hand drifted lower. She slept in a night dress, but he slept naked. She was not as comfortable with her own nakedness as he was his. She sighed and more tears fell.

Moto opened his eyes.

Her gaze gravitated to his.

He reached up and brushed her hair from her face. "Why so sad this morning, little one?"

She gave a half shrug and looked away. She wasn't certain how to put to words the magnitude of emotions swimming inside her. Sadness was just one of them.

"Kaily, look at me."

She looked up at him. "I don't know where to begin." She wanted to talk to him about her nightmares, but the words lodged in her throat. She couldn't give voice to those, not yet. She wanted to talk to him about the bonding, but he shut her down when she tried.

He sat up.

Kaily sat up with him.

Moto glanced towards the dying fire and table. "Did you mean what you said yesterday about wanting to be treated as a Kahoali?" His gaze settled on her.

Kaily frowned. Her heart skipped a beat. There was something in his tone that made her reluctant to answer his question. "Why?"

"Just answer the question, Kaily." His tone held so much frustration.

She took a deep breath and let it out. "Yes," she hesitantly replied.

He moved to kneel in front of her. He touched his forehead to hers and held her head between his hands. "I want to take you as my bonded mate."

She closed her eyes, and her heart skipped another beat. "I would like that."

He raised his head and dropped his hands to her shoulders.

Her eyes locked with his. His hands on her shoulders were gentle, but there was something in his eyes that she couldn't decipher. She wished she could touch his mind. "What is it?"

Moto took a deep breath. "I have to know that you understand what being my bonded mate would mean."

She opened her mouth.

He placed a finger across her lips. He gave her a chaste kiss where his finger had been. "I have to know that you will accept the Kahoali way." He paused. "My way."

"I do." She touched his cheek. "I do. I want this as much as you do. I may not know everything I need to know, but I trust what we have and that is enough to get us through the rest."

Moto laughed and shook his head. There was no amusement in his laughter. "I hope so. I really hope so." He pulled her in close and crushed her hard against him.

Kaily melted into his arms and gave way to his possession of her mouth as his tongue slipped in and out. Passionate heat sprung up between them. Moisture pooled between her legs. She wrapped her arms around his neck, pulling him closer, not that they could get much closer than they already were. She wanted to lay back and give him whatever he wanted.

He slowed their passionate kiss and began to pull apart.

Kaily searched his eyes for answers as she sat back on her heels. Damn their failed telepathy!

Moto took another deep breath.

Her eyes remained locked, captive of his intense gaze.

"In the way of the Kahoali, I demand retribution for the offense against me."

Kaily's heart sank. Her pulse beat faster. "What?" Fear and anger rose to the surface.

His gaze left hers and shifted towards the table and the contents on it.

Kaily pushed to her feet and slowly walked to the table. She glanced over her shoulder at him a few times as she made her way. A lump formed in the pit of her stomach as she stared down at the contents on top of the flat stone. Heat crept into her neck and settled in her cheeks. She frowned.

Moto stood and walked over to stand beside her by the table.

She glanced from him to the items laid out. There was a large pillow of sorts, a pot with a ladle, and what looked like a leather strap. She knew from her brief time with the Kahoali that it wasn't actual leather. She lifted angry eyes to meet his. "What do you intend to do with those?" She asked, pointing at the items.

"You said you wanted to be treated like a Kahoali."

"I don't care what I said." She took a deep breath. "What do you intend to do with those?" She clenched her jaw.

Moto glanced at the items on the table and back to her. "I think you know the answer to that question."

She turned around and clenched her fists. She stared at the entrance. She took a deep breath and forced herself to turn back to face him. "Why?"

"You know why, Kaily." Moto took a step towards her.

Kaily stepped back, one step back. She refused to be afraid of this man in front of her. But on the heels of her nightmare, a part of her couldn't help the fear inside her. "Pretend that I don't," she said. "Because while I have an idea what prompted this." She stabbed a finger at the items. "I don't understand. Why would you want to do that to me?" She took a deep breath.

He took a few deep breaths himself. "Because," he said, "you used your abilities in anger and threw me."

"IT was an ACCIDENT!" Her fingernails bit into her palms. She began to tremble with anger. She felt any control she might have over her temper slipping.

"The first time, yes." Moto nodded. "But the second time was not. And certainly not the third attempt. If I hadn't used my own powers to stop you, you would have thrown me off the cliff, BECAUSE YOU LOST CONTROL." He closed his eyes and took several calming breaths. He stepped back and turned away from her for a moment. He turned back to face Kaily.

She shook her head and backed away. "NO! I'm not going to submit to that." She stabbed an angry finger at the table. "NO!" She glared at him. She turned and ran to the shower room as she hastily wiped at her hot, angry tears burning her eyes.

"GET BACK OUT HERE!"

"NO!" Kaily left the shower room and grabbed a fresh set of clothes on the shelves that he stashed stuff on. "NEVER!"

Moto didn't respond. He clenched his fists and stared after her as she went back into the shower room.

Kaily quickly dressed. Her heart beat wildly in her chest. She ran her fingers through her hair and splashed cool water on her face. She stood at the entrance to the shower room and listened. She didn't hear anything. The cave had grown so quiet she wasn't positive he still remained within it. She half expected him to charge into the shower room after her. She closed her eyes and rested her head against the cold stone wall.

She took a deep breath and let out a heavy sigh. He'd been right about her almost throwing him off the cliff. She hadn't meant to. She didn't have control. She'd just been so angry at him, and he kept pushing her. She shook her head. She hadn't meant to. She stood up straight, took a deep breath, and stepped out of the shower room.

"Finished?" Moto asked in a deceptively quiet voice.

Kaily squealed.

He leaned against the wall with his arms crossed over his chest.

She could tell from the harsh set of his jaw that he was extremely angry with her. It probably was a good thing she couldn't reach into his mind.

She crossed her arms and held his harsh glare. She refrained from answering, afraid she might not be able to control her retort. She forced herself to stand her ground with this man. A difficulty under his hot gaze.

He pushed himself off the wall with a curse and turned his glare towards the cave entrance.

Kaily frowned and turned towards the same direction as he had.

Shimani and Sari stepped into the cave. They both glanced from her to Moto, and then at each other.

Kaily pushed past and ran out of the cave. She heard Sari's voice, but she didn't stick around to hear what the conversation was about. She was too mortified for them to witness what was happening between her and Moto. She ran haphazardly down the narrow path towards the pools.

She stomped around the clearing muttering and cursing Moto's stupidity. Her anger kept building. She couldn't get a handle on it. She felt her anger growing stronger, and she felt something else. She stopped in the middle of the clearing and screamed. She felt heat building in her hands. She held her hand up and without thought flung it forward. She stared at the tree that burst into flames.

"Feel better?" Sari asked from behind her.

"No." Kaily glared at her over her shoulder. She glanced back at the burning tree.

Sari touched Kaily's back as she passed her.

Kaily felt her anger drain away and something else too.

Sari walked past Kaily towards the burning tree. She held her hands up and built something almost invisible.

Kaily could see a faint shimmering ball between Sari's hands.

Sari threw it at the burning tree. The shimmer surrounded the flames and snuffed them out. She turned back to Kaily. "Ready to talk?"

Kaily sat on the ground with a heavy sigh. "There's nothing to talk about."

"Nothing? Not even what happened between you and Moto?" She sat on the ground beside Kaily and glanced at her sideways.

"No." Kaily glanced at Sari. "I'm sure Moto filled you in on the details." A tear slipped out of her eyes. She hastily brushed them away.

"His explanation was light on details. I'm interested in your side of what happened."

Kaily turned her head to look at Sari. "Why?"

"Maybe I can help." Sari shifted her position, so she faced Kaily.

Kaily shook her head. "Unless you can convince him to apologize for being a complete Jackass, there is nothing you can do." She attempted to calm her emotions.

Sari placed a gentle hand on Kaily's shoulder. "This anger isn't going to help either of you."

Kaily's eyes met Sari's. She sighed. "It was an accident."

"That's what Moto said." Sari took Kaily's hands in hers. "I know Moto, he would not ask for retribution lightly or without a very good reason. What happened?"

Kaily frowned. "He didn't tell you what happened?"

Sari gave her a smile. "Only that you lost control and accidentally sent him flying." She laughed. "I would have liked to see that, by the way."

Kaily smiled, shook her head, and looked away. "It wasn't a pretty picture. And he pretty much told you what happened."

Sari shrugged. "Technically, but what about the rest of it. Why did it happen?"

"I didn't mean to, Sari." She turned watery eyes towards her. "I was just so angry at him. He kept pushing me and pushing me. He just wouldn't stop. All I wanted was for him to leave me alone. I was tired." She shook her head.

"What was he pushing you to do?"

"Training!" She gave an exasperated sigh. "He said that if I could learn control through learning self-defense that it would be easier for me in the training room." She answered in a mocking voice. "He wouldn't let up. I was tired."

"He can be intense when it comes to combat training." Sari held Kaily's gaze. "I also know Moto wouldn't push you so hard if he didn't think it was important, and he wouldn't ask for retribution for an accident. What else happened?"

Kaily looked away. "I told you, it's because I threw him." She glanced back at Sari.

Sari's eyes narrowed. "How many times did you throw him?"

Kaily glanced down at her hands clasped in her lap. "Three times, four if you count the push into the pool. Well, maybe twice, the third time he did something to keep from flying. And the fourth time doesn't count because he threw me in first."

"I see."

Kaily's gaze drifted to Sari's.

She smiled and shook her head. "Honestly, I'm surprised he didn't beat your ass at that time." She frowned. "So, why did he wait until today to ask for retribution?"

Kaily shrugged.

Sari's features sobered. "You could have really hurt him if you'd tossed him over the cliff."

"I know." She lowered her eyes. "I didn't ask for these powers, Sari." She looked back at her. "Can you take them from me?"

Sari touched Kaily's arm and sighed. "No. I can't."

She sighed.

"Kaily, why did he wait until today? There has to be more to his request."

She shrugged.

"What else did you talk about yesterday?"

"His reluctance to bond with me."

"And," Sari prompted.

Kaily shook her head and shrugged. "He said he wished I was Kahoali, and I said I wished he would stop treating me like an outsider and it went downhill from there."

"I see." Sari exhaled. "So, you asked to be treated like a Kahoali, and now he is, and you're angry at him for it."

Kaily frowned and glanced back at Sari. "Doesn't sound right, when you put it that way."

Sari smiled. "I imagine not." She took a deep breath. "The thing is, Kaily, you can't have it both ways. You accept his reluctance to finalize the bond with you because you are not Kahoali, or you submit to our ways."

Kaily glanced at the pools. "I don't know if I can."

"Then you have much to think about." Sari touched Kaily's shoulder. "You have powers now. You have to accept responsibility for your actions and understand that you can hurt someone without learning control."

"I know," Kaily said. She glanced at Sari. "You think Moto is right, don't you?"

Sari didn't answer her right away. She glanced at the fading world above their heads, and then back to Kaily. "It is our way. You have to decide if you really want to be a part of us."

Kaily wiped at the sudden tears in her eyes. "It's not my way." She glanced up at the planet.

"That's the crux of the problem, isn't it?"

Kaily glanced back at Sari.

Sari gave her a sad smile. "Moto is not an easy man to live with. He is far too emotional for a Kahoali male and has never been comfortable with our matriarchal structure."

Kaily swallowed hard. "He told me what happened before the ceremony to him. His punishment."

Sari looked away. "That one was particularly harder on him than the past times." She glanced back at Kaily. "Shimani and I do what we can to keep him out of trouble, but," she shrugged and gave a short laugh. "Our efforts have failed lately."

"Because of me."

"Leave us!" Moto startled them both.

Sari glanced from Kaily to Moto. She accepted his offered hand to help her to her feet.

Kaily glanced at him, and then looked away.

Sari leaned into him and whispered something in his ear.

Kaily couldn't hear the words enough to make them out.

Moto nodded in response. He watched Sari go up the path towards the cave. He turned his attention back to Kaily. "Stand up!"

Kaily narrowed her eyes up at him. "Why?"

"I'm in no mood to be questioned by you. Nor do I want to argue." He held his hand out towards her as he had Sari. "Trust me."

Kaily stared at his hand for a moment. She sighed and took his hand.

He helped her to her feet. He wrapped his arm around her waist.

She looked into his eyes. Even in his anger, he was gentle with her. Well, this time.

Moto turned away, breaking their eye contact. He held up his hand.

Kaily noticed for the first time, a bag slung across his back.

He glanced back at her. "My apologies for pushing you too hard, please, trust me now." He guided her forward.

She took two steps before losing consciousness.

—ele—

"Owww." She frowned up at him. "What did you do to me?" She put the palm of her hand to her forehead and closed her eyes again. She had one massive headache.

Moto cradled her in his arms. "Portal," he tersely replied. "Here, drink this." He held the mouth of a waterskin against her lips.

Kaily drank and almost spit out the foul-tasting medicine. She drank until he pulled it away from her. "You could have warned me."

"You're right, I could have."

"What no apology?"

Moto shook his head. "Better?"

She sighed. "Getting there."

He stood, taking her with him and set her on her feet. He kept his arm around her waist for balance.

Kaily glanced around to get her bearings. They were in the deep forest in a tiny clearing with a huge stone arch. She regarded the symbols carved into the curved stone. She turned confused eyes to him. "Those are like the arch at the ruins of my home and the Agenors castle."

Moto nodded.

"You're taking me home, aren't you?"

Moto nodded.

"Why now?"

Sadness flickered in the depths of his eyes. "I should have taken you home a long time ago, and for that you have my apology."

A tear slipped out of her eye. "You have no reason to apologize for that. I agreed to stay." Emotions bombarded her.

"You did." Moto brought her hand to his lips and kissed her palm. His attention shifted to the Gateway. He covered the rune to her home world and glanced back at her. "Ready?"

Kaily frowned and nodded. Tears swam in her eyes. "Yes." She wiped at her tears.

Moto nodded and focused on the Gateway.

Kaily sensed a surge of power and saw the runes light up with a silver-blue light. The one covered by his palm glowed the brightest and the others faded. She thought she saw a slight shimmer within the interior of the arch, but she wasn't certain. She glanced down at the hand he held out to her.

"Let's get you home," Moto softly said. He stepped into the Gateway with Kaily in tow.

She emerged with him on the other side of the Gateway into the ruins she loved so much. "Thank you, Moto, thank you so much." She wrapped her arms around him. "I don't know why I'm crying."

Moto encircled her within his arms. "I should have brought you home sooner."

She sighed.

He rested his chin on top of her head. "I was selfish to keep you away from your home for so long."

Kaily lifted her head and gazed into his eyes. "It's not your fault. I wanted to stay." She frowned at the pain in his eyes.

Moto kissed her hard on the lips.

Kaily's heart caught in her throat. He was saying goodbye. She felt it with every fiber of her being.

Moto broke their kiss first.

She grabbed his hand. "I want to show you my world."

Moto glanced back at the Gateway.

"Please!" Her voice thick with her pleading for him to stay with her. She wanted her home, but she wanted him too.

He glanced back at her. He reluctantly nodded.

She smiled. She looked him up and down, and she frowned. "What?"

Kaily shrugged and shook her head. "A change of clothing probably wouldn't help anyway. You are a bit intimidating. Try not to scare the Fergusons when you meet them. They are important to me."

Moto smiled and ruffled her hair. "I'll try not to."

She smiled to herself. His genuine smile warmed her heart.

They walked in silence for a while as she led him down the path to her home. She took in the sights and sounds of her familiar surroundings. She felt beyond anything she thought possible. She didn't realize just how much she missed it.

"Moto?"

"Yes?"

"I," she hesitated. She wanted to apologize for using her abilities against him, but she didn't want to upset the fragile peace between them. "I don't want to hurt anyone here."

Moto remained silent.

She stopped them and stepped in front of him. "How do I keep that from happening?"

He glanced down at the ground for a moment. He glanced back up at her. "I don't think it will be a problem here. Can you feel the energy of your world?"

She frowned. "I don't know."

He turned her around and stepped up so her back pressed against his front. "Close your eyes." He kept his arms wrapped around her.

She glanced back up at him.

He gave her a pointed look.

She turned her head back around. She let out her breath, upset with herself. She couldn't seem to help but frustrate him at every turn. She took a deep breath and closed her eyes.

"Find the place in your center where you feel at peace." He softly spoke the words into her ear.

She relaxed into him and his embrace. "I have it."

"Good." He kissed the side of her neck. "That's my girl."

Her heart swelled at his words.

"Now, let your senses reach towards the ground and deep within your world. Search for the prickly sensation of the energy that flows within all worlds."

She frowned in concentration. "I don't feel anything. Have I felt it before?"

"Yes, you have." He stepped back, breaking his contact with her.

She turned to face him. "I'm sorry." She sighed. "My apologies for using my abilities against you, Moto." She inclined her head towards him.

"It's alright, Kaily," he said. "I know you didn't mean to."

Her heart sank at his response. There was detachment in his tone and words. She swallowed hard and turned back to the path. "My cottage is just over this hill." She started walking towards home.

He walked beside her.

She glanced sideways at him. Her heart sank deeper. She focused on her steps.

She cringed when they came closer to her cottage, and the Fergusons laid eyes on her. They ran towards her. Tears swam in their eyes. She ran the rest of the way to them. They smothered her in hugs. Tears flowed from all three. Lectures flowed about scaring them half to death. And couldn't she have called them, and so forth. She hugged them.

"Where have you been?" They both demanded when the hugs stopped.

"It's complicated." She smiled as she said the words. She wiped away her tears as best as she could and glanced back at Moto. She held her hand out to him.

Moto hesitated, but then stepped forward and placed his hand in hers.

"This is Moto, the complication." She added the last part with a spark of amusement in her tone and eyes. "Moto," she said looking up at him. "This is Mr. And Mrs. Ferguson."

He inclined his head to them both.

Mr. Ferguson held his hand out towards Moto.

Moto glanced at it, then back up.

Mr. Ferguson frowned and dropped his hand back to his side.

Kaily winced. She probably should have explained a few things during their walk to the cottage. She wished again that he would open his mind up to her. "They live in the house up the way," she said to defuse the tension building. "It is good to see you two again." She fiercely hugged them once more. She walked with them the rest of the way to her cottage.

Moto followed at a distance.

"Thank you for taking care of everything."

"Of course, dear," Mrs. Ferguson said. "Please, don't frighten us like that again. You really do need to tell us what happened and where you have been."

Kaily glanced back at Moto and frowned. She gave a small tilt of her head for him to join them.

Moto gave a barely perceptible shake of his head.

She sighed and turned her attention back to the Fergusons. "It's hard to explain what happened."

Mr. Ferguson opened the door to the cottage and stepped aside.

Kaily entered with Mrs. Ferguson. She followed the older woman to the kitchen.

Mrs. Ferguson put a pot of water on for some tea.

Kaily smiled.

Mr. Ferguson sat at the table in the kitchen.

She admired the way he stayed out of his wife's way. Kaily glanced back at Moto, who was too close to the front door for her comfort. He'd entered the cottage, but that was about it. She turned her attention back to Mrs. Ferguson. She jumped when the older woman pulled out meat and cheese from the fridge. She rushed forward to grab the meat and cheese. "Moto is," she glanced back at him.

He gave her a quizzical look.

She looked back at Mrs. Ferguson and put the meat and cheese back. "He is vegan." She glanced at Moto who was frowning with his arms crossed over his chest. Trust me, she mouthed to him.

"You don't say." Mrs. Ferguson eyed him in a way that said she was not convinced.

Mr. Ferguson muttered under his breath something about it being bloody annoying.

"I'm tired and not really hungry. I'll fix something later for us." She told the Fergusons. "If you don't mind, I really just want to settle in and show Moto around."

"As you wish, dear." Mrs. Ferguson patted her hand. "We'll stop by later this evening. Come along. Let's leave the young people to settle in." She hooked her arm with Mr. Ferguson's.

Mr. Ferguson spared Moto a harsh, warning glare on his way out the door.

"I'm so sorry about that," Kaily said in Kahoali as she walked towards him. She took his hand in hers and pulled on it until he moved deeper into the room. She led him to the couch and sat.

Moto reluctantly sat next to her.

Kaily draped her legs over his and snuggled closer to him. She laid her head on his shoulder. "Why did you shut me out of your mind?" Her question slipped out before she thought better of it.

He lifted her chin and gazed into her eyes. "I didn't, little one. Your mind has been closed to me since the training room. What happened in there?"

She moved his hand away from under her chin. She laid her head back on this shoulder. "I can't, Moto. I can't relive that."

"You'll have to relive it sometime, little one." He smoothed her hair and rested his cheek on her head.

"I know. Just not right now, please." She wiped at her tears.

"What is this vegan thing?"

She lifted her head. "You could understand them?"

He nodded. "It's something Shimani and I learned to do from our travels to other worlds. It's my traveling that led me to this world and to you."

"Why were you traveling to other worlds?" She found it strange for a people so against outsiders that one should seek them out.

"It doesn't matter." His stomach rumbled.

She sat up. "Guess it is time to eat. Vegan on this world means that you only consume plant-based foods."

Moto frowned. "What other kinds of food are there?"

She shook her head and stood. "You probably don't want to know." She walked back into the kitchen and opened the icebox. Mrs. Ferguson had always kept it stocked with fresh foods ever since she could remember. She pulled out a variety of veggies and put them on the counter. She turned when Moto entered the room.

He sat at the table.

She checked the cupboards until she found what she searched for. "I think I can accommodate your dietary needs."

He smiled at her. "You still didn't answer my question."

She winced. "Meat." She glanced over her shoulder at him.

He frowned. "Meat? As in animals?"

She shrugged and nodded.

"I did impact your life, didn't I?" He stood and moved to stand behind her. He took the knife out of her hand and turned her in his arms to face him. "I didn't mean to upset your life."

She placed her hands on his chest. "I think we upset each other's lives, didn't we?"

He nodded.

"It hasn't been all bad, has it?" She didn't wait for a reply. "I find I kind of liked eating the way you do, to be honest."

Moto laughed and hugged her hard. "I'll corrupt you to my way yet."

"One can hope," she said. "Are you hungry or not?" She eyed the vegetables on the counter.

He lifted his hands and backed away. "Far be it for me to interfere with repast prep." He sat back at the table. "It's a novelty, being served by a woman."

Kaily turned towards him with the knife in hand and narrowed her eyes at him. "Watch it, buddy! I know how to use this." She waved the knife at him.

He held his hands up in surrender.

She smiled and turned her attention back to the task at hand.

"Yes and no," Moto said.

She glanced over her shoulder. "Yes and no, what?"

"Focus on what you're doing with that knife!"

She smiled but returned her attention back to cutting up the vegetables.

"Yes, we have both changed each other's lives. No, it has not been all bad."

She didn't turn around. "Glad to hear it." She finished cutting up the vegetables and put them in a pot. She added broth and spices. Once that was done, she made up two cups of hot tea. She handed one to Moto and sat next to him at the table.

"Smells good." He accepted the cup.

"Thank you." She inclined her head. "This is peppermint tea. It's one of my favorites." She sipped at her tea while watching him over the rim of her cup as he tried the tea.

He grimaced.

She laughed and choked on her tea.

Moto patted her back. "That's what you get for laughing at me."

"Touche," she said when she could speak again. "I can get you something else to drink."

Moto shook his head. "I'll wait for the repast."

"You don't think my abilities will work here since I can't touch the energy."

He remained silent.

She instantly regretted her comment. She took a drink of her tea and set the cup on the table. She stood and stirred the veggie soup in the pot.

"No, I don't. I can't touch the energy either, except at the Gateway. I think that may be why your abilities didn't manifest sooner in your life."

"Truth?" She put the spoon down and sat back at the table. Relief swamped her.

"From what I know, granted it's only in relation to the Kahoali, most start showing signs of abilities right before puberty sets in. Sometimes sooner." He rubbed a finger to smooth the creases between her brows. "You have nothing to worry about here, Kaily."

"Thank you." She touched his arm. "How do the abilities manifest in the Kahoali?"

He tilted his head and regarded her before finally answering. "Similar to how they did for you. First, the child hears the calling, an overwhelming desire to journey to Crystal Lake. Once the child is at the Lake, they see it in an unusual way than previous visits, if they've been there before. A talisman will show itself to the child. After, they obtain their talisman, we pair them with an adult of similar powers to guide and teach them. All Kahoali children are taught control of their emotions long before the calling hits them."

Kaily winced at his words.

Moto stopped speaking.

She thought he might add more.

He didn't.

She sipped her tea. She contemplated her own journey in relation to his words. She considered her disastrous beginning in learning control. Sadness descended on her.

"Kaily?"

She glanced up at Moto.

"Do you want your talisman back?"

She heard hesitation in his question. She shook her head. "No, not really."

He frowned. "Why?"

She glanced at the contents in her half empty cup, and then back to him. "It scares me."

Moto didn't reply right away. He gave her a sad smile and took her hands in his. He opened his mouth, gave a small shake of his head and sighed. "I understand," he finally said. He let go of her hands.

She frowned.

He reached up and smoothed her furrowed brow. "Peace, little one."

She attempted to return his smile. Something felt off between them and growing worse by the minute. He was there but wasn't at the same time.

An uncomfortable silence settled between them.

Kaily was so lost in thought, she didn't notice Moto stand until he placed steaming bowls of vegetable soup in front of them. "I should get that."

Moto shook his head. "I don't mind. It didn't feel right letting you do all the work."

She snickered. "Old habits?"

He shrugged. "Something like that. Is there anything else you would like?"

She shook her head. "This is good. You?"

"I'm good." He sat and handed her a spoon.

"Thank you." She accepted the utensil. "Is all this strange to you?"

Moto glanced around. "A bit. No stranger than my Village must have been to you."

"True." She took a bite. The warm broth provided a welcome heat to her insides. After the hot, humidity of the Kahoali forest, the weather at her home seemed colder or maybe it was the, she shook her head, whatever was going on between them.

"Very good."

She blushed. "Thank you."

They talked about her life a little as they ate. Nothing of any real importance. Certainly not what she thought they needed to talk about. She was reluctant to upset what little was left between them. So, she told him stories of her childhood. He patiently listened and asked questions here and there. When they finished eating, he helped her clean up.

After, she changed into warmer, familiar clothing, and then showed him around the gardens outside. They spent the better part of the late afternoon lounging in the hammock. She'd offered a blanket, but he refused. He said her warmth pressed against him was enough. She napped, secure in his arms. It was a perfect afternoon.

The Fergusons, true to their word, stopped by in the evening. Mrs. Ferguson even made some veggie pasties. Kaily refrained from mentioning to Moto that they might have contained some animal by product. She couldn't bring herself to spoil Mrs. Ferguson's efforts, but she was fairly certain there was at least butter in the dough used for the pasties. She consoled herself with it not being the same as eating animal flesh, and he wouldn't know the difference.

After, they taught Moto a card game. He caught on well enough. By the end of the evening, Mr. Ferguson began warming up to Moto, sort of. Which was to basically say he wasn't grousing as much at him. Moto politely ignored the grousing.

Later, she and Moto walked them to the door and said their goodbyes. Moto offered to walk them home. They declined saying they walked the path often enough. Kaily closed the door and leaned against it.

"You have the most unusual accent when you speak my language."

He picked her up.

She squealed.

"You should talk. You haven't heard your accent when you speak my language."

She laughed. "Put me down."

He shook his head as he carried her to the bedroom. "Where's the light?" He growled in her ear as they entered the room.

She pointed to the switch on the wall by the door, still laughing. "Put me down. I'll get it."

He set her on her feet.

Kaily switched the light on. She turned to face Moto. "Do you want a night cap?"

His eyes narrowed at her. "Depends on what that is?"

"Now whose lacking trust?" She cringed the moment her words left her mouth. She'd almost forgot the uneasiness between them.

"Touche," he said, mimicking her from earlier.

She breathed a sigh of relief.

He sat on the bed and watched her move around the room.

She grabbed one of her sleeping shirts and headed for the bathroom. As she picked up her toothbrush and put toothpaste on it, she stopped. She glanced around the bathroom. The differences there struck her and drove home just how different their worlds were. She fell into her daily pattern so easily. She finished and found a fresh toothbrush for Moto. She always kept extra on hand since she switched them out every few months.

She stepped out of the bathroom to find him already undressed and reclining on her bed.

He'd covered his mid-section with a throw cover. His hands were laced behind his head.

She frowned, bothered by his sudden, uncharacteristic modesty. She pointed back at the bathroom. "I set out a toothbrush and toothpaste for you. We handle our hygiene needs a bit differently here."

Moto stood and moved to stand by her. "Show me!"

She glanced down at his manhood and blushed.

He laughed and tilted her chin up. "After all our time together, you're still embarrassed at the sight of me?"

Kaily shrugged.

He kissed her. "Show me."

She showed him everything he might need to know about using her bathroom and hygiene on her world. She left him to finish on his own. By the time he was done, she'd poured two tumblers of brandy. She sat in her bed with her back against the headboard, halfway under the covers.

Moto climbed into bed next to her.

She handed him a tumbler. "Night cap." She saluted him with hers and took a sip. She watched him.

He nodded his approval. "This, I like." He frowned. "Wait, is this like brey?" He eyed her suspiciously.

"Sort of," she hesitantly said.

He took her tumbler from her and drank half the contents before handing it back to her.

"Spoil sport," she muttered. She scooted closer so he was forced to put his arm around her shoulders. She sipped her brandy, at peace for now.

Moto downed his and set his tumbler on the nightstand beside the bed.

Kaily managed another sip before he again divested her of her tumbler. He set it on the nightstand on her side of the bed.

She frowned at him. She supposed she should have been grateful he hadn't downed the rest of hers.

"I want to love you, little one." He slid her down to lay on her back and covered her body with his.

"Really?" Her heart jumped into her throat. "You're ready to complete the bonding with me?"

"No," he said, shaking his head.

She couldn't hide her disappointment.

"You're not ready, little one."

"I am ready."

"I want to touch and kiss you. I want to feel your hands and mouth on me." He brushed back her hair. "If you're willing?"

She wanted the bond to be completed. If this were all he would give her, she would accept, for now. "I'm willing."

He helped divest her of her night shirt. He spent the night loving her the only way he was willing.

She tried to push aside her disappointment and give herself to his passionate touches.

Chapter Nineteen

Moto knelt beside the bed where Kaily lay sound asleep. He brushed back her hair from her face. He loved the texture and coloring in the morning light. He loved her deep sea-green eyes that changed with her moods. He loved her soft, fair skin against his darker complexion as she lay on him. He loved the fire that burned in the deeps of her center. He loved her scent that permeated his very existence.

He closed his eyes and drew in a calming breath. He took her scent deep into his lungs. He rested his chin on his hands and stared at her as though he could memorize her every nuance.

They had spent a remarkable three days on her world. But those three days showed him as nothing else could that she didn't belong in his world. She belonged in hers. He'd never seen her so happy in the short time they'd been together. She loved the Fergusons. In truth, he was growing quite fond of them as well. He loved how open and free she was with them. He loved the sound of her laughter. He would treasure these three days with her.

He kissed her forehead and stood.

He stared down at her as he gathered his courage. This decision was the best he could do for her. He picked up the bag he'd brought with him and walked to the door. He stopped and glanced back at her.

She remained asleep.

"Be well, my Kaily," he whispered. He stepped out of the room and quietly closed the door behind him. If seeing her with the Fergusons hadn't been enough to convince him she belonged on her home world, it was this. The fact that she slept so soundly on her world when she'd been so restless on his. She wasn't troubled by night terrors or any other unease that he sensed from her.

He still could not get inside her mind, which frustrated him to no end. If only he could reach her there. Maybe, just, maybe he would have been able to teach her what she required in order to learn control over her abilities. Nor could he stop her night terrors since he couldn't reach into her mind.

Determinedly, Moto forced himself to walk to the front door and through it. He shut the door behind him. His leaving was the best thing for her.

He nodded a greeting to Mrs. Ferguson who was already working in the garden.

She smiled and waved at him in return.

He returned her smile. He turned his back decisively on the cottage and Kaily. He made his way back up the path to the Gateway. Tears burned the backs of his eyes. He ignored the sensation.

He struggled to take each step away from her. The way back to the Gateway seemed to take forever. With each step he took, a piece of his heart broke off and fell by the wayside.

He wondered when she had become so much a part of him. He hadn't completed the bonding ritual, and yet it felt like he was walking away from his bonded mate. At least, how he thought it would feel. A huge chunk of himself was being left behind on her world. He resolutely continued to place one foot in front of the other until he finally reached his destination. She was better off without him.

He rested his forehead against the cold stone arch. He swallowed the lump in his throat. He left his tears sliding down his cheeks unchecked. He let go of the rest of the pieces of his heart as they dropped to his feet with each tear he shed.

When he gathered enough strength, he wiped the moisture from his cheeks and eyes. He squared his shoulders. He placed his hand over the rune of his home world without a backwards glance. He closed his eyes and took several calming breaths. He could do this, he told himself. He had to do this. She was better off.

"WHAT THE HELL DO YOU THINK YOU'RE DOING?"

Moto spun around in time to catch her fists flying at his chest. He gathered her hands in his. "CEASE!"

"ANSWER ME, DAMMIT!" She kicked him with both her feet.

"STOP!"

Kaily was beyond reasoning with. She wore her night shirt and shorts. She put shoes on and a light jacket, but that was it. Tears streamed down her face.

Her anger beat at him. His own temper rose in response to hers. He struggled for control. She was the one person who could push his control beyond its limits. He spun her around and pushed her back hard against the stone arch. He pressed his body hard against hers and spread her legs with his knees to keep her from kicking him. He pinned her hands above her head. "Stop!" He didn't quite yell at her.

"NO!" She screamed at him.

He spun her around enough to spank her hard until he felt the fight drain from her.

She slumped against his arm.

He let out an exasperated breath. He knew he probably shouldn't have spanked her like that. His anger and frustration got the better of him. He consoled himself with the knowledge that he'd left her shorts pulled up.

Her body trembled in his arms as her sobs shredded what was left of his heart. "Kaily," he spoke her name in a low whisper and with a great deal of resignation. He gathered her into his arms and sat heavily on the ground.

She turned her tear-streaked face up at him. "Why are you leaving me?"

He tried to wipe away the tears from her eyes that refused to stop flowing. He fought back his own tears. "Kaily, please."

"No, dammit, tell me why!" Her eyes slid from his. "Why would you touch me the way you do and spend this time with me, if you had every intention of leaving me?"

Moto shook his head. He gazed helplessly at her.

She raised her hand to him.

He grabbed it before she could hit him. He grabbed her hair at the back of her head with his other hand and brought her face close to his. "Do NOT hit me! Ever again!" His body shook with the strength of his emotions. "I swear that you will not sit for a very long time!"

She glared back at him. "I don't care. Why don't you want me?"

His heart caught in his throat at the utter anguish pouring from her. He'd deeply hurt her more than he anticipated his leaving would. Her pain was more than he could endure. His heartbeat increased. He kept his hand buried in her hair and lowered his mouth possessively to hers. He poured all the longing, hurt and frustration they'd both felt into that kiss. He pushed her back to the hard, cold ground and spread her knees farther apart. He freed his cock from his trousers. He pushed aside the sides of her shorts, and then surged into her with one hard, painful stroke.

Kaily cried out as he tore through her barrier.

Her pain didn't fully register in his emotionally clouded mind. All he knew was that he wanted her, and he was going to take her regardless of the consequences. He slammed in and out of her tight feminine center until he finally came. He collapsed on top of her, but remained inside, reluctant to break what little connection was left to them. He maintained enough awareness not to put his whole weight on her.

The emotions drained from both of them.

Moto cursed and moved to pull out of her.

"Don't! Please!" She wrapped her legs around his waist and locked her ankles.

Moto's apologetic gaze locked with hers. "I hurt you."

"Only at first." She held his head in both her hands to keep him from looking away from her. "Not after that." She moved beneath him. "Please, I'm begging you, don't pull away from me."

He caressed her cheek and brushed her hair back from her face. "My apologies for being so rough with you. It was not how I intended to take you the first time." Sorrow echoed in his words.

"I accept your apology. I apologize for hitting you."

Moto smiled down at her. "Apology accepted."

"Now, if you could just remain very still for a bit."

A mischievous smile crossed his features. As he moved in and out of her just the tiniest bit.

Her breath caught in her throat. She closed her eyes and squirmed underneath him. "Don't do that."

"Somebody's sensitive." He pulled out of her and slid her shorts off. He dropped them to the side. His eyes remained locked with hers.

"What are you doing?"

He smiled and lowered his mouth. He licked the outside of her opening.

She closed her eyes and arched her back.

He stuck his tongue in and out of her.

Her breath hitched.

He suckled her clit and slid his fingers in and out of her.

She yelped and buried her hands in his braids as she relaxed to his erotic touches.

"That's my girl. Give yourself to me." He alternated between suckling and nipping at her with his teeth.

She squirmed beneath his touch.

He closed his eyes and focused on her emotions. He wanted to make certain that she experienced intense pleasure this time around.

"You're killing me." She couldn't stop squirming.

Moto laughed. "No, little one. I'm making you fly."

Her eyes widened. She tensed. She forced herself to relax, to trust him.

He nodded his approval. "That's it." He penetrated her faster and harder with his fingers.

Her eyes glazed over, but she kept them open. "I'm not going to survive."

He chuckled. "You will, just a little higher."

"Please," she begged.

"Not yet."

She whimpered and squirmed.

He held her in place and picked up the pace. Her muscles clinched around his fingers. He filled her and stretched her. He moved faster in and out of her.

She cried out. Liquid poured out of her as she came.

He didn't stop. "More." He told her.

She arched into him and cried out again.

He held her tight as her world splintered around her. He felt her tremors ripple through her. "That's it." He stroked his cock as his own need to be inside her again overwhelmed him. As the last wave of her pleasure passed through her, he buried himself deep inside her.

Her eyes flew open to lock with his.

He stared down at her as he moved in and out of her hot, moist sheath.

She opened her mouth to say something. She gave a contented sigh instead. She pulled his head towards her.

He lowered his head to hers and kissed her. He started to pull back.

She grabbed his braids and glared at him.

He smiled and lowered his head to hers. He took possession of her mouth as he did her body. He stroked in and out of her until they were both on the precipice. "Wait for me," he ordered.

Tell me when, she replied.

He lifted his head and turned startled eyes to hers.

She smiled up at him.

He shook his head, and his smile grew. He kissed her hard and penetrated her deeper and faster without mercy. He pushed them both as far as he could and held them just on the brink of pleasure to the point that neither thought they could survive. Just as their shared pleasure gave way to pain, he gave the order.

It was some time before the cloud of euphoria dissipated. He pulled out, breaking the contact, despite her silent protests.

He kissed her in a way to show her reassurance that he was not leaving her. He pulled a spare vest out of the bag and first cleaned Kaily off, and then himself. He pulled her shorts back on, and then reclined next to her. He used his bag as a head rest and pulled her into his arms. "I should probably take you back to your cottage where it would be more comfortable, but I don't have the strength."

She laughed. "I don't have the strength either." She snuggled closer to his warmth. She put her bare legs between his trouser clad ones.

He gathered her closer. *Why didn't you put something warmer on, little one?*

She shrugged. *It wasn't my first thought when I woke to an empty bed.*

He winced at her words. *I thought you would be better off in your world than you have been in mine.* He felt enormous relief at being able to again reach into her mind.

She lifted her head enough, so her eyes locked with his. "I accept that your intentions were in my best interest, but please, please stop making arbitrary decision for me." *Please,* she silently added.

He frowned and touched her face. "When have I made decisions for you?"

She exhaled an exasperated breath. "All the time." She placed a finger across his lips. "You decided to leave me with the Agenors, didn't you?"

He didn't reply. The image of when he found her at the Agenors passed through his mind.

She nodded. "I see it in your mind. You asked me to stay with you on Ki, but then you were almost never around." She shook her head at him. "Please let me finish." She removed her finger and gave him a pointed look.

I will remain silent until you have finished, little one. He, through a great deal of will power, kept a smile from crossing his features.

"You decided when to take me home. You decided what I could and could not understand and withheld information from me. You didn't have the right to withhold that information. Trust me enough to let me decide for myself what I can and cannot handle. Please, Moto. I need that much from you." She held his gaze and waited.

Moto didn't reply.

She lowered her head and snuggled back into his warmth.

You're right, Kaily.

I know it isn't going to be easy for us. There is so much we still need to overcome, but I think what we have is worth fighting for, don't you, Moto?

Yes, I do.

Good. She traced patterns against his chest. *Aren't you cold?*

No. He wrapped his arms tighter around her and surrounded her with as much warmth as he could.

She sighed.

His thought drifted to the consummation of their bond and his concern that it might not have taken. No one talked about the bonding ritual, so he didn't know if what he felt was normal. He thought he'd feel different. While they were connected physically, he sensed her center merge with his. But when they separated, so did the merge or so it seemed. It bothered him. He had no information to compare it to.

Kaily reached up and rubbed her finger between his brows. *You worry too much. Has anyone ever mentioned that to you before?*

Moto laughed. He pressed her to her back and kissed her. *I have heard such on occasion.*

Just occasionally?

You're in a precarious position to be so sassy.

You think so? She laughed and slid her hand down his chest, down his stomach and beneath his waistband of his trousers.

Moto laughed and caught her hand before she reached her intended destination. He settled back to his original reclining position. *I stand corrected.*

She attempted to pull her hands out of his. *You don't trust me?* She asked, still laughing.

He shook his head. *Not in the slightest at the moment.*

Smart man. She ceased her struggles to free her hands.

He held her and stared up at the arch above their heads. For now, he was content to simply hold his Kaily and enjoy the peace between them. While he couldn't feel the energy on her world, he could feel it in the area around the arch. He drew in energy and heated the air in the space around them.

Her shivers ceased. *You have to show me how you did that. Thank you.* She smiled against his chest.

You trust me to teach you?

She sat up and looked down at him. "I do trust you. I just have issues with closed in places."

He pulled her back down. "I saw." *I just need you to trust me and to trust that I will figure out how to instruct you in the best way possible. You have to trust my knowledge and judgment in this matter, and most importantly, you have to trust that I won't let harm come to you. Can you give me that, little one?*

She nodded. *I trust you.*

He kissed the top of her head. He didn't push the matter further. He closed his eyes and tried to empty his mind. She was right. He worried too much. And he would need to include her in future decisions, somehow. Despite the hierarchy of his own world, he was not good at sharing decisions with another. For her, he would try. "Something funny?" He felt her shake beside him and heard silent giggles in her mind.

She shook her head. "No."

He rolled her to her back and tried to pull what was so funny out of her mind.

She smiled sweetly up at him.

He glanced up at the arch. "I wonder what would happen if the Gateway opened while we are laying beneath it?"

She pushed at his chest and scrambled out from under the arch. "That's not funny."

He sat up laughing. "That was funny."

"I would smack you for it, if my butt didn't still smart."

"We agreed you were not going to do that anymore."

She shrugged.

He held his hand out to her. *Trust me.*

She eyed him and glanced up at the arch.

He kept his hand held out towards her and waited. He'd learned from his time on her world, and her interaction with the Fergusons that she did not trust easily. Not even those she loved most. She kept a piece of herself in reserve. The fact that she gave him even a moment of unconditional trust, said a great deal about how much she truly did trust him. At least, on a level that went beyond her conscious decision-making process.

She took his hand and allowed him to pull her back underneath the arch and onto his lap.

"Thank you." He rewarded her with a passionate kiss. "You may smack me without consequences." He used her verbiage. "I deserve that one."

She narrowed her eyes at him but didn't lift her hand.

He shrugged. "Or not. It's a one-time offer."

She hit his chest before he said anything else.

He laughed and squeezed her. "Such a violent thing, aren't you?"

She shrugged and looked away.

He tilted her chin up, forcing her eyes to meet his. *I'm teasing you, little one.*

"It's true, though," she said with a small, sad smile. "I will try to work on that."

"Or not," he said. There was a mischievous look in his eyes. "I certainly don't mind the punishment aspect of it all."

"Hmmm." She shook her head at him. "Moto?"

"Yes?"

"Are we bonded mates now?"

He slowly nodded.

"Now what do we do?"

"We return to Ki."

"Can't we stay on my world?"

He shook his head. "You asked me why I traveled to other worlds."

She nodded.

"Some time ago, I started having night terrors about the destruction of our Villages and people. They have persisted for so long that I worry they are visions of what's to come. I searched for confirmation on other worlds and possible solutions."

"What are your people doing to protect themselves?"

"Nothing."

She frowned.

Moto smiled at her concern and hugged her tight. "Seeing future events has never been a Kahoali ability. So, my people are skeptical. I need to remain close by, on Ki, in case I'm right. I don't know what I can do, but I have to try."

"I understand." She touched his face and the furrow again between his brows. "I can't just disappear again. I have to say my goodbyes to the Fergusons and set some things in order here before I leave. Can you stay with me until I do?"

Relief washed over him followed by sadness that he couldn't give her what she wanted. He shook his head. "I have been gone too long as it is. The feeling kept growing stronger with each passing day, even though, he had not had his night terrors in a while. "I can't leave Sari to deal with the Queen on her own. She took a terrible risk for me. And I can't be away if something happens to my people. I would never forgive myself."

She glanced down at her hands. "I understand."

He lifted her chin. "How long do you need?"

Kaily shrugged. "I don't know, four maybe five days. I need to make certain that finances are set up for the Fergusons to take care of everything." She glanced out over the ruins of the castle there and the hills of the land beyond. "Will we ever return?"

Moto felt his heart breaking anew at the sorrow in her words and mind. "As often as we can."

"In truth?" Her gaze jumped to his, hope shining from her eyes.

He nodded. "Yes, Kaily. I know what it is you are giving up for me."

She wrapped her arms around his neck and hugged him hard. "Thank you." She moved as if she was going to stand.

Moto held her tight. *Not yet. Let me hold you a while longer.*

Before the day was gone, and before he left her world, he loved her again. Four or five days wouldn't be too long, he told himself. When he finally let her go, and stepped through the Gateway, he knew he left his heart and center behind with her. He would not be complete until she was again by his side.

Chapter Twenty

K aily leaned against the stone arch of the Gateway. She stared out over the land that had been her only home she remembered. She'd spent a tearful morning with the Fergusons. Despite, Moto's promise they would return to visit, it seemed as if she were saying goodbye for all time to them. They reacted to her emotions and didn't want to let her go.

She didn't give them details. They wouldn't have believed her if she'd tried to explain it. She told them she would be far away and unable to be reached, and that she didn't know when she would be back. She told them Moto would keep her safe, which seemed to offer enough reassurance, to a point.

She set up funds for the Fergusons to use to take care of everything and added them to accounts and bills they would need to access. She kept some money in an account only she knew about. It was a trust thing. Even those closest to her didn't have her full trust. She didn't understand why trusting others was so difficult for her, and she'd stopped trying to figure it out a while ago. The finances took longer to set up than she thought they would.

Which meant she was late getting back to Moto. She'd half expected him to come back and cart her off. He said he would if she didn't return in a reasonable time, although he didn't tell her what a reasonable time was to him. She had mixed emotions about the fact that he hadn't. There were nights she woke in a cold sweat, thinking she'd dreamt the whole thing up. Doubt, an ever-present demon within her mind. Like now which had her leaning against the stone arch, instead of opening the Gateway the way Moto showed her.

He'd even had her go through the steps in his presence before he left to assure himself and her that she could do it.

She pushed off the stone arch and walked around to face the runes. "Okay, you've got this," she said to herself. She took a deep breath and closed her eyes. She reached for the energy beneath the Earth as Moto taught her. She sensed the energy flowing beneath the stone arch, but she couldn't sense it entering her body the way she had with Moto. "Don't panic." She could feel the energy, so, it had to be working.

She placed her palm over the rune to Ki. She opened her eyes and focused.

Nothing. No bluish light. No shimmer.

She stepped back and took a deep breath. "Don't panic!" She took another deep breath and stepped forward. She placed her hand on the rune and reached for the energy again. "Focus."

Still nothing happened.

"Dammit!" She dropped her heavy packs on the ground and stomped away from the Gateway. She ran her hands through her short hair. She shook her head and walked back towards the Gateway. "Why won't you work?" She leaned against the crumbling wall across from it as she regarded the arched useless piece of stone.

She shook her head. She refused to let it get the better of her. She walked resolutely back towards the Gateway and again attempted to open it.

Nothing.

She moved back to the crumbling wall with some unflattering words flung at the damn contraption. She slid to the ground and glared at the Gateway. She took deep breaths, trying to calm her racing heart and panicked breathing. She couldn't do it. She couldn't open the damn Gateway. She laid her forehead on her upturned knees. She closed her eyes. She willed the tears forming in her eyes to cease. She was stuck! "Dammit!"

"Kaily?"

She lifted her head, startled. "Shimani? What are you doing here?" She stood and rushed over to join him at the Gateway.

"I thought I would check to see what's taking so long. Moto is getting," Shimani's eyes narrowed, "moody."

"Then why the hell didn't he come for me?"

"He's attempting to be patient with you."

"Fine time for him to start that shit!" Her eyes narrowed at him. "You're timing is suspiciously impeccable."

A boyish grin spread across Shimani's features. "Isn't it."

She shook her head at him. "I can't open the Gateway."

"I see that."

"I did everything Moto showed me." She shook her head. "I opened it while he watched me. What am I doing wrong that it won't work?"

Shimani's eyes took on a faraway look, and then he focused on her. "Did Moto leave your talisman with you?"

"No, why?"

"Can you sense the energy around the Gateway?"

"Yes, but I can't pull it inside me or direct it towards the rune." She lifted her arms and dropped them to her side in an exasperated motion.

"Guess Moto isn't the only moody one."

Kaily glared at him. "You're not helping, Shimani!"

He smiled. "The talisman acts as a conduit. It's what allows us to harness and use the energies of the Universe."

"Why wouldn't Moto know that?"

Shimani frowned and rubbed the back of his neck. "That's a bit,"

"Shimani, if you say complicated, I swear I will find a way to make your life miserable. I need information, answers to my questions, not lame, useless words thrown at me."

Shimani appeared a bit abashed. "Technically, he knows, but,"

Kaily crossed her arms over her chest. "Waiting."

"It really is complicated, Kaily." He chuckled. "Moto knows on instinct more than intellect."

She glared at him. "How is it you know more than he does. Isn't he training you?"

Shimani fidgeted and appeared uncomfortable.

She stepped closer to him. "What don't you want to tell me?"

"A great deal." Shimani held his hands up. "Please, don't ask me more."

"Why?"

"You'll get me into trouble."

"With Moto?"

Shimani shook his head. "In time, you'll learn everything. Until then, I can't provide you answers you're not ready to understand."

Kaily's eyes narrowed at him, and she pressed her lips together as she regarded him. "And Moto, can you provide him those answers."

Shimani shook his head.

She let out an exasperated breath. "One final question."

"Kaily," Shimani said and shook his head.

"How did I get through that damn Gateway the first time, if I needed a talisman to operate it?" She jabbed a finger at the stone arch.

Shimani glanced away.

"I didn't get there by accident, did I, Shimani."

His eyes turned back to hers. He shook his head.

"Did you do it?"

He took a deep breath.

"Shimani?"

"Look," he began, "I only tried to keep it open after Moto went through. Which isn't easy to do from another world with only a looking bowl. Balancing both worlds' energies is difficult." He held his hands up.

"What happened?"

He shook his head. "I don't know. You were supposed to exit the same Gateway Moto had."

"So, you left me with the Agenors."

Shimani shook his head. "No. I had no idea where you went. I was looking for you even before Moto realized you were missing."

Kaily turned her back on him and walked away. She clenched and unclenched her fists.

"Kaily?"

She held her hand up at him for silence.

He remained silent.

Finally, she turned back to face him. "One day, you and I are going to have a very in-depth talk." She sighed. "For now, take me to Moto. And Shimani?"

"Yes, Kaily?"

"I'm not happy."

Shimani nodded his head once at her. He turned towards the Gateway. He placed his palm on the rune to Ki. Almost immediately, the runes glowed, and the doorway shimmered. He stepped aside and picked up her bags.

She reached to grab them from him.

He turned away from her and kept a firm hold. "Moto would harm me, if I let you carry these."

"If you don't relinquish them, I will cause you harm."

Shimani tilted his head at her. "Oh Kaily, no offense, I am more concerned with Moto's abilities to harm me, than yours."

"Ouch!"

He took another step backwards. "After you."

"Don't you trust me?"

"No." Shimani shook his head.

Kaily glared at him. She slapped his chest hard as she passed him.

"Moto was right, you are violent." Shimani frowned at her.

She punched him in the arm.

"Oww. What was that for?" He asked rubbing his arm.

"Everything!" she stepped into the shimmering doorway. Shimani followed.

Once they stepped through. Shimani opened a portal to the cave.

"There you are," Moto said, coming out of the cave just as she exited the portal.

She frowned and glanced back at Shimani.

He just smiled at her.

Moto enfolded her in his embrace. He glanced at Shimani. "You can put those in there." He tilted his head towards the cave entrance.

"Welcome back." Sari said as she came out of the cave.

Kaily turned around in Moto's arms, so she faced Sari. "Thank you." She glared at Shimani as he came back out of the cave after depositing her bags inside.

What's going on? Moto asked her in her mind.

Later. She sensed him frown. "If you don't mind, I'd like some time with Moto, alone," she said to Sari, and glanced up at Moto.

Moto smiled down at her. *Thank you!*

"Of course," Sari said. She turned her attention to Moto. "Don't forget about your obligations. The Queen expects your attendance by my side."

"If you claimed your destiny, we wouldn't have to keep up the pretense."

"We've had this discussion." Sari glared at him.

"Apparently one of us wasn't listening." Moto squeezed Kaily.

"Apparently not." Sari turned away from him and opened a portal. She glanced at Shimani.

He stepped into the portal.

Sari followed.

What was that about? Kaily asked. She turned back to face Moto, still firmly within his embrace.

Nothing. He touched her face. *You're late!*

My apologies. It took longer than I expected to finalize things.

Apology accepted.

"Why didn't you come for me?" She touched the side of his face.

He shook his head and smiled. "I was trying to be,"

"Patient." She finished for him. "I heard."

He laughed.

Why are you and Sari arguing?

Why are you angry at Shimani?

She huffed and looked away.

Moto turned her face back towards him and took possession of her mouth. *Thank you for coming back to me.*

Always. She wrapped her arms around his neck. *Moto?*

Yes?

Don't ever hesitate to come after me.

He ended the kiss and smiled down at her. "Sari said I should have patience and that maybe things were just taking a while."

Kaily shook her head. "I couldn't open the Gateway."

Moto frowned.

"Evidently, I needed my talisman for that."

Moto's countenance darkened. "What happened between you and Shimani?"

"It wasn't an accident."

What wasn't?

My being on Ki.

"What does Shimani have to do with that."

She touched his furrowed brow.

Moto captured her hand. "Kaily?"

She took a deep breath. "He said he was trying to keep the Gateway open after you left so I could follow you."

"You ended up with the Agenors." Moto's features darkened.

Kaily shrugged. "He said he doesn't know how that happened only that he started searching for me even before you knew I was missing."

Moto growled.

Kaily frowned. "I shouldn't have told you."

"Yes, you should. We don't keep secrets." He pulled her close and stared out over her head.

What about Sari, what's going on?

He took a deep breath. "We have to keep up appearances of our bonding."

Kaily nodded. "As expected," she said.

He snorted. "She is the future Queen. If she revealed herself, we wouldn't have to."

"I see."

Moto glanced down at her. He swung her up in his arms. "Enough talk of those two. We'll deal with them later." He carried her into the cave and towards the sleeping pallets. "We have other matters to attend to."

Kaily laughed. "Stop."

He frowned. "Why?"

She gave him a timid smile. "We have unfinished business."

"I know. I'm trying to fix that."

She laughed. "Not that. And you're ripe. Didn't you shower while I was gone?"

Moto sheepishly shrugged. "Off and on."

"What did you do?"

"Trained."

Kaily shook her head at him.

"I had to keep my mind and body occupied with something. You were gone far too long."

She eyed him. "I was gone seven days."

He nodded. "As I said, far too long."

She shook her head. "Put me down. Go shower, while I unpack."

Moto set her on her feet. "If I have my way, my ripeness won't matter to you in a moment."

She pushed on his back, trying to make him move towards the shower room. *Moto, please. I have something important to attend to.*

He regarded her a moment. *Alright,* he said. *I'll shower and you attend to what you need to.* He kissed her and made his way to the shower room.

She stared at his retreating back. Her heart skipped several beats. She didn't know if she possessed enough courage for what she had in mind. She'd had seven days to give it a great deal of thought. If they were going to make it as a bonded Kahoali, sort of, couple, they had to overcome their obstacles together. Sari had been right. She couldn't exist in his and her world. Someone had to bend.

She waited for him to turn on the shower before she started. When she heard the water, she exchanged her sweater and jeans for a light, short dress she'd used for sleeping. She rummaged through the chest and alcove until she found the items she searched for. She laid them out on the table in the same pattern, or as best as she could remember.

Her heart caught in her throat as she stared down at them. Her pulse beat wildly. She took a deep breath.

Moto stepped from the shower room.

She turned to face him.

He sauntered towards her with only a towel wrapped around his waist. "I approve the change of clothing."

She tentatively smiled at him and ducked her head.

He stopped halfway. He dropped his towel to the floor while smiling at her.

She giggled and shook her head. A blush crept up her neck. She waited by the table for him.

A frown crossed his features.

She took a deep breath and held her hand out to him.

He cocked his head and slowly walked towards her.

Her eyes locked with his. "We have unfinished business," she said.

He took her hand in his.

Her heart pounded hard in her chest. She experienced difficulty catching her breath. She turned around. She glanced from the table to him.

Moto stepped up behind her. He took a deep breath and pulled her against his front. He wrapped his arms around her front and stared at the contents on the table.

She glanced back up at him.

He pulled her tighter against him.

She tried to turn in his arms.

He wouldn't let her.

Talk to me, please. Kaily grew uncomfortable with the silence between them. She knew he hadn't closed his mind to her, it was just blank. *Please, Moto. I need to know what you're thinking.*

Damn, little one.

She gave a nervous laugh. *I think my world had a bad influence on you.*

He chuckled. *I'm thinking you are out of your mind. Your fear beats at me.* He turned her around to face him. His gaze glanced from the items on the table to hers, and then back to the table. He began to shake his head. *No, I can't.*

Kaily glanced back at the items and back up at him. She framed his face between her hands. *It's my choice to honor your Kahoali ways, not yours.*

He took a deep breath. *Kaily.* He shook his head.

You agreed to stop making decisions for me. She took a deep breath. *I have given this a lot of thought. You bonded with me and asked me to step into your world, but I can't do that if I don't honor your ways.* She glanced back at the items. *Despite, what I feel about them. This hangs between us, Moto. We have to find resolution.*

He walked the final steps to the table with Kaily in tow. He pushed the cushion back and sat on the edge. He brought her to stand between his legs. "You have no idea what you're asking me to do." He held his palm out to her. "Give me your hand."

She put her hand in his with only a slight hesitation.

He searched her eyes. He turned his attention to her hand. He turned it over, so her palm faced up and placed it on his thigh. "Leave your hand on my thigh but take a step back."

Kaily obeyed.

He picked up the strap and laid it flat against her palm. His eyes locked with hers.

She nodded her understanding.

He lifted the strap and brought it down hard against her upturned hand.

She winced. The sting hurt from the initial blow, and then gradually intensified. She frowned. Her eyes jumped to his.

He held her hand firmly against his thigh. He took the lid off the pot.

Her eyes stayed with his every movement.

He diffed the ladle into the pot. His eyes locked with hers as he poured a minuscule amount of liquid on her palm.

She cried out. Her knees buckled as fire shot through her hand. Tears welled up in her eyes.

"Do you understand now?" He demanded.

She nodded. She sensed his anger rising. She took a deep breath. Her eyes met his. *It doesn't change anything.*

Moto set her aside, cursing. He stepped away from her and the table. He ran his hands through his braids.

Kaily sat on the edge of the table. She watched him pace back and forth. She had no idea there were so many Kahoali curse words. They put the English and Gaelic ones she knew to shame. She waited for his mind and emotions to settle. *Were you mistaken to ask for retribution in the first place?*

Demanded, Kaily, not asked. He heatedly countered.

She gave him a pointed look.

"No, but," He stopped to face her.

She glanced down. Her eyes again found his. "That day even Sari said you were within your rights to ask," she paused, "demanded," she corrected. "You were within your rights to demand retribution that day. Nothing has changed. I still wronged you, and you still have the right to retribution."

Moto walked to where she sat. He stopped in front of her and caressed her cheek with the back of his fingers.

She leaned into his caress and closed her eyes. *Tell me this won't be a thorn between us, and I'll drop it.* She locked eyes with him. *Tell me a part of you doesn't still want this from me.*

He looked away and shook his head.

She placed her hand against his cheek and turned his head back to face her. "You are not going to push me away with this. I promise, I'm not going anywhere."

He smiled at her and took her hand in his. "You are getting quite adept at reading my mind, little one."

She shrugged. "I guess, I have a good teacher."

He snorted. His gaze drifted towards the back of the cave.

She waited for him to come to terms with his own thoughts on the matter.

"Do you understand why retribution was demanded?"

Kaily nodded.

I need you to tell me, little one. I need to hear your words.

"Because I lashed out in anger and used my powers against you. I thought nothing of consequences and risked your life with my rash actions." She turned inward and thought back to that day. "Because I lost control and could have killed you."

His eyes drifted to the back of the cave again. He took a deep breath. His eyes returned to hers. "Do you yield to this process and accept responsibility for your actions?"

She nodded.

"Words, Kaily, use your words."

"I do. If you're feeling charitable, maybe we could forgo the liquid stuff." She winced at the weakness in her words.

He gave her a sad smile. "I wish we could, little one." He lifted her hand and turned it over, exposing her palm. He rubbed his thumb over where the liquid had been poured.

"Ow."

"Did it hurt, in truth?" His tone was fused with amusement.

She frowned and looked at her hand. "No, not really." She turned questioning eyes to his.

"The plant the strap is made from is mildly poisonous. If you simply touch it, there is no reaction. But when used as it is in punishment, poison is released into the skin. If left untreated the area will become inflamed with redness and eventually blisters. The liquid neutralizes the poison and heals the skin from both the beating and poison. The liquid is also used to heal open wounds, which doesn't hurt quite as much as with retribution.

She stared at him open-mouthed. "You and your people have issues."

He smiled at her. "You're part of us now."

She closed her mouth and frowned. She glanced at the table and took a deep breath. She steeled her nerves. "Let's get this over with." She glanced at him. Her eyes slid back to the table.

He touched her face.

Her eyes jumped to his.

Forgive me.

Always.

He lifted the hem up her dress and over her head.

She shifted, uncomfortable with her own nakedness.

He projected into her mind how he wanted her to lie on the cushion.

Her eyes drifted down as she attempted to gather courage. She frowned when she noticed red, angry blisters on one of his thighs. "Moto?" She pointed to his thigh. "Did that happen when you hit my palm?"

He nodded without looking to where she pointed.

"Why didn't you put that liquid on it?"

He didn't answer her.

She shook her head at him. She snatched the ladle and dipped it into the pot. "Lift your leg."

He lifted his leg, so his thigh was presented to her.

"One of these days you are going to learn to stop keeping things from me." She poured liquid on the angry blisters. She winced from the pain passing through his mind.

He didn't flinch or show any reaction on his features.

"I imagine you were too stubborn for your own good during your own punishment sessions, weren't you?"

Shame and other emotions passed through his mind.

She immediately regretted her callously uttered words. *My apologies,* she said. *I didn't mean to hurt you with my words.* She shook her head at her own stupidity and lack of thought before speaking.

You have nothing to apologize for, little one. You are right. I am stubborn, and it has not always served me. He enfolded her in his arms. *Are you certain you want this?*

She glanced up at him. *No.* She shook her head. "But I think we both know this is necessary for us to move forward."

Moto closed his eyes and nodded. *I love you.* He kissed her.

I love you too. She positioned herself on the table and cushion as he indicated she should. She took a deep breath. She jumped when Moto placed his hand firmly against her lower back.

He picked up the strap.

She trembled.

He braced her legs with something so she couldn't lift them.

Her breath caught and her heart raced.

Trust me, little one.

I do. She tried to force her panic down. Without warning, the strap came down hard against her buttocks.

Breathe, Kaily!

She nodded and tried to take a steady breath.

That's it. Focus on your breathing.

She tried. But the strap came down again and again and again.

She cried out.

Again.

Tears streamed down her face. She pressed her forehead against the cool stone.

The strap hit again.

She lost count, not that she was purposely counting. She tried to breathe. Tears kept flowing. Sobs shook her body. She lifted her head when she felt pressure on the back of her head.

Moto knelt beside her.

When had he stopped?

Tears swam in his eyes, and his cheeks were moist.

Kaily moved to stand.

Moto shook his head.

More? There was fear and dread thick in her mind.

"No. I still have to apply the healing liquid," Moto said.

A sob caught in her throat, and she shook her head. *Please no, I can't take anymore.*

Tears spilled from his eyes. *I wish I didn't have to, little one. I really do.*

I understand. She steeled herself and took several deep breaths. She nodded and pressed her forehead against the cold stone tabletop.

Moto closed his eyes. He caressed the back of her head and stood.

She covered her head with her arms. She braced herself for the wave of pain she knew was coming.

Moto dipped the ladle into the pot. He took a deep breath, and then poured the liquid where the strap hit his Kaily.

She cried out. She attempted to breathe. She whimpered and cried. Fire consumed her. Her world dimmed to nothing but pain and anguish. She didn't even notice when Moto picked her up and carried her to their sleeping pallets.

Words flowed into her mind, but she couldn't make them out.

Moto held her close and soothed her as best as he could. He sensed nothing but pain in her mind. He waited for it to subside.

As the pain subsided, she felt an overwhelming desire to connect to Moto, to feel his soul merge with hers the way she had when he consummated their bonding. She slid down his body and lay between his legs.

His eyes locked with hers.

She took his cock in her mouth.

He settled into a more comfortable position and watched her pleasure and tease him with her tongue and mouth. He caressed her head.

When he strained for release, she slid up his body and impaled herself on his hard cock. She moved relentlessly up and down, speeding up, and then slowing down.

He growled at her.

She smiled down at him but continued teasing him.

He grabbed her hips between his hands and set a faster, harder pace.

She laughed. She placed a finger against her clit. Her eyes locked with his.

He nodded.

She pleasured herself to bring her own desire to his level. *Tell me when.*

A little longer.

She held herself on the brink and waited for his order. She had fantasized while on her world, those long seven days, about pleasuring him this way. But there was fantasy, and then there was reality. She closed her eyes and gave herself completely over to the pleasure between them, and the merging of their souls.

Now!

Kaily let herself go. She felt his own release mix with hers. Pleasure rippled through them both

She collapsed on top of him while keeping him deep or as deep as possible inside her. She clung to the sensation of their merged souls. She knew he did the same.

"Thank you," he whispered against her hair. He kissed her neck.

"For what?" she lifted her head up enough for her gaze to meet his.

"Everything," he said.

She linked her fingers together and rested her chin on them on his chest. "You're slipping out." She closed her eyes as a sense of loss flowed over her.

"I know," he said. There was regret in his tone. "I wish I could remain locked with you for all time."

"Me too." She sighed. "I like the feeling of our souls merged."

Me too, he said. "I think I like this retribution thing better and better." He teased.

She narrowed her eyes at him and lifted her hand.

"Please, oh please, little one. I would love to have you ride me like that again." He looked meaningfully at the table and the contents still on top of it.

Her gaze followed his. She looked back at him and lowered her hand to his chest. She rested her chin on her hands.

"Smart girl." He caressed her head and held her close to his heart.

"Sometimes," she said with a small laugh. "You don't mind if I go to sleep on you, do you?" She stifled a yawn.

Not in the least, little one.

Good. She smiled against his chest and closed her eyes. She hadn't slept as well after Moto left her on her world. The events of the past week were creeping up on her.

Sleep well, my Kaily. He covered them both with a blanket and closed his eyes. He absently caressed her back.

You're tired too.

It's been a long seven days.

Yes, it has. She sighed contentedly and allowed herself to drift into the calm, unconsciousness of sleep.

Chapter Twenty-One

Moto's eyes flew open as he became aware of two things: Kaily was not beside him, and her night terrors had returned. Cursing, he grabbed a blanket and ran to the training room. He stopped at the entrance. He took calming breaths and slowly walked towards her. "Kaily?"

She stood, stock-still in the middle of the training room. Naked with her back to the entrance.

His heart caught in his chest as the emotional pain emanating from her hit him like a punch to his stomach. He cautiously stepped up behind her, wrapped the blanket around her, and pulled her back against him. He enclosed her in his protective embrace. "Your night terrors returned." It was not a question.

She nodded.

He turned her around in his arms and tilted her face up so he could see into her eyes.

Tears streamed down her face.

"How can I help you, Kaily?"

A sob escaped her lips. She wrapped her arms tightly around his waist and pressed into him as if she could crawl inside his skin.

Moto held her tight and swayed with her. He rubbed his hand up and down her back while her pain and sorrow poured into him. He closed his eyes. Her pain was almost unbearable, and there was nothing he could do to help her. He could still get into her mind to a point, which he was grateful for, but the images of her night terrors were unclear. He hadn't woken up when she started having them. He cursed his own exhaustion. They didn't linger in her mind. It was as if she actively pushed them away. If only he could see into her mind while she had them.

She shushed him.

I didn't say anything, little one.

You're thinking too loudly. She lifted her tear-filled gaze to his. "There isn't anything you could have done even if you did see what I see at night."

"Do you remember what they are about?" He brushed away her tears with the pads of his thumb, only to be replaced with more of her tears.

Her gaze shifted from his. She rested her cheek against his chest. "Not much, they fade so fast when I wake, not that I want to remember them." She glanced up at Moto. "They terrify me."

"I know, little one. I know." He pressed her head back down against his chest. He ran his hand repeatedly through her hair, massaging the back of her head as he did. "It might help to talk about what you do remember."

Kaily didn't say anything. Instead, she brought the one image up in her mind that haunted even her waking hours.

Moto's breath caught in his throat and his heart skipped a beat as the image of a cloaked figure solidified in her mind.

"What is it?" She didn't lift her head.

"A Druid." Moto hissed. He glanced down at the floor and noticed for the first time a complicated rune drawn in the dust layering the floor at her feet. It was similar to the ones on the Gateway arches, but more complicated in pattern. "Kaily, what is that?"

She glanced up at him and followed his gaze to where he stared. "Nothing." She wiped it away with her foot. "I doodle sometimes when I wake from," she glanced up at him. "What did you call them?"

"Night terrors."

"That's a good name for them."

"You've drawn those before? Before you came to Ki, you had these night terrors?"

She nodded, and then shrugged. "Sort of, not like these, I don't think anyway. When I was little and first came to live with my foster parents, I had nightmares. I don't remember what they were about, but I remember having them. Somehow, I grew out of them, I guess. My foster parents gave me a journal to write in at that time. I have some in there I drew when I was little and having bad dreams. Once the nightmares went away, so did my desire to doodle." She shrugged again.

He lifted her into his arms. *Are you okay in this room?* He kept touching her mind, partly to make sure he could, and partly because he needed the intimate contact between them.

She nodded. "Just leave the door open." Her eyes darted to the opening.

Done! He carried her to the far side of the entrance and sat on the ground with her in his lap. He leaned back against the wall. "You didn't always live with your foster parents?"

She shook her head. "They found me in the castle ruins when I was about seven years old, I guess. My memories are sketchy about that time of my life."

"Do you know how you came to be there?"

"No." She shook her head. "I don't remember anything before that day." She touched the crease between his brows. "What's wrong, Moto?"

He shook his head. "I don't know. There are things about you that don't make sense."

"Like?"

You dreamt about a Druid, was the first thought that came to his mind, and he quickly discarded it.

"I shouldn't have dreams about a Druid?"

Apparently, not fast enough. "No, you shouldn't even know about them."

She half smiled and shook her head. "Moto, Earth has legends of Druids throughout its history."

"In truth?" His eyebrows rose.

She nodded.

"You speak the Agenors' language."

"That's because it is the language of my childhood."

"It is?"

Her smile widened. She wiped at her tears.

"Well, at least your amusement at my expense has quieted your sadness."

You said you wanted to help.

He laughed at her and messed up her hair.

She smoothed her hair down. "I don't know where I came from, and no one ever came for me. They were great parents. We were happy, until five years ago."

"When they died."

She nodded. "It was a freak accident in their lab."

"But?"

"I don't know. It just never made sense to me. And now," she glanced around the room and back to him. "With all this that has happened to me, I wonder if there was a lot more going on than I could have known."

Moto sensed there was more, but she remained silent. "What is it, Kaily?"

She sighed. "Shimani was strange when he came for me." She shook her head. "Isn't it odd, how he was there just when I needed him?"

Moto frowned. "I had the same thought."

"I could feel the energy, but I couldn't open the Gateway. I could with you but not on my own. I know he said it was because I didn't have my talisman, but I didn't have it with you either when you had me open it before you left. And," she fell silent.

"And?"

"He said something about us understanding everything in time. I asked questions he wouldn't answer." She sighed.

"Kaily, what is it?" His tone grew strained.

She shook her head again. "It's hard to put into words what I'm feeling."

Try.

"When I put questions to him, he asked me to not ask him anything else."

"Why?"

"He said he would get in trouble."

Moto frowned.

"I asked if he meant by you, and he shook his head." She glanced away.

"Go on, Kaily."

"He isn't like other Kahoali males, is he?"

Moto shook his head. "Neither am I."

"I know, but something feels so different about him. And Sari in a way too. They don't act like other Kahoali that I observed in the village."

"How so?"

"At the pool, you avoid looking up at that planet."

Moto growled at her.

"Sari didn't. If Shimani wasn't talking about you, and getting in trouble, who was he talking about?"

"Sari?"

Kaily shook her head. "It didn't seem like it. Am I wrong here?"

Moto let out a heavy sigh. "No. I have noticed some things about those two myself lately." He half laughed. "Ever since you came to Ki, actually. Maybe the Queen."

"I don't think so. I have the strangest feeling that he is following direction from another."

Moto sat utterly still. "Who would he be taking directions from?" His tone was too quiet.

"You're scaring me."

He caught her hand in his. *My apologies, little one.*

Apology accepted. Am I wrong in my thoughts?

Moto shook his head. "I don't know, but I have sensed something strange from those two as well."

"Don't be angry at them."

"You're angry."

She shrugged. "I know, but,"

"But you like them."

"So do you."

"I do, but he and Sari have kept too much from me, and I have no idea how much more they have hidden. I don't like being manipulated." He held her tighter to him. He let out a long, heavy sigh.

"What do we do?"

"Wait and see what happens."

"You're not going to confront them."

He shook his head. "Not at this moment. As for what we need to do, aside from wait and watch, we need to train you. You should have been able to open the Gateway. I don't accept Shimani's explanation. You didn't have your talisman when you opened it with me." He rubbed the crease in his own brow.

Kaily laughed. "I don't mind touching your creased brow."

"I know." He kissed her hand.

She frowned. "I haven't had my talisman with any of the times my abilities surfaced, except the first time." She put that time out of her mind. The aftermath had been quite unpleasant. "Do you think our connection gave me the ability to draw in energy?"

Moto rubbed the crease between her brows. "Maybe." He stood and set her on her feet. "Wait here." He left the training room.

Kaily stared after him.

He returned with his talisman in his hand. "Hold out your hand."

Kaily complied.

He placed his talisman in her waiting hand. He turned to leave.

"Where are you going?"

He cringed at the fear in her voice and mind. He walked back to her. "I want to test a theory, but I can't be in the room with you."

She waited.

"And I have to close the door when I leave."

"What? NO!" She adamantly shook her head. She started trembling. She tried to give his talisman back.

Moto wrapped both his hands around her hands and closed them over his talisman. *I know what I am asking you to face with this request, Kaily. I ask that you trust me, and trust that nothing will harm you, please, little one.*

She shook her head and closed her eyes.

He saw the struggle within her mind between her fear and her desire to give him what he asked of her. He pulled her into his arms and held her close. *The first thing about learning to control your abilities, is learning to control your emotional reactions to situations. I know it is terrifying to face your fears, little one.*

Do you? She angrily brushed at her tears. *Do you really know, Moto?*

His first reaction was a resounding yes, but he held his answer. Her doubt and hopelessness beat at him. He couldn't recall a time he'd ever experience the overwhelming fear coming off his Kaily. Not even his night terrors compared to her fearful anguish. *Perhaps not in the same way you must face now.* He wished he could reassure her better, but he couldn't.

Thank you for not simply saying yes without due consideration.

I want to understand, Kaily. I really do. He caressed her cheek and wiped at her tears that just kept flowing.

I appreciate that you want to understand. She shook her head. *I don't even understand this fear I feel. I know there is no logical reason for it, but still, it consumes me.*

Trust me to help you face this fear. He held her close.

I want to trust you, Moto.

I know you do, little one. He pulled back and bent his head. He poured all his reassurance, he wished he could infuse into her being, into his kiss. He pulled back and instantly felt the loss of contact. He kissed each of her closed eyelids and brushed light caressing kisses across her lips. *Ready?*

She took a deep breath. *Isn't there another way we could test your theory? Maybe if I try to pull the energy in through you instead?*

He sensed and heard desperate, heart-wrenching hope in her heart and mind. The eyes she turned on him made his heart double over in pain. He shook his head. *I have to be certain that you are pulling and gathering the energy without me inadvertently feeding it to you. The room is shielded, which is why the door has to be closed without me inside.* He saw panic take hold in her mind. He sighed but continued. *I don't know if we will be able to speak telepathically.* He answered her unvoiced question.

She began to tremble.

He gathered her back into his warm embrace. He was torn between forcing her to face her fears and carrying her back to their sleeping pallets and loving her senseless.

I prefer the second option.

Moto smiled. *I do to, truth be told. But that does not mean it's the right option.*

I know. She took a deep breath. She took a step back, out of his arms.

Her trembles still shook her body, but there was determination in her mind. He couldn't be prouder of her in that moment. "I will count to ten and then open the door again. It will be over before you know it. I want you to concentrate on pulling in a very small amount of energy." He gave her a pointed look. "Very small, Kaily."

She nodded.

"That's my girl." He brought her hands, firmly grasping his talisman, to his lips and kissed them. *Remember, I'm right here with you. Nothing is going to happen to you.*

She nodded again.

He reluctantly stepped away from her. He walked backwards to the entrance, so his eyes remained locked with hers for as long as possible. His heart tore at the fear emanating from her. He stepped backwards through the entrance, nodded once to Kaily, and then waved his hand, closing the door.

He reached for her mind and cursed. Their telepathy wasn't working. He'd hoped but feared it wouldn't. He counted to ten and opened the door.

To his horror, Kaily was curled up in a tight, fetal position. She rocked from side to side. Uncontrollable sobs shook her body. He sensed energy surrounding her. Her mind was filled with immense pain that was nearly intolerable for him to endure.

He rushed to her as close as he could. He held his hands over her to drain the energy she'd gathered around her. He filtered the energy back to Ki. Once he'd drained enough, he reached down to pick her up.

She screamed the moment his hands made contact with her body. She blindly lashed out.

He ignored her fists flying at him. He fought through her attacks and struggled to gather her into his arms.

Kaily fought him.

Moto held her tight in attempt to keep her from hurting herself or him. He rocked her back and forth and swept her mind with calm. He kept telling her she was safe. He didn't know how long he pushed comfort and calm into her mind before her pain filled mind began to drift back to awareness.

She lifted her head and glanced around the training room. Her eyes locked with his. She threw her arms around his neck and pressed as close as possible to him.

He soothed his hand over her back.

Her sobs renewed. The intensity of them shook her body.

His heart broke repeatedly at the sounds coming from his Kaily. He attempted to hush her.

She wouldn't quiet.

Nothing he said helped. Pushing calm into her mind didn't help. He sighed. His eyes landed on his talisman. It was moist to the touch when he picked it up. He examined it to find tiny blood droplets covering it. He cleansed it with his fire ability and portaled it to the place he kept it. Moto carefully stood with her cradled in his arms. He carried her to their sleeping pallets. He sat and rocked her.

In spite of the pain that filled his heart and center, he needed answers of what happened. She needed to cry it out but finding out what happened was important. It had only been ten of her Earth seconds!

He took a deep breath and let it out. Answers would have to wait. Forcing her to do anything, hadn't ended well in the past. So, he waited, and he comforted her.

He drew in a deep sigh of relief when her sobs began to diminish. He carried her to the table and sat on a cushion by it.

Her arms remained locked around his neck.

Kaily?

She kept her face buried in the crook of his neck.

"Kaily?"

She sniffled.

He portaled the waterskin to him and set it on the table. He forced her hands to let go of his neck and lifted her face up, forcing her eyes to meet his.

Her gaze met his, and then glanced down.

He held the tip of the waterskin to her lips. "Drink."

She drank.

"Better?"

She shrugged. She wouldn't look him in the eyes.

He set the waterskin aside. He pried open her hands. He cringed at the ugly red, burn marks on each of her palms in the shape of his talisman. *Oh, my Kaily! What happened in there?*

She didn't answer his silent question.

He took the ladle and dipped it into the pot.

Her wide eyes flew to his. "Please, no," she whispered. She closed her hands into tight balls.

"It won't hurt like before." He held her gaze.

She shook her head.

He pried open one of her palms and poured liquid into it. He wanted her trust, but she was in no place to give it freely to him. He waited until the redness started to fade. *Better?*

She nodded and held out her other palm to him.

He poured liquid on her other injured hand. He put the ladle back on the table. He wanted to ask again what happened, but he didn't want to send her over the edge. They were both exhausted. He sensed the approach of another new day. He'd no idea they'd been in the training room so long.

She snuggled close to him, holding her closed hands against her own chest instead of his, like she usually did.

He carried her to the sleep pallets where he lay down with her secure in his arms. He covered them both with blankets. He didn't bother with the fire. It would probably burn completely out, but he would deal with it later.

Despite his own exhaustion, sleep did not come to him. He held her close and monitored her mind for when the night terrors returned. He had to see what she saw. It was the only way for him to understand, and hopefully with understanding, would come a path to help her.

It had been three days since the incident in the training room and things weren't getting better. Moto woke for the umpteenth time that night to Kaily's night terrors. Each time, he soothed her mind and flooded her with calm and serenity. At the same time, he reviewed the images from her night terrors.

The night terrors were not the exact same, except that cursed Druid. He remained prominent in every single one of her cursed night terrors. One image was her as a child being lowered into a pit with the sound of snakes at the bottom. He never saw a single snake. Another, she was locked in a tiny room with no escape, no discernible door, and the Druid throwing energy balls at her tiny, tightly curled up body. Her night terrors were one horrible scene after another, night after night. It was all he could do to hold on to enough calm to push them aside for her so she could rest easier, only to have them start up again not long after she settled.

Their waking hours didn't fare any better. She refused to talk about her night terrors or share how much she remembered. She refused to tell him what happened in the training room. If it weren't for his ability to connect to her mind telepathically, he wouldn't know that part of her refused to remember. It was as if her mind would not hold the information. Not that he blamed her. He would have preferred to forget what he'd witnessed in her terrors.

And now, he realized the previous day, that her mind was shielded. During the day, the shield in her mind kept a portion of her mind closed to him, but at night the shield retracted. Not enough for him to get a clear idea of her past before she was seven, but enough he was beginning to suspect that her night terrors were memories working their way to the surface.

A cold shiver ran down his spine as he contemplated these thoughts.

For the first time in his life, he began to understand the terror that paralyzed his bonded mate to an overwhelming state of helplessness. The possibility that she was somehow connected to the Druids, he shook his head. He didn't want to make such a connection, not with his Kaily.

He attempted to teach her meditation, and that was after the enormous struggle to get her back into the training room. She fought him until she had no strength left, at which point, he would carry her into the training room and begin the lesson.

His temper flared more than was good for either one of them. His exhaustion and her night terrors made for a dangerous combination. His own control slipped more and more with each passing day. Thankfully, Sari and Shimani had stayed away. He didn't think he could control his temper around those two yet. There were too many unanswered questions that he wasn't prepared to pursue, not yet.

Training her had become a losing battle, and he was running out of ideas to try. The only peace either one of them had was when they made love each night. They both craved the merging of their centers or souls, as she called them. But each time they separated physically, so did their centers. A part of him, he resolutely ignored, wondered if the bond didn't properly take. He was beginning to believe they hadn't formed a true bond, and maybe it was impossible to create one between them. He didn't want to face that possible reality either.

He was running out of time with her. He didn't know how he knew that, but he did. He had to break through her barriers somehow, and soon. There was only one time she was somewhat open to him, and the only time his last resort idea might work.

He waited and monitored her mind for when she began to wake.

When her awareness started to surface, and just before she completely woke up, he slipped his cock inside her. He pleasured her to wakefulness and drove back her night terrors.

She moved restlessly beneath him.

He took possession of her mind and body and flooded her mind with his erotic emotions and the demands of his body. He didn't give her a chance to retreat, not physically or mentally. He filled her completely and ruthlessly drove their pleasure higher. He took every advantage to drive her demons back. He knew the moment he partially succeeded when he sensed their centers begin to merge.

She silently begged him for release.

Not yet. He remained brutal in his possession of her. He kept her relentlessly close but refused to allow her release.

Finally, she stopped begging, and simply gave herself over to their shared pleasures.

Their centers fully merged.

As a reward, he gave her a small release, and then built her up again. He repeated the process until she was so sensitive that she came at the slightest touch. Then and only then, did he give them both a final, overwhelming release.

He breathed a sigh of relief when he found no fear in her mind, just a fleeting thought of her demise by passion.

You are very much alive, little one. He kissed her neck and smiled down at her.

Are you certain? I can't feel the floor beneath my back. Isn't floating something you do when you die?

He laughed. *No. Just enjoy the sensation.*

Don't leave me, she pleaded.

He closed his eyes and took a silent, deep breath. And there it was again, her fear, her doubt, her barrier. *Look at me!* He ordered.

She hesitated.

Look at me!

She slowly lifted her eyelids.

So much pain shone from her eyes.

His effort to give her a reprieve this day, failed. *I am never going to leave you. Do you hear me, Kaily? Never!*

She nodded. Tears trickled from the corners of her eyes.

His temper flared. *Enough!* He ordered. "You are stronger than this, Kaily. I know you are."

She looked away.

He forced her gaze back to his. "You are." He spoke the words aloud and pushed them into her mind.

She attempted to give him a smile.

Moto stood. "I said enough!" He pulled her to her feet. "Get dressed."

She looked as if she were going to protest.

He swatted her bare ass and shook his head. "I have tried letting you come to terms with these night terrors your way.

Now we do it my way." He wasn't going to give her a reprieve or a chance to withdraw into herself again. If he could help it.

Kaily gave him a lost, forlorn look. She shook her head. "I can't, Moto, not yet." She didn't move to get dressed.

He grabbed her by the upper arms and pulled her hard against him. He leaned down so he could whisper in her ear and mind. "I gave you an order, woman. Don't make me spank you into obedience." His tone was overly harsh, but he was not going to let her hide, not anymore. She had to face her terrors.

Her temper flared.

He kept from smiling, barely. A temper he could deal with far better than her withdrawal.

"Fine!" She ground out between clenched teeth. "One of these days, I'm going to be the one giving you orders." She stepped out of his grasp.

He crossed his arms over his chest. "I'd like to see you try."

Her face flamed and her eyes flared with heat.

"You have five of your world's minutes to obey me. Get dressed, and then present yourself to me in the training room."

She crossed her arms over her chest and glared at him.

He portaled his clothes to him and turned to walk to the training room. "Your time starts now." He called over his shoulder. In the training room, he dressed and started his count down.

A fully dressed Kaily entered the training room before he'd finished.

"Well done."

She stomped to where he stood. "Now what?" She crossed her arms over her chest. "More meditation crap?"

No. While he waited for her, he'd slowly drawn in energy, and now held it at bay. He waved his hand, closing the entrance.

She spun around. Panic gripped her mind.

He didn't let up. He bombarded her mind with images from all her night terrors. Rapidly passing each one through her mind. He hoped he could catch her by surprise, that the room would enhance his abilities to project. Even untrained, she was strong enough to block him. The Universe help them if she ever really got a handle on her abilities and the immense power he sensed just below the surface. He hoped, by forcing her to face them, that they would lose their hold over her.

She turned anger filled eyes on him.

A wave of immense power hit him so fast he couldn't react. The power threw him hard against the wall. He fell to the floor. His breath was knocked out of him, and his head spun. He struggled to remain conscious. He pushed the ringing in his ears aside. His talisman burned so hot it scorched him through the material of his vest.

He removed his vest and dropped it to the floor.

He erected a shield and came unsteadily to his feet. He used the wall to maintain his balance and to remain standing.

Wave after wave of power emanated from Kaily.

The power bombarded his shield. He lost his concentration to project into her mind. It was all he could do to maintain his shield. He'd expected the room to protect him from any power she might hurdle at him. Shimani said the walls would absorb the energy. He tested it himself.

He'd been foolish to think such.

His attention snapped up as a cracking sound echoed in the room. There was an indention in the domed ceiling directly above her. Cracks spread out, like a spider web. He cursed as options filtered through his mind.

KAILY! STOP! He shouted into her mind, but nothing coherent remained to connect to. He glanced up and struggled to keep his own panic at bay. The spider web cracks continued to spread outward. He sensed the room's shield buckling.

He took a deep breath. He circumvented his talisman and drew energy from Kaily's power to reinforce his own shield. He realized too late that she was not connected to the energy through any conduit. Somehow, she pulled from the shield of the room, and from deep within Ki. She'd accessed unlimited amounts of energy.

"STOP KAILY!" He shouted at her. "YOU'RE GOING TO KILL US BOTH!" It was no use. She was filled with nothing but anger. Not even a remote awareness of her surroundings remained within her mind.

He sensed the room was moments away from collapsing in on them. He took several calming breaths. He drew in the energy from Ki in the same way that Kaily did. He built the energy around him and tied his power with Kaily's through their bonded connection. Thankfully, he'd made her his bonded mate. Any doubt it wasn't true evaporated with his connection of his power to hers.

He sent a silent prayer to the Universe that they would survive what he was about to do.

When he held enough energy, he sent a massive backlash of power along their connection.

Kaily screamed and grabbed her head. Power drained from her. She collapsed in an unconscious heap.

Moto didn't waste time. He grabbed his vest and Kaily, and he ran from the crumbling room. His erected shield protected them from the debris. He collapsed in the center of the main cave with Kaily secure in his arms. He focused on the back of the cave, specifically the walls and ceiling until he was convinced the main part of the cave would remain intact.

He left Kaily where he'd fallen and forced himself to his feet. It was a struggle to remain coherent and conscious. He felt the energy of Ki pulling at him, trying to somehow lay claim to his being.

He pulled the pallets and blankets closer to the cave entrance. After, he picked Kaily up. He gathered what little strength he had left and carried her to the pallets. His will power and fear for her demise provided him the strength he required.

He carefully placed her on the pallets and collapsed beside her. His head pounded. Before he lost his battle with remaining conscious, he reached out to Shimani and Sari for help. He didn't know if it would work, but he had to try.

His breath left him, and darkness claimed him.

"When is he coming back?" Sari asked.

"How should I know? It's not like he tells me where and when he is at any given time!" Shimani angrily replied. "Sari, you can do this, I know you can. He has trained you well. You have a gift for healing, and I will be here to help you." Shimani said in a gentler tone. "Moto?"

"He will be fine," Sari said. "In fact, he's coming around now. You know what I need, get them, and hurry back before we permanently lose her."

Moto opened his eyes as Shimani hurried out of the cave. He sat up and put his hands to his throbbing head.

"Drink this." Sari placed a cup in his hand.

Moto held the cup with two trembling hands and downed the contents. He set the cup aside. He glanced at Kaily. She remained unconscious and laid too still for his comfort. He reached for her mind but encountered emptiness. He turned paid filled eyes to Sari. "Is she going to live?"

Sari's gaze met his. "I don't know. She's locked deep within her mind."

Moto cursed.

Sari laid a reassuring hand on his shoulder. "It could have been worse."

"How?" Moto asked.

Sadness filled Sari's eyes. "The energy could have claimed her." She picked up a small handful of his now silvery-white braids. "What happened?"

Moto took his braids from her hands. He frowned at them. He dropped them and glanced at the back of the cave, now rubble. "An accident." He touched the parts of Kaily's hair that matched his silvery-white. He caressed her too pale skin. He laid his hand against her chest.

Her heartbeat was too weak.

"Moto?"

Moto's eyes met Sari's intense gaze.

"Did Kaily do that?" She tilted her head to the destruction.

Moto maintained eye contact with Sari. "Can you help her?"

"Yes, she can." Shimani said from the entrance of the cave. He handed her a bag.

Sari pulled crystals from the bag. She turned her attention to Moto. "I need Kaily's talisman." She glanced at Shimani who nodded just once. "And yours."

Moto frowned and glanced from Sari to Shimani. He'd heard part of their conversation when he came to, but not enough to determine about whom they were discussing. He considered demanding answers from them, but Kaily's motionless body beside him, quieted his desire to know what was going on with them. He held out his hand and called both talismans to him. He handed Sari his talisman and the pouch which held Kaily's.

She held the pouch over Kaily and emptied its content so that the talisman lay on Kaily's abdomen.

Moto noticed that she still refrained from touching it, and yet, touched his. While the Kahoali were protective of their talismans, there was never an issue with touching anyone's.

"Please lie flat on your back next to Kaily. Make sure that your body touches hers as much as possible and lock your mind with hers."

"I only encounter emptiness when I try to touch her mind." Moto stretched out beside Kaily and interlaced his finger with hers. He scooted so that her side touched the full length of his.

"That's to be expected," Sari said. "Just keep a lock onto that space. When she starts to come back to us, lock her mind with yours. Do you understand what I'm asking you to do?" Sari set Moto's talisman on his abdomen the same as she had Kaily's. She stood over him with her eyes locked with his.

"Yes." Moto didn't understand what had happened to make her mind so empty. He knew what happened, just not why she was the way she was now.

Sari inclined her head. She placed seven crystals in a circle around Kaily and Moto. After, she took a waterskin out of the bag and poured some of the contents into her hand. She sprinkled drops between each of the crystals.

The same spicy, floral aroma that was found at the meadow of Crystal Lake permeated the air. His eyes continued to follow Sari. He buried his questions to the back of his mind.

Sari nodded once to Shimani and stood outside the crystal circle at Moto and Kaily's heads. Shimani stood at their feet, also outside the circle. Both lifted their arms and stretched them towards each other.

Moto glanced from Sari to Shimani.

Close your eyes, Moto. It was the first time she'd spoken mind to mind with him.

Moto was so shocked by the telepathic communication that she had to repeat her command before he comprehended what she told him. Reluctantly, he closed his eyes.

Almost at once, he felt the surrounding air charge with energy. He sensed the energy remained contained within the crystal circle. His talisman warmed and pulsed against his abdomen. He sensed the same emanating from Kaily's talisman. He locked his mind to that empty space within her mind.

Their talismans became a beacon within her empty mind. He marveled at the power surrounding them. Peace infused his mind, and Kaily's.

He found the process painstakingly slow. He didn't know how much time passed before he sensed a glimmer of Kaily surfacing within her mind. He knew that Sari said Kaily was locked within her mind, but he couldn't help but feel her statement was not entirely truthful. He didn't want to believe that Sari would intentionally lie to him either. Kaily seemed outside herself.

He waited for Kaily to surface within that empty space to latch on to her mind. The waiting was excruciatingly painful.

Patience, Shimani projected into his mind.

Moto frowned. He focused to maintain control over his actions. He kept his eyes closed and focused within Kaily's mind. He didn't know where her consciousness had slipped off to. He didn't know how much she would remember.

Stay focused on task! Shimani said.

Moto took a deep breath and refocused on Kaily. He attempted to quiet his anger rising as he learned more about Shimani and Sari that he hadn't known. *That's it, little one. Come back to me.* He whispered into her mind. He sensed a part of her was reluctant. A part of her didn't want to leave the safety of where she had retreated. He poured warmth and love into her mind and wrapped her consciousness within the warm embrace of his overwhelming love for her.

He pushed aside his fear her reluctance sparked within himself. He vowed he would never lose her again, never. He continued to pour his love into her mind.

He sensed the moment Kaily consciously embraced him. *Kaily?*

She didn't respond in words.

He sensed her mind with his, it was enough for now. He was so focused on Kaily that he didn't notice when the energy surrounding them dissipated or when Shimani caught Sari before she collapsed to the ground with exhaustion.

"Moto!" Shimani called to him as he shook him.

Moto's eyes flew open.

Relief crossed Shimani's features.

Moto was surprised to find himself sitting with Kaily cradled in his arms and lap. Their talismans lay beside them, his on top of hers.

Shimani picked up the talismans and held them up for Moto to see.

They were connected as if by a magnet. He also noticed that Shimani only touched Moto's. As he looked at them, Kaily's talisman dropped to the floor. Whatever connected them had dissipated.

His eyes met Shimani's. "What happened?"

"Sari healed Kaily." Shimani glanced to where Sari sat on the floor holding her head. She drank something from a cup. Her hands were shaking.

"Sari," Moto called to her.

She lifted a tired gaze to his. She was pale, and her eyes were dull. She appeared extremely exhausted.

"Are you okay?"

Sari nodded. "I just need a moment."

"Kaily's going to sleep for a while, but she is out of danger," Shimani said. He handed Moto back his talisman. Shimani picked up Kaily's talisman with a cloth and put it back in the pouch. He started to slip the pouch inside his own vest pocket.

"Both," Sari said.

Shimani glanced at her.

Sari gave a minute shake of her head.

Shimani handed the pouch to Moto.

Moto's eyes narrowed. "Seems there is much for us to discuss."

Shimani glanced at Sari again, who again shook her head.

"You two have a telepathic connection like Kaily and I do?"

Shimani smiled and shook his head. "Not like you two do."

"But you are speaking telepathically, aren't you?" Moto glared at both of them and waited for an answer.

"Yes," Sari said. "We do. Shimani, gather up the crystals."

For a moment, Moto thought that Shimani was going to protest, but he didn't.

Moto turned his focus to Sari.

Sari regarded him for a long moment before speaking. "I know you're angry."

"You think?"

She glanced at the cup in her hands. She sighed and glanced back at Moto. "When it's time."

"It's time."

Sari shook her head.

"Don't," he said. "Don't tell me you'll explain later."

Sari held his gazed while she finished the contents in her cup. "The Queen is getting suspicious."

"Why should I care?"

"I care, Moto."

Moto looked away. He'd agreed to her plan, and then disappeared from her life when Kaily hurt herself. Sari was in this difficult position because she helped him out of yet another tricky situation. While Kaily had been on her world, Sari convinced him to spend time with her to help put the Queen's mind at ease. Apparently, not enough time. He'd learned that Sari spent some time away from her Village, she said to give the impression they both were elsewhere. Something was off with her lately. As long as she wouldn't take her place as future Queen, they had to keep up their ruse. "What do you need me to do?" Moto asked, looking back at Sari.

Relief passed over her features.

"She has invited us to this evening's repast, as her honored guests." Sari stood on shaky legs.

Shimani helped her walk closer to where Moto sat with Kaily in his lap. He helped her kneel in front of them.

"Shimani can stay with Kaily tonight. She will most likely sleep through the night."

Moto shook his head. "I can't leave her."

"Why?" Sari asked.

Moto took a deep breath. "She is having night terrors. I have to be here to help her through them."

"How long has she been having those?" Sari touched Kaily's forehead and closed her eyes.

"A while," Moto said. He didn't like the strain on Sari's face as she concentrated.

"How long?" She repeated her question.

"They started ten or so days before we went to her home world. She didn't have them there." Moto was taken aback by the curse that she uttered.

"Why didn't you tell me!" She demanded.

"Why would I tell you? I had no idea of your abilities," Moto retorted. "Can you help her or not?"

Sari shook her head and rubbed her temples. "Not permanently. Only Kaily can help herself by facing them." Sari's gaze met Shimani's.

Moto brushed the hair back from Kaily's face. "So, I keep telling her."

"I can keep them from bothering her this night."

"How?"

"By putting her into a deep sleep."

Moto could not decipher the look she gave him or the emotions within her.

Sari turned her attention to Shimani. "We need to put Kaily into a deep enough sleep she won't dream, and right now, I'm too tired to pull enough energy to do it. Do you think you can if I show you how?"

Shimani cast a similar look at Moto that Sari had before answering. "I already know how." He knelt in front of Moto and Kaily. He placed his hand on Kaily's forehead.

Moto glared at him and Sari but remained silent. They both could already sense how angry he was at them. Fortunately, for them, Kaily's well-being took precedence.

Shimani finished. He inclined his head to Moto.

Moto's censoring glare remained fixed on Shimani, who had the good sense to look away.

Shimani stood and picked up the bag with the items he brought for Sari.

Sari placed a hand on Moto's shoulder.

Moto glanced at her.

"Rest with Kaily, you look exhausted. Shimani and I will return this evening before the repast begins."

Moto nodded.

Shimani helped her stand. He kept his arm around her waist for support.

Moto remained where he sat and watched them leave. Once they were out of the cave, he settled Kaily on the sleeping pallets. He stretched out beside her and gathered her into his arms. He covered them both with blankets. He attempted to maintain his lock onto her mind. It was difficult to keep that level of concentration when his body cried out for sleep. He was half afraid to allow himself to rest. He didn't altogether trust what Shimani had done to keep her from her night terrors. But he was exhausted and badly needed sleep.

His mind drifted towards his dilemma with Sari and Shimani. None of what he'd witnessed was Kahoali abilities, none of them. The power and ability both displayed confounded him. The peace he'd sensed in Shimani as he put Kaily into a deeper sleep still lingered within her mind. There was no remnant of her night terrors.

He'd always thought the Kahoali were capable of more as evidence by his own abilities. After what he'd witnessed, he shook his head. His abilities were pale by comparison.

Somehow, he would find a way to force answers from them both.

He needed rest. He sighed and let his mind drift to sleep.

Chapter Twenty-Two

Kaily exhaled as the fog of sleep receded from her mind. A dream like state lingered, but she couldn't recall what she might have dreamt. This sensation was not the same as with her night terrors, so, she was fairly certain she hadn't had those.

Her heart pounded in her chest. A thin sheen of sweat covered her body. She shivered from a bone-deep cold surrounding her, in spite of hearing the crackling of the fire and the heat at her back.

"We need to talk," said a sharp, male voice.

Kaily's eyes flew to the entrance where Shimani leaned against the stone wall. His arms were crossed over his chest. She pulled the blanket up to her chin, acutely aware that both she and Moto were naked. "Moto is not going to be happy you're here when he wakes." She wondered why Moto was still asleep. He usually rose before she did. She reached for Moto's mind and encountered peaceful slumber.

"Moto is not going to wake until I wake him." Shimani didn't move from his position by the entrance.

"Why?" She frowned. "What did you do to him?"

"I left a cup for you on the table to help with your headache."

"What headache?" Her hand touched her forehead as she became aware of the pain behind her eyes. It worsened by the minute. She closed her eyes. "Oh, that headache."

"I'll wait for you by the pools." Shimani pulled the covering back over the entrance as he left.

The energy crystals embedded in the wall gave off a soft bluish glow. Still, the soft light was beginning to pain her eyes and making her headache worsen. She sighed and began untangling herself from Moto. She moved slowly to keep from jarring her head too much. She managed to sit up before she had to take a moment. She glanced at the covered entrance. She didn't like Shimani's tone, not that they'd had the best exchange the last time she saw him.

She glanced at Moto. She brushed his braids back from his face. He appeared so peaceful, but she didn't like that he still slept. A frown creased her brow as she picked up one of his silvery-white braids. There was a handful of them on the underside of his hair. She looked from him to the entrance. It dawned on her just how close the sleeping pallets were to the entrance.

She half turned and stared at the massive pile of debris at the back of the cave where the hall leading to the training room used to be. "Oh god," she whispered. Her hand flew to her rapidly beating heart. Dread surfaced inside her. Her gaze drifted to Moto as she struggled to remember what might have happened. She couldn't imagine sleeping through something like that.

She took a deep breath and stood. She walked to the table and picked up the cup. Normally, she would have preferred dressing first, but her head was not going to wait. She drank the foul contents, staring at the wreckage. She had a sneaking suspicion she might be responsible for what she saw. She struggled to remember.

She remembered Moto waking her in the most delicious way, and then pissing her off. She thought they'd ended up in the training room, but she couldn't recall leaving it. No matter how hard she tried to solidify her memories, she didn't remember anything after entering the training room.

"Please, no," she whispered. She closed her eyes. She opened them again. Her eyes focused on the destruction. She downed the remaining contents and set the cup on the table. She wiped at her tears.

She turned to face the covered entrance of the cave. Shimani might have answers. She straightened up and pushed her shoulders back. She needed answers, and he was the only one around to provide them.

Kaily paused by Moto. She knelt beside him and placed a soft kiss on his lips. "I love you." She stood with purpose.

She took a quick shower and dressed in clothing she'd brought from Earth. Her body felt too grimy to skip washing up. Plus, the water helped wash away the stubborn remnants of her tears. After she was ready, she stopped back by one of her bags. She pulled an old, tattered journal out. She stared at it a moment, before slipping it into the back pocket of her jeans. She hurried down the narrow path to the pools.

She found Shimani standing near the edge by the pools, staring out over the cliff ledge. She sensed a contemplative quiet in him that she had not before noticed. She frowned. Her senses seemed to be on hyper drive. She was not completely oblivious to other's emotions, but neither was she empathic like Moto and his people. Except this day, it would seem.

Shimani turned towards her as she stepped from the path on to the soft grass covering. "Please join me." He nodded his head towards a low table with two cushions set by it. There was a variety of food items on top of the table and two cups with a waterskin nearby.

"What's going on, Shimani?" She crossed her arms over her chest and remained where she stopped.

He calmly walked to the table and sat in one of the low cushions. He didn't say anything. He simply gazed at her and waited.

She glared at him.

He remained silent, waiting.

She shook her head, took a deep breath, and glanced back at the path. Being stubborn wouldn't help her obtain answers. She walked to the table and sat on the other low cushion.

Silence.

Her anger brewed beneath the surface.

Shimani filled her plate first and placed it in front of her, and then his own. He poured a portion of the waterskin's contents into their two cups.

"Brey?" Kaily asked.

Shimani shook his head.

"Nectar of brey?"

He shook his head again.

She loudly sighed.

Shimani handed her a cup. "This will help with the nausea."

"I don't," she started to deny. Her protests were silenced by a wave of nausea hitting her. She narrowed her eyes at him. "What's going on?" She forced herself to swallow the bile suddenly in the back of her throat.

"Drink!" He ordered.

She glared at him. "This is," she swallowed. She huffed in frustration and drank from the cup. The taste wasn't as bad as his other concoctions. She finished the contents and waited for the worst of the nausea to pass before finishing her comments. She took a deep breath. "This is the second time you have given me medicine to help with a symptom I did not have." She narrowed her eyes at him. "Not until you told me I had them."

Shimani gave her a humorless laugh. He smiled, but it did not reach his eyes or seem particularly happy. "I have kept the symptoms in check for you so we can talk. Unfortunately, there are certain side effects." He saluted her and downed a second refill of his cup. He took her cup and refilled it, then handed it back to her. "That is a horrible sensation."

"Don't expect sympathy from me." She downed the refill he gave her. She held her cup out for more. The pleasant tasting concoction reminded her of iced tea on Earth. Not exactly the same, but close enough to satisfy and settle her stomach.

Shimani refilled both of their cups with the last of the liquid in the waterskin. "We can talk after you eat."

"I'm not hungry."

He gave her a mischievous grin. "Are you sure about that?"

"Damn you, Shimani." She grabbed her stomach. Hungry didn't cover it. She was ravenous. Her stomach rumbled and clenched in pain. She narrowed her eyes at him. "Exactly how many symptoms are you keeping from me?"

"That was the last one," he said around a mouth-full of food. His plate already more than half gone.

She shoveled several bites into her mouth before she said anything. When she had enough to settle the worst of her hunger pains, she lifted her eyes to him. "Why did I have those symptoms?"

He paused between bites and regarded her. He lowered his eyes. "Eat."

She frowned.

He glanced up at her. "I will answer your questions after you eat."

She shook her head but focused on finishing what was on her plate.

They ate in silence. She glanced from time to time at Shimani. His gaze seldom met hers. He seemed so far away in thought. She focused on her second plate full of food, more pahini than anything, to be honest. She'd developed quite the liking for it. When she was finished, that's to say, had her fill, she grabbed another slice of pahini and nibbled on it while she waited for Shimani to finish his third plate full.

She watched him finish his last bite and push his plate aside. He sipped on his drink and sat in silence.

She waited.

The silence grew more uncomfortable by the moment.

He did not speak or give any indication he was going to.

She turned her attention to the pools and the open ledge they were a part of. Her eyes kept drifting thoughtfully back to Shimani. There was something very different about him. He seemed somehow older. He wasn't the easy-going, fun-loving person she'd met not so long ago.

Finally, he handed her a square parchment paper. "Have you," he paused for a moment, he sighed. "Have you seen that before?"

Kaily took the parchment from him and stared at the symbol on it. One symbol only, a complicated rune. She let the parchment drop from her hands. "I have not seen paper of any type in the Kahoali village."

"No, you have not."

She regarded him.

He remained silent and watched her.

She glanced down at the parchment. Her hands began to shake. She swallowed the lump in the back of her throat. Her eyes lifted to his. "Is that what you really want to know, Shimani?" Her heightened senses communicated more to her than his words.

He shook his head. "No." He glanced out over the pools. Again, he seemed faraway.

She waited.

He returned his attention to her. He took a deep breath. "I want to know if you have ever drawn that symbol."

She reached for the journal in her back pocket. She held it in front of her. She stared at it. She took a deep breath and handed him the journal.

Shimani's frown grew deeper. He opened the thin book and thumbed through the pages. He handed it back to her. "I see." He stood and stepped away from the table. He stopped by the pool.

Kaily remained sitting at the table. She waited. She opened her journal and compared what she doodled to the parchment paper. There was no mistaking that her doodles and that symbol matched. She glanced up at Shimani when he uttered some Kahoali curses.

He still stood by the pool.

"What's wrong?"

"I wish I had guidance in this," he said more to himself than her.

Her eyes followed him as he made his way back to the table.

He sat on the cushion he had vacated.

"I don't understand." She handed the parchment paper back to him. "What is this?"

"Before I answer that question, I need to talk to you about your night terrors."

She pulled her trembling hands back and put them in her lap. "No." She shook her head for emphasis. She didn't talk to Moto about her nightmares, why would he think she would him!

"I'm not asking, Kaily."

Her eyes flew to his and narrowed.

"I won't be as nice about this as Moto was." His tone held no small measure of warning.

She would not have expected such a warning tone from Shimani. "Nice?" She almost laughed. "You think Moto was nice about my nightmares?" She frowned. He kept wanting her to talk about them. Had he done something to her? Her mind struggled to remember something. She sensed anger, almost rage at Moto, when she thought about how he was with her nightmares, but she couldn't solidify any harsh memory. Not one that would be logical for her words or anger.

"I have to understand the source of those night terrors, before I can decide what the best course of action here is to take." His tone softened but not by much.

Kaily sensed a strong resolve in him. He was not going to let this go. She swallowed hard. She shook her head. "I can't talk about them. I can't." Damn tears stung her eyes.

"You have no choice, Kaily. It's important."

Tears slipped from the eyes, down her cheeks. "Please, Shimani, I can't."

His smile held a measure of sadness. "It's the only way. As long as you continue to avoid talking about them, they have power over you."

She looked away. She hastily wiped at her tears.

"Let's start with the night terror you woke from today."

"I didn't wake from one."

"You did." Shimani walked around the table and crouched in front of her. He took her hands in his. He refused to relinquish them when she tried to pull hers out of his. "I'm right here with you, Kaily. Please, it's important."

She angrily wiped at her tears. She stared at the ground. "I," she started and then shook her head. She glanced at the pool.

Shimani wiped at her tears with a cloth. He handed her the cloth. "Talk to me. You remember them, don't you?"

Kaily nodded. "Maybe not all, but enough."

"Tell me." He squeezed her hand he still held.

The cloth resided in her other hand. She glanced down. "I'm like I am now, and not." She shook her head.

He waited.

She used the cloth to catch more tears. "In the," she wiped more tears. She swallowed again. She lifted her eyes to his. "I think I was a child when those things happened to me. I feel like an adult in them, helplessly watching, but I feel what the child feels." She shook her head. "I,"

Shimani patted her leg. "It's alright. I have what I needed to know." He let out a heavy sigh. "I was afraid they might be memories surfacing."

"They are, aren't they."

"It seems that way." Shimani closed his eyes.

She shook her head. "I didn't think I had woken from any this morning, but there is one lingering in my mind."

"Tell me about it."

She glanced down. "It was of a woman," she paused.

"It's okay, Kaily, I'm here. Talk to me."

Her eyes met his. "She saved me, the woman. I was a young child, I think. She woke me, and then," her tears began in earnest. A sob escaped her lips. "I begged her to leave her sleeping. I begged her, Shimani." She shook her head. "She wouldn't listen to me. She should have left her sleeping."

Shimani brushed back her hair. "The night terror cannot hurt you now. It's only a memory."

Kaily gave a small laugh. "It hurts here, Shimani." She placed her hand over her heart. "They hurt me here."

Shimani gave her a sad smile.

She focused on the cloth she twisted in her hands. "She woke her up too and took us to a room. I think it was a library." She lifted her eyes. "It looked like the room in the Agenors' castle with the stone arch."

Shimani nodded. "Go on."

"Honestly, I don't know what's real about those nightmares and what might not be. I feel like I can't tell anymore what is real."

"What happened next?" He prompted.

She took several deep breaths. "I saw the woman throw a vile at the door. It shimmered. She took me by the hand and whispered to me," she shook her head. "I don't know what she said to me, but she wanted me to step through the door even though it was closed." She turned pain-filled eyes to him. "I didn't understand. The door was closed. I hesitated because I didn't understand."

"It's alright, Kaily." Shimani rubbed her arms. "It wasn't your fault."

"She died, Shimani, because I hesitated. How is that not my fault?"

"What happened next?"

"I hesitated. The other one started screaming for help. The woman," she paused as the pain tightened in her chest and another sob escaped. "My mother, she was my mother,

Shimani." Pain filled her eyes. Her gaze locked with his. "She pushed me through the doorway, but not before I saw him. She took a deep breath and wiped at her tears. He entered the room and grabbed her by her hair. He yanked her away from me. He killed her. I know he did. Because of me. He killed her, because of me. I hesitated. If I hadn't," she shook her head and tears fell. Sobs wracked her body.

"Shhh." Shimani wiped at her tears. He wiped at his own tears slipping from his eyes. He gathered Kaily into his arms. He held her while her sobs shook her body. "It's not your fault, Kaily," he said when her sobs slowed enough for her to hear him.

"It is." She pulled back.

He shook his head. "No, it isn't! You were a child, Kaily. It's not your fault you didn't understand. Who is the other one?"

She looked at the pool.

He turned her face back to him. "Will you allow me to see the night terror, Kaily?"

She wiped at her tears with the too damp cloth. She slowly nodded.

Shimani placed the palm of his hand against the side of her head. He closed his eyes.

A warm sensation spread through her at his touch. The image of the nightmare played through her mind. There were details there that she missed remembering. She let her tears fall unchecked as she relived the horrible memory within her mind.

Finally, he released her and sat back on his heels. "I would like to try and pull more memories of your mother to the surface. Will you let me?" His tone held immense tenderness.

She shook her head.

"I think it is important, Kaily." He brushed back her hair.

She wiped at her tears and raw cheeks.

Shimani took the ruined cloth out of her hands and handed her another.

She wiped anew. "Why couldn't I remember all of what you saw earlier?"

"I will attempt to answer your question after we try to bring more to the surface. Will you let me?"

She glanced down. Honestly, she didn't want to remember. Except a part of her wanted to remember more about the woman who gave birth to her. Her gaze lifted to his.

She nodded.

He placed his palm of his hand against her head, like before. This time, he placed his other hand on the other side of her head. Shimani looked deep into her eyes. "This may get uncomfortable. Don't pull away. No matter what happens, do not shut me out of your mind. I think it is important we pull her memories to the surface of your mind."

"Why?" There was a deep sorrow in her voice.

"I don't have an answer yet. Call it intuition if you wish."

"Men don't have intuition."

Shimani smiled, a real, amused smile. "You actually believe that after all this time with Moto?"

"No." She dried her tears and blew her nose. She took a deep breath. "I'm ready."

He nodded once and closed his eyes.

The same familiar warmth spread throughout her body and mind. There was a brief moment her urge to pull away was strong. She forced herself to remain still and focus on breathing.

Suddenly, memories of her mother flooded her mind. She had no idea so many memories existed. They passed so quickly she couldn't get a hold of any of them. Then as suddenly as the flood started, it stopped. One memory solidified and stayed in the forefront of her mind.

She wiped at her tears.

She lay in bed in the big house the Fergusons now occupied. It was the house she grew up in with her foster parents. She looked so young. Kaily frowned. It must have been shortly after she came to be with her foster parents.

Tears trickled down her cheeks.

Her mother sat on the edge of her bed. She brushed back the hair of the sleeping girl. Her mother placed a crystal on her forehead. She whispered some words, the crystal glowed, and then stopped. Her mother picked up the crystal, kissed her head. She told the young child she loved her and to be well. She left her room.

Tears flowed. She pulled her knees to her chest and rocked back and forth.

Shimani walked some distance away, lost in his own mind and thoughts.

When her tears slowed. She looked up expecting to see Shimani crouched in front of her. He wasn't. She searched the clearing for him.

Shimani turned towards her.

She stood and walked to join him by the pool.

He met her halfway, and held his arms open to her.

She walked into his embrace and laid her head against his chest. Her tears started up again.

He held her in silence.

Kaily had no words to describe how grateful she was for the gift he gave her. Her mother escaped. Where was she? Why did she leave her there on Earth?

"I don't know, Kaily. Maybe she left you on Earth to protect you."

She stepped back from his embrace. "Maybe," she thoughtfully replied. If her nightmares were memories, it would make sense. "Why was the memory there like that, as if watching events unfold. I was asleep as a child. I would not know she was there to even remember it."

Shimani tilted his head at her. "I don't know for sure, but I think she put that memory in your mind. Maybe she knew you would think she died and would blame yourself. Maybe there's more to the memory you'll discover later. It's hard to say."

"How is that possible?"

Shimani gave her a sad smile. "You have so much to learn, my young friend."

Kaily frowned at him. "You can't be that much older than I am."

"In Earth terms, years?"

Kaily nodded.

"You're how old?"

"Young, Shimani, I'm young."

Shimani laughed.

"Twenty-three."

"I'm thirty. So, yes, I'm close to your age physically."

"But?"

Shimani shrugged. "Age is relative. I've had a very different upbringing than you have."

"Hmmm." Kaily hugged herself. "What did she do to me?" she wiped more tears away.

"I think she somehow shielded you from your memories, maybe even your abilities."

"Moto mentioned a shield in my mind." Kaily mused aloud.

"Did he?" Shimani frowned.

Kaily nodded.

"I wish he would have told Sari and I all this stuff about you." He growled.

"You can't blame him, Shimani. He is quite upset with the two of you. He doesn't feel like he ever really knew either one of you."

Shimani sighed. "It couldn't be helped."

"You should have helped it. I think a part of him feels betrayed by you two."

Shimani closed his eyes a moment. "He still should have talked to us about all this."

Kaily sighed. She didn't add more. "Did you remove the shield?"

Shimani shook his head. "No. I pushed it back enough to allow some of the memories to surface. If my theory is accurate, and no, I'm not giving you all the details of what I suspect. Your shield will come down on its own when you are ready to face what they are keeping away from your conscious mind."

"What if I'm never ready?"

"Kaily, please hear me on this." Shimani put both his hands on her shoulders, silently demanding her full attention. "Please try to understand. You must, and I repeat must face those memories. You no longer have the luxury to choose not to. It is imperative you face them. I am certain that is why your abilities are so out of control, at least, part of the reason."

"And the other part of the reason?"

"Part of my theory I'm not willing to share."

Kaily groused at him.

"Picking up Moto's temperament, I see."

Kaily stuck her tongue out at him.

Shimani smiled and shook his head.

"I destroyed the training room, didn't I?" She sighed. Her eyes met his. "I'm the reason part of Moto's hair turned white, aren't I?"

"His hair wasn't the only one."

Kaily tentatively touched her hair. She closed her eyes.

"I don't know what happened, and Moto wouldn't say more than it was an accident." Shimani sighed. "But yes, I believe so. I don't know how." He shook his head. "To be honest, the power it would take to do such a task, truly impressive." He held up his hand to stay her words. "A devastating result, but impressive. And the reason you have to get control of your abilities."

"I try, Shimani. I do. I just don't know how."

Shimani handed Kaily back the parchment paper. "This is the rune that will open a doorway to Celtan, the Druid home world." He glanced at the fading world above their heads.

Kaily glanced up at the planet. She looked back at Shimani. "I'm not Druid." She took the parchment paper.

"Who was the man in your night terrors, Kaily."

She turned to walk away.

Shimani grabbed her arms and turned her back to face him. "Who was the man?"

She fought to break his hold on her.

He didn't let go.

She settled down. "The Druids would call him my sire." Hatred infused her words. "Why didn't you just open the portal to Celtan instead of here?" She demanded.

"Kaily, we've been over this, I didn't open it. I just tried to keep it open to Ki."

"You shouldn't have. Then I would never have been brought to Moto."

Shimani sighed. "Is being with Moto so bad."

"No. That's the problem." She pulled back to break his hold. He let her go.

"Why was I brought to Moto, Shimani? It was orchestrated, us meeting, wasn't it?"

"You are too perceptive. You know that, right?"

She crossed her arms over her chest.

"It isn't as simple as you think."

"Then clarify it for me."

"First, you need to understand that Moto found you. We had nothing to do with that first meeting."

"We?"

"Patience."

Kaily glared.

"Moto told you about his own night terrors?"

Kaily nodded.

"Your world was the first he kept returning to. I was sent to find out why."

"By whom?"

Shimani gave her a pointed look.

Kaily held up her hands.

"I found out that he kept returning to you. There was an obvious connection between you two. We waited for him to bring you to his world, but he didn't."

"He watched me."

Shimani smiled. "He did. All the time. When it became apparent your connection went beyond even a Kahoali bonding pair, and that he was not going to do more than watch, we decided to create a meeting. Which, admittedly didn't work out the way it was intended."

"You think." Kaily smiled at Shimani's glare. "How does that answer not sending me to Celtan in the first place instead of here? Why pair us?" She held up her hands. "I know, you didn't, but really, orchestrating a meeting between us, knowing the pull we have on each other amounts to the same thing as pairing us."

Shimani nodded, sort of. "Fine, I'll give you that one. As for here instead of there." He looked up at the world. "We hoped Moto could train you after he made you his bonded mate. The bonding between you two was inevitable. The Universe wouldn't create such a strong connection between you two if you were not meant to be together. We needed you trained before sending you to Celtan."

"Why?"

"That's where your destiny resides."

Kaily shook her head at him. "I don't believe in destiny or fate."

Shimani shrugged. "Doesn't matter if you believe. They both find you, eventually."

"You think I'm Druid?"

Shimani came to stand behind her. He put his hands on her shoulder. "I know you are."

She turned to face him. "Moto hates Druids, Shimani. Hates them. You should have left me and my destiny well enough alone." Her hands balled into fists. "You had a purpose in coming here today, what is it?"

Shimani nodded his head once. "You need to carve that rune," he nodded to the parchment in her hand, "and go to Celtan."

"When?" She asked from between clenched teeth.

"Now."

She shook her head. "No."

"Kaily?"

"No!" Her heated gaze remained locked with his. "And what about Moto?"

Shimani took a deep breath. "We would prefer he went with you."

Kaily harshly laughed. "You and I both know he won't. Not with his hatred of Druids and not with his night terrors foretelling emanate doom of the Kahoali people." She turned away. "When he finds out what I am," there was a catch in her voice, "he will hate me too."

"Kaily, he,"

Kaily turned heated eyes on him. "Don't, Shimani. We both know the truth. He won't." She took a deep breath. "On Celtan, will I learn what I need to control my abilities?"

Shimani shrugged. "Maybe. You're Druid, learning as a Druid might make a difference."

"How can you not know?" She waved her hand. "Never mind, you're Kahoali, why would you know about Druid stuff?"

"That's not the reason, Kaily."

"Then what is?"

"It has been over three thousand years since a Druidess has stepped foot onto Celtan. Most of the knowledge about Druidesses has been lost since that time. There is a complicated history on Celtan that only a handful even have some knowledge about."

"I see." Kaily rubbed her closed eyes. "Tomorrow."

"What?"

She glanced up at Shimani. "I will leave tomorrow. Today," she smiled to herself. "I want today with Moto. One perfect day to take with me." She wiped at her tears.

Shimani nodded. He held his hand out to her.

Kaily stared at the pouch in his hand. Without seeing inside, she knew what the pouch contained. "I don't want that."

He started to say something.

Kaily adamantly shook her head. "No. I won't take it." She brushed away the tears falling. "I won't need it for the rune to Celtan will I?"

Shimani shook his head.

"It's a Gateway of sorts, isn't it?"

"A doorway." Shimani corrected.

Kaily frowned. "I have images in my mind, and knowledge about that rune. How?"

"The innate knowledge is passed down through the bloodlines and surfaces when a Druid is called home. It's why you drew the rune long before setting eyes on your home world."

"Don't give that back to Moto either." She nodded her head towards the pouch. "I don't want him to have painful reminders of me when I'm gone. Promise me!" She locked her eyes with his.

Shimani nodded his head in agreement.

"The stone pillars in my mind, what are they? They remind me of Stonehenge on Earth but different somehow."

"That's where the rune should open up to on Celtan, but it won't. The current High Druid, Deykin, altered the path. You will find yourself in his throne room when you exit the doorway. You will be in a circle of light. Whatever happens, Kaily, do NOT step outside that circle. Deykin has unpleasant surprises for unwanted guests, and his surprises do not distinguish between friend or foe."

"Nice." She sighed. "How will my presence be received?"

Shimani shrugged. "It's hard to say. As far as anyone now believes, only males are Druid."

"Right, three thousand years, you said. So, male dominated world, to an extreme."

"Something like that. There are risks, Kaily. I won't lie to you about that. I don't know how Deykin will react to you, but you will have one ally."

"Really?" Kaily frowned.

"His name is Ethan. When you arrive, you will enter the throne room where your presence will trigger a summons to Deykin and the Council. Your ally is on the Council. He can be trusted." He lifted Kaily's face to his. "Do exactly what Ethan tells you to do, Kaily. Your life will likely depend on it. Celtan can be a dangerous place."

"How do you know Ethan can be trusted?"

"I just do. In reality, you have little choice. This environment here is not helping you with your abilities. I don't know if your bond with Moto is helping or hurting the process." He regarded her a moment before continuing. "Once Ethan gets you past Deykin and the Council, he will start training you on how to use your abilities."

She regarded him in silence for a while.

He waited, patiently.

"Why do you think Ethan can train me when Moto couldn't?"

"As I said, Druid training Druid may make the difference."

"And if it doesn't?"

"It has to."

She closed her eyes. "You should have left me where I was." She turned away from him.

Shimani turned her around and pulled her into his warm embrace. "Believe me, today, I wish I had."

She gazed up at Shimani. The look on his face turned her heart over in her chest. She gave him a sad smile. "I can't go back, can I? I can't just return to my life and pretend none of this happened, can I?"

Shimani shook his head. "No. I wish it otherwise, Kaily. I really do." He wiped the tears falling from her eyes. "I will find a way to help Moto accept what you are."

She harshly laughed and shook her head. "I appreciate you want to, Shimani. But I don't want Moto to want me or honor our bond out of some sense of duty or obligation. I know you could convince him too for those reasons, and he would. Damn his honor! He would face his greatest enemy," she paused. Her voice caught on a sob she tried to hold back. "He would stand by me for his honor, even though he wouldn't want to." She sighed and shook her head. "I don't want that. I want him to want me as I am. I want him to want me in spite of what I am. Do you understand?"

"I do." He hugged her tight against him. "My apologies, Kaily. I wish I could change it, all of it."

She pulled out of his embrace. "I accept your apology, Shimani. What's done is done. Promise me that when I leave, you and Sari will give Moto the time he requires to heal, before dragging him back to his Kahoali way of life."

"I will, but I can't promise that Sari will do the same."

"Try to convince her otherwise, please." She didn't want either of them pushing Moto. He will need time. She will need time.

"I will try, I promise."

"How long will Moto take to wake after you release him from whatever you did?"

"Not long." Shimani followed Kaily. Once at the table, he waved his hand, and the food disappeared.

"Hey!" She turned on him.

Shimani smiled at her. "I sent the food to the table in the cave. You wanted to take some to Moto, didn't you?"

She smiled. "Yes." She inclined her head at him. "Thank you."

He gave her a half bow. "Let's see about waking Moto."

They walked up the path in silence. During the walk back, she put her conversation with Shimani out of her mind. She built a shield in her mind as best as she could. Not that she really knew what she was doing. Sometimes, she thought she did, and others she knew she didn't. For the shield, she imagined a wall and placed the things she didn't want Moto to sense behind it.

When they made it to the cave, she knelt beside Moto and nodded towards Shimani.

He placed his hand on Moto's forehead.

She watched as he closed his eyes, and a stern look
of concentration crossed his features. She sensed power
surround them. The energy dissipated.

Shimani stood and walked to the entrance. He stopped and
turned towards her. He inclined his head. "Be well, Kaily."
He opened a portal and disappeared.

"Goodbye, Shimani," she whispered to the empty space
where he stood just seconds before. Her attention shifted to
Moto as he stirred. "Good afternoon, sleepy head."

Moto bolted up. "Afternoon? Are you kidding me?"

She laughed and shook her head. "Afraid not."

"Why didn't you wake me?"

Her gaze shifted to the back of the cave and back to Moto.
"I don't know what happened back there, but I figured the
least I could do was let you sleep for as long as you could."

Moto's gaze drifted to the back of the cave. He looked back
at Kaily.

Her heart skipped a beat at the pain reflected in his eyes.
She straddled his lap and caressed his cheek. "I don't want
to know, Moto. Today, I want to forget about everything,
my nightmares, whatever happened back there." She waved a
dismissive hand in the direction of the destruction. "I want to
forget about everything." She repeated. "I want to swim and
make love to you as many times as possible." She shrugged.
"Or as many as you're capable of loving me." She gave him a
mischievous smile.

Moto pressed her back against the pallet and covered her body with hers. "Is that a challenge I hear, little one?"

"Is it?"

"Sounds like one to me." He undid the buttons on her jeans. "You have far too many clothes on for me to make good on the challenge you issued."

She laughed and wiggled to help him remove her offending jeans. She sat up at his urging and helped him remove her sweater. "If you need strength, there's food over there." She pointed to the table.

Later, Moto said as he claimed her mouth with his. *Exactly how many times are you challenging me to, little one?*

She smiled against his mouth. *All. Day. Long.*

Challenge accepted.

That was the last coherent thought she allowed herself for the remainder of the day and a good portion of the night too. She gave herself completely over to Moto in a way she had not yet done. Tomorrow she would break their hearts. Today she would take every single experience and commit them all to memory. The memories of this day would have to last her a lifetime. Moto was her one and only true love, and always would be, even if he wouldn't be a part of her future life.

From the Author

Thank you for embarking upon this journey with me to the *Center of the Universe*. I hope you enjoyed this first novel of the **Druidess Trilogy.**

To continue the journey, please check out **Druidess Forged** which is available on Amazon.

If you just can't get enough, please check out this first behind the scenes story, **Night Escape** which can be read for free by joining my newsletter at my website machellehanleigh.com.

The behind-the-scenes stories pair with the main novels and provide additional points of view, scenes, and other tidbits that didn't fully make the cut.

To help me grow as an author, please tell your friends and family about my stories. Leaving an honest review on **Amazon** and/or **Goodreads** is a great way to encourage other like minded readers to find their next favorite author. As word spreads about these amazing, page turning novels, my career as an author grows, but not without help from my loyal readers!

I also invite you to join my **Author Machelle Hanleigh Official Fan Group** on Facebook to be part of the conversation about my stories and life as an author.

As always, please enjoy the Journey!
Machelle Hanleigh

Made in the USA
Columbia, SC
11 March 2023

13647735R00321